The Richebourg Affair

THE RICHEBOURG AFFAIR

by

R.M. CARTMEL

The Richebourg Affair © R M Cartmel

ISBN 978 0 992948 60 3
eISBN 978 0 992948 61 0

Published in 2014 by Crime Scene Books

A CIP record of this book is available from the British Library.

Printed in the UK by TJ International, Padstow

À Papi.
Je vous ai promis un roman policier,
et maintenant, cinquante ans plus tard,
le voici.

Thank You

To the family and friends who read the various drafts of *The Richebourg Affair,* and whose honest criticism made it a far better book as a result. My sister Hilary; Vanessa, Dave and Harry; and Maggie.

To David Clark at Domaine David Clark in Morey-Saint-Denis, a couple of miles or so north of Nuits-Saint-Georges, who checked the manuscript for viticultural howlers, as well as providing the house and the Vosne-Romanée that took such a prominent part in the story.

To Sylvie Poillot, Pierre Vincent and Nathalie Bergis-Boisset, at Domaine de la Vougeraie in Prémeaux-Prissey, a mile or so south of Nuits-Saint-Georges, whose warmth on my visits, and quarterly notebook on their wine, *La Lettre,* has been so helpful with the viticulture.

To Christine Tournier et fils, in whose café in Nuits-Saint-Georges, Charlemagne Truchaud appeared, fully formed, one summer morning and where much of the action takes place, and yes, I like what you've done to the place.

To Nicholas Marquez-Grant for all your suggestions and corrections concerning the forensics of the book.

To Sarah Williams, my editor and her gang at The Book Consultancy in Woodstock, who helped turn an old man's dreams into some sort of reality.

To Alain Ampaud and his family in Dijon, who have provided an alternative reality for my family for the best part of a century now.

To Jean Taupenot-Merme of Morey-Saint-Denis who introduced a young student to the taste of fine Burgundy wine on the assumption that he would, one day, be able to afford to buy some himself. To all the other Vignerons in the Côte de Nuits who sold me their nectar, ensuring I kept coming back, especially Jean Grivot who made the majestic bottle of Richebourg that David Clark and I shared one evening in the Millésime in Chambolle-Musigny.

Burgundy

Châtillon
sur-Seine

N

Auxerre

la Seine

Yonne

Dijon

la Saône

la Loire

Nuits-Saint-Georges

Nevers

Beaune

Autun

Châlon-sur-Saône

0   60km

Mâcon

Nuits-Saint-Georges

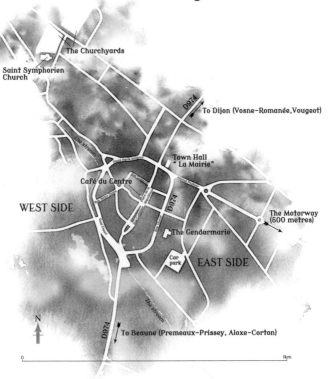

The Churchyards

Saint Symphorien
Church

D974

To Dijon (Vosne-Romanée, Vougeot)

The Stream

Place Marie Noirot

Town Hall
" La Mairie"

Café du Centre

Avenue Jofffen

WEST SIDE

Rue Sofia Dame

D974

The Motorway
(500 metres)

The Gendarmerie

Car
park

EAST SIDE

The stream

N

D974

To Beaune (Premeaux-Prissey, Aloxe-Corton)

0   1km

Chapter 1

Paris, Wednesday

'Commander Truchaud?'

Truchaud looked up. It was Constable Dutoit, waving her telephone at him. Her spectacular blonde head looked considerably less gorgeous after last night's celebration session, following his team's capture of the much-hunted and semi-mythical 'Fox'.

'There's a telephone call for you. It's a Madame Albrand from Nuits-Saint-Georges. She says you know her and it's very important.'

He remembered Madame Albrand; a rather severe woman from the generation between him and his parents, who had lived just round the corner when he was growing up. She'd always been there and his mother, bless her, had always used her as a threat if he did or didn't do whatever was the topic of the moment. He couldn't remember now what the threats had been, but he still remembered the combination of Madame Albrand and the severe, slightly sideways expression from his mother.

'Madame Albrand; it's Truchaud. You said it was important?'

'Oh, thank goodness I've found you. Are you sitting down? I'm afraid I've got some terrible news.'

'Imagine I'm sitting down.'

'It's your brother. I don't know how to say it any more gently … but Bertin died in his sleep last night.'

There was a stunned silence for a moment. 'What happened?' he asked.

'They don't know,' she said. 'The ambulance came to take him away, and there has been rather more gendarme activity in the village than usual. But that's all I know.'

1

'How're Dad and Bruno taking it? Michelle?' he added as an afterthought.

'You know your father,' she replied. *Not really any more,* he thought. Over the years they had drifted apart. Once they had both realized that there was more family than there was room for in the family business, it had become necessary for him to find his own path in the world. As a result, they found they had less in common to talk about on the occasions they did meet. It wasn't hostility, just separation.

Bruno was Bertin's son. He would be the next generation of *Domaine Truchaud Père et Fils.* Being the elder son, Bertin had had first dibs on whether to follow Dad into the business. Once Bertin had made his decision, it had then been up to his younger brother to make his choice about what he was going to do with the rest of his life. He did his national service in the Gendarmerie, and having completed that, he went straight on to Police College. A career in the police beckoned. His recruitment into the civilian National Police Force, known at the time as the *Sûreté,* was an easy step for him to take from there.

'Are you likely to be seeing them shortly?'

'Yes, I expect so.'

'Can you tell them I'll be down this evening? We've just finished a case, and I'm sure the squad can spare me for a few days. I'm owed some holiday.'

'I knew we hadn't seen you down here recently,' she replied slightly tartly. It wasn't that he hadn't taken any recent holidays in Nuits-Saint-Georges; it was more that he hadn't taken any holiday at all. They passed a bit more inconsequential trivia and bade each other farewell. He put the phone down.

Michelle … his brother's widow. He chewed those words over in his mind. He had never really seen her as his brother's 'wife', although he had been at the wedding. She had been a plain dumpy girl when they got married, and had remained a plain dumpy woman, until motherhood had made her plainer and dumpier. Now she was his widow. Their son, his nephew, was an amiable lad of twelve years old, who at times, rather embarrassingly, hero-worshipped his uncle, because he was a detective in the police in Paris.

'Uncle Shammang, Uncle Shammang, who have you caught this time? Did you shoot him?' was something he didn't really want screamed the length and breadth of the *Côte d'Or* as soon as he had arrived. He had always wanted to feel he was well and truly off duty when he arrived home. If someone said the word 'home' to him, his mind would always conjure up the vineyards round Nuits-Saint-Georges, never the flat in Paris, despite the years he had lived there.

He tapped on the Divisional Commander's door. The rather round and ruddy face of his senior officer looked up at Truchaud's entrance. The Chief raised a silver grey eyebrow. Truchaud started straight off, 'I wondered if I could take a few days' leave, Chief?'

The Chief looked up slightly bewildered. He stuck a pencil into his ear and scratched at it a little with the blunt end. 'I'm sorry,' he said, 'Could you repeat that? I didn't quite catch it.'

Truchaud did so and the senior officer chuckled at him. 'You know, Commander, that's the first time I can remember you asking for any leave at all.'

'No, Chief, it may be the first time I have asked *you* for any leave, but I'm sure I've asked previous bosses for some from time to time.'

'And when did you have a different Divisional Commander from me? During which century was that?'

Truchaud chuckled politely. The Chief had to be allowed his jokes, especially if he was to get a few days off as a result. 'My brother has just died in Nuits-Saint-Georges, and I would like to take a few days to be with my family and help them set up the funeral and stuff.'

'Of course, you can have those days off,' said the old man, and then continued. 'In fact, I want you to take a month off.'

Truchaud looked up aghast, 'What? I mean, why?' he spluttered, 'What's gone wrong?'

'Absolutely nothing, dear boy,' continued the Chief. 'It's just the perfect opportunity for the rest of us.'

Truchaud looked at his boss, increasingly puzzled.

'Well, it's like this. Firstly, you need a holiday. Secondly, you're so damn clever, you frighten people, and I could use a few fewer frightened flics around here at the moment. Thirdly, there are a couple of promotion holes coming up, and I would quite like to see how a couple of members of your squad handle themselves, without your being there to support them, so to speak.'

'May I ask who you're talking about?'

'Well, Leclerc is an obvious case. He's arrogant, bumptious, and may be just the ticket for Vice. They need a new man, and I think he might just fit the bill.'

'They'd never recover! What have they done to deserve him? And the other?'

'Your extremely wholesome and delicious Constable Dutoit.'

'You're not sending her to Vice, surely?'

'No, no, no. But from what I understand from your reports, her extreme good looks appear to hide a razor of a mind. Now, I don't think for a moment that you'd be biased in her favour because she's so damn pretty. In fact, if anything I suspect that that would be a disadvantage in your eyes ...'

'May I ask very politely and respectfully, of course, what exactly you mean by that?' Truchaud gave his boss a piercing eye.

'Well, you've never really shown any interest in the opposite sex ... or the same sex for that matter. As far as I know, you've never been married or anything. Umm ...' The Divisional Commander appeared to feel uncomfortable, and Truchaud let him wriggle on the line for a few moments longer.

'Actually, I was married once,' Truchaud replied, 'but she ... escaped. I have to say I didn't resist her departure very hard. I suppose she had never been my first choice in the first place, and when she made it fairly obvious that I wasn't her first choice either, we went our separate ways amiably enough.'

'What happened to your "first choice?"'

'Do you remember "The one that got away?"'

'You mean the old song?'

4

'Yes, that's the one.'

'You mean, old chap, you've been pining for a girl all these years, and we've never known about it?'

'Pining is not a word I would ever use, nor is it appropriate in this case. But there is a woman I have known for a very long time, and when my wife left, I realized that I had never really wanted to be with anyone else in the first place.'

'But what happened to her, old chap?'

'She married someone else.'

'Well, that makes you a free man then.'

'Not really. It would still be most unfair of me to ask anyone else to try to compete with someone who isn't even playing. If I ever met anyone that I wouldn't abandon in a trice — if she were to snap her fingers and say, "Hey, Truchaud, it's me, and I need you" — then that would be a different matter, wouldn't it? The fact remains that I don't think I've met such a woman yet.'

'This woman who got away, she didn't actually call you "Truchaud", did she?'

'Well, you wouldn't expect her to call me "sir", would you?'

The Divisional Commander smiled. 'You, know the whole time I have known you, Truchaud, I don't think I have ever heard anyone address you by your forename.'

'I don't suppose you have,' he replied. 'I can't ever remember using it in Paris either.'

'You know, without actually looking in your records, I don't know that I know what it is.'

'Is that a question?' the Commander asked, his head cocked on one side.

'It now is,' replied the Divisional Commander.

'If I were to tell you it's *Charlemagne* you'd understand why I don't use it much.'

'Charlemagne? You mean you were christened after an old barbarian king?'

'Indirectly, I suppose,' replied Truchaud. 'I was actually christened after a Grand Cru wine.'

'I don't follow.'

'Well, back in the mists of time, the Franks, who originally came from Belgium and further east, had a King called Charles the Great, or as his name has come down from those days, Charlemagne. History or legend also tells us that he was partial to the great wines of Burgundy; in his case, the wine made by some local Benedictine monks, who called it Corton. However, legend has it that Charlemagne used to dribble his wine, and it used to stain his beard red. It is also said that his queen found a red-stained beard just a little off-putting, and instructed the monks to plant white grapes instead. Just to prove the point that behind every great man, there is an even more fearsome woman, she persuaded Charlemagne to only drink the wine that did not stain his beard. Twelve hundred years later, wine from that vineyard is still rated amongst the greatest of white wines. Queen Litgarde was a very good judge of *terroir,* as well as being a terrifying woman!'

'But why did your parents think that Charlemagne was a suitable name for a child?'

'Being rather young at the time, I wasn't conscious of very much when I was being christened, and it never really came up later in conversation. Mind you, they had already christened my brother "Bertin", which wasn't much better for him, so they obviously had some sort of obsession going on there.'

The Divisional Commander looked all the more intrigued, 'Go on,' he said, 'You've got me interested, you can't possibly leave it there.'

Truchaud smiled again, he was enjoying giving his boss a history lesson. 'Well, move on 400 years from Charlemagne, and there was a farmer called Bertin, who was very impressed with the wines that another group of monks made in their walled vineyard next door to his farm, and it was called the Clos de Bèze, after their monastery. The word *clos* in the local patois means a walled vineyard. Bertin thought that they made such good wine, and on top of that, such a good income, that he thought he might plant similar grapes in his field, to see if he could make wine like theirs. So he did, and he could. When he died a richer man, he left his field to the monastery, in the hope that this act of munificence would guarantee him a place in heaven. To differentiate the wine from the new unwalled plot from that from their old plot, they called the new plot "Bertin's Field" in his memory. Over time this *Champ de Bertin* contracted to *Chambertin,* which, nowadays, is hailed among the greatest of all great red wines, and, in the nineteenth century, it added its name to the name of the village where it comes from. So now the village is called Gevrey-Chambertin. My brother was christened "Bertin"; another person who instinctively understood the concept of *terroir,*'

'My dear Truchaud, I'm not even going to ask you about this "concept of *terroir*" you keep talking about, or I have a feeling we'll still be sitting here at dawn tomorrow, and I'm sure we both want you on the road south. Do you mind if I don't address you as Charlemagne, and stick to Truchaud?'

'I would be most grateful, sir, if you did just that. After all, it's not a name I would recognize as me if I heard it shouted across a room.'

'Go on, man, you're off duty as of now. See you when you get back.' Truchaud stood up, and placed his sidearm and warrant card on the Chief's desk. He saluted, and left the room.

Chapter 2

Paris, Nuits-Saint-Georges. Wednesday

'I'll keep an eye on the flat while you're away.'

Truchaud had always wondered how his landlady seemed to know what he was going to do before he actually thought about doing it. He was aware he really didn't understand the innermost workings of the female mind, but somehow this particular elderly lady's ability to predict his most private thoughts, he found most disconcerting. He thought about it logically for a moment. Well, yes he had parked his tatty, rather elderly BX outside the front door, and he only tended to do that when he was going to load it. His landlady ought to have been a detective!

The Citroën hadn't always been old and tatty. When he had first bought it, it had been brand new. Somehow they had remained friends, and the car had never given him a reason to change it. They had grown into comfortable middle age together. Admittedly, he had not used the car an enormous amount, but when he had driven it in the city, it had never looked like a policeman's car. It had been far too new to be one to start with, and then, one day, out of the blue, it had become far too old to be one.

'You're going to see your family,' she said, 'I'm sorry for your loss.' *How did she do it?* he wondered. 'Do you want me to forward your post?' she asked.

'Only the important stuff,' he replied, knowing immediately that she would understand what was important.

'Do you want me to pay the bills?' If there was any doubt that she just knew about the contents of his mailbox, this was the confirmation of it. But then he asked himself, *Why am I concerned?*

'I'll keep the baker and the grocer sweet,' she smiled. That one was a no-brainer. Anyone who lived in the same building as him knew that *café au lait* and croissants at breakfast were important to him, and the croissants had to be really fresh.

He went upstairs to pack a case.

'I'll see you soon,' he reassured her, 'and if I'm staying longer than expected, I'll give you a call.' He threw his cliché of a trench coat on to the back seat of the car. He looked at it for a moment, it was almost as tatty as the car, but because it had so many pockets in all the right places, it was his ideal accessory.

There were times it felt like crossing an international border, coming home. He had driven through the hills and corners of Morvan, which had appeared quite subalpine in nature. Suddenly the road dived straight through a cutting onto the plain below. There was his junction, just to the north of Beaune. The motorway itself headed off to join the great French cities of Paris, Strasbourg and Marseille further on. The peel-off swung sharp left, over a bridge, and guided him between marker cones to pull into the tollbooth area.

As he pulled up under the half-arch of the kiosk, he amused himself by wondering whether he should wave an identity card. If there ever had been someone actually in the box that person might also have found it faintly amusing, but it never seemed to be manned when he went through. *Who looks after the cones,* he wondered? He could, of course, have driven through the automatic path, which would have registered his car as a police car, and charged the Police Headquarters the fee, as he was sure someone like Commander Lucas would have done. He didn't like Lucas, and he thought Lucas probably didn't like him much either. He wasn't bothered, but somehow he felt that, as he was on his own time, he should pay the fee required. That sort of honesty made him feel in some ways superior to Lucas who was at least a head taller, and looked down at him.

He pulled away from the kiosk as the barrier went up, and turned right onto the main road. Corton hill appeared on his left. It had always reminded him of a monk, though of course in reverse, with its tuft of trees on the top instead of a tonsure. Below this tuft were the vineyards of Corton and Charlemagne. Definitely wine country now, and then, just as suddenly as it was, it wasn't again. In the villages of Corgoloin and Comblanchien, there were lorries and dust from the marble quarries, with rather sad little vineyards on either side of the road, which he somehow felt sorry for. He had lived ten kilometres north of these villages for the best part of the first two decades of his life, but had never knowingly tasted any wine from there. He wondered whether anybody ever did stop at the houses in the middle of those villages offering a free tasting. In fact, unless you were looking to buy marble, he wondered why you would stop there at all.

He rolled through the dive and climb of Prémeaux, and into Nuits-Saint-Georges itself. Compared to the sleepiness of the villages to the south, Nuits felt awake. There were people on the street, some even in animated conversation with each other.

He turned off the road he had always called the 'Seventy-Four', as most people still did, despite the bureaucrats' declassification of it from a national road to a departmental road. He was old enough to remember the time when it had been the main road to the South of France. He drove into the chaos of Nuits itself. His part of the little town had obviously been conceived before the advent of the automobile, with corners of buildings jutting out into the street, which turned blindly to the left or the right. He turned left through a gate that someone had left open, into a little courtyard. There was a tractor asleep under the eaves. He got out and went up to the back door on the right. He tried it and, as it was open, he called out and went through into the kitchen.

'Is that you, Shammang?' came a choked voice from inside.

His brother's widow was red and puffy round the eyes. She had certainly been crying, but didn't look like she could cry any more. He was not sure how to greet her. There hadn't been a course in how to greet a bereaved close relation during his training, and the last time he had been in this situation was

11

when his mother had died so many years before, while he was still at school.

'Let me make you a coffee,' she said, 'It's on the hob.'

'How's Dad?' he replied.

'Oh you know Dad,' came the response. *Why does everyone keep telling me that I know Dad?* he wondered. Anyway, he had absolutely no idea how his father might respond to the loss of a son. When his wife had died, he had just become very quiet, and didn't appear to respond to anything very much for quite some time.

Much as his father had not appeared to feel anything, all those years ago, all Truchaud felt was numb. He had been calm back at the *Quai*. Back then all he had probably felt was disbelief. Driving down from Paris, he had sort of half-expected his brother to leap out of the front door and shout, 'Gotcha!' on his arrival. Not that it was ever the sort of thing that his brother would have done, even when he had been alive.

Concerning his father, Michelle added, 'He's been off in the *clos* all day, making sure that the last bits of pruning get done. You know how he feels that the pruning should be done just as the sap starts to rise.' Truchaud smiled a little. It was a quotation from someone that his father often used. He had no idea who had originally said it, and he was fairly sure his father didn't either.

'And Bruno?' he continued.

'He'll be upstairs in his room on that computer you gave him.'

He was about to call upstairs to his nephew when there was another knock at the front door. 'Monsieur Truchaud?'

Truchaud walked to the door, as his sister-in-law was still busy with the coffee, to find a tall man in his middle fifties.

'I've got a couple of friends who have suddenly turned up,' he said, 'and I haven't got any half-decent bottles of wine ready to be opened. I wondered if you had a couple of your Vosne ready to drink?' The Vosne was a wine from the next village north of Nuits-Saint-Georges. It was a small village with a wonderful pedigree, and the Truchauds were justifiably proud of their Vosne. Within a few hundred yards of their little plot were some of the most desired and expensive vineyards in the world. Wines such as Romanée-Conti and La Tâche changed hands for several thousand euros a bottle, and that was before they were really ready to drink. Richebourg, just up the slope a little from their plot, was pretty exclusive too.

'I'll check,' Truchaud replied, and went back into the house to ask his sister-in-law. 'Have we got any of that '99 Vosne still in the cellar?' he asked.

'Yes, I think so,' she replied.

'What's the current asking price?' he asked, and she told him.

He went down into the cellar and found a couple of bottles, put them into a double bottle bag, and took them out. Cash changed hands and they bade each other good day. Truchaud put the cash on the table and sat down. Michelle opened a door in the massive sideboard and took out a large cashbox, which she unlocked, and taking out a notebook from within, made an entry in it. She then put the cash in the box as well and locked it back in the sideboard, and came and sat down again.

'Life must go on,' she said. 'That sounded like Étienne,' she said.

'Étienne?' he asked.

'Lives round the corner; never has any stock of his own,' she said. 'He always claims to have stuff maturing in his cellar, but if he has, he certainly didn't get it from us. Don't know why you gave him the '99. He'd have been perfectly happy with the '04.'

'Sorry about that. I gave him what I would have bought if I had been at our door.' He sat down again at the table thinking he would like to find out about his brother before the room was full of twelve-year-old boy. 'So what actually happened to Bertin?'

'Well, after dinner, he said he was tired, so he'd go up to bed. I had a few papers to do before I turned in, so I told him I would follow him up when I'd finished. It must have taken me an hour or so. I'm always trying to keep up to date with the taxman; it's so much easier in the long term. And anyway our taxman has a habit of just turning up out of the blue, especially when he is in

13

urgent need of a cup of coffee. When I did finally finish and go up he was already asleep, so I slipped into bed without disturbing him and went to sleep too. When I woke at about five in the morning, he felt cold and rather clammy, so I shook him,' she started to cry again, 'and he was stiff.'

Truchaud was beginning to feel quite uncomfortable about behaving — at least in his own eyes — more like a police inspector and less the concerned relative.

'I called the *SAMU*, and they sent an ambulance with a paramedic, but there was nothing they could do. They said he'd been dead for hours.' Truchaud was sure they were right too. The way she described it, it sounded like rigor mortis had already set in, so he might have been dead even before she got into bed. 'So they called the gendarmes, who were here pretty much immediately, and they took him away.

'They've taken him to the coroner's lab in Dijon. They left a nice young woman in uniform behind, who talked with me for a while, but I don't really know what we talked about. She left when Bruno woke up. I have no idea how he managed to sleep through all that. I told him what had happened, we cried a bit, and then we both went across the courtyard to tell Dad. He still gets up at dawn.'

There was movement at the door behind him, and in walked his father, grubby from the vineyard where he had been kneeling. His father nodded at him as he passed to the sink. 'Oh, it's you. Thought we'd be seeing you soon.' Somehow the curt greeting didn't particularly upset Truchaud. He had been used to the patriarchal grunt for most of his life, and knew the old man didn't mean anything offensive by it.

'How are you doing, Dad?'

'Well as can be expected,' he replied still from the sink. 'Vines are looking well this year. Very few of them died last year, so we didn't have to replace many of them. The sap is definitely rising, so who knows … maybe we'll be in for yet another good summer.' Truchaud was aware that they hadn't had a really bad summer for over fifteen years, but you would only really know what sort of summer it had been once the bottles had been counted and the wine tasted. The old man took the lid off the coffee pot, which was still on the stove and sniffed at it. 'That smells burnt,' he said and poured it straight down the sink.

'Oh,' said Michelle, 'I meant to make that for Shammang; I must have forgotten it.'

'Well, neither of us would have drunk it now. It would have made us both ill.'

'But how actually are *you?*' Truchaud pushed.

The old man looked at him severely. 'I'm not sure I want to talk about it at the moment. When I do, I'll let you know.'

There was a creak at the door and the family was complete. Bruno, twelve years old, but right now looking younger than his years, with eyes swollen as if he had recently been chopping onions. He spotted his favourite uncle — not difficult as Truchaud was his only uncle — and rushed to him. 'Uncle Shammang — it's Dad — he's dead!'

'I know, mate,' replied Truchaud, holding his nephew, aware that the boy was sobbing. There had always been a subtle relationship between the policeman and his nephew, which transcended age. They related as pals of the same generation, rather than a generation apart. In his rather deluded thought process, Truchaud considered Bruno to be the closest thing to the son he had never had. It had of course been easy for him, as, when he had gone back to the stews of Paris and its criminal underworld, he had simply returned the boy to the care of his parents and promptly forgotten all about him. It had been all the warmth and none of the responsibility.

'So what are we going to do?' the boy asked. Truchaud looked up at that one, aware that Michelle and his father were looking at him as if he had an immediate answer to that.

Rather uncomfortably he replied, 'I don't know yet, but we will get through this.' He fished around for another platitude, but one didn't immediately spring to mind. He didn't want to make any promises to anyone else; that would mean making them to himself too. He realized that the grief in that front room had finally reached him too.

There was another tap on the door. It was Mrs Albrand from next door, armed with a large casserole. 'I have made a large *pot-au-feu* for everyone,' she said. 'There's even enough for the prodigal son as well.' She looked straight at the Commander. Was there accusation in her eyes?

'Thank you very much, Madame,' he said. 'You didn't have to.'

'Yes, I did,' she replied. 'Somebody has to keep this family alive, and that's what neighbours are for. Neighbours rally round in time of need.' She looked away from Truchaud and back to Michelle, 'Is there anything else I can do for you tonight, dear?' she asked.

'No, I don't think so,' she sniffed. 'Thank you so much for all you're doing.'

'It's what a good neighbour does,' she replied. 'See you in the morning.' And giving Michelle's shoulder a gentle squeeze, she turned on her heel and left.

'I'll go and get a bottle of wine,' said the head of the family, and followed her out. A couple of minutes later he was back with a dusty bottle of wine in his hand. 'Somebody's been at the cellar,' he said. 'There're a couple of bottles of Vosne missing.'

'Oh,' said Michelle, 'those may have been the bottles that Shammang just sold to Étienne on the corner.'

'Really?' said the old man tetchily. 'Back here for five minutes, and he already thinks he can go around selling our wine.'

Truchaud was beginning to realize there was more than just grief in his family; there was tension as well, so he switched on his watchful mode.

Chapter 3

Vougeot, Thursday

Spring was in the air, and the winter was finally over. The vines were beginning to wake up after their winter's rest. The winter was the time for new wine, fermenting the last harvest and passing the one before on to the merchants. Meanwhile the vines themselves slept. With the advent of spring it became vine time again. Slowly they woke up, and the first shoots would soon be appearing. Any vintners would be completing the pruning by now, as indeed his father — who was often jokingly known as 'the last of the late pruners' among the local winemakers — had been doing yesterday.

As Truchaud walked slowly down the row of vines, he stepped back into the life he had lived so many years before. During his youth, this had been his life, and had also been the direction he had expected to go in the future. Many of these vines had been his friends, and they had changed a lot less than he had.

The feeling of spring was so completely different on the *Côte d'Or* than it ever felt in Paris. Paris was busy, amused, humorous, and he could hear laughter even near Police Headquarters. The scents of Paris were also so different. Contrary to the marketing patter, Paris didn't smell like perfume; it smelled like any big city, grubby with petrol fumes. Burgundy was quiet and serene as opposed to the noisy, fizzy streets of Paris. *And its scent,* he wondered? Apart from near where certain winemakers, who might remain nameless, had sprayed some chemical fertilizers recently, at this point it remained scent-free.

The ground was moist under his feet without actually sticking to his shoes. His father was further down the row, kneeling down and it looked like he was pruning a vine. He walked slowly up to him, breathing in the clean air and feeling the sun on his face.

'Morning, Dad.'

The old man looked up from the gnarled twisted pieces of wood in front of him. Vines produced one of the most sensual of stimulants for at least three of mankind's special senses, but at no time could they be described as pretty.

'Oh it's you,' the old man said. 'What are you doing here?'

'Well, I thought you might like a hand,' he replied. 'Tell me what you want me to do.'

'You?' the old man replied. 'Why you? Your brother will do all that. Do you know where he is? He should be here by now.'

Truchaud stopped and looked at his father. 'Dad, do you remember why I'm here? Bertin isn't here any more!'

'Well, where is he then?'

'Dad, Bertin died two nights ago. Why do you think I'm here?'

His father's expression did a complete about-turn. His mouth turned into a very unpleasant snarl. 'It doesn't take a dead brother to get you out of the sin parlours in Paris, does it? If you haven't got any more brothers, I suppose that's the last we'll see of you too.'

'What?' Truchaud was stunned. His father had never spoken such nonsense to him before. He remembered that his father had been quite odd when his wife had died all those years ago, while Truchaud was still at school. But to a hormonal teenager in those days, every adult's behaviour had seemed somewhat unpredictable.

His father returned to the vines, taking no further notice of his confused son, who turned on his heel and walked back towards the chateau, through the gates in the wall surrounding the *clos*. One of the elderly winemakers in the vineyard, known as 'Uncle Louis', was tending the vines that ran along the wall, on the other side of which ran the single-track road that led up into the hills, passing the fabulous vineyard of Musigny. He wished that his family had a parcel of Musigny in its portfolio. Bertin would love working that vineyard. He stopped for a moment, realizing what he was thinking. At that moment he became aware of Uncle Louis at his elbow. 'I am so sorry to hear about …'

Truchaud let him commiserate. *There's an obvious reason why it's called the 'grapevine' here,* he thought. The old man had finished saying whatever it was he felt he had to say. Truchaud would never have admitted it, but he wasn't really listening. Instead, he was thinking how he was going to phrase his next question about his father. Using an open question that he had been trained to use when he was a junior detective, he asked if Uncle Louis had noticed any changes recently in his father.

By his reply, it rapidly became obvious that Uncle Louis hadn't really seen a lot of his father since the harvest at the end of last year. That, of course, was the way of things on the *Côte* during the winter; the winemakers went undercover, tending the maturing new wine in the tanks rather than out in the vineyards with the vines. From what he understood from Uncle Louis, however, his father had been well at the harvest. So whatever change had taken place, it had happened after his previous visit during the autumn of last year.

He wandered out of the *clos,* up past the chateau and along the cobbles to the gate. He had left his car down the track outside the wall of the *Clos Blanc,* on the other side of the road. The *Clos Blanc* was that rare vineyard in the northern part of the Côte d'Or, which grew grapes for white wine. The monks who had owned the famous *clos* in the eleventh century, and had made the great red wine in the Clos de Vougeot itself, had also planted and walled this much smaller vineyard next to it, and grown white grapes. In both cases they had got the grapes right. Truchaud got back to his car and drove slowly back home, thinking quietly about the 'diamond in the nest of rubies' as the winemakers' publicity read for the *Clos Blanc.*

Michelle was at home. 'You wouldn't mind doing a spot of shopping would you?' she asked.

'What sort?'

'Well, if I give you a list for supper, then you can nip down to the grocer's. We can't go on being looked after by Mrs Albrand.

19

It's not fair on her. The grocer's will understand, and if you tell them it's from me, then they won't try to palm you off with produce that's going off, because they don't know who you are I've had that sort of problem before, when I've sent the students off shopping. It's particularly difficult when we get students at harvest time that don't speak a lot of French.'

Truchaud thought about that. She was right; Nuits was far more familiar to him than he now was to Nuits. While she was making her list he asked, 'Is Dad all right?'

'You've noticed?' she replied.

'Well, everybody's been telling me "well, you know Dad", and I have realized that I don't really any more. Is this all recent?'

'Um, no, not really. I spotted the change over the past six months or so.'

'I didn't see anything when I was last down,' he replied.

'Well, you didn't talk much to any of us when you were last down,' she observed drily.

He thought about that for a moment, and reflected she was probably right. Bertin and Dad had had their usual two students, who were staying to help with the harvest. They had actually been French last year, and had therefore joined in the dinnertime conversation, which had been about the harvesting of grapes, and not a lot else. They didn't even discuss sport very much. Maybe they had already discovered that they were interested in different teams, or maybe in different sports. However much he liked to talk about his family making wine when he was away in Paris, he really didn't understand much of the conversation round the family dining table. Everybody else had seemed so excited about that vintage, and he had definitely felt the one out of place.

The students had appeared slightly tense about him too. Usually their living quarters expanded into the room where he was staying, so that time they were sharing a room. He also wondered whether the presence of a policeman in the house had restricted some other of their usual out-of-hours activities. Mind you, he hadn't even really known if they were the same students whose space he had missed invading the previous year. To him they were just generic students. He didn't even remember their names.

The conversation went back to his father. 'Has he seen a doctor?' he asked.

'Well, we've pointed him in that direction, but I have no idea what they actually talked about. Neither he nor the doctor would tell us about the consultation. The doctor used the word "confidentiality" an awful lot when I tried to bring up the subject. I have to go and see the doctor myself, from time to time, about my diabetes. I have no idea whether he will actually write my prescription if I don't go and see him, but I'm not prepared to take the risk. However, my conversation with him remains strictly about me, and Bruno of course.'

'Bruno? What's the matter with him?' Truchaud looked up in alarm.

'Bruno? Absolutely nothing. But I am his mother and Dr Girand is his doctor.'

The Inspector thought no more about that, but his thoughts went back to his father's health. 'Is Dad taking any medicine?' he asked.

'Not as far as I know,' she replied. 'Mind you what he gets up to in the little flat across the courtyard is anybody's guess. The back half involving the bedroom and the bathroom is strictly off-limits. He occasionally brings sheets and towels over to go into the wash, but he takes them back himself.'

Truchaud thought it was time to change the subject again. 'Had Bertin been to the doctor's at all himself?' *Did he die of a heart attack in his sleep?* he wondered. If so, they might have had some sort of warning that he had known nothing about.

'He'd had some silly nonsense about not getting to sleep over the last few weeks, and the doctor gave him some sleeping pills or something, but I don't think he took them very often. The gendarmes took them with them when they took him away. Nothing else as far as I know.'

Truchaud tried very hard not to look 'detectively' interested. Sleeping pills were always things that interested detectives, especially when they had been prescribed for 'the deceased'.

'What was that all about then?'

'Well, we hadn't been having it very easy with Dad since the harvest, as you can understand with Dad's behaviour becoming a little … shall we say, unpredictable, and while he wouldn't go into any details with me, it had made him more tense, and he was finding it difficult to get to sleep.'

'I know this is a difficult question, but are there any money problems?'

'Not that I know of. The Domaine bank account is fine, and I know that for sure. Our joint account is fine. I have access to both of those. The taxman appears as happy as a taxman can be, I guess. Why do you ask?'

'I was just trying to figure out what was worrying him,' he replied. 'Was there anything else keeping him awake?'

'If there was he didn't talk to me about it,' she said, 'and I thought he talked to me about pretty much everything.'

Truchaud thought quietly about this. He couldn't help himself. His brother had died unexpectedly, and there was a mystery about any unexpected death. He was a policeman whose life was built round solving mysteries. There was an emotional link he had to be careful about here, but, he thought sadly, not as much as there ought to have been. With this family with whom he shared so many genes, he shared very little else. He felt even guiltier about that thought as the image of Bruno passed in front of his eyes; the Bruno who had gone back to school that morning. When he thought of Bruno in Paris, as he did from time to time, his thoughts were of teaching the boy how to be a policeman like him, not about teaching him to be a winemaker, like his father and several generations of Truchauds before them.

'Have you got that list?' he asked. 'I'll go and do the shopping.'

She gave him the list. At least he knew where the shops were, he thought as he wandered out.

Chapter 4

Nuits-Saint-Georges, Thursday

'Commander Truchaud?' asked a rather gruff voice down the phone.

'Technically, yes,' he replied, 'though while I'm in Nuits I'm only an off-duty policeman. I only answer to "Commander" when I'm in Paris. Who's this?'

'Someone who is very relieved to hear you say that before you were even asked. I'm Captain Duquesne at the local gendarmerie. Are you doing anything in particular this morning?'

'Not that I can think of. Is there anything I can do for you?'

'Well, I was wondering whether you might be willing to pop down to the local station. There are a couple of things I would like to clear up.'

'When would be convenient?'

'Right away, if you wouldn't mind. You do know where it is?'

'Of course. I'll be down right away.'

What a ridiculously English conversation, he thought, as he walked out of the house; both of them being extremely polite. At least he doesn't think I'm guilty of anything, otherwise first contact would have been made by a couple of armed gendarmes hammering loudly on the front door, using phrases like 'behind yer back', 'now', 'on the ground,' and 'mush'. This appeared to have nothing to do with the intense competitiveness between the civilian and military branches of the French law-enforcement system, and having been on both sides of the fence during his life, he could do without such barricades being erected here in Nuits-Saint-Georges.

It took him barely ten minutes to walk from the house to the square in the town centre, dominated by its water feature. It was a long narrow space, not a square in a geometrical sense at all. Listening to the rippling water all around him, and, walking across the narrow dimension of the square, he headed past the walled car park and from there crossed the Seventy-Four to the gendarmerie.

It looked all very secure behind a tall spiked fence, but the gate in the fence was unlocked and he walked through and up the steps. He rang the bell as instructed by the sign next to the door, and then walked in. The young man in uniform behind the counter was just opening his left eye, so the bell had obviously done its job and woken him.

'Yes?' he asked lazily.

'Someone called,' he checked his notes. 'Um Captain Duquesne asked me to come down to see him,' he replied.

'And you are?'

'My name is Truchaud,' he replied. The gendarme was perhaps as young as he had been when he was a lad doing his national service all those years ago. He called into the microphone on the desk. 'Captain Duquesne, sir. Got a chap out here called Truchaud, who says you want to see him.'

'Tell him I'll be right out,' replied the desk, loud enough for all to hear.

Truchaud sat down on the chair near the main entrance. He didn't have very long to wait as a tall solid man, past the first flush of youth, but not yet turning grey at the edges, came out from the office. He was wearing the badges that announced his rank as 'Captain' on his uniform.

'Come on through,' he said cheerfully enough, and Truchaud followed him. He was well aware the gendarme was at least half a head taller than him, and that would be a vaguely comical addition to the unspoken question marks coming from the uniformed youngsters as he walked past.

'I'm Captain Duquesne, and I'm the local Chief of Gendarmes. I think we know why you're here,' he continued, following up on one of the usual expressions of sympathy for his loss, which hadn't really come from anyone's heart and were becoming increasingly tedious.

24

'Do you?' asked Truchaud drily. 'I mean, do you know what happened?' He corrected himself quickly, beginning to wish that everyone would be a little less polite.

The gendarme looked at him quizzically, so Truchaud asked him if he had already received a report from the coroner, and perhaps that's why he had been summoned.

'Oh, no, no, no,' the gendarme replied quickly. 'What interested us was that we knew you were here, and yet you hadn't contacted us. We were wondering what you perceived your role down here to be.'

'I am down here being a dutiful son, to be with my family because my brother has died. No less and no more.'

That was very obviously the right thing to have said as Duquesne broke into a smile and surveyed him slowly and intently, giving nothing away, assuming he had something to give away in the first place. 'Have *you* any reason to believe that his death may have been untoward?' asked the gendarme.

Truchaud shook his head. 'I haven't been looking. Why, do you think that might have been the case?' he replied, beginning to feel slightly uncomfortable. He was trying to work out whether Duquesne was attempting to recruit him as an extra pair of experienced eyes that he didn't actually have to budget for. That immediately raised the question, why? Was there something that Duquesne knew that he didn't? He felt that this was going to be a potentially tricky next few minutes, which would require playing just right.

'This is our problem: a senior police officer arrives from the capital, more highly ranked than any of us here, immediately after the unexpected death of a prominent local. You can see how that might look?'

'Oh, for heaven's sake! I was born here. I grew up here. He was my only brother. His father is my father, and his son is the only nephew I've got. We are a small family.'

'So why aren't you working in the domaine with your father and brother?'

Truchaud explained, without going into fine detail, the family dynamics and economics. After being pushed a little, he also told the story of how he had become a policeman. He described his national service in the Gendarmerie, and then described his time in the formal police training school and beyond.

'Tell me, are you working in your family business?' he asked slightly tersely.

Duquesne grinned. 'No,' he replied. 'I grew up in Tours, where my father was employed as a stonemason. There wasn't a family business so, like you, I joined the police. Ironically, my father's still working the marble, and he actually moved down the road to Comblanchien several years ago.

'I'm surprised that you're here,' said Truchaud. 'Usually people in the gendarmerie are posted to command places far from their family homes. How did you pull that one?' Truchaud was pushing back a little.

'My parents moved here after I got here, if you must know. The National Gendarmerie isn't going to move their officers around when their parents take an opportunity to move nearer to their kids, just to be difficult with everyone. But when you come to think about it, the two municipalities around here, Beaune and Nuits-Saint-Georges, all scream 'wine'. Part of my CV talked about my dad being a stonemason, and that I was born in Tours. I suppose the computer or the clever little chap driving it didn't understand that Comblanchien stone is a really important component of the local *terroir,* and in the middle of all this wine there is a village where the stone is allowed express itself as well. I wasn't going to complain now, was I?'

Truchaud felt relieved, the tension of a few moments before appeared to have passed, and his relationship with the gendarme was back on an even keel. He felt that the score was now Gendarmerie 1–Truchaud 1. He felt he had learned very little to his advantage, apart from the fact that each was better informed about the other's family dynamics. He wasn't likely to hold the captain's local status against him. Still, it might be useful if anything went wrong.

'Is there anything more I can do for you at the moment, Captain?' he asked.

'Not at the moment, but can I ask you to be available if we need you?'

'In other words, you're telling me not to leave town?'

The Captain smiled, amiably enough. 'Something like that. And while I think about it,' he added, opening a drawer in his desk, 'my card. Take one and give me a call if anything crops up, or occurs to you.' He produced a business card, which Truchaud slotted into his wallet.

'If my Chief calls me back,' Truchaud replied, 'I'll give him your number.' He stood up and, like Elvis, left the building.

All the way home he ran a potential conversation with the Divisional Commander in his head. So, when he got home, he made the telephone call himself.

He was greeted with a fruity chuckle from his chief. 'Knew you couldn't resist finding out what was going on since you left. We had a sweepstake on it actually.'

'Oh. Who won?'

'Don't know off hand,' replied the Chief. 'It wasn't me anyway. My euro was on Saturday for you to be calling back.'

'Well, tell you what, you keep your money in your pocket, and I'll call back in three days' time, and we can both pretend you've won. I would much rather you won the bunce than Commander Lucas.'

'Lucas, eh? I often wondered why you two don't get on.'

'Call it a clash of characters,' replied Truchaud, his mind's eye drifting back to the tollbooth kiosk at Beaune. 'But that's not actually why I'm calling.'

'Oh? Go on.'

'I've just been interviewed by the local gendarmerie.'

'Already? What on earth have you been up to? And how did you find the time already? I thought you were down there on compassionate leave with your family.'

'Nothing in particular, but the local captain did tell me not to leave town. I thought he was going to confiscate my passport, but then I remembered you don't actually have to show your passport when you come off the motorway at Beaune.'

'Tell me more.'

'Well, you know my brother died? Well, his remains are at the coroner's lab in Dijon.'

'And they think you murdered him? If you like, I can trot out the arrogant young Leclerc, and the exquisitely fragrant Dutoit, who will give you an alibi and swear blindly that you were having dinner with them in Paris on the night of your brother's demise.'

'But actually, Guv, I was having dinner with them. It isn't just an alibi, it's also the truth.'

'So you were. Well, there's a thing. It's not something you get to see in our line of business: an alibi that's genuine. Do you know something else? Perhaps I'll have to take the lead of your squad while you're away.'

'I sincerely hope I'll be back in Paris long before that becomes necessary. I was only phoning you to let you know that I might not be allowed back quite as quickly as I had originally hoped.'

'Well, keep me informed, and don't worry; we'll do just fine. If we really need you back quickly, I'll have a word with your Captain Duquesne and pull rank or something. Come to think of it, you could pull rank yourself, you know.'

'Yes, but that is something I'd rather not do. I don't want to look guilty. This is my home town after all, and I do want to be able to come back here from time to time.'

'I take your point, Commander. If any rank-pulling needs to be done, you can count on my support.'

And with that the telephones were put down. Truchaud looked at the phone and shook his head rather sadly. He was concerned that his old boss was beginning to age rather disgracefully, and he hoped that his judgement was still in the right place.

Chapter 5

Nuits-Saint-Georges, Friday

Truchaud stirred his cup again. He wasn't quite sure why he kept doing this. The coffee was getting cold, after all. At least at home there was the machinery to make a strong cup of coffee, with cream on the top; coffee with a kick. Laid out in front of him was the local newspaper. Had anyone he had once known said something funny, or perhaps been caught shoplifting, or been caught in bed with someone who ought not have been there? Were they local *slebs* even? He liked the word 'sleb'; an abbreviation of the word 'celebrity', with all the contempt built in. The concept of being famous for no good reason whatsoever, apart from being famous, was so built into those four letters. What else was a local paper for, but to be a source of gossip?

However, there was nothing in it at all about his brother. He found some relief in that deep down. At least his brother was not to be trivialized. He had even looked through the sport pages, just because they were there. Still nothing of interest. Mind you, he wasn't interested in soccer, he wasn't fit enough for cycling, and the paper didn't seem to be interested in rugby. There was a short article about pharmaceutical assistance in professional cycling, and the paper seemed more surprised about that than he was. *Nonetheless,* he thought, *as everybody in Nuits-Saint-Georges seemed to know everything about his brother's demise already, perhaps there was little point putting it in the paper anyway.*

There was a knock at the door. He was getting quite used to this happening; somebody popping round the corner for a bottle of wine to drink on the spot, and perhaps to take a gawp at the grieving family. Domaine Truchaud Père et Fils, like many other domaines, was being used as a public cellar for people

29

who couldn't really be bothered to keep their own. There were the wine shops in the town centre, which had a much greater variety than any single domaine, but being shops, they had overheads. If you wanted a bottle of Truchaud, then the cheapest place to get it would be at his own back door, and Truchaud himself wouldn't be out of pocket either. This was someone who wanted a couple of bottles of the Nuits, and Michelle had left out a price list for this very reason.

The door to the cellar was out in the yard, down two steps and then through a locked door. He picked up the bunch of keys from the big chest of drawers in the dining room. The man followed him and then stopped respectfully as he reached the top of the steps. Truchaud went down the steps to the cellar door, unlocked it and then descended into the darkness. The light switch was still where it had always been, and he twisted it on. The cellar was laid out systematically. To the left of the steps, and indeed, under the steps themselves, was the Truchaud family's own personal stock, and where the family kept their own supplies, including a ham and a couple of dry sausages hanging from a hook. Straight ahead was another door. Through that door, the light was already on, where labelled bottles were racked horizontally on the left of the cellar. Some bottles lay in cases; some were in diagonal racks. These racks probably didn't contain more than twenty bottles resting on each other.

Domaine Truchaud and Fils made all of these bottles, to sell from the premises. Some of them looked very old and dusty, but most of them looked much younger. One or two of the very old-looking bottles had a fresh capsule on them. He assumed Dad or Bertin had recorked them recently. However, as this was the only actual cellar on the premises, in the family compartment there were occasional oddities, such as a couple of bottles of Gewürztraminer from Alsace, which had obviously been bought somewhere else and brought in. Maybe Bertin had a taste for spicy white wines from outside the area. He didn't think Michelle would drink sweet wine, being a diabetic. Mind you, the pack of plastic bottles of mineral water under the steps was probably hers.

Truchaud let his eyes wander deep into the centre and right of the cellar, where the barrels of wine from the last vintage were quietly letting the wine mature, in preparation for bottling next autumn. There were a few new barrels and a few not so new. Dad put about half of the *Clos* into new barrels, and half in the barrels from the previous year. It had certainly been the family policy not to 'over-oak' the wine, which meant that each barrel had several years of use, before it was passed on to the Scots.

Several years before, Bertin had arranged a deal with a whisky distiller. They took the barrels that had been used several times by the domaine, to put their whisky in for a decade or more, to let it 'mature in wine casks', somewhere deep in the Highlands of Scotland. Dad had a bottle of twelve-year-old malt whisky, matured in Burgundy casks, which he was very proud of. Truchaud wasn't a particular fan of the faintly pink stuff himself, but it contributed just a little to the cost of the new barrels that they would use that year. The Scots were more interested in having well-wined barrels, than new ones.

There at the back of the cellar was the Clos de Vougeot Grand Cru, and next to that were the Nuits. You could tell what was what as they had identifying marks on the barrels. The Nuits barrels had already been used at least twice for the *Clos*, and sometimes they had also had a year of Vosne in them too. They were in their last run before they went to Scotland. He was suddenly confused. Where was the Vosne? Every year the wines were laid out in geographical, or as Truchaud saw it, *ranking* order. The Vosne should be in barrels between the Clos de Vougeot and the Nuits. It wasn't there. There wasn't a hole where the wine from that vineyard in Vosne-Romanée should be. There just weren't any barrels from the previous harvest marked V-R in the cellar.

He was about to have a look round to see if it had been put somewhere else for a change, when he remembered he had a customer upstairs. He put a couple of bottles of Nuits into the wire bottle carrier, noting that the bottles of Vosne from earlier years were in the place they usually were, and wandered back up into the sunlight. Money changed hands, pleasantries were exchanged, and the customer commiserated with Truchaud about his loss, and wandered off clasping his bottles. Truchaud made a note on the piece of paper on the table for Michelle to put in her books, then went back down the cellar steps to lock up again. But before he locked up, he had a further look round the cellar for the missing barrels.

In the end he checked every single barrel in the cellar. He was right. All the barrels from the previous harvest were from Le Clos and the Village Nuits, and a couple of barrels that had nothing at all on them. Were they the missing wine? He tapped the barrels with a knuckle, but they were obviously empty. It hadn't been quite the productive year that some had been, hence the empty barrels, but he had never seen zero barrels from a *climat*. If a *climat* had completely failed to produce a single grape, it would have been public knowledge all over the Côte, especially if a neighbouring winemaker's *climat* had produced a normal harvest. There wouldn't have been a different topic of conversation anywhere. If they'd sold the vineyard, surely someone would have told him. He couldn't imagine Dad selling one of the family's three prize plots without telling him about it; especially as Dad knew that the Vosne was his favourite. Had they sold the Vosne to buy a Premier Cru? If one of those had come on to the market, as they did from time to time, then surely the new plot would have been on everyone's lips? A new Premier Cru *climat?* Even the thought made him excited, especially if it was a Vosne. But if his father had acquired one, he couldn't imagine anyone in the family talking about anything else. The Premier Crus were in the front rank of the village wines, hence the name, and were second only in status to the Grands Crus, which were deemed to come from such good *terroir*, that they were accorded an *appellation* all of their own.

Feeling more upbeat about the missing wine, he decided that must be the reason until it was proven otherwise. He turned out the lights, locked the cellar and went back up the stairs back into the house. Michelle had just got back, and was busy unpacking carrier bags.

32

'Where's the new patch?' Truchaud smiled at her.

Michelle looked at him completely uncomprehendingly. 'What?' she asked.

'The new patch,' he replied.

'What new patch?' she asked.

Oh, he thought sadly. A new premier cru plot wasn't the reason for the missing Vosne. He asked her what had happened to the last year's barrels.

'Oh that,' she replied. 'You spotted that.'

Truchaud was amazed. 'Err, yes. Was it planned that I wouldn't?'

'I think your father had rather hoped you wouldn't,' she replied.

'I think I need to understand exactly what's been going on here,' he said frostily.

She looked uncomfortable. 'Well, you've already seen that Dad is not very well. So, this year, it was decided that Bertin was going to make the Vosne himself, so that Dad could concentrate on the Clos. Sooner or later Bertin was going to have to make all three of the big wines anyway, so he thought he'd better start now. At the vintage, Dad seemed perfectly happy with the Vosne. However, after the first fermentation, Dad tasted it and blew a gasket. He said it was foul, an insult to the domaine and to the village. He called the dealer who buys all the grapes we grow on the other side of the Seventy-Four and gave him all the barrels of Vosne to take away. He told him he was declassifying it down to basic Bourgogne, or lower if the dealer liked, and that he could "take that muck away".'

'How did Bertin take that?'

'He was devastated.' Tears came to the corners of her eyes. She opened her bag for a tissue. Truchaud suspected she was currently well-practised in sorting tears, and she dabbed them away.

'Was the wine that unpleasant?' Truchaud couldn't imagine Bertin making a complete mess of a barrel of wine. He'd always had great respect for his brother's winemaking skills.

'I never actually got to taste it so I really don't know. Bertin said it was a little different, but that he was actually quite proud of it. But then he would have been. After all, he made it, not Dad.'

An idea crossed Truchaud's mind. 'Was that the beginning of the problems that Bertin and Dad were having?'

'Well it didn't make things any easier between them,' she replied sadly. 'But things had already begun before then.'

'Go on,' he said, beginning to realize that all had not been well at Chateau Truchaud for some considerable time.

'Well, Dad had been getting poorly during last summer. At times he seemed to be coping all right, especially when he was doing his usual things, like working with the vines, but at other times, he became upset for no obvious reason, and sometimes he just lost his temper. It always seemed to be Bertin's fault too.'

'Did he shout at you or Bruno at all?'

'Oh, he adores Bruno. He'd never shout at him.'

'And you?'

'Not like he popped off at Bertin, no. But then I do all the things that the men don't do. I'm sure that if he'd ever been involved in the paperwork side of things, he wouldn't have been so easy with me. Bertin had all the contacts with the dealers, at least until Dad gave them the Vosne, and I did all the paperwork for the taxman.'

'So, he shouted a lot at Bertin?'

Michelle nodded. He had no idea that his home had become such an unhappy place. His father was obviously suffering from some form of dementia, and was taking it out on the others. Moreover, in a relatively stratified dynamic like this family domaine, it had become increasingly difficult for the team members to cope.

'I know I asked you earlier, but did Dad go to the doctor?'

'And I'm sure I told you, yes. But the doctor wouldn't tell me what they had talked about.'

Truchaud felt that that was the problem with doctors behaving correctly: it could be extremely unhelpful to those closely involved with the patient and their care. He would have to go and see him himself. 'Garand, you say his name is?'

'Yes,' she replied, looking up at him. 'Bertin said that he married a friend of yours.'

He remembered that day. He had been unable to get to the wedding, even if he had wanted to. He had been in the middle of his training, and taking time out to go to a friend's wedding would have been frowned on. And he had not wanted to discuss how close a friend it had been … especially as she was marrying someone else.

'Something like that, yes,' he replied. 'You know something? I've never actually met the man himself.' *I must change that,* he thought to himself.

Chapter 6

Nuits-Saint-Georges, Friday afternoon

Bruno was back from school and appeared brighter. He was very keen to spend some time with his uncle, who, he had been boasting to anyone who would listen, was a very important policeman in Paris. There was still a wistful air about him concerning his father, but he was pleased to see his uncle, who was another family member to whom he could show off his knowledge of the family business.

'Uncle Shammang, can I take you out to the Nuits plot? I want to show you something.' *Bruno is growing fast,* he thought. *Every time we get together, I have to look a little less far down to see him. We'll soon be standing eye to eye. I hope he wants to run a domaine.*

'Your wish is my command, *mon capitaine,* lead on.'

It was a ten-minute walk from the domaine south to the vineyards of Nuits-Saint-Georges, and Bruno was now at least as fast on his feet as his uncle. They were heading out to what Truchaud always considered the 'Third Plot'. Not that there was anything second-rate about it, anything but, but he had always been of the opinion that the Vosne would have probably merited a Premier Cru rating if it had been in any other village, and would possibly get one if there were to be a new selection process today. Then again, he also felt that there were probably one or two Premiers Cru vineyards in Nuits itself which were worthy of Grand Cru status. Truchaud reckoned it was all a matter of the taste buds of the 'delimitation committee' that had doled out the rankings in the early thirties, or possibly their interpersonal politics.

Bruno suddenly accelerated and broke into a run. 'Granddad!' he shouted. 'Granddad, stop it!' He rushed on towards his grandfather who was bent over a vine with a pair of secateurs. 'You've already pruned that one once.'

The old man stood up looking at Bruno, somewhat confused. 'No, I haven't,' he replied. Truchaud caught up with Bruno and his father. His father was probably right actually, the policeman thought sadly, as the vine over which he was brandishing his secateurs wasn't one of his. He said softly in the old man's ear, 'Come on, Dad. Let's go home.'

'But I haven't finished the pruning.'

'You've finished that one,' he replied. 'That vine was pruned by its owner a month ago.' Truchaud took him by the elbow, looking around to see how many of its neighbours had been double-pruned by his father. Fortunately, not many, but he would have to run that vintner to ground and apologize, and arrange some sort of recompense. Production roughly worked out at a bottle per vine per year. If those vines weren't as productive as they might otherwise have been there might be questions to answer.

'Thank you, Bruno,' he said to his nephew. 'That could have been embarrassing.'

'I know,' said the boy. 'That's what Dad was saying too.'

So Bertin had been aware that his father had been 'working' on other people's vines too. That would have been a cause for discussion between them certainly.

This time Dad came meekly with his grandson and son back to the domaine. 'Dad, you can't go working on other people's vines like that.'

'But they needed pruning.' A tone of petulance entered the old man's voice.

'Even if it makes them better than they would have otherwise been, you can't go around attacking other people's vines without asking them first. There may have been all sorts of reasons that they hadn't discussed with you, as to why they wanted those vines to remain just exactly how they were. Did you know that they weren't our vines?'

The old man bristled. 'Well, of course I did! Do you think I'm some sort of fool?'

Truchaud looked at him sadly, 'You're not very well, are you, Dad?' he replied. 'How would you feel if someone else was cutting bits off our vines without first asking our permission? We wouldn't be very amused.'

The old man shuffled his feet and looked embarrassed.

'Now, what I want you to agree with me, is that you won't wander off into the vineyards without telling me where you're going first.' Truchaud was very concerned that this would trigger an explosion. However, if his father were to be caught cutting bits off vines that weren't his own in the *clos* the repercussions would be enormous, and probably very expensive. The vines in the *clos* were of high value, and high maintenance.

His father looked at him coyly, almost playfully.

'I'm not messing about with you, Dad,' he said. 'This is potentially very serious.' He looked at him down his nose, picked up the secateurs off the dining-room table and put them into his pocket.

'You're not confiscating the secateurs are you, son? Not from your own dad?'

Truchaud looked at him in despair. *What a ridiculous situation to be in,* he thought. One thing was becoming abundantly obvious; he wasn't going to be able to leave his father alone to run the domaine on his own. His brother's untimely death had come at exactly the wrong time. A moment or two of locked gazes, and his father looked down and wandered off to his own flat on the other side of the courtyard.

'What are we going to do, Uncle Shammang?' asked Bruno.

The policeman looked at his nephew fondly. 'I don't know exactly,' he replied. 'We're going to need to work this out.'

'Have you spoken to the doctor yet?'

'No, not yet. I think that's something I have to do really soon. Smart thinking, *mon capitaine*. Changing the subject a little, do you know if there is any work that actually needs to be done on the vines at the moment? A smart lad like you would know that.'

Beaming with importance, Bruno looked at his uncle, 'Not as far as I know. All the pruning's been done. Dad and Granddad

39

had already attached the canes to the lower wires of the trellises at the same time as they did the pruning. Granddad always liked to wait until the sap was rising. It makes the plants softer and more bendable.'

'Anything else?'

'Well, we've always got to be on the lookout for spiders and mildew.'

'But that surely means walking round the *climats* each day with your eyes open?'

'Just that. Great fun on a good day with nice weather; not so much when it's drizzling and cold.'

'So, Bruno, that's going to be our project over the next few days. We're going to walk the vineyards together, and you're going to have to point out to me what I should be looking for.'

The boy beamed at his uncle in pride. Suddenly the domaine had become his responsibility. At least someone in the family took him to be a man, even if he didn't sound like it yet. He glowed as he watched his uncle leave the room. 'Stay here,' his uncle told him. 'I'll be back in a moment.'

Truchaud, himself, went back down into the cellar. On the left-hand side of the cellar, there was a wooden case marked 'Charlemagne'. He had once thought it looked like it might have contained bottles of Le Charlemagne, the great white Corton, and he worried that the taxman would think that they were making it themselves and would impose more tax. As it was, his case was full of his own bottles, tax all paid and totally above board. There was also a case marked 'Bertin', which was his brother's box of bottles. He opened his own case and removed a bottle of Vosne 1996 made by the domaine, which he had been keeping for a special occasion. He looked back and didn't think that this would have been the sort of occasion he had had in mind when he had laid it down, but then he hadn't decided what would have been the right time then anyway.

He took the bottle back upstairs and put it on the table. Bruno looked at the bottle. 'That one's older than me,' he said.

Truchaud got a couple of glasses down and a corkscrew, and cut the foil off the top. The cork looked dry, so he put the corkscrew in the cork and withdrew it gently. 'On an ideal occasion, we would go away and let it breathe for a while,' he told his nephew.

'But this isn't an ideal occasion?' his nephew volunteered.

'Something like that,' he replied and poured a small amount of brick-red liquid into each glass. He picked up the glass by the stem and put the opening to his nose. He inhaled deeply and held his breath, then looked at his nephew, who did the same.

'What do you think?' he asked.

'Nice,' replied the boy.

'But what did you actually smell?'

'Cherries, violets, perhaps blackberries, and something more earthy perhaps,' replied the boy.

The detective, keeping the bottom of the glass on the table, and just holding the bottom of the stem, rotated the glass, such that the wine swirled in the glass for a moment. 'Yes, I agree,' he said. 'There's a sort of gamey scent in there too, like well-hung venison.'

Again the boy copied his uncle. Again he agreed.

'People pay a lot of money for the experience we've just had. Your grandfather made that, and in time you will be doing so too. Think about it; we've started a conversation about it and the liquid hasn't even been in our mouths yet.' He put the glass to his lips and took a small pull into his mouth, sloshed the wine round his mouth and waited. There was no unwanted extra acidity, no unpleasantness. If he were at a tasting, as occasionally he had been in Paris, at that point he would have found a spittoon and spat the wine back out. But he was at home and so he swallowed. The flavours stayed in his mouth. He looked at his nephew, who again followed his uncle. His eyes widened as the tasted also stayed in his mouth. 'That's what critics call a mouth-filler,' the uncle explained to the nephew.

'I really liked that, Uncle Shammang,' said the boy.

'I thought you might. What I've just shown you is the bottom line of what the family actually does. We're not a factory; we're artists. Think about painters. They design pictures. In the olden

41

days, some of those pictures were like photographs of things that they'd seen, but once the camera had been invented to actually provide that sort of memory, paintings then became individual artists' comments on what they'd seen. Some artists' comments became very, very famous.

'Wine is fermented grape juice. Some grape juice, however, is very different from others. It is from these different breeds of grapes, growing on different lands in different places, that produces the concept of *terroir*. That is how *climats* are ranked. Different people put their own touch on that *terroir* and its juice. Then a great wine artist comes along, to put their own stamp on a *climat*. I happen to believe that your grandfather is a great wine artist.'

'Was my dad a great wine artist?' asked the boy.

'I think that is one thing we will never know,' replied the policeman sadly. 'We never had any evidence that he wasn't,' he added tactfully, but then he really did not know the answer. There came a 'harrumph' from behind him.

'Oh hello, Dad. We were talking about you.'

The old man glared at the next two generations of Truchaud balefully. 'What about?'

Bruno chipped in. 'We've been tasting some wine that you made before I was born, and it's very good.'

The old man went over to the sideboard and took out a glass. He too poured himself just a splash. Bruno was fascinated that he too did the routine: sniff, swirl and then another sniff. Then having thought about it for a moment, he took a mouthful and sloshed it around his mouth. Unlike his son, he did spit it out into the sink.

'Very nice,' he said. 'Chap who made that can be proud of himself.'

'Why did you spit it out, Granddad?' asked Bruno in despair, 'Uncle Shammang swallowed his and so did I.'

'That's because you two knew that's all you're getting.'

The policeman chuckled. 'One of the disadvantages of tasting wine,' he said, 'is the strength of the alcohol. Only the first mouthful is the perfect one to judge. All the other mouthfuls are blurred by the memory of the first, and of course, by the alcohol, which dulls all the senses.'

The old man was looking at the label. 'Where did you get this?' he asked.

'From my box in the cellar,' replied the policeman.

'We could have sold this and made some money,' snapped the old man.

'You already sold this,' replied the policeman levelly, 'to me, many years ago, so the money was already earned.' Ignoring his father, he looked at his nephew again. 'Two things happen to a bottle of wine once it is sold: it is either drunk in its time, like this bottle will be by the end of the day; or it will be traded as an investment, and sooner or later, the label will be worth more than its contents. Isn't that an unpleasant thing to happen to a bottle of wine? I am glad to say that that won't happen to this bottle.'

He turned back to his father, 'Dad,' he said, 'you made a very good bottle of wallop there. What I suggest we do with the rest of it, is to put a vacuum cork in the top and honour it by saving it for supper. What do you think?'

His father harrumphed again, and muttering something about poultry, wandered out again.

Chapter 7

Nuits-Saint-Georges, later Friday afternoon

'You must be Bertin Truchaud's brother,' said the receptionist looking up. 'I'm so sorry for your loss.'

Truchaud looked surprised. He hadn't even opened his mouth yet. He didn't really think he looked that much like his brother. 'Is it possible to see the doctor?'

'Dr Girand is out at the moment. Is it urgent?'

'Well, I'd like to see him sooner rather than later. I would imagine that he knows what has happened to my family over the past few days, and I'd really value some advice as to how to handle things under the circumstances.'

'Do you want to book an appointment now, or would you like to phone back after lunch? I'll see, in the meantime, if I can persuade him to slot you in sooner.'

'That would be perfect. I'll call you at two.'

By 3:45 p.m. he was in Dr Girand's consulting room. Even though the doctor remained sitting down, Truchaud could tell that he was somewhat taller than himself and broader at the shoulders. His eyes were alert, dark and clear. He had a full head of dark hair, just beginning to grey at the temples. However, despite his imposing presence, his face seemed gentle and kind; just how Truchaud felt a country doctor should look. The policeman reckoned that they must be of a similar age, so the touch of grey, something that Truchaud felt added a little gravitas to his own image, suited the doctor too.

'As you probably understand,' Truchaud began, 'my brother has recently died, and my father, with whom the rest of my family lives, appears to be suffering from some sort problem of his own. I am down here for a few days, as I work in Paris, and

45

sooner or later, my sister-in-law and nephew are going to be looking after both him and the family business, on their own. What I really need to know is do you know about what's going on with Dad, and what can be expected from him over the coming weeks to months?'

The doctor leaned back. Somehow he had expected at least a bit more 'me' in the first statement from Truchaud. He had probably expected a bit more of 'tell me what happened to Bertin' in there as well. However, he didn't appear to need to refer to any notes, and the policeman was quite impressed that the doctor had either prepared this conversation or just carried his family's information in his head.

'Your father has a progressive form of Alzheimer's Disease,' began the doctor gently. 'If I say anything you don't understand, please stop me, and I'll try again.'

The bottom line, he explained, was that his father's dementia was going to get steadily and increasingly worse. 'At this moment in time, there isn't a cure for it, and certainly nothing to reverse where he has got to now. There are some drugs available, however, that might slow the progress down a bit, but even with them nothing is guaranteed.'

'Where does it come from?' Truchaud asked. 'Is it an inherited thing? I don't think any of my grandparents had it.'

'There is a variant of the disease that runs in families, but it's not common, and that one tends to start raising its head at a much younger age than your father's; that one is more likely to appear at our age. We don't really know what causes any of them. Most of the current treatments are built round what is actually happening in the brain once you've got it.'

'How do you mean?'

'Well, I'm getting into tiger country here, towards the limits of my own understanding. If you want greater details then I think you will need to see either a neurologist or a psychiatrist. Do you know what a chemical transmitter is?'

'Vaguely,' replied the policeman.

'It's a chemical that one brain cell uses to send a message to the next brain cell, usually to tell it to do something. There are also transmitters that tell other cells not to do something, but that's not relevant here.'

'Okay,' said the policeman cautiously, 'go on.'

'There's a chemical transmitter in the brain called acetyl choline, and in Alzheimer's disease there seems to be less of this stuff about. In a normal situation, you make acetyl choline when you need it, and then when you've finished with it, you break it down again with a different chemical called cholinesterase, which is, I suppose, like taking your foot off the accelerator pedal when you're driving a car. This is the same system the body uses for a lot of different chemicals we use called hormones. Switch on when you need them, and then, when you've finished, switch them off again. The current treatments for Alzheimer's that seem to work best are the drugs called cholinesterase inhibitors, which slow down the breakdown of acetyl choline in the brain, so that even when you take the foot off the pedal, there still is enough of the stuff around generally. But that isn't perfect, as it slows down the switching-off process or putting on the brakes.'

'Go on.'

'Well, imagine you're on a mountainous road going uphill. You need to put your foot down, or you won't go up the hill at all. But when you reach a twisty dip, you need to be able to take your foot off again in a hurry. We can't do that yet with anticholinesterases. Still, it's better than nothing.'

'I don't really follow all that. Are you saying that he will have to take pills for the rest of his life?'

'I expect so.'

'What happens if he won't take them?'

'A very good question. Personally, I think the best treatment is not actually pharmaceutical, but, at this moment a social treatment, called Active Stimulation. There was an article I read about the therapeutic nature of chess or cards, particularly social card games such as bridge or Tarot. They stimulate the mind and the social interaction seems to help too. And to prove the point, it appears that solitaire card games don't seem to be anywhere near so helpful.'

47

'I used to play Tarot when I was at school and we used to play at Police College.'

'Yes, it was a game we enjoyed at medical school too. Four or five of us would all get together to discuss what we had learned that day, while looking out for the one-eyed Knight of Diamonds.' He grinned.

'Worth three points,' chuckled Truchaud. It was some years since he had picked up a pack of French Tarot, to play a game of cards. A couple of years before there had been a case up in Paris, involving a fortune-teller and their pack of mystic Tarot cards, but those had been somewhat different in design, having suits like cups and swords. He had thought at the time that it would have been perfectly possible to play the game with them, although they were somewhat more papery than the rather lacquered style of playing cards.

'Do you still play?' asked the doctor.

'I haven't played recently, but I suppose it's like riding a bike: you don't forget these things once you start playing again.'

'You must come round some time and we'll play a few hands. My daughter, who's a student, is forever trying to recruit me into playing Tarot at the weekends. You can help me shut her up.'

'If I'm going to get Dad playing, I'm going to have to teach Bruno too. He's the right sort of age.'

'I can see I'm going to regret this. Soon I'm going to be more in demand as a Tarot player than as a family doctor.'

And like ships passing in the night they bade each other farewell, agreeing to see each other soon, perhaps socially, and with that Truchaud wandered off.

The next objective Truchaud had on his list before the evening meal was to touch base with the wine merchant. He felt he really had to know what Bertin's Vosne had been like. A neutral judgement would be valuable, especially as there was now so much at stake here. They were going to have to make a decision, sooner or later, about employing a winemaker to take over, until Bruno was old enough to take on the business himself. He was worried that the cost of employing someone, and the cost of looking after Dad was going to be beyond what the family could afford. However, the first thing was the dealer. Most dealers were based fifteen minutes south by road in Beaune. The one that Bertin and his father had picked was based on the outskirts of Nuits-Saint-Georges itself.

The house was built on a grander scale than his own domaine, with a shop front in the courtyard. He went through the door into the shop itself and rang the bell. Behind the counter there were rows of bottles all standing up, with the wine certainly not in contact with the cork, keeping it moist. Truchaud was pleased he wasn't actually buying wine from here. There was something distinctly 'for the tourists' about the place.

'Can I help you?' came a voice from behind him. The girl had obviously followed him in.

'Yes, I was looking for the merchant himself,' Truchaud replied, fully aware that he sounded a little patronizing, as if he was too grand to be talking to a mere slip of a girl.

'He's out at the moment, but I'm sure I can help you find the wine you're looking for.'

He thought for a moment, and, then slightly provocatively he said, 'Well your boss had a few barrels of Vosne-Romanée off my dad after the last harvest, and I wondered if you'd bottled it yet, and if so whether you'd sell me a bottle. I'm fascinated to know how it turned out.'

The girl looked uncomfortable. 'Sorry, what was the name again?'

'Truchaud Père et Fils.'

She looked up and down various lists shaking her head. 'No, I can't find anything here. Are you sure he bottled it under that name?'

'Not at all sure, that was all part of the question.'

'No, you're right. You will have to come in when he's back. Who shall I say called?'

'Charlemagne Truchaud,' and by this time he was positively twinkling with mischief. She swallowed it hook, line and sinker poor girl.

'Oh, I can find you a bottle of that. Yes, here it is,' she said brandishing a bottle of crystal clear white wine.

'No,' he replied gently, 'I was telling you my name, Charlemagne. You can understand why I don't use it very often, especially round here. Do you know when the owner will next be in? I'm only in Nuits-Saint-Georges for a few days or so, and I would like to see him while I'm here.'

'Hang on a moment. I'll take a look in his diary. He keeps it on the laptop on his desk.' She walked through the door behind the counter deeper into the building. *Hmm,* he thought, *very trusting, I could be anybody and just help myself to a couple of bottles, and walk out.* He hadn't spotted where she had got that bottle of Charlemagne from, but it looked beautiful. It was always possible that it had been sitting bolt upright in the warm like the others in front of him, but its lustre was undeniable.

Suddenly there was a shriek from behind the door. 'Oh, oh my God!' It was the girl's voice. She came rushing out, her olive complexion now ashen, her mouth open and struggling to breathe.

'What's happened?' he asked.

'It's young Mr Laforge. I think he's dead.'

'Where?' he asked walking round the counter and through the door. There in the office on the other side of that door, slumped over a laptop on the desk, with his back to him was a man. Truchaud was completely in agreement with the girl. You didn't get a hole that size in the back of your head without being dead.

He pulled out the card from his wallet that Duquesne had given him earlier that day, and called him on his mobile.

'Captain Duquesne? Truchaud here.'

'Hello Commander, a pleasure again so soon. What can I do for you?'

'I think you'd better get round to Laforge's wine shop. I'm looking at a dead body which appears to have a gunshot wound to the back of the head, and under such circumstances, I think I'm supposed to inform the local senior police officer.'

'You haven't touched the body, have you?'

'Believe me, I didn't need to.'

'I'll be right there. Don't contaminate the crime scene, and don't let anyone else do so either.'

Truchaud went back into the shop to comfort the sobbing girl. Within a few minutes or so, the sound of a two-tone siren filled the air.

Chapter 8

Nuits-Saint-Georges, Friday afternoon

Truchaud had realized very early in his life that he wasn't very good at comforting people. He was well aware that in the current situation he was showing little improvement. He also felt uncomfortable holding a slightly built teenaged girl so closely, who was considerably younger than he was. It wasn't as if he knew anything about her at all, apart from the fact that she had just found her employer very messily dead.

There was one other thing he knew; she had just failed to sell him a bottle of wine. All right, so he didn't actually want any, and that wasn't why he had come into the shop in the first place, but she wasn't to know that. He hadn't even consciously looked at her face. He could see from the position of her head on his right shoulder that she had brown shiny bobbed hair, but that was about as much as he had worked out by the time the gendarmes arrived.

'Good evening, Commander. I see you're busy,' said Captain Duquesne drily as he walked through the door, followed by a couple of uniformed gendarmes he recognized from earlier in the day. They were armed to the teeth and looking as they might actually bite.

'Good evening, Captain,' he replied. 'The body's through there, in the office.'

The Captain and the male gendarme walked through into the office. Truchaud watched the younger officer walking in first with his gun at port. The other gendarme, a red-headed woman, remained at the door of the shop, brandishing her weapon just to make sure that Truchaud and the shop girl didn't try to escape.

They were back out again very quickly, with the Captain already barking instructions into his handset. When he had finished he looked at Truchaud and the girl coldly.

'Do we know who he is?' he asked.

'Jérome Laforge,' said the girl. 'He's the owner.'

'And how do you know that? Did you actually touch the body?'

'No,' she wailed. 'It's his office, and that's the same old jacket he always wears. Who else would it be?'

The Captain ignored her question and the desperation in her voice. He continued. 'Who discovered the body?'

The girl looked at him. 'Well I suppose that was me too,' she said rather brokenly, still crying.

'And you are?' asked the gendarme, still ignoring her distress.

'Suzette Girand. I work here.'

'What do you actually do?'

'I'm a salesperson. I try to sell wine.' She emphasized the 'try', and looked up over her shoulder straight at Truchaud. He caught his breath. He had not seen eyes that green since he had last looked at 'the one that got away', so many years before.

'So, can you tell me exactly what happened?'

Truchaud told him the story from when he had entered the shop to the moment of the Captain's own arrival. The Captain then interrogated them rapidly: first the one, then the other.

'Did either of you hear any shots?'

'Not that I'm aware of, and I like to think I would recognize a shot if I heard one,' replied Truchaud.

'So would I, Commander, so would I. Now, I noticed you mentioned that you had entered the shop before Miss Girand here. How exactly did that happen?' There was a pause, and then he added, 'Miss Girand?'

She tried to speak amid the sobs. 'Well, it had been a quiet afternoon, so I crossed the road to have a cup of coffee with my friend who works in the café over the road. We were sitting where I could easily see the entrance to this place if anyone should actually come in, and I could get back to the shop long before they managed to leave again.'

'Your friend will corroborate that statement?' enquired the gendarme.

'Of course,' she said. 'Ask her.'

'I'm quite likely to do that,' he said. 'When did you last see your employer alive?'

'Yesterday.'

'So how did you get in today?'

'I have my own set of keys, so I let myself in after lunch and opened up.'

'Been a busy afternoon?'

'No. As I said, very quiet. This gentleman was only my second customer.'

Duquesne harrumphed. 'Well,' he said, 'it's not going to get any busier. We're going to have to shut the shop up for the moment, as it's now a crime scene.'

The girl let out an explosive wail, and pushed her face again into Truchaud's shoulder for a moment. Then she looked up again, more frightened. 'I'm not under arrest, am I?' she asked, her eyes opening even wider.

'Not at the moment,' he said, 'but I don't need to tell you … don't leave town.'

'But I'm due back at university in Dijon on Monday,' she said desperately. 'My tutor is expecting an essay in then, at the latest.'

'Then what you have to do is get that essay done. What will happen on Monday, we will have decided by Monday. And the same thing about leaving town goes for you too, Commander Truchaud.'

'I wasn't planning on leaving town. I've told you that already.'

The gendarme noted down their names and addresses, looking up at Truchaud when he gave her his address. He wondered whether she was the same policewoman who had sat with Michelle awhile after she had discovered Bertin's body.

Duquesne looked at the crying girl with increasing irritation. 'Commander Truchaud, can I trust you to make sure Miss Girand here gets home safely? That way I can hang on to my gendarmes to investigate the crime scene. I think you had both better have one of my cards.' He issued them both with one of his business cards: Truchaud's second of the day.

'Now once you have got her home, go home yourself. If I need to see you tonight, I'll know where you are. If I don't come and see you tonight, can you come down to the gendarmerie in the morning?'

'Of course.'

'And, mademoiselle, may I also request that you stay home tonight? I would rather you weren't off gallivanting with boy-friends. I may need to be able to find you too. I will make a telephone call when I want to see you, and as soon as I know what we're to do about university on Monday.'

Truchaud and the girl left the shop, and she directed him where to go. He decided not to tell her that he had grown up in Nuits-Saint-Georges, and that he knew every street in the place.

'You don't have to take me home,' she said, looking up again with her magical green eyes.

'I promised that nice gendarme I would,' he replied. She laughed hollowly. 'After all, I too am a policeman; just one who's not on duty.' In the end he couldn't resist the question. 'Tell me, those eyes, are they real?'

She smiled just for a moment at him, before they all watered up again. 'No, they're contact lenses. My mum has eyes this colour naturally, and I think they're so pretty that I got these lenses, so that mine can look like hers.' With that smile, he knew exactly who she was. The whole shape of her face was so like Geneviève's; it was almost like falling backwards into a time capsule. He may not have seen her for years, but he had never forgotten what she looked like, and this girl had to be her daughter.

'What are you studying?' he continued with the inconse-quential small talk in the hope it would calm her distress.

'Modern Humanities, in Dijon. I share a flat near the uni-versity campus, but I usually come home at the weekend. It's easier to walk to the shop. It earns me a little pin money. You know, helps me buy books, and my food tickets at the

Restaur-U.' Her face crumpled. 'I can't believe what's just happened,' she said and burst into tears again. She pushed her face into his right shoulder again, sobs racking her body.

He felt quite honoured in a strange sort of way; he had met this girl bare minutes ago, and she already trusted him enough to sob into his shoulder. He really hadn't held anyone this close for a long time, apart from the occasional off-duty moment in Paris. But that was an inappropriate thought that wandered across his consciousness unexpectedly. 'Go away!' he commanded the thought silently, 'especially in the presence of this girl.'

They walked up to the door of her house.

'Daddy, Daddy,' she wailed as she opened the door. 'Someone's just killed Mr Laforge.'

The person who met them at the door was the doctor in whose surgery Truchaud had been not more than an hour ago. 'Mr Truchaud?'

'Doctor Girand? I thought I recognized the name.' The girl had now transferred her interest to her father, and was sobbing into his right shoulder.

'What on earth happened?' asked the doctor.

Truchaud explained. The doctor made all the right noises and said finally, 'Well, now you've met the daughter, who plays Tarot.'

'What on earth is all this noise about?' came a voice from behind him that Truchaud may not have heard for years, but he recognized as if it had been yesterday. The hairs stood up on the back of his neck, and he almost didn't dare look round.

'Oh Mum, it's been so awful!' said the girl through her tears, as she rushed from her father, past Truchaud, to fall into the arms of the voice behind him. 'Somebody's shot Mr Laforge, but this kind man brought me home.' Truchaud turned round slowly. She hadn't changed at all. He had been right when he told his Chief that there had never been anyone like her. There hadn't. She hadn't changed a bit. She was exactly as he remembered her, right down to the piercing green eyes.

'Charlie?' she asked as her magnificent eyes widened.

'Jenny,' he replied. He had, after all, had a few minutes' notice of this meeting.

'You know each other?' father and daughter chorused simultaneously.

'We were at school together when we were kids,' they replied, also in perfect two-part harmony.

This conversation needs redirecting very quickly, both protagonists thought. 'Why don't you stop for supper? We can talk over old times.'

'Much as I would like to, I've promised Michelle, my brother's wife, and she will have already started cooking. I also promised the gendarme that Suzette likes so much, that I would be at home for the rest of the evening, in case he wants to see me again. Incidentally, he also asked your daughter to stay at home too in case he needs to see her again as well.'

'Oh, he was horrid,' wailed the girl, 'so rude.'

'That's what we police tend to be like,' he said gently. 'I think it's to make sure the criminals, such as whoever killed Mr Laforge, don't think they can get away with it.'

'Well, sometime soon, you must come round,' she added, to which her husband interrupted, 'and play Tarot.'

The daughter then interjected into the cacophony of speech, 'Oh you play Tarot?'

To which the doctor then replied, 'Yes, I was going to tell you about him. This chap actually plays Tarot and he wants to teach his family.'

'Well there's a coincidence.' Truchaud said nothing, and waited a moment until all went quiet again, give or take a sob.

'I'm going to need to see you *all* again very soon. You,' he said to the doctor, 'are going to need to help me sort out my dad.' He looked at Suzette. 'And your father tells me that you're just the person we may need to help us with him.'

Finally, he looked at Geneviève. 'And you and I have a lot of catching up to do. But right now,' he said, 'I have a bewildered father, an excited nephew, a widowed sister-in-law and supper on the table: all of which are where they were expected to be an hour ago. I must go.'

They let him out the front door, and as he walked back west into the older part of town, he had a spring in his step and he could not remember the last time he had felt like whistling.

Chapter 9

Domaine Truchaud Père et Fils, Friday evening

'I'm home!' he called out, throwing his trench coat at a peg in the hall.

The smell coming from the kitchen suggested that cooking had been going on for some time. It was the smell of cooking wine, with herbs and garlic. This was definitely home cooking, not just putting the finishing touches to a Mrs Albrand creation, started next door. 'I needed to start cooking again,' Michelle said. 'I was beginning to feel guilty about being waited on hand and foot.' She sounded more cheerful in herself too; creating does that to you.

'Uncle Shammang, Uncle Shammang,' came an excited voice from round the corner, followed by a rapidly hurtling Bruno. 'You'll never guess what I've just heard.'

Truchaud raised a surprised eyebrow, wondering what this good news could be that made the lad sound so happy too. 'You're probably right, I won't.'

'Somebody bumped off Mr Laforge at the wine merchants.'

'Oh, Bruno, don't go telling your uncle stories,' said his mother gently. 'Just because your uncle's a policeman, it doesn't mean that everything is a crime.'

Truchaud glanced at Michelle, 'Unfortunately, this time, it's true. Where did you hear that, Bruno?' he asked, thinking that was quick news circulation, even in a small place like Nuits-Saint-Georges.

'One of the lads was walking past his shop, and the whole street is teeming with gendarmes, even in the coffee shop across the road, and one girl in the coffee shop is his sister, and she told him. Weren't you going to see him today, Uncle Shammang?'

'Yes, I did.'

'Was that you they were talking about? You know, the off-duty policeman who was also there? You didn't bump him off, did you?'

'I might well have been that off-duty policeman, and no, I did not kill anybody!' The second clause was emphatic.

Michelle looked up surprised; 'You mean you were actually there?' she asked.

'It'll be all round the town in the morning. Yes, I was there. I was one of the people who found him.'

'What happened?' she asked.

'I have no idea at the moment,' he said, and while that wasn't strictly true, it would do for the time being. 'We found him in his office, and, as Bruno says, the local gendarmerie is involved. They may come round later this evening, I suppose, wanting to interview me further. Meanwhile, is the supper ready?'

She smiled. 'Right away,' she said.

'Then I'll reopen that bottle of wine.'

'Go and get your granddad, Bruno,' said Michelle. Bruno rushed off out. She looked at her brother-in-law quizzically. 'Really? Murdered?'

'It appears so,' he replied.

'That sort of thing just doesn't happen in Nuits-Saint-Georges.'

'Well, it appears to have happened now. What was he like? I mean I never actually met him alive.'

'I never really knew him either. He did all his dealings with the men, mainly Bertin. Until that last Vosne harvest, they mainly talked about the parcels on the east side of the Seventy-Four. They tended to meet sometime during the summer to look at how the grapes were doing, and would haggle over a price for the harvest. They would then meet again during the harvest, in the vineyards, and haggle a bit more. The whole conversation was in numbers. Finally, they would shake hands, having come to some sort of a mutual agreement, down an aperitif or a brandy, and that was it.

'They would probably talk again in very early spring, when the occasional vine that needed replacing was replaced. I know we pay for any new vine stocks we need. They come ready

62

grafted nowadays, and we usually plant them at the end of March. The few we've needed to replace this year have all gone in. They're not much good for wine in the first couple of years.'

'Ready grafted?'

'Do you remember the stories of the *Phylloxera* aphid?'

'Only too well.'

'Well, the insect larvae killed all the French vines in the 1870s, so we had to import *Phylloxera*-resistant rootstocks from America, and graft French vines on to them; a process that continues to this day. Every single vine, pretty much throughout France, is a French vine hand-grafted onto an American root. The larva, ironically, was a resident of America, which was shipped to Europe by mistake in the 1850s. They live in the American roots too, but don't kill them, hence the grafting process.'

'Hasn't that changed the taste somewhat?'

'I have no idea. I wasn't around 150 years ago.'

'So, Granddad, what do you think?' Bruno and his grandfather were coming through the front door.

'Is it true?' he asked Truchaud.

'I'm afraid so,' the family detective replied.

'Hell of a thing,' the old man mumbled. 'What is the world coming to?'

Truchaud pulled the vacuum cork from the Vosne, as Michelle passed round bowls of coq-au-vin, tasty chicken pieces on the bone stewed in wine with small pieces of bacon and onions. The meat fell off the bone as if commanded. He really hoped she hadn't used a bottle of old Vosne to cook it in; they hadn't got a lot of that left. The bread was a crisp baton, and must have been made at the baker's late that afternoon, it tasted so fresh.

They ate in silence, partly out of respect for the chef, and partly because they had always told Bruno it was unpleasant for everyone else to talk with your mouth full.

The baker, wearing his *patissier* hat, had also made the apple tart that followed. 'I never really bothered to learn how to make these things,' Michelle said. 'Why should I bother when we've got such an artist living three doors down?'

They then followed it with some cheese and a little marc.

'What do you think, Dad?'

'Good marc,' he replied.

'About the murder.'

'Murder, what murder? Who's been murdered?' The old man looked around in alarm.

'I just told you, Granddad,' said Bruno exasperated.

'Oh, that murder,' he shrugged, as if he had understood what they'd been talking about all along. 'Well, these things happen, don't they?' He then announced he was going out for a walk and left the room.

'Have we still got his secateurs?' Truchaud asked his sister-in-law, who nodded and pointed at the sideboard where they kept the cutlery and glasses.

'Bruno, time for bed.'

'Oh, Mum, I want to be here when the gendarmes arrive.'

'I'm not sure they're coming,' said Truchaud. 'They only said that they might, and that I should be here in case they do.'

'But that's not fair.' They could almost imagine the boy stamping his foot.

'I don't think it's fair on anyone,' replied his mother firmly, 'least of all on poor Mr Laforge.'

'I don't think you need to worry,' added his uncle. 'We're not going to keep you out of the picture. As soon as we know anything more, we'll be the first to tell you; that is, provided you don't know already.' They grinned at each other, both fully aware that the one had sources of information to which the other had no access.

'Okay. Well, goodnight everybody.' And with that, the boy also left the room.

There was a moment or so of silence while they cleared the table and washed up. Aware that he wouldn't be driving again that night, the detective helped himself to another splash of marc. 'You want one?' he asked Michelle.

'No thanks. I may start crying again. What on earth is happening Shammang? Since the beginning of this week, it hasn't been a very good thing for anyone's life expectancy to actually

64

know me. My husband and then someone he did business with are both dead.'

'Do you think there's a link?' he asked gently, aware of the moisture in her eyes.

'Well, you always say you don't believe in coincidences. don't you?'

'If you think that's the case, then you're suggesting Bertin was murdered. Surely you don't think that. Why would you think that?'

'Well, the only reason I wondered whether that might have happened was after what's happened to poor Mr Laforge. I mean, you do think Mr Laforge was murdered, don't you?'

'Almost certainly,' he agreed. 'Did they know each other socially? Were they friends outside their business relationship? Did they play cards together or support the same team or something?'

'Not that I know of, no.'

'So how did their business relationship actually work?'

'Well, as far as I know, our link with his firm, and it is quite a big firm, is that in the autumn, they come and harvest our vines on the east side of the Seventy-Four with their mechanical harvesters, and take those grapes back to Laforge's. They then turn those grapes into whatever they need them for, and pay us for them. We continue to look after the vines throughout the year, until the next harvest.'

'Why don't they just buy the vines off us and do it all in-house?'

'I think Mr Laforge put that suggestion to Bertin and Dad more than once, but neither of them would sell. Every now and then the harvest is good enough that they make some wine from there themselves and sell their own 'hand-made' Bourgogne. By continuing to own the vineyards, that remains an option. I suppose if they had ever wanted to turn that vineyard into cash for any reason, it's quite handy to know there was someone ready to buy it. If anyone else bought it, then they would probably have a use for the grapes that might not involve Mr Laforge and his firm.'

'So what would have happened with last year's Vosne? Certainly the girl in the shop didn't seem to know.'

'Oh, you've met Suzette? Nice girl.'

'Difficult to form an opinion,' he lied. 'One moment she was trying to sell me wine I didn't want, and for the rest of the time she was crying.'

'You're a hard man, Shammang Truchaud. Death is not part of everyone's daily life experience.'

Truchaud thought about that for a moment. She was right. If he had married Geneviève then he very much doubted that he would be a policeman right now. He would have been somewhere very different. He also wondered whether he would still be married to her. *Different paths in different universes,* he thought.

'Well, if it was as bad as Dad said,' he went on, not following his own train of thought, 'would he have poured it into the vat of Bourgogne to be sold to the masses?'

'Depends what he paid for it,' she replied.

'Surely you would know that?' Truchaud looked up at her.

'No, they kept those business transactions away from the domaine business.'

'I don't follow.'

'The business I dealt with was all the owner/grower/harvester side of the business where we made the wine, literally from the ground up to the finished bottle, down to the label design. We took full responsibility for all that, including all the duty involved. We might sell the wine on our doorstep like last night, or to individual merchants. Most of the merchant sales are done before we do the bottling and labelling, but not all. When they collect from here the labelling is all already done.

'They might have done their own personal deal with the taxman, and therefore bought from us in advance of tax, and put their own tax capsule on top of the bottles. Certainly in good years, a merchant might come and buy more as if it were doorstep trade. Some of the merchants come and see us from England or America even. We might even sell stuff from our cellar that's two or three years old. We have a good reputation with some of them. I'm pretty sure that if they sell in England, they get the tax capsules redeemed by the French taxman, before they then charge their English customers the English levels of duty. That's the business that I do. Bottles that go through my books are bottled in-house and are usually taxed at source. I can track any bottle that has left here untaxed anyway.'

'And the sale of grapes before they are fermented doesn't attract any duty?'

'Right, and therefore it is not our *wine* business, it's our *grape* business, which is a different thing altogether. I had little or nothing to do with that.'

'So who runs that now?' he asked. *Bertin's dead, and Dad's not in a fit state to do any business,* was an unvoiced thought that passed between his ears.

'You know, I have no idea. I haven't really thought about that yet.'

'One last thought. The Vosne had been fermented, so it was wine and not grape juice. Therefore it would have attracted tax, even if Dad did give the wine to Laforge free of charge.'

'Oh, good lord, I never thought of that!' Michelle looked alarmed.

'It may be that they agreed that Laforge would take responsibility for that tax bill. I wonder who would know the answer to that.'

And that, he thought, *is where we need to start exploring next, both on behalf of Bruno and the family's future.* Also, being a policeman, he had a personal need to solve the mystery.

Chapter 10

Nuits-Saint-Georges, Saturday morning

'Did the gendarmes arrive last night, Uncle Shammang?' asked Bruno over breakfast.

The croissants were still warm from the bakery down the road. *When I go back to Paris*, Truchaud thought, *I'm going to kidnap this baker and install him in the basement of my block of flats.* Nowhere in Paris had he ever found such perfect croissants. They were light, fluffy, and made with enough butter to need nothing more, apart, of course from the coffee.

Making sure he didn't talk with his mouth full, he waited until he had swallowed until he replied in the negative.

'So what happens now?' asked Bruno.

'I finish my breakfast in peace, help your mother do the washing up, and then when all is neat and tidy, I go down to the gendarmerie in the town centre as instructed and see what's going on.'

'Are you in charge of the case, Uncle?'

'Anything but,' he replied. 'At the moment it's the Captain who's running the show. Then there will be an investigating judge whose job will be to pull the case together for the prosecutor to try in court. Quite when the judge appears, I suppose, will be up to them. In Paris some of our judges are more hands-on than others. I have been asked to go down to the gendarmerie, and therefore that's what I will do. It's a good trick for you to learn when dealing with the police: if you do exactly what they tell you to do, you can't go wrong, even if they're not prepared for you to actually do so.'

'What will you say?'

'I don't know. That really depends what questions they ask me. While we were all asleep, they will have been assessing the

69

crime scene. They won't have had time to go through any of the papers they have found yet.'

'Will the post-mortem results be back yet?'

'Oh, Bruno!' exclaimed his mother in disbelief. 'He is really getting into American television police procedurals. Every time he's in front of the telly, he's watching *CSI* or something grim like that. Why can't you watch a nice French farce?'

'There aren't any nice French farces on telly.'

'Well, how about a nice variety programme or something?'

Bruno rolled his eyes and his expression begged his uncle to wade in to help him out. He accepted the cry for help. 'I suppose that depends whether they were willing to pay the pathologist to stay up all night. Mr Laforge wasn't going on his own anywhere beyond where they took him, so perhaps the pathologist will have just gone in this morning, after a breakfast of coffee, ham and, if he has access to them, some of these delicious croissants. It would certainly put me in a better frame of mind than having to go in and work all night. On the other hand, however, he may have just bought a new car and be in need of the money.'

It was a bright day, and showing no signs of rain as he walked into the centre.

The young gendarme on the desk recognized him this morning. He was the one who walked into Mr Laforge's office, armed and loaded. Truchaud wondered how much sleep he had got last night. 'Good morning, Commander,' he said politely. 'I'll tell the Captain you've arrived.'

'Thank you.'

'Commander,' came from within the office, rapidly followed by the form of Captain Duquesne, 'come on through. Coffee?'

'No thanks. I've just had breakfast.'

'I never like to be without a cup of coffee to hand, otherwise my stomach thinks I'm out on a case and it gets grumpy. I can do without too much of that.' *Hmm,* thought Truchaud, *he's a morning person; very chipper.* The gendarme gestured to a rather gaunt looking silver-haired man who was sitting behind the desk where the Captain had been sitting yesterday. 'May I introduce you to the investigating judge, Mr Lemaître?'

'Monsieur le Juge,' said Truchaud politely, 'my name's Truchaud.'

'I understand from the Captain here that you're a policeman too.'

'When I'm in Paris, yes. My role in this room is as a simple witness to this very unpleasant killing. Is this something you're getting a lot of down here now?'

'What? You mean you get a lot of this sort of thing in Paris?'

'Executions? Yes, quite a few.'

'How do you make that out; that it was an execution?'

'To get a hole in the back of the head like that, someone has to walk up behind the person, aim and fire,' Truchaud explained, making a pistol with his right hand and fingers, firing and then blowing across the top of them. 'That's an execution. I would be willing for the post-mortem to prove me wrong, but the way I saw it Laforge was sitting quietly in his chair working on the computer, when someone walked in, pointed a gun at the back of his head and pulled the trigger. He may have been totally unaware of anything before he was absolutely aware of nothing. Did the shell come out the other side of his head? I didn't see.'

'No, it didn't penetrate through,' replied the Captain.

The judge leaned forward and said, 'I'm interested in your thoughts and experience, Commander. Do go on.'

'Well, that should tell the ballistics experts in the lab some-thing. Off the top of my head that suggests that he was shot with a low-velocity round, or perhaps a shotgun, though the relative lack of spread suggests it wasn't. And if it was a low-velocity round, then it will need to have been fired from very nearby to have penetrated the cranium at all, and, there should therefore be gunshot residue on the back of the scalp.' Truchaud looked the gendarme in the eye.

'Now, if someone walked up to him that closely, the chances are that the victim knew what was happening. That sort of execution, bullet to the back of the head, was the common way, for example, for the Khmer Rouge in Cambodia to execute their prisoners. Do you want me to see how far I can think this?' The judge nodded, so Truchaud continued. 'Do we know how old Laforge was?'

'Early sixties, I think,' said Duquesne. 'You're not suggesting he was in Indochina at the time of the First Indochina War, are you?'

'No,' said Truchaud. 'But from what you say, the killer might have been, or was trained by someone who was.'

Duquesne replied dismissively, 'No, I wasn't suggesting anything like that. However, Laforge would have been a young man in the seventies, and perhaps involved in the counter-culture of that time.'

'A hippy you mean?' Lemaître rolled his eyes.

Truchaud thought for a moment about the music of the counter-culture: late Beatles, Jacques Brel, the Grateful Dead, and Serge Gainsbourg. There were a fair few LPs of those back in his flat in Paris, plastic discs a foot across, which were played with a fine-pointed diamond needle. They were immensely fragile, and most of his LPs had at least one scratch on them, which nowadays added to the authenticity of the sound when he listened to them, which he did when he wanted to switch off. He sometimes wondered what he would do when they wore out.

'I can't see anyone being executed for being a lapsed hippy,' he said after a moment's thought, 'but it might be interesting to take a dig into his past and see what rolls out.'

The judge cleared his throat, and the tone of his voice became altogether more business-like. 'So Commander, getting back to the point, can we get started? Why were you at Laforge's in the first place? You say yourself that you weren't there to buy wine.'

'He was the wine merchant my family dealt with so I went to talk to him about how my brother's death affected all that.'

'I hope you aren't going to tell me you were there actively investigating your brother's death.'

'Of course, I wasn't,' he protested tactically. 'What I had wanted to do was to find out exactly where the business stands. You may be aware that my father, who runs the family business, isn't very well at the moment?'

'Nothing serious I hope?'

'Tragically, very serious. He's got Alzheimer's, and it's getting worse. There's no way he's going to be able to run the business on his own in the future. That means it looks like my brother's widow's going to have to run it herself from here on in.'

'Or, you're going to have to help her,' Duquesne added.

'You catch on to my problem fast, Captain,' he replied. 'I'm going to have to find a winemaker to employ to run the place for the next ten years until my nephew Bruno's old enough to run the business. But before I can do that, I need to know exactly what I'm going to have to ask this putative employee to do. I also need to know how hands-on I'm going to have to be from Paris. It's a half-day drive, or an hour or so on the TGV to Dijon. I don't think it's going to be any quicker to fly, with all the messing about at either end at the airports. If, therefore, communication is going to be virtual, over the phone or over the Internet, I've got to know in my own head exactly who and what I'm dealing with.'

'I follow,' replied the judge. 'Not guilty there then?'

'Of what?' enquired Truchaud, slightly alarmed.

'Of impersonating a police officer. What did you think?' Lemaître threw that line out with a smile behind it, but Truchaud was well aware of the underlying threat.

'Going back to your original question, Monsieur le Juge,' he pushed. 'Do you think there is anything in my brother's death that needs investigating?'

'You tell me,' replied the judge inscrutably. He then relaxed a bit, 'As far as I am concerned, there is one death I am investigating at the moment and that is Mr Laforge's. The only reason that your brother's death might interest us too, is the fact that they are sudden unexpected deaths of two people that happened only a couple of days apart, and that before their deaths both lives were closely linked together commercially. You are trying to find out the state of your family business, and the relationship between your business and Mr Laforge's. We are trying to find out who killed Mr Laforge and why. Do you follow me so far?'

'Yes,' replied Truchaud cautiously.

'May I suggest, gentlemen, that you separately pursue your individual investigations, and yet at the same time, share information with each other where appropriate, so that when one of us acquires some information that might be of assistance to the other, then that information might find itself available to the other's hands.'

'Would we be allowed to do that?'

'Share information? You might think not officially perhaps, but if either of you felt the need to put your relationship on a more formal footing, then the situation would have changed anyway. By that time all that information will have been shared with me.' He stood up from behind the desk. 'Gentlemen, I have another appointment I must keep. Commander Truchaud, it was good to meet you, and I will see you both again soon.' And with that he left the room, and could be seen through the window a few moments later walking out to the gate.

Duquesne looked at Truchaud quietly for a moment. 'Did you follow all that?' he asked.

'I think so,' replied Truchaud. 'Do you know what he's like under the grey suiting? He seemed pleasant enough.'

'He's always been easy to work with. This is a new angle for me. You're effectively a private eye investigating a different but linked case. The argument is that when I leak information to you, that you need to be trusted to treat it with the utmost discretion, and at the same time you may well be in a position to help the official investigation in return.'

'You're taking a lot of me on trust. I'm sure there are senior police officers around and about France on whose word you might not be able to rely.'

'Ah, but yours I think I can,' the gendarme grinned positively. 'I am quite skilled in the use of a clever device you may have heard of, called a telephone. When I called an old friend in the gendarmerie in Paris, and mentioned your name, he was positively effusive. It appears you have quite a reputation with the gendarmerie up there. He did say that, as well as being trustworthy, you are also downright clever. Mind you, he did ask me if we wouldn't mind keeping you down here as long as possible! What was that all about, I wonder? All I need to do, therefore, is to get you to agree to state publicly that this is my case and not yours, and thus I can bask in your reflected glory, pretending it's my own.'

'Not a problem,' Truchaud replied. 'My side of the deal is that my time is my own, and that I'm not at your beck and call every part of the day and night. Moreover, if I'm playing Tarot at somebody's house, it may be socially, or I may be doing a bit of investigating, but that is on my time. I won't be further away than Dijon to the north or Beaune in the south without telling you first. So call me on my mobile phone. You've got the number, and I'll arrange that we meet up as soon as possible. If you really do need to see me immediately, I am prepared for you to need to arrest me, but you to be prepared to be able to justify your actions.'

'I was about to ask you how far east or west you might roam, but I realized that sounded unnecessarily flippant in my head.'

'From one monastery to the other; from Autun to Cîteaux; no further.'

'You know, Commander, I think this could be the beginning of a beautiful friendship.'

'I suppose that depends, Captain, on whether you are called René.'

'I don't follow.'

'They were the last words in the film *Casablanca*, when Rick says that line to Captain Renault. I've got the trench coat and you're the one in uniform, so it's obvious which parts we're playing.'

The gendarme rolled back in his chair and laughed, 'So,' he said, 'where are you planning to go from here?'

'No further than central Nuits-Saint-Georges. There's a man who has a parcel next to one of ours, who deserves a grovelling apology from a Truchaud. I think that as it is likely he will know me the least well of us all, perhaps it should be me doing the grovelling.'

'What's that all about?'

'My dear old dad was caught by my nephew, pruning vines that weren't his yesterday afternoon and protocol dictates that I apologize and offer some form of restitution.'

Chapter 11

Nuits-Saint-Georges, late Saturday morning

Truchaud pressed the button marked *'Sonette'*. This was also a domaine, like Truchaud's, which sold at the door. To his relief — as once again he was not planning to buy any wine — it wasn't the wife of the family who opened the door. He was uncertain why wives made him uncomfortable, but it had been ever thus, unless crime was involved. He seemed very much more confident in himself when he was being a policeman, than he would have been knocking on some strange woman's door to say 'sorry'. A tall healthy outdoors face looked out at him, blinked, and looked out again.

'I know you,' said the outdoors face. 'Your face has aged a bit perhaps, and worn a bit since I last saw it.' Truchaud also thought backwards and then realized that this was Geneviève's brother Jean, who he hadn't seen for at least twenty-five years. They recognized each other's identity at the same moment, and threw their arms out. 'Come on in, old man. Come and have a glass.'

A little early in the morning for a glass of whatever was on offer, thought the policeman, but a friendly face was a positive first step in his mission. Jean took out a couple of tasting glasses, and an unlabelled bottle with a rubber bung in the neck. As he twisted the bung there was a *pfft* as the vacuum was released.

'We had a buyer from an English wine merchants last night, and he tasted this.' He poured a splash of a deep ruby coloured liquid into the glass. It almost looked clear with very fine ruby jewels suspended in it. They both sniffed it, and it really didn't need the swirl they both gave it. The smell of cherries and raspberries leaped out of the glass up his nose, and perhaps there was even a reminder of fresh ground coffee in there. Then they both sipped it and swirled it round their mouths. All sorts of flavours rushed out and made themselves known, exotic fruits such as lychees and guavas, and then hid, leaving space for others to announce their presence.

'Now that is *nice!*' said Truchaud, as the extraordinary mix of flavours filled his mouth. 'Let me guess,' he said. 'It's very young of course.'

'Oh yes, that was drawn from the barrel into that bottle yesterday afternoon, with the turkey baster we keep down in the cellar just for that purpose.'

'This is from Gevrey-Chambertin up the road,' Truchaud told him, 'and if it isn't a Grand Cru, there is no justice in this world.'

Jean smiled. 'Right first time. It isn't a Grand Cru, but it is from Gevrey, and I'm so glad you like it. You know, I haven't seen you for over twenty years, but you come waltzing in here out of the blue, and tell me my little Village Gevrey deserves Grand Cru status. Where have you been all my life?'

Truchaud trotted out his life story. He was getting quite good at this by now, and had got it down to a minute and a half's patter, starting from his first days as an intern doing his national service in the Gendarmerie, to his current service in Paris in the National Police.

'So what are you doing down here now?'

'Well, my brother died the other day.'

'I heard about that. Very sad. He was a friend, as well as being a good winemaker. We used to meet up at all the local get-togethers. What happened?'

'We don't know yet. He's still being examined by the pathologist. My dad isn't very well either, and that is part of the reason why I'm here now.'

'Oh?'

'Well, you know that nice little parcel of vines you've got on the south side of Nuits-Saint-Georges?'

'Yes?'

'We caught Dad pruning a few vines in it yesterday.'

Jean took on a grin. 'He probably did a better job of it than the clown we actually paid to do that job,' he replied. 'That's the problem with being bigger than a small operation, run entirely by the family. We don't get to do it all ourselves. What your dad doesn't know about pruning probably isn't worth knowing anyway.'

'That's what everyone says, but I'm not sure he is that good any more. He's got Alzheimer's, and he's not doing very well with it.'

'If it isn't a crass thing for me to say, I've heard that with Alzheimer's you first forget the tricks you learnt last of all. I'm sure his pruning is fine.'

'You know, I was hoping you would take it that way. However, if it does turn out that those vines aren't as productive as they should have been, you must let me reimburse you in some way.'

'On the other hand, if they do better as a result of his intervention, will you ask me to pay you a fee instead?'

'Let's just cross those bridges when we come to them, hey?'

'So what are you going to do now your brother isn't here and your dad really isn't up to the job anymore?'

'Well, that's exactly the problem that I'm having to think about.'

Jean looked at him carefully. 'I'll put this on the table. You'll refuse, but at least it's out there. If you want to sell the domaine, I'll buy it and I'll make sure it's a fair price. I could certainly use a parcel of good Clos de Vougeot like yours in our family portfolio, and that parcel of Village Vosne you've got is to die for.'

'Let me think through my response carefully,' Truchaud replied slowly. 'You're right, I will turn it down. First and foremost, it isn't mine to sell; it still belongs to Dad. You have to add in the fact that Bertin has a son who, when Dad dies will presumably inherit Bertin's share. But even if it were mine to dispose of right now, I'm not sure that it's something I would want to do. However, if I ever did come to sell,' he added, 'I can't think of a family I would rather took it over. So may I store your offer in the back of a mental filing cabinet somewhere?'

Jean smiled softly. 'Of course,' he said, 'Hey, I haven't forgotten that you and my sister had a thing for each other once upon a time.'

Truchaud looked up in surprise. Jean was a couple of years older than him, and at school, two years was an age. Anyway in those days Jean had always been more a friend of Bertin's than his, but they had got along okay. 'You mean she had a thing about me too?'

'You mean you didn't know?'

'There's a life-changing moment,' said Truchaud slowly. 'If I had known, I'd probably not have joined the Gendarmerie to do my national service. I'd have tried to do something less career-generating and sexier, like say, joining the Alpine Infantry. I'd have then come back here, and in the fullness of time it would have been me you'd have been calling the clown who prunes your Nuits so indifferently.'

'Wouldn't you have been working at Truchaud's?'

'I really don't think there's enough of Truchaud's to gainfully employ the three of us. There are only three decent plots, and all the other vines we've got are on the wrong side of the Seventy-Four.' He chuckled for a moment as a thought, unbidden, crossed his mind. 'Besides if we had got together then, Suzette wouldn't exist.'

'Oh, you've met Suzette, have you? Nice kid.'

'Yes, we met for the first time yesterday. Satisfy my curiosity. Why doesn't she work for you instead of Laforge's?'

'More her choice than ours. She wanted to work for a firm with whom she hadn't got any family ties, as she thought she would learn more that way. Besides, they're a bigger operation than we are. They have their own industrial wine plant as well as a hand-made operation. She felt it would be a good experience for her to see both sides of the coin. Mind you, that Laforge is a funny bloke; I'm not sure I would trust him with my daughter.'

'Really? How do you mean?'

'Well, do you remember that medical problem we used to joke about in school? You remember: Desert's disease. You know … wandering palms.'

'Has Suzette complained about this?'

'No, she hasn't. At least, so far she hasn't. But one of her friends, who worked for Laforge's, told her the other day that he couldn't keep his hands to himself, and that's why she stopped working there.'

'Yet despite knowing that Suzette went to work for him?'

'You know that was something that always puzzled me too. I'll never understand women.'

'Well, of course, Laforge's taste may have been particular that way. Mind you, that won't be a problem now, bearing in mind the fact that Laforge is dead.'

'Laforge too? Whatever is happening in Nuits-Saint-Georges? Is there a plague or something? What am I missing?'

'No plague,' replied Truchaud. 'Keep it under your hat for the moment, but somebody shot him. I'm not being indiscreet. It was Suzette who actually found him, so you will hear it very soon on your family bush telegraph anyway.'

'But a shooting! Is that why you're down here in Nuits-Saint-Georges?'

'As far as I know, my presence here is totally irrelevant. But you know our family has had many dealings with Laforge over the years, which is why I'm involved with this. The whole shop and everything is closed up at the moment, as it's a formal crime scene.' He stopped for a moment, an idea crossing his mind. 'Satisfy my curiosity. Do you know who I would talk to at Laforge's now, and how?'

'Well, like most domaines in Burgundy, it's a family owned show. Old Mr Laforge is still alive — he's the father — but I don't know how active he still is in the business, as he must be well into his eighties. There was a brother who was killed in a car accident about twenty-odd years ago. I don't know what happened to his wife, but they had a daughter before the accident, and she's still in Nuits-Saint-Georges and has a son.

81

'I think they're involved in the business too somewhere, probably not the son, as I think he's still in high school. Jérome, old Mr Laforge's younger son, however, was the overall manager. There's also a team they employ. I think if I were to want to talk to anyone, even when Jérome was still alive, I think it would have been Simon Maréchale, who seems to be the general go-to guy at the operation. I don't think he's related to anybody, and I don't even think he's a Burgundian by birth, but he certainly knows his stuff.'

'Someone who's actively keen on the place, rather than just born and bred?'

'Yes, something like that.'

'You don't happen to know where I might find him?'

Jean grinned at him. 'You remember one of the things everyone knew about me? I know stuff. Be reassured that although I've got older, I haven't changed that much.'

'Go on.'

'Simon can usually be found taking his lunch at the Café du Centre in the Place de la République, here in Nuits. If you fancy a spot of lunch, they do a very good *boeuf bourguignon*, which I can whole-heartedly recommend.'

'Why not? Let's do this.'

'Hon,' Jean called upstairs. 'I'm going off to the Central Café for a spot of lunch with young Truchaud here. Do you need me to do anything while I'm out?'

'Not that I can think of. If I think of anything, I know where you are,' came a female voice from within the house. 'Morning, Bertin,' she added.

'Bertin?' asked Truchaud.

'Well, I didn't know what had happened until you told me just now. Why should she? Come on. Now I've started thinking about food, my stomach won't stop reminding me.'

Chapter 12

Nuits-Saint-Georges, Saturday lunchtime

The central square in Nuits-Saint-Georges was a long narrow open space, surrounded by shops and cafés. At its centre was an open area, with large cut pieces of Comblanchien stone, and a culvert of water flowing through the middle of it. When the sun shone, like today, the cafés put out tables and chairs in front of their open doors, with large parasols over them. These parasols were large enough to keep the sun off the heads of diners eating outside, and it could get really hot out there, even in early spring, as there was rarely much in the way of breeze in an area surrounded by buildings. When it rained the parasols also kept most of the rain off diners too foolish not to rush for the cover of proper buildings if the heavens decided to really open. It didn't look as if that were likely to happen, but you never knew at this time of year.

Jean led him into the café and spotted Maréchale straight away. He looked a lot younger than Truchaud had been expecting, perhaps in his late twenties. He had a rather boyish face with carefully cultured stubble, and fairly long dark hair, which, Truchaud expected, would be everywhere if the wind got up. Considering that Jean said that he was not of Burgundian extraction, Truchaud was impressed that he had got as far, as fast as he had. *Some people are just gifted winemakers,* he thought, *and born lucky. I've got a dad like that.* He wondered whether he came from wine country like the Bordelaise or Champagne, or somewhere else with nothing to do with viticulture at all. 'May we join you?' Jean asked.

'Sure,' replied Maréchale, and waved his hand at two chairs at the table. Maréchale was sitting on the bench seat looking

83

across at the bar, and the collection of foreign banknotes pinned on the wall behind it. 'Bonjour, Jean,' he added.

'Simon, this is Charlie Truchaud, Bertin's brother. Charlie this is Simon Maréchale, the power behind the throne at Lafurge's.' This was the second time in two decades that anyone had called him 'Charlie'. The first time had been the night before, and his knees were still suffering a little from that moment.

Simon nodded at Truchaud. 'So sorry for your loss,' he said. *Well*, thought Truchaud, *at least he had heard about it.*

'And I for yours,' he replied. Simon looked at him with more interest.

'Gentlemen?' came a female voice from behind him. Truchaud turned to see a middle-aged woman smiling at them.

'A carafe of wine between the three of us?' said Jean, and the other two nodded. 'A carafe of the Patron's best.' He looked back to his fellow diners. 'It's always an interesting challenge to a café or a restaurant,' he remarked, 'especially as they know we are winemakers ourselves. She has the opportunity to show off, which will be all the better for us. You don't sell wine here, do you, Simon?' Maréchale shook his head. What Truchaud did not yet know was that Parnault was talking to the Patron, Christine Tournier, the owner of the bar. On the other hand, Maréchale almost certainly did, and shared a surreptitious smile with the owner.

'Not so far as I know.'

'And you would know?'

'I think I would yes.'

'And to eat?' Mrs Tournier chipped in assertively to prevent the conversation drifting too far from the menu.

'I'll have the Burgundian menu, with a half dozen snails and the *boeuf bourguignon*,' said Simon. He looked at the other two. 'Most of the people who come in here and ask for snails are tourists. They tell me it's rare for them to serve the snails to the French apart from on high days and holidays.'

'You like to be the exception to the rules,' remarked Jean.

'Always,' came the reply.

'I'll keep him company,' said Truchaud. 'Same for me.'

'Oh go on,' said Jean. 'I haven't had snails this year at least. Count me in too.'

'And for dessert?'

Truchaud took the mixed cheese board, and the other two ordered crèmes caramels.

She walked off into the back of the café to give their order in to the kitchen, and said something to the tall girl standing by the entrance to the bar. 'Well,' said Simon, 'company at lunch. This is a novelty. Normally people leave me well alone.'

'Might be something to do with the snails,' replied Jean with a chuckle. 'That or the garlic butter. Why did you think we ordered them too?'

'I think you're the solution to my next question,' Simon said to Truchaud, 'Why are we all sitting here at the same table?'

'I imagine so, yes. I went round to your shop yesterday and was there when we found your boss.'

'Ah!' he replied, 'That must have been an unpleasant experience.'

'Pretty grim, though Jean's niece found it infinitely more so. She was the person who actually found him.'

'Yes, so I understand. Like any good employer, Laforge's looks after those who work for them. I popped round to see her at home this morning. She's up and about, with her mother in the kitchen. We've had to keep the shop closed today while the police turn the place upside down. Wouldn't be surprised if the inventory turns up a little short after they've finished with it,' he remarked drily.

They stopped for a moment while the tall girl from the bar arrived with three glasses, and a carafe of red wine. She picked Parnault as the expert and offered him a mouthful to taste. He sniffed it for a moment, and said, 'That'll do.' She poured half a glass for each of the men, and put the carafe down on the table, and wandered off.

The conversation resumed as if it had never been interrupted. 'Do you really think they'd steal stuff?' Truchaud asked.

'Oh come on. The only way to stop people stealing stuff is to give them enough money so that it doesn't hurt to buy it. I suppose it's partly our fault for pricing the good wine the way that we do, but why make it cheap when fat cats are very willing to pay loads for it? I would even go so far as to think the fat cats wouldn't buy ours if it were cheap. There would be no exclusivity. That's what they are really paying for, you know; a label to which the plebs don't have access.'

'That's a very cynical view on life,' said Jean. 'I like to think that we make the stuff that the buyers actually like.'

'I look at bottles every day that I cannot afford myself yet. It's my objective, one day, to be able to buy them, not just to taste a mouthful with a well-heeled customer, but to actually buy them for my own consumption. Whether I will actually do so when the time comes, of course, is another matter altogether. There will be a new pleasure available by then, which with any luck will still be legal. It probably won't be of course; politicians don't like people having too much fun. If alcohol had been invented recently, it wouldn't be legal. They're busy surreptitiously making tobacco illegal, by making it almost impossible to find a place to have a cigarette. It wasn't so long ago you recognized France by its own aroma.'

'The Gauloise?'

'Spot on. Now, the young man on his VeloSolex, with a Caporal in his mouth is a thing of the past.'

Truchaud wondered whether this young man had ever seen a VeloSolex outside the cinema. He himself had seen them as a child, but had never ridden one of those strange bicycles with a little engine that went '*tuc-tuc*' that sat on the front wheel that it was driving. The rider also had pedals as well to add extra human power on top when a mild incline became all too much for the little motor to cope with. 'It all reminds one of those Jean-Paul Belmondo films. You have an image of the sixties right there,' he said.

'I would think you're probably right, but doesn't that make you yearn for the days before France was the fifty-second state; before the likes of MacDonald's, Mobil and Starbucks?'

'Is that what you're trying to do with Laforge's? Are you trying to revive the old ways of making wine?'

'No, not to revive it, because we've still got it. I'm trying to retain it. I've been to California and Australia, and seen the massive wine factories they have.'

'But,' interrupted Jean, 'Laforge's is not exactly small itself. It's hardly an artisan's cottage industry.'

'In comparison with some of the big New World places, it is. What we're trying to do is to keep a French label on the product in the mass market. The man in the street doesn't want to pay 150 euros for a bottle of Le Chambertin. He wants to put his hand in his pocket and pull out a fistful of washers for a bottle of plonk to accompany the family dinner. That's the market that the New World is tapping into, ask the taxman. The taxman knows the market, and the highest percentage of tax is on the cheaper bottles everywhere, except in France. Once the Government catches on to that as well, no one will be buying *vin ordinaire* anymore; they'll be buying cheap beer or alcoholic lemonade.'

'You are so cynical,' said Truchaud. 'Why do you deal with us then?' he asked, pouring glasses from the carafe that the waitress had put on the table.'

'You want to sell your grapes, we want to buy them, and the prices seem to suit us both. Easy.'

'You know my father gave you all last year's crop of Village Vosne? Or he may have sold it to you as basic Burgundy, I suppose. I wondered what it was like, as I never got to taste any.'

Maréchale shook his head. 'I don't remember any of that,' he said. 'That would have been some sort of private arrangement that he came to with Jérome himself, I would think.'

'Would you be able to find out if there is some about?'

'I could have a look in the papers. The gendarmes would have messed about that sort of information, but I doubt that they would have wandered off with it. Oh, thank you.' He acknowledged the arrival of the snails.

'Bon appétit,' wished the waitress.

'Thank you,' they all replied.

At that point the conversation stopped. The little steel holders were clicked in to place so that the snail shell could be held firmly. Once secure, the snail itself could be winkled out with the small fork that came with the holder. The chewy snail was then popped into the mouth with the fork and the garlic butter in which it was bathed dribbled down the chin. Any excess garlic butter was then soaked up by a piece of bread dipped into the plate that held the shells. Truchaud took a sniff and a mouthful of wine. He was reminded of the Beaujolais back in Paris, not by its taste but by its effect on the meal. Was it really only three days ago? This one was pleasant enough too, but nothing to write home about. It certainly wouldn't have taken part in a dinner table conversation. It would clear the palate for the next snail perhaps.

Once the snails had done their job of amusing the mouth and preparing it for the meal itself, the conversation started up again. As is its wont under these circumstances, the topic changed. Truchaud wasn't sure there was any point in reviving the previous one. Maréchale hadn't got any more information off the top of his head about the Vosne, so he backed off and let the other two do most of the talking. He did note that Jean's comment earlier that morning about Laforge's taste for physical contact with younger females in his employ was never brought into the conversation. It didn't appear that the family firm was going to have any further problems following the man's demise. Maréchale certainly expected to take over as the business manager forthwith. He would have to be able to talk to the fat cats, however much he disliked them: fat cats from the capitals of wherever wanted to spend money at wine merchants among other places, and fool the merchant who wouldn't relieve them of it.

The *boeuf bourguignon* was delicious, just as Jean had promised it would be. The sauce was rich and thick, the meat fresh and not overcooked, and the little pieces of bacon contributed a smoky overtone to the flavour, with the pieces of potato giving it extra fullness. A further mouthful of the patron's wine added to the beef supported the flavour without detracting from it.

The conversation once again died while the beef was being eaten. *Shame Bruno isn't here*, Truchaud thought, *this is a good lesson in why table manners work.* He promised himself he would bring the whole family here someday soon. Michelle couldn't be expected to do all the cooking for the family now. The final remains of the bread were used to absorb the final part of the gravy, and with shiny clean plates, the men sat back. 'That hit the spot,' remarked Jean looking up.

Truchaud nodded and took another mouthful of wine. The tall girl had obviously been watching the progress of their dinner, as she was suddenly at the table clearing the plates, and asking for feedback on their meal. They replied in the affirmative but Truchaud had often wondered what would have happened if he had turned round and said, 'No actually, I thought that was positively foul.' The first one to pick, of course, would be one that actually was pretty revolting.

She returned with the crèmes caramels and Truchaud's cheese plate. 'Coffee?' she asked, and all three said 'yes'.

The cheeses were a small piece of soft goat's cheese, a firm piece of *Comté* from not far east in the Jura, and a piece of local, very strong, ripe *Époisses*. The last was so liquid in that it could almost have been poured onto the plate; not exactly like the milk it once had been; more the consistency of thick honey. He tried to think of a wine that would successfully compete with it. Certainly nothing from Burgundy would win that one. Perhaps something from further south might have a hope, but this cheese wasn't subtle, and so a wine to accompany it would have to be fairly assertive too.

Three espressos, black and very strong, arrived in tiny cups, with a little wrapped sweet biscuit. They were offered liqueurs or a brandy to finish, but all declined.

At this moment Truchaud's mobile phone went off. 'Yes? Yes I'm in the town centre having lunch. No, just about finishing, so I can be with you between five to ten minutes. Bye.'

Truchaud looked up and caught Mrs Tournier's eye almost immediately. *When was the last time that happened in a restaurant?* he wondered. 'Can we have the bill?' he asked.

'Together or separately?' she asked.

'Bring it all on one,' he replied. 'I'll pay this one, that way you should at least feel duty bound to rustle through your records for any trace you might have of our Vosne.' He grinned at Maréchale.

Maréchale smiled back. 'My philosophy is that if someone offers to stand you a meal, then accept and see what happens later. That isn't corruption, it's just lunch.'

Truchaud drank the last of his coffee, paid the bill, leaving the waitress a tip, for which she said, 'Thank you', and walked out of the restaurant leaving the other two still deep in conversation.

Chapter 13

Nuits-Saint-Georges, early Saturday afternoon

The telephone call had been from Captain Duquesne, and the gendarmerie was no more than two minutes' walk away, provided he didn't have to wait an age to cross the Seventy-Four. It had been a summons to a further conversation.

He pressed the button outside the door to wake up the gendarme on the desk and walked straight in. The young gendarme grinned at him as if he understood the unspoken game Truchaud had been playing, and that he had won that round, as he had been awake all along. 'Good afternoon, Commander,' he said, 'I'll tell the Captain you're here.'

Duquesne was right out. He was effusive in his greetings and this time Truchaud decided to accept his offer of a coffee, even though he had just had one. 'That's right,' said Duquesne, 'A policeman can never have enough coffee.'

'So?' enquired Truchaud, 'What's up?'

'You mean, what's afoot, my dear Lestrade?'

Truchaud raised an eyebrow. 'Sherlock Holmes, the famous English amateur detective, had a colleague in the Metropolitan Police called Inspector Lestrade. I have always imagined Lestrade to be in uniform. Whether or not I can picture you in a deerstalker hat, I'm not sure.'

'I would rather you didn't,' replied Truchaud. 'Your timing was perfect, lunch was over, but if you'd been earlier, in the middle of it say, I would have been most disrupted.'

'Especially as all I appear to be doing is making platitudes about Sherlock Holmes.' The door opened and one of the gendarmes came in with a tray on which steamed two small cups of coffee. As national service was now a thing of the past, he wondered how the system tolerated young coppers being

91

used as batmen for more senior officers. It wasn't something he would have expected his juniors to do. Truchaud chuckled, 'I thought for a moment that was the judge coming back, catching us in flippant mode.'

'Actually Mr Lemaître's an okay sort of chap. He's aware that we have a potentially unpleasant job, and that a little gallows humour behind closed doors is sometimes needed to prevent us all going mad.

'Right,' he said. 'Now that's over and we're not expecting any further disturbances, let's get down to business. I've been having a preliminary chat with the coroner. One of the items, you have a right to know. The other is part of our agreement with Lemaître.'

'Go on.'

'Firstly, he has done the autopsy on your brother. He couldn't find any cause of death anatomically, so he's sent off the usual toxicology screen.'

'He didn't have a heart attack?'

'No, it doesn't appear so. Did your brother take drugs or anything?'

'Not that I know of, apart from the odd drop of wine. But he was always very sparing with his wine, because he knew how destructive it can be, if you let it get hold of you. Dr Girand told me he had been having a little problem sleeping, so he had given him a small box of sleeping pills, but Michelle told me he hardly ever took them. So, apart from the occasional glass of wine with a meal, and an occasional tasting, not a lot.'

'As far as the sleeping pills are concerned, we found the box when we came to the house that night. There appeared to be no more than five missing from the box. The worst that could have happened to him, even if he'd taken them all at once, was that he would have woken up in the morning with a bit of a hangover.'

'That's a relief. So what else?'

Duquesne looked uncomfortable for a moment. 'One of the first things the pathologist looks for when he's doing an autopsy on a winemaker, are signs of excessive consumption, cirrhosis and the like. He saw none of that. He has taken some pieces to look at under the microscope too, but he isn't expecting to find very much.'

'So?'

'I expect he will release the body very soon for you to plan the funeral.' Truchaud looked at him sadly. This was his brother they were talking about after all. From Duquesne's point of view it would probably be a piece of cake, discussing the last mortal remains of a man with his brother who was also a senior police officer, who as part of his job, had been associated with death the whole of his life.

'I will have a word with the undertaker and the priest,' the detective replied.

'Was your brother a religious man?' enquired the gendarme.

'Not that I know of, but Bruno's granddaughter might turn out to be a nun, and might be terribly disappointed if her ancestors hadn't done the right thing for great-granddad 100 years before. It would all come out while she was writing her version of the family history.'

'Right. She could of course end up a Sunni Muslim ... the granddaughter I mean, and be even more disappointed,' said Duquesne. 'And now to the police thing. The pathologist's also done a preliminary autopsy on Laforge.'

'And?'

The gendarme picked up a piece of paper on his desk and scanned it for a moment, making sure what he was about to say was on the money. 'Well, you were right. There were traces of powder residue on the entry wound, like you suggested. It was a low-velocity round that did indeed struggle a bit to get into the head in the first place, and certainly wouldn't have had the energy to get out again. So it bounced around a bit in the cranium, turning much of the brain into porridge. There was no chance of Laforge's surviving that attack.'

'Was there any evidence of his being aware of what was about to happen?'

'You mean the shooter told him he was going to kill him, and then killed him?'

'Something like that. He could have walked in quietly, gone up behind him and pulled the trigger.'

'At this stage there is no evidence one way or the other. There was certainly no immediate evidence of a struggle,' continued Duquesne, looking at Truchaud to take it from there.

'The only way you could have come in quietly without being seen would have been from the shop. Even then you would have to have been careful where you put your feet, as there was a lot of clutter — cardboard cases, some full of bottles, some empty — between the door and right behind someone sitting at the desk.'

'Moreover, if the killer walked into the shop from the street that would have automatically rung the bell, announcing his arrival. The killer would then have to have been let into the back office by whoever was manning the shop.'

'I take it that you assume that the killer was a man?' asked Truchaud.

'Well, that's the trouble with French. We haven't got a gender-neutral pronoun. Even the English have *it.'*

'Though when you do use *it*, it isn't usually complimentary,' replied Truchaud, who then returned to the discussion. 'Therefore the person who let him in would have to have been aware that the killer was at least in the office. That would suggest that the person working in the shop was in league with the killer.'

'Or would have had no idea what the killer was about to do until after he, or she, had actually done it.'

'But nevertheless, surely the person in the shop would still be aware that something had just taken place? Even if a silencer had been used, the noise would have been enough to attract some attention, and whoever was in the shop would surely have been interested enough to go into the back office to find out what had happened, especially as today was so quiet. If that person in the shop was not in league with the killer, they would have phoned us immediately they saw the hole in the back of Laforge's head.'

'Another scenario,' continued Duquesne, 'might be that Laforge opened the door himself. He recognized the killer, and for whatever reason took him straight into the back office. It may not have crossed his mind what the killer was about to do, of course. The killer might have asked him a question that Laforge would have had to look on his computer to find the answer, and while he was doing so, the killer pulled out his pistol and shot him.'

'That is still more gentle than a further option, which would have been: "Laforge, I have come here to kill you. Sit down at that desk!" He then executed a man who was fully aware what was going on, picked up the spent cartridge case and left.' Truchaud drew a breath and continued.

'I can't help thinking that's the least likely scenario. The street is busy and the café over the road is always fairly full of people. All he would have needed to do was shout.' Truchaud was aware that he really didn't want Suzette to be involved.

'Could the killer have entered the office from the house?'

'If the killer had come in through the house, then as he entered the office, he would have been facing Laforge the whole time. That does make the "I've come to kill you scenario" more likely. I think the one thing that we are both agreed on is that this was an intentional assassination,' Duquesne said. 'I assume you have quite a lot of experience of this sort of thing up in Paris?'

'A bit,' said Truchaud.

'What should I be looking for?'

'Money, sex, silence, revenge mainly. It's unlikely to be racial or religious down here. Who was he bonking? Presumably she was someone's daughter. Did that someone know and object? I did hear someone say that he had a taste for teenage flesh. If someone was bonking your rather young daughter, I imagine you'd be a little piqued.'

'I'd be more than a little piqued,' replied Duquesne drily. 'My daughter's only seven.'

'Ah! I heard that he liked them young, but perhaps not that young. Then again, was he having an affair with someone's wife? Furthermore, had he stumbled on to some sort of business malpractice, and the only way that he could be kept quiet would be permanently? Or maybe he was blackmailing some-one, and they had reached the end of their rope.'

'Or had he welshed on a debt one time too many?' Duquesne continued. 'There are still so many questions to be asked. Where do you think we should be looking next?'

'Well, firstly, we could contact Paris and see if their records can throw anything up about Laforge. They have access to the biggest database of information in France, and I am sure they'd let me put what's left of my team to work on it under a formal instruction of an Investigating Judge,' said Truchaud.

'I'm sure I could get Mr Lemaître to rubber-stamp that and I could get my Parisian contacts to access it too.'

'Secondly, I have just created an opening, which I'm quite happy to walk through, with your permission, of course.'

'Go on.'

'I've just been having lunch with Simon Maréchale, who's supposed to be the general factotum at Laforge's. He's prom-ised me he would take a look for the missing Vosne that Dad gave them.'

The gendarme cleared his throat, obviously in need of more coffee. 'Remind me, what was the business link between the Laforges and your family again?'

'We sold them grapes from the east side of the Seventy-Four so that they could make their industrial wine from them. Sometimes, of course, they sold wine we had made and bottled under our own label in their shop.'

'Not something you are especially proud of, I imagine, sup-plying the petro-chemical wine industry.'

'Probably not. You'll find the product of our vines in every hypermarket throughout France in bottles labelled 'Laforge'. Hopefully they will be called 'Bourgogne' rather than 'Grand Ordinaire' or even 'Methylated Spirits'. Anyway, I asked him to look out for what happened to those barrels of Village Vosne. After all it was wine, somewhere between its first fermentation and the malolactic fermentation …'

Duquesne put a hand up. 'Hang on, I don't understand that bit.'

'The first fermentation turns the sugar into alcohol. It's caused by the action of the yeasts on the grape juice.'

'And the yeasts come from?'

'Usually, they're already on the grapes here in Burgundy. In September go and take a look at the grapes when they're just about to be picked, and you'll see a bloom on them. That's the yeast just waiting to get to work. Once that happens, the winemaker then tastes and tests. The *malo* is done by the action of bacteria on what is now wine. Malic acid is sharper than lactic acid. Your winemaker decides how soft he wants his wine to be, and then bubbles sulphur dioxide through the wine, or simply chills it to slow the *malo* process down, or stop it altogether. He will have already separated the wine from the marc.'

'Marc?' enquired the gendarme, 'I thought that was some kind of fire water that the locals concoct to keep them warm on a winter night.'

'Well, it is, but it's made from the skins, pips and other solid detritus that were so important in creating the taste and colour in the first place. Winemakers often turn that stuff into a rather nutty tasting brandy. Dad quite likes the stuff if it's well made.'

'Satisfy my curiosity. Did they teach you all this in the Police College?'

'No, this was all I was learning when I was growing up, and you never forget what you learn as a kid. Anyway, going back to what I was talking about, which was what I understand Dad passed over to Laforge's.'

'So, as it already contained alcohol, it was liable for tax.'

'That is my understanding, yes.'

'Did you pay any tax on it?'

'No, but then it was still in a barrel, and the angels had not yet had their share.'

'The angel's share?'

'It's an old Scottish phrase which Dad heard and liked. When we've finished with our barrels, Dad flogs them off to a family of mad Scots who mature their whisky in them. There is a moderate amount of evaporation from those barrels, and, many years ago, when the taxmen came up from London, they accused the Scots of selling the stuff off on the side, or even drinking it before taxation, when all the time it had just evaporated. The whisky men being as religious as the English taxmen, blamed the angels for the loss of whisky volume, and suggested to the English that they applied to the church, as the angels' representatives on Earth, for the missing revenue. Now wine doesn't disappear in anywhere near the same quantity as whisky, but in France the wine accrues tax when it's bottled.'

'But there was alcohol in the wine?'

'Well, I assume so. My brother Bertin made it, and Dad tasted it. He deemed it so foul he gave the whole lot to Mr Laforge.'

'Was it that bad?'

'Who knows? That's why I was round at Laforge's yesterday, and that's why I'm going back round this afternoon to see Simon Maréchale, to see if he can find the wine, or at the very least any record of it. I'm rather hoping that Laforge realized that Dad was losing the plot, and decided to steal it and sell it as his own batch of Vosne … at minimal cost to himself.'

'And if he did, what do you intend to do about it?'

'We will no doubt talk, but I doubt that there's a lot I can do about that. I guess we will just make sure the taxman doesn't get to accuse Truchaud Père et Fils of any malpractice. It would be nice to taste it. After all, it was the last thing creative my brother ever did in his life.'

'Okay, I've got that. Now our gendarmes are still rummaging through the shop looking for evidence.'

'I understand that yes. Maréchale was fairly dry about them and their ethics.'

'You mean he was accusing my lads of petty pilfering?'

'Not in so many words, but that bottom line was certainly there.'

'Commander, please be aware that I don't much like Mr Maréchale very much either.'

'I'll take that as read, Captain, and if it comes to a fight, I volunteer to be the referee.'

'Okay, Commander. It's been delightful, and as educational as ever seeing you again. You can guarantee we will meet again soon.'

'Any decision yet about Suzette going back to university on Monday?'

'Not yet, but there's still a day between now and then. Perhaps she will have written a really good essay while she's waiting to hear from me.'

Chapter 14

Nuits-Saint-Georges, Saturday afternoon

'You're back,' called Michelle as Truchaud walked through the door. 'The gendarmes kept you a long time.'

'Ah yes, well,' shuffled Truchaud, 'not exactly. I've actually had two separate meetings with them today, and I've seen the chap whose vines Dad was busy pruning, and then had lunch with him and the manager at Laforge's, so I've had a busy morning.'

'Oh, did the chap have a problem about Dad pruning his vines?'

'Actually no. He knew Bertin quite well, and I knew him from school too. He said that in all probability Dad's activities would have improved the vines. You know Jean Parnault?'

'Oh, yes. Bertin's often round his place ... er ... he *was.*'

'Well, they were his grapes. He wasn't particularly upset.'

'That's a relief for all of us. So,' she asked changing the subject, 'what else did the gendarmes have to say?'

'Why don't you sit down?' he suggested. 'I've had a preliminary path report on Bertin.'

Michelle sat down on the sofa and looked at him. Truchaud couldn't see any tears at that moment so he carried on. 'The pathologist didn't find any obvious cause of death. He's taken some samples to study more closely in the forensics lab, but the gendarmes are going to release the body shortly, so we can get on with planning the funeral. I'll go round to the undertaker's on Monday morning, when they're open, to get the ball rolling.'

She looked at him, wide-eyed and sadly. 'They didn't find anything?'

'Nothing yet.'

'What does that mean? He must have died of something.'

'It means they don't know anything yet. No heart attack; he wasn't shot or stabbed; no signs of a head injury or liver disease ...'

'How odd. When they find something will they tell us?'

'Of course they will.'

'Why don't they keep the body till then?'

'Well, in Paris we would rather not hang on to a body for a long time. There are storage space issues, and also it upsets relatives not to have a funeral. It's the way for loved ones to say goodbye. I imagine in Dijon, the storage issues are even more acute.'

He looked at her for a moment. He wondered whether she was trying to hold back the inevitable. While the funeral had not yet happened, she could persuade herself that her husband was still alive. Once the funeral had happened, he had gone.

Perhaps he needed to move on to the next phase too. Sooner or later he was going to have to make a decision about Dad and the vineyard, for Bruno and the future. He had been trying to put himself in Bruno's shoes. Would he have wanted to be uprooted at the age of twelve; to leave all his friends, and the one place whose mechanics he understood? Would he have wanted to go to Paris, which was really the only option? Truchaud himself thought that he had never been as amiably close to Michelle as he had these last few days, but there was no emotional tie there. The links were Bruno and Dad. He had to decide how to support them both.

He couldn't expect Michelle and her family to look after his father on their own as things got steadily worse ... as they inevitably would. That was a group of people he had never consciously met. Who, and moreover where, was Michelle's family? He was only aware of having met them the once, at the wedding, and they had made very little impact on him. However, Bruno might know them and care for them. That might be the solution for the growing boy, and if so, then Jean's offer might be a possible solution. But he wasn't going to put that to Michelle yet.

He changed the subject. 'I've just had an excellent lunch at the Café du Centre, and it did occur to me that you have been doing more than your fair share of the domestic duties since I arrived. Why don't I stand the whole family dinner? It's the least I can do.'

She looked at him gently, 'Not tonight,' she replied. 'I've got everything in, and it's three-quarters prepared already. If we don't eat what I've already done, the only thing we'll be able to do with that food will be to throw it away, and that would be a waste. However, hold that thought; tomorrow night it might be a very nice idea.'

Truchaud felt relieved. At least he would be able to contribute. 'Well,' he said, 'before I go out again, I'm going to make a quick phone call to Paris and then I'm going to nip round to Laforge's to see if Simon Maréchale has found anything about the Vosne. Then I'll probably wander round to the Girand's to see if Suzette is all right, and then I'm home for the evening. Do you need me to pick anything up from anywhere?'

'Not that I can think of,' she said.

He wandered over to the trench coat hanging in the hall, and had a rummage in its pockets. He found his phone, pulled it out, and grabbing a piece of paper and a pencil from the mug on the sideboard in the dining room, he parked himself at the dining table and started dialling.

'Hello, it's Commander Truchaud here. Is there anyone there from my squad I can talk to?' he asked.

'Putting you through, sir,' replied the disembodied voice at the *Quai* switchboard.

There was a click, and then a softer and rather less automated voice replied, 'I'm sorry, Commander Truchaud isn't here right now, but I can take a message for him.'

'Is that you, Sergeant Dutoit?' he asked.

The voice giggled, and then replied, 'That's you, sir, isn't it? And you know I'm only a detective constable.'

'There isn't an only about it,' he replied, 'but I'm delighted it's you, I've got a job for you. Can you slot in a little research for me, in between what the old man has got you running around doing?'

'Are you working down there?' she asked in the sort of voice you use immediately prior to delivering a severe scolding.

'Sort of,' he replied. 'There's been a shooting,' and he told her all about it.

'So you're on the gendarmerie's payroll?' she said. 'I'll keep quiet about that.'

'Actually this chap's all right. You'd like him. I do. And there really isn't any interdepartmental rivalry down here, as his squad's effectively the only form of policing there is in Nuits-Saint-Georges. Anyway, what I would like you to do is to rummage around in the files and see if you can find any reference to one Jérome Laforge, born 1949 in Nuits-Saint-Georges. I gather he was at one of the Parisian Universities when the counter-culture all kicked off. I haven't met anyone down here yet who knows which university, but that probably only means I haven't found the right person to ask. I do know he reappeared here in the late eighties, to help his father out with the family business when his brother died in a road accident. It would be interesting to know if he got into the records in between those times, and if so, might his activities have led to his being formally executed yesterday.'

'Yes, sir. I'll tell the Divisional Commander that I have some real police work to do, and he's just going to have to take comfort from the fact that he's won the Truchaud sweepstake.' She stopped for a moment, and then explained. 'You first called us about police stuff on Saturday.'

A surge of memory swept over him. He'd forgotten all about the sweepstake, and decided on the spur of the moment to pretend ignorance. He did feel that the old man could afford to not win this one, and hoped he hadn't taken the younger police for more than a token euro, just for amusement. 'You mean you were having a sweepstake on when I called?' he asked, feigning surprise.

'Er, yes, sir. Sorry, sir.'

'Never mind. I'm really not cross.' He wondered whether the old man would do the right thing and not let on that he already knew, especially as he had actually forgotten all about it. 'Now you know my phone number. Either call me or text me directly if you've got anything for me. I have another number that is instantly contactable, if I'm not.' He gave her the number on Captain Duquesne's card. 'Introduce yourself as one of my star squad, and if he's not polite, tell me when you next speak to me and I'll thump him. Give me a call in about twenty-four hours just to let me know how you're getting on.'

She chuckled down the phone at him. 'Will do, sir.' And the phone clicked off.

Michelle looked up. 'Who was that?' she asked.

'One of my squad in Paris who I've just recruited to do a little research for us.'

'Oh right.'

'I'll be off out then. I'm going to see Simon Maréchale about Bertin's Vosne, as I said,' he added. 'I'll see you soon.' Collecting the trench coat from the peg, he dropped his phone in the left hand pocket. He pulled the coat on, but didn't do it up; it was too hot for that. It waved behind him as he walked out.

Chapter 15

Nuits-Saint-Georges, later Saturday afternoon

Laforge's was still fairly full of members of the gendarmerie when Truchaud walked in later on that afternoon. The young strawberry blonde gendarme who had manned the door when they discovered the body was among them, and greeted him politely.

'You haven't been here for the past twenty-four hours have you?' he asked her gently.

She laughed nervously before saying that they had allowed her time to take a quick nap, and the gendarmes had been working in shifts to make sure the place was still manned 24/7. Mentally he translated the new slang into 'round the clock'. She asked him why he was there and what she could do for him. He explained that he was looking for Mr Maréchale, and asked if he was around somewhere.

'Last time I saw him, he was out the back,' she said. 'Do you want me to go and rustle him up?' She was obviously uncomfortable about letting him into the back of the shop unattended, so he followed where she led.

'Mr Maréchale, you've got a visitor.'

Maréchale came out from the recesses of the building. 'Oh, it's you,' he said tersely. 'Come on through.'

Truchaud picked his way past various gendarmes and a great deal of clutter in the back office. It looked infinitely less tidy than it had done the evening before, and it hadn't looked that tidy then, especially considering the body on the laptop. He passed into the hall, and followed Maréchale down the stairs into a suddenly much older part of the building: the cellar. The first few flights of the stairs were made of concrete, and then suddenly on a bend downwards, they turned into slightly worn stone blocks. It appeared that the cellar had been built a considerable time before the house above. Presumably the current house had been rebuilt on the foundations of a previous one, but the cellar beneath those foundations had been left intact. The cellars were, after all, the point of a domaine.

Once he passed through the thick wooden door into the cellar itself he was impressed. The temperature was cool, but slightly damp; the perfect ambience for the maturing of fine wine. Row upon row of barrels disappeared off into the distance, slightly downhill he felt, but maybe that was just a trick of the eye. They walked on for a moment and then turned left into another doorway and there were more barrels. Truchaud wondered how far this catacomb went under the streets of Nuits-Saint-Georges. He didn't have time to ask. Maréchale turned a full 180° on the ball of his foot and glared at Truchaud.

'I am seriously unimpressed,' he snarled. Truchaud jumped back in surprise. 'I don't take my lunch with flics, and certainly I don't let them pay for it. I thought you were just the brother of a winemaking colleague who's just died.'

'But that's who I am,' he replied.

'But you're also a flic.'

Truchaud struggled to explain that he wasn't down in Nuits-Saint-Georges in his role of a flic, and that Maréchale already knew why he was there. While he was struggling to appease the situation, he couldn't help thinking that this argument wasn't strictly true anymore. A snapshot of his relationship with Duquesne would look like that of a policeman and his informer. However, that really was between him and the gendarme, and had little to do with the angry winemaker in front of him.

'However, if you had told me you were a flic at the beginning, I could have decided whether I took my lunch with you or not. It was an unpleasant surprise when Jean Parnault told me who you were. You never let on at all.'

'I wasn't actually trying to hide it from you. The topic never came up during the conversation.'

'I would question that,' replied Maréchale, still furious. 'I can distinctly remember commenting on the fact that I thought those gendarmes upstairs might well be light-fingered. You didn't bat an eyelid.'

'But they're nothing to do with the gendarmes I work with. I'm in the National Police in Paris. I have no police business at all in Nuits-Saint-Georges, and wouldn't have unless somebody currently in the village is involved in a crime in Paris.'

'A likely story! What makes you think I'm going to bother to look out some barrels of Vosne for the likes of you?'

'Well, I was seriously hoping you might. We may not be friends — that is up to you — but those barrels belonged to my family, and so did their contents. I think, at the very least, you owe me a tasting, if you still have an unadulterated one. If you haven't got anything unmixed any more, then, surely you'd still keep a paper trail to keep the taxman happy.'

For a moment Maréchale wore an expression as if he was going to stamp his foot and say, 'Well I haven't, so there!' like a petulant child. Then a loud voice came down the stairwell from above. 'Maréchale? Are you down there?'

A quite extraordinary transformation came over him. He appeared to nearly jump out of his skin, and his cheeks lost their entire colour. His tone changed too from being that of a surly brat to that of a rather frightened little boy. 'Coming right up,' he shouted back up.

He turned back to face Truchaud and softly, almost apologetically he said, 'Please keep quiet down here.' He pointed to a gap between the rows of barrels far down the left-hand side of the cellar. 'You might find something of interest through there.' He then turned and trotted back through the doorway, pulling it gently to behind him.

Truchaud looked along the rows of barrels away from the door and spotted the gap between them. Finding the ends of the barrels he walked towards it. There appeared to be a waist-high archway between the barrels. Then the lights went out. Now very carefully he felt his way round the barrel. He realized how difficult it must be to be blind, especially when the floor wasn't there anymore and from his already crouching position, he tumbled forward into the darkness. He didn't fall far, just down a few steps he thought, but his knees and hip ended up in considerable pain.

Bloody stupid, he thought. *Anyone in their right mind would have gone back to turn the lights on again.* He flexed his wrists to make sure he hadn't broken either of them. *Sore but mobile,* he thought, *so far so good.* Then he moved his left leg, first the toes, then the ankle. The knee hurt like the blazes, but the leg moved when he asked it to. He did the same with his right leg. *So,* he thought, *I'm bruised but not broken.*

The next thing he needed to do was to reorientate himself. There had been steps down, but he had not crashed into anything, so presumably there was an open doorway at the bottom of the steps. He felt behind him, and found the steps. They were like the lower steps of the main staircase into the cellar, cut from stone and worn in the middle, so they too had been in place a long time. He moved along the steps to the right and felt a wooden doorframe. He then climbed up it so at this point he was standing upright. There was still no light. He followed the frame round to a wall. Leaning against that wall was another barrel. So this was yet another room in the cellar. He carefully walked out of the doorway. When he reached the other side of it, he found a wooden case. He tapped it and it clinked. *Hmm,* he thought, *glass.* They didn't sound empty. He was almost amused. He had been imprisoned in a cellar containing perhaps a great deal of money's worth of merchandise. He wasn't going to break anything yet, but there were police somewhere upstairs, and one of the properties of wine is that it flows, like the water he could hear flowing in the background. The contents of a barrel would go under a door, and had an attractive smell to it.

He returned to the doorframe and felt around it, further up. He was right, there was a switch; a round switch, which you twisted to turn it on, rather like the one in the cellar at Domaine Truchaud. He twisted it, muttering quietly to himself, 'Let there be light!' And there was.

This room was much the same size as the cellar he had just fallen out of. There were precisely three steps that he had fallen

110

down. Not far, he agreed to himself, but enough to make the audience laugh in an old slapstick silent film. This cellar had a mixture of barrels, large wire baskets with bottles in, and to the side of him, wooden cases with the lids already nailed down. He walked over to one of the large baskets. The bottles were full, but there were no labels on them, and no tax capsules on the necks. On the end of the corks were simply the last two numerals of last year's vintage burnt into the end.

He turned on his heel and looked at the cases by the door. They were more interesting. A label stuck onto the front of the case read: *Richebourg appellation controlée. Bottled on the premises by Chateau la Nuitoise. Well,* he thought, *that's a load of hogwash.* Richebourg was a Grand Cru from Vosne-Romanée, just up the road to the north, and one of the most valuable pieces of real estate in the whole of Burgundy; the whole world even. On the other hand, he had never heard of a domaine called Chateau la Nuitoise, so it would be highly unlikely that such a firm would own a parcel of Richebourg.

He could understand that Laforge might lease some cellar space to another winemaker, especially as he appeared to own so much of it. One other thing occurred to him: he very much doubted that any of the few vintners who actually did own parcels in the vineyard called Richebourg would be able to make this much wine in a year, or indeed all of them put together. He delved into the pocket of his trench coat. On the ring where he kept the key to his car, his flat in Paris, and the key to the domaine, he also kept a Swiss army penknife, which had all sorts of widgets on it. You never knew when you might need a corkscrew or something to winkle stones out of a horse's hooves. He also had a tool on it with which he could ease the lid off a wooden case.

He opened the blade, and slid it in under the wooden lid, lifted it and the lid obligingly rose up until he could get his fingers underneath. The top came off. There were two rows of three bottles. The top bottles lay on a nest of what called to mind chewed cardboard. It looked as if it had been soggy once, but had been dried round burgundy bottle shapes. He lifted

111

one of the bottles out. The label was quite colourful, but carried the same information. The capsule on top did not carry any French tax details, and was a plain, dark red painted foil. The neck label contained the date 2009. *That wasn't from our barrel,* he thought. So this Chateau la Nuitoise was planning to export this Richebourg from France, was it?

They made a very good 2009 Vosne themselves and sold a good deal of it *en primeur* to dealers even before they ever got round to bottling it. Bertin and Dad did the bottling themselves, down to the very last drop. He was very interested in the provenance of this lot. He had begun to understand exactly what was going on down here; it was wine fraud on quite a colossal scale. He wasn't sure where one might get away with selling an obviously fraudulent Grand Cru wine, but the person on the receiving end obviously wouldn't understand the small print of the provenance of Burgundian wine, and probably wouldn't speak French either. It was easy to separate a fool from his money.

What was it really? If you were going to be fraudulent about the contents of a bottle, why be sensitive about its vintage? 2009 was the best of a fairly good cluster of vintages, and was also the largest, so if you were going to call your fake wine 'Richebourg', why not go the whole hog and say it came from the 2009 vintage? He dug into a different pocket of his trench coat to get out his phone to see if he had got a signal down here in the cellar. Failing that he could at least take a couple of photos of this. He pulled out the wreckage of his phone. Damn! He had obviously landed on it when he fell. No wonder his left hip felt so sore. The touch screen was cracked in several places, and he could no longer activate it or use it. He slid open the back. The battery and the SIM card seemed intact, so it may actually still be sending out a locator signal, but as far as being a communication device or a camera, his phone was dead.

He looked around. There were rows and rows of cases. No barrels this time, just cases. Around to the right there was what appeared to be a dumb waiter to the room above. Presumably the top end of the dumb waiter would have been further along behind some of the cases. Piled up against the wall beside the steps were a couple of planks that barrels could be rolled down from the cellar he had originally come from. You'd never get anything like the size of a barrel into the dumb waiter, but you might get a full case.

The running water sound came from the far side of the cellar off to his left, where there was an archway. There was a switch again by the arch, which he turned on, and walked through the archway, down the next few steps onto a wharf.

The patch of water must have been no longer than fifty metres, and reminded him of a Métro station in Paris with its semi-circular bricked roof, except instead of the pit containing a railway, it contained water. It was not running particularly quickly, but fast enough not to be silent. At either end of this strip of water was a gate. The gates appeared to be locked by large loops of chain, secured by equally impressive padlocks through stone posts. There would be no escape that way.

For a moment his thoughts drifted off into wondering about the history of these cellars and this waterway. It must have dated back to the Revolution, and might have been a way for aristocrats to hide from the Terror. It may have been built even earlier, to smuggle wine out of Nuits-Saint-Georges to escape the royal tax collectors, maybe even from the Valois dukes themselves some 500 years ago. The chain, gate and padlock all looked pretty new, so whatever this place had been designed for originally, it was under a different use today. There were no cases on the wharf at the moment, and no boats moored to the wharf either, but there were a couple of large stone posts that boats could be moored to. Any such boats wouldn't be tall, the tunnel wasn't tall, but a punt or a small rowing boat would fit the bill. He went back to the archway, and turned off the lights to the wharf. He didn't think there was any necessity to advertise his presence to anyone who came in that way from the outside.

He looked at some of the cases as he walked back into the cellar. Some of the labels looked perfectly genuine. Some of them read 'Bourgogne, Domaine Laforge'. He wouldn't be at all surprised if they carried a French tax capsule on the bottles, and were to be sold, quite legitimately throughout France. There were more cases claiming to be 'Richebourg' as well.

The next couple of minutes were spent walking to the locked door, turning on the lights for that room at the timer switch. He tried the main door; it was locked. *When did that happen?* he wondered. Had Maréchale come back down when he was out on the wharf, and seeing no one, had assumed Truchaud had left, so he had simply locked up and gone home? He went back to the steps he had fallen down and turned off those lights. He wasn't going to take out his spleen on those blameless bottles of wine, whatever their birthright. They didn't want to be exposed to light any more than strictly necessary. He took a final look at the archway and across the room, trying to etch it indelibly into his memory.

The mechanics of this were becoming fairly clear to him. The wine was made, and then put in the barrels at the top end of the cellar. The wine was then bottled after the end of its designated time in oak, and moved to be encased in the room he was beginning to think of as the 'smuggle cellar'. From there, the wine went out via the wharf and the tunnel on the next part of its journey. There were enough genuine cases of wine in the smuggle cellar, to mask what was going on if a customs officer took a cursory glance. If, like Truchaud, he took a serious look at the merchandise, then Laforge's was in trouble. Truchaud resolved that when he got out of his enforced prison, Laforge's the firm, would be brought to book.

He picked up the bottle of Richebourg he had examined originally, and went back up to the top room, and hammered on the locked door, hoping to attract some attention.

He secured his bottle down between the barrels by the door, just in case it was not Maréchale who came back, and waited.

No one came.

Chapter 16

Nuits-Saint-Georges, Sunday morning

There was a hammering on the door. 'Commander Truchaud, Commander Truchaud, are you in there?'

Truchaud opened one eye, and then he opened the other. He could sense light, but nothing was in focus. He shut them again and then tried again. *So that's what a barrel looks like,* he thought. *Well, that's a start.* He started to stretch and realized everything hurt. His mouth felt as if some bird with a rather unpleasant disease had recently been roosting there. He felt also that he had been hit round the back of the head with a sandbag filled with drying porridge. 'Hey,' he tried. Not a lot of sound came out. He tried again. 'Yes, I'm in here,' he croaked. Yes, that was better.

'Are you hurt?'

'No, not as far as I can tell, just creaking in places I wasn't aware that I did before. I don't think I'm working very well at the moment.' His voice was still protesting, but was giving him grudging permission to try to use it.

'Hang on. We'll find someone to let you out.'

He stood himself up and stretched further. Then he remembered the bottle of Richebourg he had hidden away, and tucked it into one of the pockets of his trench coat. He didn't want to be seen to be carrying that one out, by whoever was on the other side of that door. Someone was working on the lock with a bunch of keys, which, annoyingly, were not fitting. First one key and then another either didn't fit or, those that did fit, wouldn't turn. The voice outside said, 'Be back in a minute.'

It was a considerable time later when the voice returned. 'I should stand at least fifty metres away from the door, people, and cover your ears. This may get a little noisy.' *Oh my god!* he thought. *They're going to blow the door.* He rushed to the steps he had fallen down, went down them, and poked his head back round the frame. 'Ready!' he shouted, relieved that the ability to shout had now returned, and disappeared back round the corner.

There was an encouraging *bang* and the sound of solid material raining down onto wooden barrels. He looked round the corner again, and behind the remains of the door stood the two young gendarmes he was rapidly becoming distinctly fond of: the young man who wasn't asleep behind a front desk this time; and the stocky strawberry blonde girl, who just seemed to be on duty more hours than a normal day was designed to have. 'That seems to have done the trick,' she remarked. 'Are you all right in here?'

'Yes, indeed. Thank you for warning me what you were going to do.'

'What actually happened down here?'

Truchaud explained that Maréchale had taken him down to the cellar and then been called away. Somehow he had got himself locked in.

'You mean you haven't got Mr Maréchale in here at all?' she asked looking about. 'We assumed he was locked in here with you.'

'No, he was on the other side of the door when it got locked.'

'So, he must still have the key with him, which explains why we couldn't find it. Come on. We must get you out of here and back upstairs. There's a terrific hue and cry going on up top about your disappearance.'

Back upstairs in the shop the Lieutenant in charge was very pleased, almost amused to see him. 'You mean you were locked in the cellar all night?'

'If now is tomorrow morning,' replied Truchaud, 'then yes.'

'Your sister-in-law's been inconsolable. Apparently losing a second Truchaud brother in a week was more than she could take. Before we do anything else, Lenoir, can you and Montbard take him round to show him to his family in his current condition? I don't think his sister-in-law's in any state to believe

116

us if we just tell her he's okay. Once you've done that, I know the Captain wants to see him, so you know where to take him after that.'

The gendarme who was still not behind a desk, set off with a squeal of tyres, and once they were in the little courtyard of the domaine, he whirled the blue lights for a moment. Bruno and Michelle came rushing out, just as Truchaud got out of the car.

Before Truchaud could even open his mouth, Lenoir said, 'We are just showing you he really is fine, before we take him down to the gendarmerie. Our Captain also wants to find out how a Commander of the National Police managed to get himself locked in a cellar overnight.' Both gendarmes grinned at Truchaud.

Meanwhile, Bruno had wrapped himself round his uncle. Truchaud slipped him the bottle of Richebourg, and whispered to him to take it indoors and hide it somewhere safe.

Michelle, smiling again, said, 'You really are unhurt?'

'Completely,' he replied. 'Just aching a bit. I slept on a very old, cold, and rather damp stone floor in my trusty old trench coat. I have to go down to the gendarmerie to explain myself, and I'll be back when I can. When I do get back are there any croissants left over from breakfast, or shall I pick some more up on my way home?'

'No, there're still a couple left over.'

He then climbed back into the Mégane, and soon Truchaud found himself once again in Duquesne's office, face to face with a chuckling Captain of the Gendarmes.

'Well, Commander! Coffee?' At this point Truchaud would have been very disappointed if the Captain had not offered him a hot drink. His mouth still tasted as if someone had been using it for arcane plumbing purposes. 'Two coffees,' he said down the intercom, 'I think the Commander would like a big strong one. Milk?' he asked.

'Yes, please,' replied Truchaud.

'Milky, like a latte,' he shouted. Turning to Truchaud, he started, 'So, Commander, tell me all about it.'

And Truchaud did. He told Duquesne about getting locked in the deep cellar he had christened the 'smuggle cellar', and asked him what had happened to Maréchale.

'At the moment he's AWOL,' Duquesne observed. 'When you were reported missing by your sister-in-law, before supper last night, the other person we went out to look for was Maréchale. You had, after all, told us that that was the next place you were going to go. We assumed, at the time, that you were still together, as you had been when you were last observed by Constable Montbard here.' He nodded in the direction of the strawberry blonde girl. 'We couldn't find anything or anyone last night, when we went down there. At that point in time we didn't know anything about there being a deeper cellar, and the door into it just looked like an old locked door. We ran Mr Laforge's niece to ground this morning and she told us about the deeper cellar behind the locked door, so we came back.'

'And blew the door off its hinges,' remarked Truchaud.

'As you say … we blew the bloody hinges off. Now, where is Maréchale?'

'That's exactly the question I asked you. I certainly think we have uncovered a counterfeit wine business. I think he was trying to tell me about the fake wine, without actually telling me about it.'

'You know,' said Duquesne. 'I'm beginning to find this very intriguing.'

At this point Truchaud told him the rest of the discoveries, especially the quite impossible quantity of Richebourg in the basement, attributed to a Chateau he had never heard of. He also told him about the wharf and the padlocked dock. Duquesne's eyebrows rose as the Commander talked.

'Do you think,' Truchaud continued, trying to sound like an excited narrator, 'that Maréchale contacted the "international gang" and told them that I was locked in the basement, and would they send round some muscle to do me in and then dispose of the body?'

'Is this "international gang" you are talking about, any specific gang, or is it just any old international type of gang?'

'Oh, the latter. It is a sort of generic phrase my mum used to use when I was a child. When I'd lost something, my dad used to say it was where I had left it, which was about as helpful as a car accident. My mum, however, used to say that perhaps "the international gang" had stolen it. It was no more helpful, but a lot more amusing to a small boy.'

'Well, if it was a real international gang, it isn't very good at the job on hand. They locked you in the cellar all night and then no one turned up to dispose of you.'

'Oh,' said Truchaud, slightly sadly, and becoming a little less excited. This was one story he shouldn't be telling Bruno.

'I take it that this Richebourg is quite expensive stuff?' asked the Captain, getting to the nub of the matter.

'Expensive and exclusive. You won't ever find it on a hyper-market shelf,' agreed Truchaud. 'Despite the ancient graffiti on the walls as you go into the village, very few people have ever tasted the real stuff. I have this fear that a great many more people will think they've actually done so, especially if their shop or restaurant has Laforge's as a dealer.'

'Do you think we ought to be involving the customs department yet,' Duquesne raised an eye at Truchaud.

'At this moment all we have is an intent to defraud the customs. While the bottles remain in that cellar, that's all it is, an intention. Customs will need to be involved sometime, but at this moment the only thing that we definitely have on paper is the murder of the perpetrator of an intended fraud, and the temporary deprivation of an officer of the law of his liberty, albeit intentional or accidental. We've found some bottles wearing labels to which they're not entitled, but then nobody is entitled to wear those particular labels. At the moment, no one's attempted to move any of them off the premises, so I don't think that any actual breach of Customs law has happened yet.' Truchaud was of course aware that he himself was in breach of that one.

'It is my thought that, sometime before the shop next opens for business, that wine needs to be *arrested*, so to speak. And the best way to do it is to go back down to that wharf and rechain both entrances with a gendarmerie official padlock. I think that ought to be done today, and also that a twenty-four hour guard should be put on the top end of the warehouse.'

'That certainly means involving the regional gendarmerie office in Dijon.'

'Or pulling in your colleagues from Beaune. They should certainly know a bit about wine fraud. They must've been involved in a few cases of that in their time. My friends in Paris are certainly jealous of the wine fraud cases they hear about down here, and what you all appear to get up to.'

'So, will you take me back there now, and show me what you found?'

'Okay.'

'Lenoir, Montbard, you're with the Commander, and me,' called Duquesne as he rushed out of his office into the front of the gendarmerie. 'Bring some chains and padlocks. We're going to need them. And we may need torches.'

They all piled back into the Mégane, and Lenoir raced them all back to Laforge's. Truchaud at least now knew the surnames of the amused young man on the desk, and the young gendarme with the strawberry blonde hair, who may, or may not, have sat with his sister-in-law after they had taken her husband away. They were greeted on their arrival by the Lieutenant, who was, himself accompanied by another couple of gendarmes. Duquesne told them not to worry too much about him and his, and that they were all going into the cellars. The Lieutenant cocked an eye at Lenoir who now bore a more than passing resemblance to a Greek demi-god in a dramatic painting weighed down with chains as he was. 'Yes, sir,' he said.

They walked through the wrecked doorframe with Truchaud at point. 'You see the first gap on the left? That's the one that opens on to the wharf. The second one's just a dumb waiter.' They went down the steps. The room had been stripped. There were no cases of Richebourg left at all, nor were there any wire baskets with unlabelled bottles. The few cases of Laforge's own Bourgogne were lying miserably all on their own, not stacked in any particular order, just there. Truchaud rushed across the room, through the archway onto the wharf. He looked both ways. Both gates were still secured with the chain. 'I should leave those chains down here, Constable Lenoir,' he said. 'We may be back down here in a moment anyway. Come on.' He led the way back up the stairs. The barrels were still there, but the cases of bottles were gone. In particular, the case he had opened, and from which he had stolen the bottle wasn't there anymore. In horror, he thought of Bruno and the bottle, and members of the *international gang* turning up at the domaine.

'Come on,' he shouted, and shot up the stairs again. The others followed him breathlessly.

'Where are we going?' asked Duquesne between breaths, as they got back out into the street where the Mégane was parked.

Truchaud explained that he had pilfered a bottle of the fake Richebourg, and that he had left it at the domaine. 'It may be the only hard evidence we've got left.'

They dived into the unfortunate little car again, with only Montbard able to get into the back with any modicum of comfort. Lenoir drove alarmingly round to the domaine. Quite how he avoided making contact with all sorts of brickwork en route was anybody's guess. On arrival they all rushed into the kitchen. Michelle, if this had been an old-fashioned Keystone Cops movie, would have tapped her foot on the parquet flooring. 'Explanations, gentlemen?'

'Where's Bruno?' asked Truchaud.

'He's gone round to see a friend.'

'Did he put a bottle somewhere? One that I gave him when I was last here?'

'Last here, as in last autumn or an hour or so ago?' she asked drily.

'Just now.'

Michelle shook her head. 'No I can't remember him with a bottle an hour ago,' she said slowly. 'Don't know where he'd have put that.'

'Where did he go? Which friend did he go and see?'

'I don't know. He didn't say. He just said he'd be back for lunch in an hour.' Truchaud had noticed that she and Montbard had not in any way acknowledged each other, so perhaps the red-haired gendarme was not the girl who had sat with her during the night last week.

'Madame,' barked the Captain, 'could you compile a list with my officers here, of the friends your son might have gone round to? Their addresses too would be most appreciated.'

Michelle and the two constables sat down at the table with a ballpoint and a piece of paper. 'I think that's all that's likely. If they've gone anywhere else, the resident parent will probably know where they've gone.'

The two gendarmes waved the piece of paper at their Captain. 'Fine,' he said, 'now be off with you, and when you've found him, bring him back here. Take the car!'

The two constables rushed off out, and there was the squeal of tyres, but much to Truchaud's relief, no thump of metal on anything more solid.

'Now, Madame,' continued Duquesne, 'my good friend, your brother-in-law is desperately in need of breakfast, and if you were to be making a cup of coffee for him, I would really appreciate a cup for myself.'

Duquesne sat watching Truchaud as he munched on the slightly aging croissants. Hmm, he thought, even croissants as good as these didn't stay fresh for long. 'Captain?' he said, with the flakes of croissant coming away.

'Hmm?' came the reply.

'If we can find this bottle, I think now might be a good time to get it tasted.'

'What do you mean?'

'I'd like Dad to taste it, to see if he can remember what Bertin's Vosne tasted like and whether this Richebourg might contain any of it. There were far more bottles of the fake Richebourg down in that cellar than could possibly have been made just using our Vosne, but if there is a high percentage of Bertin's wine in the mix, then it might dominate any blend. I know that this is more a personal family issue, rather than a criminal one, which is why I am asking you for permission to do this.'

'So if your dad were to taste it and declare that there was indeed Bertin's Vosne in there, then at the very least I will have witnessed a statement of its provenance.'

'Exactly, and then after we had all tasted it, you could have the bottle with its label to lock away somewhere safe.'

'Sounds like a plan,' agreed the gendarme. 'So all we need now is the bottle.'

'And Bruno.'

'And, of course, Dad. Michelle?'

She put her head round the door. 'Breakfast okay?'

'Yes, fine. Do you know where Dad is?'

'He's gone off to walk round the vineyards, but don't worry, he hasn't got the secateurs. He should be back for lunch.'

'Is there enough lunch to include Captain Duquesne?'

'Oh no, no, no,' said Duquesne. 'I won't stay to eat if you don't mind. If we can have the wine as an aperitif so to speak, then I'll leave you to it.'

'So,' said Truchaud, 'we wait here for Bruno and Dad,' and they parked round the dining table to wait.

Chapter 17

Nuits-Saint-Georges, Sunday from late morning onwards

Bruno seemed very excited to have been brought home in a police car. He wasn't in the slightest bit anxious, despite the antics of the driver. His friends had been equally amused, after the first moments of concern as a police car screeched up to the front door. Of course Laforge's demise was big news around all the kids in Nuits-Saint-Georges, and Bruno was right in the thick of it.

Truchaud had finished his plateful of croissants by the time Bruno was brought back.

'Bruno, remember that bottle I gave you?'

Bruno looked at Duquesne out of the corner of an eye, and then with a slightly sly look at Truchaud, said slowly, 'Bottle? When exactly?'

'About an hour ago, when these good people brought me round to show you that I hadn't been in any way hurt.'

'Oh, you mean *that* bottle.' He grinned. 'I'm sure I could find it if you wanted it.'

'Yes,' said Truchaud, 'I do.'

'Hang on a moment. I'll go and look for it,' he said and disappeared into the house.

'Feisty young man that one,' remarked Montbard drily. 'I'm glad he's on our side.'

'Here it is,' Bruno cried cheerfully as he returned. 'Just where I hid it.'

'No,' said Truchaud sternly, looking at a perfectly normal bottle of Domaine Truchaud wine. 'The bottle that I gave you a couple of hours ago!'

'Oh, that bottle! Why didn't you say so!' Once again the boy disappeared back into the house.

Truchaud was relieved that this time it was the bottle that they were all talking about that Bruno produced. 'Well, I had to be sure that you actually wanted me to bring this one. There seemed to be so much cloak-and-dagger stuff going on: what with your not coming home last night, and then being brought home by the gendarmes, who then promptly took you off again. I thought you might be in all sorts of trouble.'

'Cute!' remarked Montbard. 'Are you going to join the gendarmerie when you grow up?'

'Not that I know of,' he said, giving her a slightly sly look. 'I think I'm going to be a winemaker like the rest of the family, apart from my uncle here. I think I know more about it.'

Duquesne and Truchaud were both amused watching this play between a girl in uniform and a twelve-year-old boy, who was just beginning to get a handle on the concept of subtext. Truchaud got up and got out some tasting glasses, and a corkscrew. Now all they needed was Dad.

Duquesne was studying the label. It was fairly uninformative, but for the most part true. The phraseology of bottling was wide and varied, and often not very helpful. This one said 'bottled in our cellars'. It did not in any way state that they had grown the grapes and vinified the wine themselves, although in fact that may have been true as well. Nowhere did it suggest that they were the growers or the harvesters. In fact, the only overt falsehood on the label was in the biggest print: 'Richebourg'.

'Now that's what you call lying in plain sight,' remarked Duquesne drily.

Truchaud suggested they pulled the cork to allow the wine to breathe a little, as it had already been fairly well shaken over the past twenty-four hours, in one way or another. *Allowing it to develop the bouquet it had to offer would be a reasonable apology to the contents of the bottle, if it were well enough bred to deserve it. And,* his thoughts continued, *if it isn't, then there will be riots when its siblings come to be consumed at the other end of their journeys.*

They both sniffed the cork. There wasn't much wine at the bottom of the cork. It hadn't been bottled very long, but then it didn't claim to have been. There was a pleasant cherry and blackberry aroma coming from it. Both men screwed up their faces and nodded appreciatively at each other.

Fortunately, Dad didn't take forever. He was a little worried about the police car parked in the yard, and even more concerned to find three uniformed officers in his dining room, two standing politely at the door and one having the temerity to be sitting in his chair. 'What's happened?' he asked. 'Who else has died?' and spotting his son also sitting at the table he remarked, 'Well, at least it's not you then.'

'Dad,' his son replied, 'these people are my friends. We would very much value your opinion on this wine.' And without further ado, he poured a small tasting mouthful into each of four glasses. He passed one to Michelle, another to Duquesne, another to his father, and kept the fourth for himself. He nodded at Lenoir and Montbard, as if to say, 'yours will come in a moment.'

All four of them first lifted the glasses to the light. The wine was a deep strawberry red, glinting almost like rubies in the glass. It was clear and there was no sediment. Then they sniffed their glasses. *At least this one's not corked,* thought Truchaud, *that would be the ultimate disaster after all this.* The fruity nose was actually quite delicious. As well as the cherries and the blackberries, there was just a touch of violets on the nose too. Swirling the glass didn't achieve much more, apart from further aerating the wine. So then came the tasting itself. Yes, it was young and vigorous. It was not sour, but there was fatness to the tannins. For a young wine, it had a good deal of class.

'Well, Dad? What did you think of that?'

'Quite nice. What is it?'

'Well, we wondered if you recognized it. We've just lifted it from Laforge's,' replied Truchaud. Suddenly his father looked shifty. 'We wondered whether there might be some of last year's Vosne in this.'

'What exactly are you saying?' asked the old man suspiciously.

'Could the Vosne you gave to Mr Laforge have ended up in this wine? Do you recognize the taste in this wine?'

The old man thought for a moment, and sniffed his glass again. 'Could be, could be. What are they saying it is?'

'Something for any number of reasons it can't possibly be. What we are trying to find out is what actually did Laforge put in that bottle that's pretending to be a Grand Cru. I'm asking you, because you tasted it and I never did. Could that be our Vosne in that bottle?'

'But that's fraud,' the old man spluttered.

'Hence the police,' explained his son.

'Are we in trouble?'

'Not at the moment,' replied Duquesne, 'but I would like you to formally confirm that this tastes like the wine that you gave to Mr Laforge in the winter.'

'I certainly can recognize some of its flavour in this glass,' he replied very carefully.

At this point Captain Duquesne's mobile phone rang. 'Hello? Yes, I'm Captain Duquesne. Truchaud? Yes, he's here. Do you want to talk to him? I'll pass you over to him.' He looked at Truchaud, 'I think this is Paris for you,' he said. 'Why are they calling you on my number?'

'Ah,' said Truchaud taking the phone, 'I'll tell you about that in a moment.' He spoke into the phone, 'Constable Dutoit? Is that you?'

'Yes, sir,' replied the phone. 'I was a little worried when I couldn't get a reply on your number.'

'Ah yes, my phone had a little accident and it will be out of action until tomorrow morning. Any news?'

'I've got something to start with,' she said. 'It appears your man Laforge was a freshman at Nanterre University in Paris in 1968. We couldn't find anything to suggest he was active prior to the university administrators closing the university on 2nd May, the day the strike kicked off. But once it had done, his name does crop up from time to time in the reports. The most interesting thing is that, although his name is mentioned some-times, it never has a political faction attached to it. It just seems that he was never very far from the action, but just far enough away to keep out of trouble. Does that make any sense to you, sir?'

'I think so. You're saying that he wasn't a fanatical revolutionary, with a capital 'R', just a grubby little rebel with a small one?'

'Well, that's the bottom line in one, sir, but it's all I have got so far.'

'I think you can pat yourself on the back for getting that much in twenty-four hours. I have no idea how helpful it will be in the long term, but it will be very interesting to see how our disruptive student's behaviour links up with our executed corpse over forty years later. I'll talk to you again soon, and I'll give you a call tomorrow, when I've revived my telephone.'

'May I ask what happened to it, sir?'

'I slipped down some steps and landed on it.'

There was a sound of a giggle down the phone at him, and a snort of laughter from Duquesne. She said, 'Don't worry, sir, I won't ask any further. I'll talk to you again tomorrow,' and disconnected the line.

Duquesne looked at him. 'That sounded an interesting conversation from the gaps at your end,' he remarked, still chuckling.

'She's one of the constables from my squad in Paris, with a mind like a steel trap, who's doing a spot of legwork for us on Laforge. Did you know he was involved in the Paris riots in May '68? She hasn't got any further yet, but it might turn out to be relevant.'

'Keep me informed, Commander, if anything comes up. Meanwhile,' he said turning back to Truchaud senior, 'could I ask you to put that you may have recognized the wine into a written statement?' asked Duquesne.

The old man agreed, and Montbard stepped forward with her notebook and pen. Truchaud meanwhile poured three more tasters into three clean glasses. 'Bruno,' he called, 'can you give these to Constables Lenoir and Montbard, and then when you come back …' — he looked up at Michelle for her approval; she nodded — 'the other one's for you to try.'

He looked up at his sister-in-law. It had sunk in that this had been perhaps her one and only experience of Bertin's last work, and contrary to what Bertin had been told, the wine was truly excellent. How she would cope with that remained to be seen. Would she forgive her father-in-law's fading intellect? Bertin's last days had not been happy. Right now, on his seat in Purgatory, he might be furious, but fairly upbeat. The tragedy was that they wouldn't have more of this wine to drink at his farewell next week, unless the local police were very lucky and the local law was very generous.

His father finished making his statement with Montbard. Duquesne stood up. 'Right,' he said, 'I think that's it for the moment. Commander, as I always seem to be saying: please don't leave town yet.' Duquesne picked up the bottle, 'I must take this with me I'm afraid. Evidence.' He looked at Truchaud senior, 'Very nice, sir, very nice indeed.' He also bowed graciously at Michelle. 'If you were to invite me to your house again, Madame, I would graciously accept.' He winked at Bruno, and ushered his constables out. The last the family heard of them was the squeal of tyres, again without the impact of car on stonework.

'Well,' said Michelle. 'I've only got bread, charcuterie and cheese for lunch if that's okay. I'm sure we can dig up some wine from somewhere.'

'What was that all about?' asked Truchaud's rather bewildered father. Truchaud tried to explain to him simply and without accusing him of anything in particular what had just happened. He seemed rather upset that the police had gone off with the wine. Ownership was becoming a difficult issue to get across. He looked across at his nephew. 'You know that other bottle you produced, may I buy it off you for lunch?'

Bruno grinned. 'Oh, that was one of yours anyway.' Truchaud pulled the cork, and took all the used glasses and put them in the dishwasher. He was pleased it still worked. He had given the machine to the family as a Christmas present a good ten years ago, when it had been given to him as a thank you for his part in solving the White Goods Bullion Robbery. While he had little use for it himself, his brother and his wife, with a new baby, had appreciated some labour-saving equipment.

The bread was very fresh, the butter was firm and the pâté complemented them both. While the wine wasn't as exciting as what they had just tasted, at least this one was ready to be consumed now. That one had been a taste for the future.

After lunch his father announced he was going to put his feet up for a nap. The boys cleared the table much to Michelle's pleasure, while she made a couple of coffees.

'So what are you two going to do this afternoon?' she asked.

'I thought I might ask Bruno to come with me to walk the vineyards, to see if he can spot if anything needs doing. Would that be okay?'

'Provided you don't get him locked in a cellar,' she smiled.

'Okay with you, Bruno?' he asked.

'Yes, please,' said the boy, and they went out.

Chapter 18

Nuits-Saint-Georges, Monday morning

The following morning was Monday, and France reopened for business. Following breakfast, Truchaud set out on his shopping trip into the town centre. The first spot would be the shop to get a new phone. He had put the old broken one in one of the pockets of his trench coat, the old phone still being the safest place to keep the valuable SIM card. He and the young man in the shop talked lots about mobile phones, about a third of the content of which he actually understood and considerably less of which he found even vaguely interesting. The number of things you could do with a mobile phone nowadays was astonishing. Some of the things that appeared to excite the salesman Truchaud couldn't imagine ever wanting to do ever, at any time, with anything at all, let alone a telephone. It made him shudder.

He decided on a fairly simple model, checked that it was compatible with his SIM card, and that you could actually send and receive telephone calls on it. Its ability to take high-definition photographs could be useful. They switched the SIM, and he took the display model, which had already been charged. To test it he phoned the gendarmerie. Montbard answered, 'Just letting you know, I'm back on the phone again, so you can call me if you need me.'

'Good to know,' she replied.

Truchaud paid the young man who looked slightly disappointed about the whole affair. He had got out all his best patter about the most wondrous piece of miniaturized wizardry and all this old buffer wanted was a telephone to talk into that took a few snapshots. How dull his life must be!

The next stop on Truchaud's list was a visit to the funeral

parlour. He walked into the little shop at the bottom of the Place de la République. The woman with sad but gentle eyes looked up at him. 'I would like to arrange to bury my brother in the family crypt,' he said in reply to her, 'Can I help you, sir?'

'I'm so sorry for your loss,' she replied.

Truchaud smiled back, and said, 'I've always wanted to be able to say, "Oh no, he's not dead, I just want to stick him in the family crypt", but I'm sorry to say that he is. The crypt is in the cemetery on the other side of the road from St Symphorien's Church.'

She nodded. Obviously, she knew the place. 'Would you be wanting a church service with the curate officiating?'

'I think the family would like that,' he replied.

'Where is your brother at the moment?'

'They tell me that he's in a fridge in the Coroner's lab in Dijon. The local police have told me that we now have permission to arrange the funeral.'

'Would you like him to be embalmed before the burial? The bodies tend to keep better that way.'

'I was rather hoping they would hang on to the body until the day of the funeral. The bed in which he was sleeping when he passed over is still occupied at night. I think his wife might find it quite difficult to sleep if he was there too, especially as he has undergone a post-mortem exam.'

'I understand completely,' she replied gently. 'Is there anything else we need to know?'

'How do you mean?'

'He didn't die of some infectious disease that might put our employees at risk did he?'

'No, no, no, nothing like that,' he replied. 'In fact we don't know what he died from yet.'

'Does that mean that there may have to be an exhumation?'

'I think that's no more likely than for an ordinary burial, but I suppose it's always possible, yes. I thought that is what these family crypts were all about. My family's been buried in there since the Third Republic. We aren't a very reproductive lot, which is why there is still quite a bit of unoccupied space in it.'

'Shall we take down some details then? Would Thursday or Friday be acceptable?'

'I think either would suit us just fine. I've been given a free hand to set this up.'

'I'll get our stonemason in to lift the stone from the crypt so we can gain access to it.'

From thereon they discussed the finer details of exactly what would happen, the hymns that would be sung. He agreed that they would have a farewell to Bertin, at the domaine afterwards. The undertaker would take over the catering, so that the widow wouldn't have to do that, and that they would sort all the plates, knives and glasses too. 'Wine?' she asked.

'I think it would be nice if we used his own wine; you know the wine he made while he was still alive.'

'A nice touch,' she agreed.

'I'll bring that up from the cellar.' Not however the wine he would have really wanted; *that Vosne,* he thought sadly.

The third activity on Truchaud's list of things to do was shopping for lunch and supper that night. He had more or less volunteered to be responsible for both. Lunch would be easy. The first stop was the baker's. From the man who made those croissants that would get the young man kidnapped and abducted to his *arondissement* in Paris, he bought bread, a quiche and some apple tarts. From there he went to the cooked meat delicatessen and bought some pâté and some rather strong local cheese. Some slices of ham would add to the lunch and some pickled salads.

The next stop was the greengrocer, who provided lettuce, tomatoes and a cucumber. They were all for lunch, because he had decided already on dinner, and he knew he didn't have the culinary skills to do it himself. Armed with food and the papers, he walked up into the square. At that time in the morning the Café du Centre had a distinctly 'opsed' air to it.

If anyone had asked him about the word 'opsed' he would have taken them to the old Castrol signs in front of the petrol stations of his youth. They had a flap, and when you moved the flap to the left, they read 'open', and if you moved it to the right, they read 'closed'. Now if, owing to some misfortune, or to vandalism, the flap had been torn off, it read 'opsed', hence the word; meaning neither one thing nor the other. The owner-manager was moving about in the back. He decided to take lunch home and come back.

When he got home, the house seemed quiet. Bruno was at school, no doubt telling all his mates about having played cards with Suzette Girand last night. He knew that the name would have to be both words; this was not any old Suzette, but the Girand variety that would give his social standing an upward kick. His father had gone for a walk, but Michelle knew the secateurs were still safely out of harm's way. He unloaded the lunch onto the kitchen table. The charcuterie and cheese went straight into the fridge, as did the apple tart. The bread was also stored in the usual place.

'I'm booking us in to the Café du Centre for supper tonight, or at least I'm trying to,' he said. 'Must go back there in a few minutes. It wasn't open yet.'

'You could just phone,' Michelle replied. 'Remember? You've got a nice shiny new one,' she added. What he really wanted was a coffee, sitting out in the town square, watching the world go by. The Place de la République in Nuits-Saint-Georges was one of his favourite places in all the world.

'No,' he said, 'I'll go back and see them. That way I'll ensure the booking is taken, or we'll suddenly have nothing to eat tonight.'

So back he went to the square. There was a bit more life at the café, but it was hardly what you would call open. The tables were out, but the parasols had not yet been erected, and there were no paper tablemats or racks of menus out. He walked up the square and bought a local paper, to see if the dramas of the weekend had actually hit the press yet. He parked himself with his paper in one of the chairs in front of the café and started to read. This finally activated the tall girl who had served him lunch a couple of days ago with Maréchale and Jean Parnault. She came out from the café and told him that they weren't open yet.

'Not a problem,' he replied. 'I'll just sit here and read my paper, and when you are open, I'll have a large creamy coffee. I'd also like to book a table for dinner, but there's really no hurry, and this paper might be very interesting.'

The girl went back into the café. A few minutes later the front door opened, and Mrs Tournier herself came out with a large cup of coffee, and a little sweet biscuit in the saucer. She also took his booking for four for dinner that night. 'Inside or out?' she asked.

'It will probably have cooled down again by this evening,' he said, 'so given the choice, we'll eat in.'

He stirred the coffee and perused the paper.

'Charlie?' he heard from one side. It was Geneviève, with whose daughter they had been playing cards the night before. He thumped himself mentally. As if being Suzette's mother was the most important fact he knew about this woman. He stood up and motioned her to the table. 'May I join you?' she asked.

'Of course,' he replied. It was her town, so if she didn't mind being seen having coffee in the town square with someone other than her husband, the doctor, then that was fine by him.

'I gather Suzette had a nice evening last night,' she said carefully.

'I think we all did,' he replied, 'even Dad.' It was the most extraordinary thing how, a quarter of a century after he had last seen her properly, she still gave him butterflies in his stomach. To him she didn't look her age, but was still the creamy skinned angel he remembered from so many years ago. He couldn't see the crows' feet at the corners of her eyes or the flecks of silver in her hair. One thing that hadn't changed over the years was the emerald green of her eyes. 'Coffee?' he asked. 'They seem to be serving it to me to keep me quiet.'

'Yes, that would be nice.' The tall girl was obviously watching him to make sure he didn't get up to any mischief, as she reappeared when he looked up. Maybe she recognized Geneviève as a friendly native. She took her order and went back into the café. 'So,' she asked, 'are you down here working, or for pleasure?'

137

'Well it's hardly pleasure with a brother who has died and a father who's no longer firing on all cylinders.'

'Sorry, that was a singularly bad choice of words.' She caught herself. 'I hope you know what I meant.'

'Forgiven,' he chuckled. 'How much do you have to do with Jean's wine business?' he asked changing the subject.

It was her turn to take a little mock offence. 'His wine business? It's every bit as much mine as his! When we inherited it, we decided to keep it as a single firm between us, rather than split it in half. It kept it alive for the time being. As I married outside the wine trade, that really solved all the inheritance problems. I can also think of a number of siblings who don't get on anywhere near as well as Jean and I do. Most days you will find me round Jean's place poring over paperwork with Élodie.'

'Élodie?'

'Jean's wife. Have you met her?'

'I don't think I'd recognize her if I saw her, but I exchanged a few words with her out of line of sight the other day. She took me for Bertin. But then she wasn't expecting a different Truchaud from the one she knew. Shows how the mind can play tricks.'

With exquisite timing the coffee arrived and his phone rang simultaneously. He looked at his phone and it told him it was Captain Duquesne on the line. He looked at Geneviève, 'I must take this,' he told her.

'Do you want me to go?' she asked.

'Never,' he replied, and then spoke into the phone. 'Captain, how are you? Where am I? I'm sitting outside in the middle of the Place de la République drinking a coffee. No, I have no objection to you joining us.' He looked at Geneviève. 'You've no objection if a policeman in uniform joins us?' She shook her head. 'No, come on over. How do you want your coffee? A double espresso it is.'

Geneviève cocked a green eye at him. 'The policeman that Suzette positively hated forty-eight hours ago,' he said, 'I think he's an okay human being actually, but you can judge for yourself shortly.'

'Are you working with him?' she asked.

'A very good question, to which I'm not sure I know the answer yet,' he grinned.

Truchaud looked over his shoulder. The uniformed Duquesne was walking past the post office into the square and walking alongside him was a dapper man of about their age with a pencil-thin moustache. All of this new character's clothes hung just as they were told.

Truchaud again stood up, and Geneviève from a sitting position watched this little play with amusement. She knew exactly who the dapper man was, even if Truchaud didn't. 'Captain Duquesne,' he said.

'Good morning, Mrs Girand,' both men greeted her. 'Commander Truchaud, may I introduce you to Inspector Molleau, from the local Municipal Police here in Nuits-Saint-Georges.'

Both men shook hands and both acknowledged each other. 'Ah,' said Truchaud, 'you must excuse me, I only ordered one coffee. The Captain didn't warn me he was bringing company.' He waved a finger at the tall girl.

'I see you share the Captain's obsession with coffee,' said the Inspector drily. 'I suppose being addicted to coffee is less damaging both physically and mentally than other addictions I could mention.'

'I've told him you are not in Nuits-Saint-Georges on police business,' explained Duquesne, 'But you're here looking after your family's wine interests, which is inextricably involved in this mess.'

Geneviève looked at him. 'Inextricably?' she asked. 'I shall have to tell Jean to be more careful with his offers of help in future.'

'Commander,' began Molleau.

'Please talk to me as a civilian, it is so much easier. Mister will certainly do.'

Geneviève giggled, 'Oh Charlie, you are still ridiculous.' She looked at the local policemen, 'Charlie and I were at school together. We've known each other all our lives.'

'Mr Truchaud,' Molleau bristled, with considerable emphasis

on the 'Mr', 'may I request that you come over to my office in the town hall, say 2 p.m. today?'

'I will be there on the dot,' replied Truchaud.

Molleau stood up, and Duquesne shrugged and got up and followed him, just as his coffee arrived. The tall girl looked anxiously at them, and then the coffee, and at the fast disappearing gendarme.

'Oh, don't worry about them,' said Geneviève to the girl. 'We'll take it anyway.'

Chapter 19

Nuits-Saint-Georges, Monday lunchtime

Truchaud wandered back home to have a spot of lunch before his planned interview with Inspector Molleau.

'Home!' he said as he walked through the door. Michelle was just on her way out as he arrived. 'I've got a meeting at the town hall at two,' he explained.

'I'm off to see someone and won't be back till way past one,' she replied.

'In which case,' he replied, 'if you don't mind, I'll make my lunch now.'

'If Dad gets back soon from the vineyards can you put something together for him?' she asked. 'If he's later, and I'm already back by then, then I'll sort him out.'

'Fair enough,' he replied.

'Got to go. See you later,' and rather more jauntily than she had been for … well … ever, or so he thought, she left the house.

Truchaud wandered into the kitchen, and raided the bread bin, and cut off a couple of hearty pieces from a baton. He put a slab of butter on the plate and cut a hunk of sausage and some pâté from the sheet of greaseproof paper. He cracked a clove of garlic and crushed it, then put the crushings, some mustard, honey, vinegar and walnut oil in a small jug and beat them together with a fork, creating an instant vinaigrette dressing. He poured some of this over a few lettuce leaves and a couple of tomatoes. It was an instant lunch for a busy policeman. He thought for a moment about looking for an opened bottle of wine and decided against it; he was being interviewed by Molleau in an hour and a half.

He took a quarter of an hour to eat his lunch and made a coffee to finish off with, and then dialled Natalie Dutoit in Paris again on her personal mobile phone.

'Oh good afternoon, *chef*,' she said. 'I've just sat down to lunch.'

'Do you want me to ring you back when you've finished?' he interrupted her.

'No no,' she replied, 'I'm just fine. It's only a spot of bread and cheese.'

'Well then, have you got any further?'

'Oh yes. He was quite a busy little fellow during the seventies, was our Jérome Laforge. It appears he was rather more generally involved with a number of Autonomist groups that became intermittently active around that time.'

'Autonomist?' asked Truchaud. 'I have a feeling I should know what you're on about, but I really don't.'

'Autonomism, sometimes known as Autonomous Marxism, is a set of left-wing political theories that first raised its head in Italy in the early sixties, though the name itself was actually coined nearly 400 years earlier. Various political factions then hijacked this set of theories by the end of the sixties for their own personal, rather more aggressive reasons. Certainly the May '68 General Strike had Autonomist components in its leadership, and the Red Army Fraction and the Italian Red Brigade were all well-armed, spin-off organizations that, at the very least, used the Autonomist template as an excuse for their behaviour. Although what they actually got up to would probably have made the original founders shudder. Are you with me so far, sir?'

'Bewildered, but so far I'm following you. Go on,' Truchaud replied.

'Well, *les évenements* of May '68 really didn't last much longer than the end of June that year, when De Gaulle actually did call the election that the strikers had demanded, and promptly won it hands down. The strikers took it on the chin that it was the national will that De Gaulle should hang on to the presidency, and everything on the outside appeared to calm down again. It appeared that there remained a pool of anarchism smouldering quietly in Paris, attached both to the left-wing and to the right. It appears that our man gravitated towards these pools, with apparently a very balanced perspective as to which wing he was flying under on any particular day, if you get what I mean.'

'Left-wing, right-wing; he wasn't unduly bothered.'

'Quite! Anyway while he was playing one faction off against the other, probably without either side realizing it, he was also getting on with his studies. Having got his degree, he moved to Germany for a while, ostensibly to learn how to cultivate grapes, but his name also cropped up in conjunction with an urban guerrilla training camp at a local cadre of the Red Army Faction. The Communist Party was made illegal in West Germany in 1956, so it went underground. Ten years later, a young party member called Andreas Baader, in response to some ex-Nazis putting their heads above the parapet again, took to open revolt to get his points across, and much of the disaffected youth rallied to his clarion call. Among the European youth, one Jérome Laforge found his leadership charismatic, and gravitated into his field. Laforge's name didn't appear in any police reports of direct action, apart from the fact that his membership was acknowledged from time to time. In 1977, the whole Red Army Faction disintegrated with the death of Andreas Baader himself, in what became known as the 'German Autumn'. It was a bloodbath on both sides, but our man was nowhere near the epicentre, and as far as I could ascertain he had already been in Paris for quite some time.' She took a few breaths, apparently perusing her notes. 'Still following so far, sir?'

'Oh yes, though I'm finding it difficult to believe that all this happened under our noses.'

'Don't blame me, *chef*. I wasn't even born at that time.'

Momentarily he contemplated the attractive, creamy voice at the other end of the phone. *She was very young, wasn't she?* 'Yes, and I was still at school,' he said, excusing his thoughts, mainly to himself he suspected. He wasn't that much older, surely? 'So by the time we'd appeared it had all gone quiet, then?'

'Perhaps, as it appears to be a sleeping tiger today. Anyway, getting back to your Jérome Laforge. For a while he appears to have kept his head down, but then he became involved with the French left-wing group Direct Action in the early eighties, which allied itself formally with the reborn Red Army Faction Mark Two in 1985. He appeared to be highly skilled in keeping his name out of any reports at the time, and if you were to actively look for him — if you could find him at all — he would always be somewhere else completely. This fellow seems to have been far more tricky than the "Fox" ever was.' Truchaud thought momentarily about that case they had just wound up. Was it really less than a week ago?

'Then, at this moment of high international tension,' she continued, 'soon after the two factions set up a formal alliance, Louis Laforge went and died in a road accident, and, without further ado, his father summoned Jérome back to Burgundy to take over the running of the domaine, where he appears to have been ever since.'

'It's not a very left-wing thing to do, running a wine business.'

'Especially as the slogans of May '68 criticized bosses of such companies with "Don't negotiate with bosses, abolish them".'

'Wasn't that the same organization that had the slogan, "I'm a Marxist, of the Groucho variety?"'

'The very same. Not all the slogans were political or violent. Some of them were just very witty. One asked people to leave the Communist Party in the same condition they would wish to find it! Anyway, that's where I've got so far. I'm wondering about what happened to brother Louis, and with your permission, that's what I'm going to look into next.'

'That is quite exceptional work, Constable. Is there anything in any of that explaining where he got the money to feed himself while he was indulging in all those activities?'

'Not obvious. He was being paid as a labourer when he was working in the vineyards in Germany, so that might have covered his income while he was a Red Army cadet, but there was little else suggesting he was gainfully employed during the seventies. There's certainly nothing in his French tax records. Mind you, there are a couple of chunks of time where his name doesn't crop up at all, so he may have been gainfully employed in another country at the time.'

She chuckled for a moment. 'Of course he could have been cooling his heels in a prison somewhere I haven't found yet. I suppose he could have been involved in a robbery, which funded one of those left-wing groups. People tend not to declare the proceeds of a robbery to the taxman. I suppose it was possible that his father was funding him from the shop. Your guess is as good as mine. Would you like me to look into that as well?'

'That would be handy.'

'I'll do that too, *chef.*'

'I'm full of curiosity. Firstly, does anyone else at the *Quai* know you're doing all this, or is this something you're doing on the q.t.?'

'Well, I'm piggybacking it onto some research I am doing for Inspector Leclerc, who's been seconded over to Vice by the DC while you are away. I don't think he's enjoying it very much, I think they expect him to understand more than he actually does. I don't think he's anywhere near as vice-riddled as he would like us to believe.'

'Have you been allocated anywhere in particular?'

'No, sir. The squad appears to have been mothballed, and the DC is just using us as general factotums as needed. Poor George is driving about all over the place playing at being a courier. I think he rather hopes you will be back in Paris again soon, so we can all sink our teeth into a nice juicy murder again.'

'And you?'

'I'm still working for you, aren't I, and if the issue crops up, I've got all sorts of notes to prove that I'm actively doing so, while you have been seconded to the Nuits-Saint-Georges crowd. I must come down some time and see what the place looks like. I have quite a vivid imagination, as you well know, but it would be interesting for me to find out how off-beam the picture of Nuits-Saint-Georges that my imagination has painted actually is.'

'That you must, but not while I'm undercover down here. It's a small quiet town and a girl as pretty as you, that nobody knows, would stand out like a sore thumb. Everybody would want to know everything about you, down to your shoe size and your favourite colour. Let's just wait until we've unravelled whatever it is that's going on and we're having another of our famous debriefing dinners. I've found just the place for it incidentally. Anyway, you're doing a grand job up there, digging up information that I wouldn't be able to lay my hands on down here.'

'I'm sure you could at the University in Dijon.'

'But then I would be somewhat less undercover if I was to be seen sitting in a forensic part of the university library. And it means I can get you to do the donkey work and keep the squad alive while I am on compassionate leave. Incidentally, satisfy my curiosity, where do you get all this stuff from? You say Laforge's name doesn't show up anywhere, and yet you've found out all this information.'

'Oh, his name shows up just fine, it's just when something goes off bang, that's when his name doesn't appear. His name also features in the German police archives, which are still in Bonn, but again the same pattern. When something went off, there he wasn't. I think he used to be a very slippery customer.'

'Bonn?'

'Used to be the capital of West Germany, sir.'

'Don't patronize me, I do know that. How did you get information out of the old *Bundespolizei?*'

'Ah well, there's this chap in Bonn called Karl-Heinz, who sometimes needs information from what used to be the *Sûreté,* and sometimes we need information out of him.'

'Do we approve?'

'On the whole, *chef,* yes. On this occasion he has been helping us.'

'How did we get the information?'

'I use the telephone, *chef.*'

'Should we need paper copies for the trial will they be available?'

'I'm sure Karl-Heinz will oblige.'

'What's he like?'

'I don't know, sir. I've never met him face to face. He seems amiable enough. We just talk on the phone every now and then. Anything else I can do for you at the moment?'

'Not that I can think of. Bye.' Truchaud disconnected almost out of breath. He had been completely thrown by that telephone conversation. It was very interesting indeed.

He stirred the coffee that had cooled down slightly while he was on the phone to Constable Dutoit, and sipped it. It was cool enough to swallow down in one draught, but he decided against it. It wouldn't take more than fifteen minutes to walk from the domaine to the Place d'Argentine, and he didn't want to appear overkeen. On time was good, fifteen minutes early was not the image he wanted to give out. One thing he could therefore do was the washing up before Michelle got back.

He swallowed the last of the coffee, and walked through to the kitchen. He had already rewrapped the pâté and put it back in the fridge as he had also done with the sausage and vegetables. There was nothing left on the draining board to be washed apart from the cutlery and crockery he had used for his own lunch. These he washed, dried and put away, just as Michelle came back through the door.

'There's something I'm not used to,' she remarked, 'someone else doing the washing and drying up. What have you done with Shammang? Truchaud men aren't that domesticated. I should know; I married one, gave birth to another, and regularly look after a third.'

'I shall think about whether you want me to meow or purr all the way down to the meeting I am off to shortly,' he grinned. 'The pâté's delicious by the way, so I would tuck in before it goes off. Did your meeting go off okay?'

'Fine, fine,' she said, but didn't elucidate further. So he told her all about the plan for the funeral that he'd set up, and that it was to go for Thursday. She seemed okay with what he had done so far. He then explained that he had been called to formally meet the local Police Chief in the town hall.

147

He set off on foot out of the gate, out of the narrow streets of western Nuits-Saint-Georges, and down the street past St Symphorien's Church and its churchyard. He looked through the gate back at the church on his left. It stood tall and rather sandy coloured in the sunlight. He also quietly cast an eye over the ornate tombstones in the churchyard, then looked at his watch, and realized he had to get a move on. He walked to the end of the Rue de l'Égalité, and turned right, away from the second churchyard on the other side of the road where his brother would soon be interred. He headed right to the Place Argentine and the main entrance to the town hall, where he was due next.

He looked at his watch; perfect, on the dot.

Chapter 20

Nuits-Saint-Georges, Monday afternoon

Truchaud wasn't at all sure what to make of Inspector Molleau. He had seemed to be dragging Captain Duquesne around behind him like an unwanted dog that morning. More surprisingly, Duquesne had seemed willing enough to follow.

He walked through the front door, which opened obligingly when he pushed at it, presented himself at the desk, and addressed the rather constipated looking girl sitting behind the desk. 'Yes?' she asked.

'I've got an appointment,' he replied.

'Name?' came the next monosyllable.

'Truchaud,' he replied in kind.

She looked at her desk, and pointed at a chair on the other side of the foyer. 'Sit,' she instructed, and then spoke what was an enormous sentence for her into her intercom. 'Your two o'clock's here.'

Molleau sent someone wearing the badge of 'sidekick' to find him, who led him through to his office. The dapper inspector had at least made the effort to watch the door. As Truchaud walked through it, he was gestured into a rather more comfortable looking chair than he had been offered in the reception area. 'Coffee?' he offered.

'No thanks,' replied Truchaud. 'I've just had lunch, and coffee was part of that.'

'I understand from the Captain of the Gendarmerie why you're here. I'm not quite sure, given your background and the department in Paris you work for, why you called in the gendarmerie, rather than us first.'

'Simple,' he replied. 'They made contact with me, and gave me their telephone number, so when I came upon the body, so to speak, I'd already got a number to call, should I have need to call someone in an emergency.' He fished around in his wallet and finding Duquesne's card, gave it to him.

Molleau looked closely and rather suspiciously at it, and then gave it back. 'I suppose I had better give you one of mine as well.'

'In case I come up with another body?' Truchaud looked concerned. 'I really hope not.'

'So do I. I would start becoming suspicious of your motives for being here in the first place, were that to start happening. How long are you planning on staying here, by the way, before you return to Paris?'

'I don't know yet. There are issues I have to sort out at the domaine. As you know, my brother died very recently. What you may not also know is that my father isn't very well either, and with my nephew not being old enough to take over the firm yet, I think I may need to take on an overseer of some sort.'

'Have you any one in mind to be this overseer?' asked Molleau with notes of interest in his voice.

'Oh several,' Truchaud told him almost jauntily. 'But I don't think they suspect I'm considering them as an employee as yet. That's all part of the game, isn't it?'

'I suppose you're right, yes. Do you think any of them might accept such an offer, if one happened to be made?'

'You know, I haven't the faintest idea. As I've just told you, I haven't asked anyone yet. But until I'm sure of the identity of my preferred candidate, I don't really think I'm going to start offering jobs about.'

'May I know your candidates?' asked Molleau.

'I do hope you wouldn't take offence if my reply to that question is "No". I haven't even discussed it with my family yet, so I certainly don't want to tell anyone else. I think you can be sure that I won't be offering it to Jérome Laforge.'

'I would doubt that, his being already dead!' So at least he knew that much about the case.

Truchaud pushed again. 'Why, had you got someone in mind?' Was this why Molleau had asked to see him? Had he got a nephew in need of a job?

Molleau sat back in his chair and looked slightly uncomfortable. 'Er, no,' he said, 'not offhand.'

'Well, if you think of someone, feel free to give me a call. I have a phone permanently in my pocket. It occasionally gets broken when I fall on it, but that's not something I make a habit of doing. Now, what is it I can actually do for *you?*' It was time, Truchaud thought, that he took control of this conversation, which didn't seem to be going anywhere.

'There's been a murder,' Molleau announced gravely.

'Yes, I'm aware of that,' replied Truchaud, airily. This man had so far succeeded in irritating him all the time he had been in his company. The only reason he had been summoned apparently, was because he was a bit miffed that Truchaud had chosen to call Duquesne first when he had found Laforge's body.

'We've got to solve murders, we police, and lock up the guilty parties involved.'

'You sure have,' came the careful reply. 'That's certainly how things happen where I work, in Paris.'

Molleau made a steeple of his fingers and rested his chin on it. 'Here too,' he replied gravely, and thought silently for a moment. 'I have spoken to your Divisional Commander,' he said quietly.

'Oh, yes? How is the old boy?' asked Truchaud breezily, wondering where the conversation was off to now he had lost control of it again. It was interesting that Molleau was making it sound like he had instigated the conversation with the Divisional Commander, and that he was apparently giving out the orders. Bluff the old buffer might be, but he didn't make life easy for people in Paris who behaved like they outranked him, even the very few who actually did.

'Difficult to tell, from where I was sitting. I've never actually met him, you see.'

'So what did the old buffoon have to say for himself?' Truchaud attempted a similar technique, just to ensure that his

151

superior and Molleau had no actual relationship, like being uncle and nephew, or something Truchaud knew nothing about.

'He told me you were available to work for us. Moreover, he offered us the services of one of your assistants as well. What do you think of that?'

'Firstly, as you probably understand, I am on compassionate leave. My brother's just died, you remember.'

'Yes, he did mention that, but he also said that whatever leave you were on, you would be unable to resist sticking your nose into a trough if there was a crime on offer.' *Yes, that sounds just like the Divisional Commander all right.*

'So who did he offer to send down to help?' If he'd offered Leclerc, the whole thing was off. Obviously Vice had failed to get anywhere with him.

'He mentioned a Constable Dutoit. He says she's as sharp as an operating theatre full of scalpels, and will be of considerable use to you and us.'

Truchaud laughed out loud. 'Now you know he's laughing at both of us,' he said.

Molleau looked up quizzically, 'Why?' he asked.

'Because she looks like Bardot in the fifties, and despite her detecting skills, the one thing she really can't do is go discreetly undercover unless it's on a film set or in a bordello, and anyway the old man can't keep his eyes off her. I really cannot imagine him sending her down here out of his sight for no benefit to him.'

'Well, that's what he said,' replied Molleau sounding slightly petulant. 'Are you armed?' he asked, suddenly leaning forward.

'Armed?' Truchaud asked somewhat surprised.

'Armed,' Molleau repeated. 'You know, have you got a side-arm?'

'Not on me, I haven't. I carry a pistol very rarely, even when I'm on duty, and as I've already told you, I'm not on duty.'

Molleau withdrew a pistol from his desk. He systematically dismantled it into its component pieces, like a child deconstructing a model kit. When he had finished he looked at his handiwork laid out on his desk. He then swept all the pieces off the desk into the top drawer. At that point he locked eyes with Truchaud, and an 'assembling things' type of metallic noise emanated from the top drawer again. Within a minute or so the pistol was reassembled on the desktop, and he had not broken Truchaud's gaze once. Truchaud was fairly sure he hadn't blinked either. Truchaud, trying not to laugh at the ridiculousness of the whole thing, broke his gaze.

'There,' said Molleau.

'I hope that thing is safe,' said Truchaud caustically, noting that if the gun went off it was pointed directly at his midriff.

Molleau scrabbled around in the drawer again, and produced a handful of live bullets, and deposited them on the table beside the gun, without moving the direction in which the gun was pointed.

Truchaud was not satisfied. 'And there isn't a live round in the chamber?' he asked drily.

Molleau broke the pistol again and demonstrated the chamber was empty.

'Safety catch?' Truchaud was making it absolutely clear that he was not impressed with Molleau's display of machismo.

Molleau slipped the safety catch on. 'What I was trying to find out is whether you had a sidearm available should you need one.'

'And what you were trying to show me is that you have one, and that you know how to fiddle with it. Are you trying to tell me that you want me to be armed?'

'If you are going to work for us, we need you to be properly equipped for the job.'

'Somehow I don't follow all this. What I need to know, if I'm going to be more involved, is: a) my status in all this; and b) whether you or Duquesne is my nominal commanding officer, and thus who do I report to? Also, which of you two is expected to report to me?'

'What I understand is that your role is to be an independent advisor to both forces.'

'A sort of official private investigator you mean?'

'Yes, a police private eye if you like. After all, in that coat, you look like one. At the moment the gendarmerie is in charge of the case, especially as Maréchale is missing, and they are out there looking for him. Furthermore, as I think you know more than all of the rest of us put together about the winemaking underworld out there — being one of them, or at least born into that stock — I think you can take that as your responsibility. I suspect all three of us will meet up on a regular basis to share information.'

'So you want me to spy on my friends and family?'

'Spy?' He appeared to chew over the word for a moment. 'I think that's the bottom line of it, yes. What do you think?'

'Well, for the first thing, I don't know anything about the *winemaking underworld*, as you so graphically put it, and I will have to talk to my boss about this myself. I need to know what rights and restrictions he will put on me, we all know the rights and restrictions *you* will put on me. I also want *you* to know that I need to do things for the family and the domaine in the meantime, which is, after all, why I'm here at all.'

'We would expect nothing less. We would definitely like you to be seen working with and for your own domaine. People won't think you're being a detective, even when you are. They're far more likely to talk to you, and you're more likely to understand what they're on about.'

When he left the town hall, instead of walking straight home, he wandered back via the Place de la République, via the Café du Centre, which had rapidly become a favourite watering hole. Lunch was over, and there were few people in there still, and the back was empty. He asked for a large creamy coffee, and felt very 'breakfastish', or ' English'. Some time, he thought, he ought to try their beer, but wasn't in the mood for a drink-like drink right now. He sat back and slurped the coffee while making some notes. The notes and coffee finished, he paid the bill and walked the short distance back home.

Once he had got home, he dialled the Divisional Commander in Paris.

'Hello, old boy,' said his boss. 'You sound different.'

Truchaud explained what had happened to his original

154

phone, and that he was talking into a brand new one. 'Yes, your young fellow down there has been telling me you've been getting yourself caught up in all kinds of a kerfuffle on his manor. You're becoming a regular chaos merchant, aren't you, Truchaud. I'm beginning to wonder whether these sorts of thing follow you round, rather than you being where dogs' dinners are created so you can tidy them up.'

'Why? Has it all gone quiet since I left Paris?'

'Pretty much,' replied the Divisional Commander. 'Obviously there are the usual issues going on, the usual gutter-press rubbish about some politician being caught in bed with the wrong wife. You know that sort thing, but otherwise nothing much.'

'So that's why you said you could spare me?'

'Only for the length of your compassionate leave, old boy, then we'll want you to come back and stir Paris up again. After all, it's still three months to go before Bastille Day.'

'What puzzles me is that you told Inspector Molleau I could have Constable Dutoit as an assistant if I wanted. Surely that was a joke?'

'Was a bit, I'm afraid. I thought you'd get it.'

'Oh, I did. You're telling me I can go undercover, here in my hometown, and then you offer to send me a lighthouse to get everyone looking at me. There's no way that young Dutoit could go undercover here in Nuits-Saint-Georges; it has a small population, and most people know most people. Everybody would want to know all about her and who she is.'

'Well, you could always pretend that she's your wife.'

'Here in Nuits, they would expect me to sleep with her: that's what men do with their wives down here in the provinces. There would be people tweaking their shutters to make sure we did too, to find out exactly what techniques we were using. I don't think either Dutoit or I, or indeed *you* would find that acceptable.'

'As I said, nothing going on in there, old boy, as you well know. I accept, however, that you don't actually need a sidekick down there. Nevertheless, if I were to come down to see you and how you're getting on, I trust you could find me a hotel.'

'Anything from the grotty to the sublime, with matching prices to boot. I've never been in the building, but there is a hotel in Vosne just down the road called the Richebourg, and considering what the case is all about, that would be most appropriate. Anyway, I'm happy to do this. Will you courier down my warrant card, which I left with you when I came down here? I also have a feeling that the inestimable Inspector Molleau would like you to send me my sidearm too.'

'Will do, old boy. Will you be at home this evening?'

'We're booked into the Café du Centre in the Place de la République for dinner, but thereafter we'll be home playing cards. Bruno, Dad and I have quite got into playing a few hands of Tarot in the evening before bed. It's better than plugging in to mindless television.'

'Three generations of Truchauds playing cards. If I wasn't so busy, I'd do the courier job myself just to see that,' he chuckled.

'Do you know how to find us?'

'All the police cars have up to the minute satnav, so no problem there.'

'Tell them to come into the domaine. They can park in the courtyard. At the moment the locals expect to see and hear police cars coming and going from our house. What's going on down here is pretty common knowledge on the street. There's nothing yet in any of the papers, but everybody knows anyway. Oh, and by the way, will the courier need putting up for the night? We've got a spare room that we offer out to the students who stay over during the harvest.' He felt guilty offering to put a policeman up in the house: yet more work on the already overworked Michelle, particularly if that person turned out to be someone like Leclerc. And with the DC's sense of humour that was exactly who he might send.

'Remember, old boy, the bottom line is that you still work for me and Paris. It's only your wits that are on loan to the locals.'

'Anyway, I'm still on compassionate leave.'

'Exactly that. I'll see you soon.' The phone went *click* in his hand, and he disconnected and put it back in his pocket.

Chapter 21

Nuits-Saint-Georges, Monday evening, Tuesday morning

'Well? How did it go?' Michelle asked as he got in.

'He's asked me to do a bit of work for him while I'm here.'

'Is that a good thing?'

'To be honest, I'm not sure. I'm not sure I like Inspector Molleau a great deal. Duquesne's all right, provided you're not Suzette Girand, but Molleau, not so much. What has come out of that is that they're sending a courier down this evening from Paris with my warrant card. We may have to put him up overnight.'

'Oh, Shammang. We're not a hotel!'

'Well, I can send him down to the Ibis on the edge of town if you'd prefer.'

'No, it's all right.' The argument collapsed, but it still left him feeling very guilty, and hoping that it really wasn't someone disagreeable who he didn't know that the old man sent down. It might be anyone. He was, after all, in charge of a number of squads in the Paris area. Even worse, it might be someone disagreeable he *did* know.

'What are they asking you to do?'

'Ear to the ground stuff from what I understand; nothing much.'

'Nothing dangerous, I hope.'

'Hopefully nothing involving falling down stone steps again, that's for sure. I've got a new mobile phone by the way, so if anyone calls me while I'm out, or you need me to do something, then I'm contactable again.'

'Yes, you said that at lunchtime.'

'Sorry, I forgot. It's been a busy day. One thing I have remembered is that we've got a table booked for dinner for all of us at the Café du Centre.'

'But what you didn't remember was that you said that too,' she replied.

'I nearly didn't when I was talking to the Divisional Commander on the phone.'

'That might have been embarrassing.'

Truchaud spent the rest of the afternoon walking the vineyards on the east side of the Seventy-Four, in much the same way that he and Bruno had walked the Clos, Vosne and Nuits the previous day. At this point in time there was little to choose between the sites, apart from the obvious fact that the eastern patch was considerably larger. He pulled up the odd weed by hand and perhaps the odd tuft of grass, but there certainly wasn't enough of anything to fill the shoulder bag he was carrying.

The vines east of the Seventy-Four were, like their more illustrious bothers, sprouting tiny green tufts of life out of the top of the twisted wood; almost a cheeky appearance in the hope that no one was watching. These may have been the lesser-ranked plants in their holding, but the Truchauds always treated them exactly the same as they did their flagship vines. They stood in disciplined ranks, reaching just below the trellises towards which they were aiming. The greenery would grow quite fast in the pleasant weather that they were having at the moment. He would need lessons from someone in how to clip the shoots to the wires without doing any damage, probably within the next week or so.

He would also need to check with Dad to see that they had all the sprays ordered. It would be a combination spray of copper and sulphur, to suppress mildew, spiders, odium, and all the other blights that were the winemakers' enemies, even in good years. Sometime during the next few days, it would probably need ploughing over, partly to aerate the soil and partly to disrupt the grasses that were beginning to appear, so he would need to get the tractor serviced, if it hadn't been already.

The evening meal was delightful. It was probably the first mouthful of wine that the domaine hadn't made that Dad had drunk for a long time, apart from yesterday's mouthful of Richebourg, although there was a case for saying that the family had made a considerable amount of that bottle too. This was a bottle of Village Nuits made by a friend of the family, and Dad was full of complimentary remarks about the wine-maker. As the family was tucking into the cheese course, a face appeared through the door that Truchaud recognized: George Delacroix, one of his own squad from Paris.

Truchaud invited him to sit down and join them, performing the introductions, 'Do you want anything to eat?' he asked.

'No thanks, I stopped at a L'Arche on the way down. They're not a bad way to stop a rumbling stomach when you're driving, and as I knew you were eating here there was no pressure on time. And yes, I kept the package in my pocket all the time, and the Mégane's parked in your courtyard.' He turned to Dad. 'Your son has told us lots about you, sir, and it's an honour to meet you.' Dad turned bright red and didn't know where to look.

Bruno looked excited; another police Mégane at the house. Truchaud let him down slowly. 'This one's unmarked,' he said. 'It will flash blue in places if you really want it to, and does have a siren, but you won't notice it if George doesn't want you to see it.'

'So you work with my uncle in Paris?' Bruno asked the detective.

'I do.'

'Is he as difficult up there as he is down here?'

Delacroix looked at Truchaud. 'You know I've no idea how to answer that one. Is your nephew always this sharp?'

'The answer to both questions is probably "yes". As far as being able to answer him when he is being particularly difficult, better men and women than me have failed … abjectly.'

Following coffee and a cognac, they all walked back to the domaine. Delacroix had charmed Michelle utterly that Truchaud's offer of a bed was no longer a bone of contention, and it was becoming a pleasant evening. Bruno went up to bed, Dad followed him off to his room, and Michelle made herself scarce, leaving the two policemen talking in the dining room.

Delacroix pushed the package across to Truchaud. In it was his warrant card, his SIG SP 2022 pistol and a box of rounds for the pistol. There was also a notebook written in Natalie Dutoit's copperplate handwriting. He looked at the gun, broke it to make sure it wasn't loaded — it wasn't — then closed it up again, and flicked the safety catch to 'on'.

'You may not believe this, but the only thing I've ever done to this particular device since I was issued with it is to clean it. Even on the practice range, I fire the range's weapons. Truth be told, I'm not a very good shot, and I have this feeling that if I were to start brandishing it, I'd probably shoot an innocent bystander by accident.'

'You could, of course, spend more time on the practice range,' said Delacroix with a grin, his dark eyes alight with amusement.

Truchaud smiled gently back. 'Perhaps you're right, but while I'm undercover in Nuits-Saint-Georges I can't. People round here hear a bang, and they all start looking round for the wreckage of the engine of an old *Deux Chevaux* van. Did the Divisional Commander specifically want me to have that?'

'I have no idea, *chef*. He's the Divisional Commander; I'm a lowly constable, who does what he's told, even by junior inspectors, without quibbling. When the likes of the DC speaks to me, it is all I can do to stop myself grovelling in gratitude for being allowed into the presence of his Magnificence.'

'You are joking?'

'Of course I am, but it does make a point. What's the job down here?' he asked changing the subject.

'What did Natalie tell you about it?'

'Not much. She just gave me that notebook and told me to tell you it was the next instalment. I think she's somewhat disappointed that she didn't get to do the courier run.'

'Well,' Truchaud replied, 'she's doing a little research in Paris on one of the characters in my little adventure down here. He's actually the victim of the murder. He was the wine merchant my family had dealings with. I'd been down here for precisely a day and a half when he ended up with a bullet in his head. Cause and effect has yet to be proven, but it's an unpleasant coincidence.'

Truchaud went on to explain his understanding of what was going on, and why. He explained that he was going to need to be down for the best part of another week at least, as the funeral was another four or five days off. He asked Delacroix what time he was expected back in Paris on the morrow.

'I don't think they've told me a time as such, or if they did, I wasn't listening. I suspect the later I am the more likely it will be that the DC will have a couple of jobs steaming quietly on the hot plate, wailing quietly "do me next". Why?'

'Well, I wondered whether you'd join me in Captain Duquesne's office tomorrow morning before you go. There's something I would like you to do for this investigation when you get back to Paris.'

Once he was in his bedroom, Truchaud turned his attention to Natalie Dutoit's notebook. There wasn't a lot in it, but what there was looked extremely interesting. It appeared that Laforge had had access to some offshore bank accounts, though what sort of access and where, she hadn't put in the notes. Perhaps she hadn't known when she had written them. Perhaps she still didn't know. He dialled her personal mobile phone number. A pre-recorded voice spoke to him.

'Hi there, this is Natalie. You have lucked into my special beauty secret: sleep. If you want to leave a message, feel free, and I will give it the treatment it deserves when I wake up. Good night.' Truchaud chuckled, but didn't leave a message. He resolved to give her a call when he had a moment to himself the following day, and went to bed.

Breakfast was quiet. As usual, Truchaud munched on fresh croissants, digested the contents of the morning paper, and slurped coffee. Delacroix was offered the sports page, but didn't bother. He had bought yesterday's edition of L'Équipe on the way down and was busy perusing its pink pages, which contained all the sport anyone could ever want, provided those sports didn't include cricket or hurling. Bruno had already disappeared off to school, and Michelle and Dad said little. Following breakfast Truchaud fed the dishwasher, then climbed into Delacroix's little Renault, to be driven round to the gendarmerie. They pressed the bell and walked in. Constable Lenoir was back at his usual post at the desk again. 'Has he banned you from driving again?' chuckled Truchaud.

'Oh no, sir I practise at every possible opportunity. At the moment I'm just driving this desk.'

'Can you tell the boss I'm here, and it would be handy to see him?'

Lenoir spoke into the desk, and then looked up. 'Go right in.'

Truchaud nodded at the plain-clothes officer accompanying him, 'Detective Delacroix from the National Police in Paris.'

'Good morning, sir,' replied the young detective, sounding entirely automatic.

Duquesne looked up from his desk. 'Good morning,' he said. 'Coffee?'

Truchaud explained to Delacroix that the gendarme Captain did not feel in any way intact without a cup of coffee to hand.

Delacroix replied that he wouldn't say no, so Duquesne bellowed for a further two cups of coffee for his guests.

Truchaud smiled. 'I'd like to explain why I brought the good detective in here to see you. It wasn't just to show you off to each other. Do you still have that bottle to hand; the fake "Richebourg"?'

'I think I can find it. Why?'

'I wondered whether it would be possible to do a photocopy of the label for the detective here to take back to Paris with him.'

'I think we can sort something like that out. Lenoir!' he shouted into his desk.

Lenoir leapt through the door, landing at attention. 'Sir!' he snapped.

'Can you arrange a copy of the label of the Richebourg for the detective here to take away with him? Now if possible. He's got to be off shortly.'

'Sir!' said Lenoir and having performed a very disciplined about-turn he marched out. Truchaud couldn't help thinking that Lenoir was grinning, even though all he could see was the back of his head.

'What I'm hoping is that our office in Paris will be able to trace any bottles of these that may have already drifted into the Paris market. London is probably the biggest single wine market in the Western world, but Paris isn't far off the top of the ladder either. Moreover, Paris has close links with the London market anyway. My feeling is that if we can find any other bottles claiming Chateau la Nuitoise as its provenance it will be a step in the right direction. Do you think we can do that from our end?' he asked Delacroix.

'I think it's a reasonable idea,' he replied. 'Our intelligence department would probably find it interesting.'

'I think so,' agreed Truchaud. 'Explain to them that this is the fake, but bribe them with the idea that they may even get to drink the real McCoy, if they get a positive result.'

Constable Montbard, ever on duty, brought in the photocopy for Delacroix. They locked eyes, longer than immediately necessary. Maybe sparks had flown, but Truchaud wasn't that good at picking up those sorts of signals.

Montbard snapped to attention, just like Lenoir previously, about-turned and marched out.

Delacroix then stood up, clutching his precious paper. 'I think I'd better be getting back to Paris then,' he said. He then snapped to attention, imitating the local gendarmes, but looked a bit ridiculous performing such a drill in civilian clothes. 'Sirs!' he saluted and left the room.

'You've not been drilling them?' grinned Truchaud.

'I just thought the unit was getting a little sloppy, so I thought we might smarten things up a little.'

'Silly boy. They were all laughing at you, my detective included, though I don't think any of it was meant particularly disrespectfully.'

'Doesn't do them any harm to know who's the boss from time to time.'

'I think you've got a couple of very good kids there. Don't break them. Anyway, going back to what I understand is going on. You've recruited me as a detective down here, and I have access to the full strength of the forensic unit in Paris. Let no one that's clever take you for a fool, Captain.' He thought for a moment and then asked, 'Any news about the missing Maréchale yet?'

'I've not heard anything yet, no. We've got officers out asking questions about where he might have gone. He doesn't appear to have had much of a past does young Maréchale, and seems to have appeared as if by magic in Nuits-Saint-Georges a couple of years ago. The people we've asked so far all heard that he had come from somewhere else, but nobody was exactly sure from where or when.'

'Surely he would have references on file or something.'

'You would have thought so, but it appears that the only person who might have known where they might be had his brains blown out a couple of days ago.'

'For being part of an international gang, Laforge's seems to be awfully amateurish about its paperwork. Either that or deliberately obscure.'

'I think, Commander, as far as Laforge's is concerned, it's more likely to be the latter. If they were stupid enough to think they could get away with the fraud we appear to have caught them at, they had to be fairly incompetent. If the misfortune that caused the collapse of the whole house of cards was your brother's unfortunate death, then that was an unlikely occurrence.'

'But why would my brother dying have triggered the execution of Jérome Laforge? That's what I don't understand.'

'That may be the bottom line of the whole mystery, Commander. That may be the nub of it all.'

Chapter 22

Nuits-Saint-Georges, Tuesday morning

Truchaud told Duquesne he was going to wander round to Laforge's to see if he could find anything in the filing system, but first he had a telephone call to make to Natalie Dutoit in Paris. He picked up his phone and dialled. This time the silky voice did not sound pre-recorded. 'You know I'm beginning to think we talk more now on the phone, than we ever did face to face in Paris,' he said. 'I got your note about Laforge's banks.'

'Yes,' she replied. 'He has at least two, but I don't know how he uses them. One of them he can use to stoke up on his tan while he's cashing a cheque.'

'Huh?' enquired Truchaud, not following.

'It's in the Cayman Islands. The other is much closer to home, being in Switzerland. La Chaux-de-Fonds is just across the border from where you are.'

'Yes, I suppose it's an hour and a half's drive on a good day. Satisfy my curiosity, where did you come by this information?'

'I'm beginning think you're more interested in the provenance of my information that the information itself,' she said, but continued. 'Karl-Heinz; he put a tracker on Laforge's account in Beaune. The tracker took him through the account in the Caymans to the Swiss account where it was caught and arrested. The Swiss are rather more watchful about monitoring devices attached to their accounts.'

'How much money was being moved?'

'That's just it. It really wasn't a lot; a few hundred euros, that's all. It seemed an awful lot of palaver for very little money. It'll be a very clean few hundred euros though.'

'When did that transaction take place?'

'A couple of days before Mr Laforge was killed.'

'So Karl-Heinz was already watching Mr Laforge?'

'Well, now you come to mention it, so he was. I wonder why,'

'That's the sort of question you might ask him next time you two get talking.'

'That's the sort of question, *chef,* that will get us talking again, in the very near future, I suspect.'

'In which case I'll leave you to it, and I suspect one of us will be calling the other later in the day.'

'Speak to you soon, *chef.* Bye!'

He looked at the phone for a moment, and then as it went back into stand-by mode, he put it in his pocket and set off for Maison Laforge. The place was still closed and there were a couple of gendarmes he hadn't seen before wandering about rather aimlessly. Sitting at the desk in the office was a fairly severe looking woman who could scarcely disguise her annoyance as yet another policeman walked into the shop. She almost growled at him as he introduced himself as a 'Commander', but her expression softened a little as he added the 'Truchaud'.

'Any relation?' she asked.

'Bertin was my brother,' he replied.

'I'm so sorry for your loss,' she said. 'Jérome was my uncle. I'm Marie-Claire Laforge.'

Truchaud softened too. So this was the niece that Duquesne had been talking about. He did, however, make a mental note that she still used her maiden name, and he glanced at her hand: no wedding ring, or mark where one had been. He replied the formulaic condolence, and both of them then explained to the other that they understood what was going on, and how it had involved their respective families. 'I'm here today seeing if you have any information about where Simon Maréchale had come from, or more usefully, where you think he might have gone.'

'You're not the first policeman who's asked me that question today. I don't think I ever knew where he came from. I know that seems daft, but it's true. His background and his reason to come here to Laforge's never seemed to be an issue. As far as we were all concerned, he appeared to know exactly what he was doing and Uncle Jérome seemed to be very happy he was around.'

'Where would Jérome have put any of the documents pertaining to his employment?'

'Well, that's just it, I've no idea.'

'Where would he have put anybody else's paperwork that he had taken on?'

'In their employment files.'

'And they might be where?'

She pointed at the row of box files up on the wall opposite, all lined up in alphabetical order. The people who were ex-employees were on the top shelf, and the current ones on the row below. There was a complete absence of 'Simon Maréchale' on the spines of any of the files. There was also the complete absence of a hole where a 'Simon Maréchale' file may have been taken from. 'Computerized payslip?' he asked.

'Can't find anything,' she said. 'I'm not sure where else I should be looking.'

'Would the secretary or payroll clerk know?'

'Well, Celestine was asked by various people earlier on today, but she didn't know, no matter who it was who asked her.'

'Is she still here?'

'I think so. She shouldn't have gone off to lunch yet.'

Celestine was a mousy young woman, her face defended by severe horn-rimmed spectacles. She didn't look as if she would hurt a fly, unless it flew in the near vicinity of her teeth, and then woe betide the fly. She did look rather unsettled about confronting a Commander however. Constables she could handle; Commanders, less so.

'We're looking for Mr Maréchale's payslips,' said Marie-Claire.

'There aren't any,' she replied quietly. Her tone was certain. She had been asked the same question very recently and had checked.

'May I ask why not?' enquired Truchaud.

'You may inquire,' replied the girl, 'but I'm afraid I don't know the answer. I did ask Madame's uncle about this before his

'… ah … misfortune, but he told me it was nothing to worry my head about.' *That reply confirms something,* Truchaud thought; it validated the accusation that Jean Parnault had made a couple of days previously; that Jérome Laforge shouldn't have been allowed anywhere near young women. She may not have quoted him exactly as telling her not to worry her 'pretty little head about it', but that was certainly the implication.

'So who sent the final accounts to the Revenue?' asked Truchaud.

'That would have been the late Mr Laforge himself,' she replied. 'I just gave him all the figures I had.'

'So you wouldn't have known anything about the individual wines you make?' He stopped for a moment, and then added, 'Like Richebourg.'

'Oh, sir, you're having me on. We don't make anything like Richebourg here.'

'We don't,' agreed Marie-Claire. 'Those sort of elite Grand Crus are way out of our league. The best we sell from this domaine is some of our Echézeaux, and when we can persuade your father to part with some of his Clos de Vougeot, we get some of that too for the shop. Mind you, the Clos is badged under your domaine's label and not ours.'

'So you know nothing about Chateau la Nuitoise?' asked Truchaud.

'Chateau la Nuitoise? What's that?'

'Two days ago, there was a large number of bottles down in the bowels of your cellar, whose labels read "bottled in our cellars; Chateau la Nuitoise".'

'I'll have to take your word for that. Generally, Burgundies aren't bottled under Chateau names; that's more of a Bordeaux way of doing things.' She chuckled. 'We Bourguignons aren't grand enough to own big things like chateaux. We own domaines or have part-shares in a *clos* or two if we're lucky, but that's about it. Whereabouts did you find those bottles?'

'Down by the underground wharf,' he explained.

Both women looked at each other as if Truchaud had lost the plot. 'Underground wharf? Where's that?' So Truchaud told them. In the end, as they still didn't believe him, he had to show them. He was quietly relieved that the wharf was still there even though the 'Richebourg' itself was still most definitely gone. Truchaud certainly believed them that neither of them had any idea before that moment that such a wharf existed at all, or even knew about the depth of the cellars.

Soon all three of them were back upstairs and drinking tea. It was, after all, by now late morning. They talked of needing to explore the rest of the cellar. The women had never been anywhere near as deep into their cellar as Truchaud had, and, as they were all becoming aware that there was some serious skulduggery going on in their domaine, they wanted to know more. They therefore decided to explore the depths of the cellars between the three of them. At least, Truchaud and Mrs Laforge did, and Celestine didn't want to be left outside what was going on.

'The most astonishing thing to me,' remarked Truchaud, 'is that nobody seems to know anything about this business, even the family that owns it. There are great chunks of the cellar that nobody knows are there, and yet it's on, or rather right under the premises. There are bottles of wine that nobody knows anything about and yet this is a wine merchants. There is a very senior employee about whom there is absolutely no evidence that he exists; nothing on paper whatever.'

'Oh, I'm sure I can find some paper proof Mr Maréchale exists,' said Celestine, diving back into her office. She came out waving a receipt. 'See,' she said, 'he signed this.' It was a paper receipt for some white wine from the Chablis from a wine merchant called Maison Dubois, in Auxerre, to sell at Laforge's. It also showed it was paid for with an equivalent quantity of Échezeaux and Bourgogne. Included in the barter transaction was a VAT certificate, so it all appeared pukka and above board. Maréchale had countersigned the receipt. Truchaud looked at it carefully, and wrote down the address in his notebook. He also took a photocopy of the document on the company photocopier and stuck it in his wallet.

'Well, that's a relief,' he remarked. 'I was beginning to think that young Mr Maréchale was a figment of an overactive imagination that I never knew I possessed. Now, as far as this cellar is concerned, we need to see exactly the lie of the land.'

Truchaud called Duquesne on his phone, and explained their plans. He asked if he would send Lenoir and Montbard down, to explore the deeper cellars with them, and just in case, he wondered if they might be armed. Duquesne said that he imagined that they would both be very excited, especially as they would have real bullets in their weapons for a change. The gendarme asked why he hadn't just asked the police who were already there on-site. Truchaud replied that if they disappeared for a while down into the basement, then once again there would be no one on guard up top. And if no one was up top, then who would raise the alarm, should anything go wrong down below.

'Unimpeachable logic,' Duquesne replied. 'I'll send them both over.'

'If you can't raise me on my phone,' continued Truchaud, 'then remember I'll be underground so call the gendarmes up top.'

The two gendarmes arrived in ten minutes, in the usual squeal of tyres. Truchaud wondered whether Lenoir would be made responsible for their replacement himself when that time came, which would be fairly soon. He introduced them to Marie-Claire and Celestine, and all five of them went back down into the cellars again. This time, for the moment, they did not turn left through the shattered door, but carried on deeper into the outer cellar. There were two further locked doors to the left, which responded to being opened with keys, and opened into small cellars which looped round back onto themselves, containing more barrels, and some cases of bottles marked Echézeaux by Maison Laforge.

There were also two doors right at the bottom, which did not respond to the use of any of the keys on the ring. Marie-Claire had no idea where the keys to those doors were hidden. Nor did she know anything about the door deep to the right.

Some of the barrels in the first cellars looked old, and when Truchaud tapped them they sounded empty. Some of the bottles of Echézeaux looked old enough to be very interesting now, and there was nothing in particular about the labels to suggest they weren't the genuine articles. What was hiding behind the locked doors, however, was what Truchaud wanted to know, and so did Marie-Claire.

His first temptation was just to launch a rampant Lenoir at the doors, and let the devil take the hindmost. The owner's granddaughter, however, was less tempted to use mindless violence on them, and before she let the police go ahead, she felt she would rather discuss things with her grandfather first; he being the titular owner of the place.

So they walked back out of the cellars again and back up top. Once they were there, Truchaud and Montbard sat down with a pencil and paper to try to draw a map of the catacombs from memory. It looked complicated and, in particular, it didn't show where the underground waterway came from or went to, just the location of that portion of the stream at that point. In an ideal world they would have had access to a three-dimensional pencil and paper.

Marie-Claire Laforge was talking to her grandfather on the internal telephone system, asking where he had hidden the keys to the back cellars. He was obviously being difficult, if her end of the conversation was anything to go by. 'But Grandpa, you must have some idea where the keys are, or at least where Jérome may have kept them? No, they're not on the master bunch. If they were, I wouldn't be asking you.'

Truchaud had an idea, and looked up at her. 'Ask him if they're a locked barrier between the cellars of what are now two completely different domaines. You know … at one time the whole thing belonged to one single domaine, but then, after someone's funeral, it got divided in half, and each new domaine was allocated half a cellar each.'

She passed the message on to her grandfather. 'Yes, that could be it,' she replied.

'In which case, ask him whose domaine is on the other side of that door. It would be only fair to warn the owner we're going to blow his cellar in if he doesn't let us in to his side of that door.'

The conversation carried on down the phone for a while. 'He doesn't know, but he really, really does not want you to blow the doors down.'

'He must know who is on the other side of a personal border. This is ridiculous. It's like the Alsatians not knowing who the Germans are!'

'He says it has always been there throughout his life. Before he was old enough, he didn't think to ask about it. By the time he was in charge of the domaine, he had no idea who to ask.'

'Why didn't he stick a note under the door? One day someone would have come upon it, and replied.'

'Why don't we do that now?'

'Nobody might come upon it maybe until the vintage after next, and that'll be far too long.' Truchaud could well understand that she was trying to prevent him from blowing those doors apart, just as she understood that that was what he wanted to do. Why was she worried? They would protect her barrels. That was unless, of course, she knew what was on the other side of those doors, and didn't want Truchaud to know.

Truchaud's phone rang. He pulled it out from his trench coat, and answered it. 'Hello?'

'Duquesne here. We've got a problem. There's been an accident.'

'Go on.'

'On the motorway somewhere up near Auxerre.'

'Auxerre? We've just been talking about Auxerre.'

'Well, your Detective Delacroix apparently lost control on the motorway up there. They've taken him off to the hospital.'

'Near Auxerre?'

'Why do you keep going on about Auxerre, man? It's the departmental capital of the Yonne. The motorway goes right past it.'

'Yes, I know, it's just that we were talking about it a moment ago. Apparently, Maréchale had recently been doing business there.'

'I don't believe in coincidences,' replied Duquesne drily.

'Nor do I,' replied the detective. 'I think I ought to be heading to Auxerre. Do you want to come?'

The Captain replied in the affirmative. 'Then wait there,' Truchaud said. 'I'll be round shortly to pick you up.'

The Captain demurred. 'I'm sure Lenoir will drive us in the Mégane.'

Truchaud shuddered, having no urge to suffer the same fate as the young detective. He was not the most content of passengers, and certainly not now. He was going to do the driving. 'I'll be round in my car in a few minutes,' he replied drily.

'I'm afraid I have to go,' he announced to the company in the office. 'There's been an accident to which I have to attend. Meanwhile, you two stay with the ladies and see what further information you can glean from the cellars here. I'll walk to my domaine to pick up my car, and Captain Duquesne will be answering my phone if you need to talk to me while I'm gone.'

Chapter 23

Auxerre, Tuesday afternoon

Auxerre was a small town with a famous football team to the west of the Chablis, and therefore was technically in Burgundy. Truchaud was just as dubious as its claim to ownership of Burgundy's northern border, as Beaujolais lay to its southern reaches. However, back in the distant mists of time, Auxerre had been the seat of the Dukes of Burgundy, until they were frightened off by packs of gigantic marauding wolves, and had retreated to the considerably less lupine Dijon. There they remained until they were formally defeated in battle by no less than the King of France himself, in 1477.

Truchaud's thought about the status of the territory of the Chablis was in no way a criticism of the wine. The best accompaniment to a plateful of fish, Truchaud thought, was a cold steely glass of Chablis, if a Premier Cru Puligny was outside your pocket-money range. Chablis was almost entirely a white-wine area, though, like all rules, there were exceptions such as Irancy Rouge, though Truchaud wasn't aware he had ever tried any, unlike the crystal white Clos Blanc de Vougeot from the predominantly red area of the Côte de Nuits from where he hailed, which had passed his lips from time to time, usually at somebody else's expense.

The hospital was not in the first flush of its youth, but the staff were pleasant, and he hoped efficient. The girl in casualty didn't admit to know anything about a George Delacroix until after they had produced their warrant cards, even though Duquesne was in uniform. They directed them up to his ward.

George was not easily recognisable: his left eye was very bruised and swollen shut, there were dressings on his cheek, and a bandage round his head. A drip was letting clear fluid slowly into his left arm. The parts of his body below the neck were not in direct view, being covered with sheets, but Truchaud did note that he was not wearing an oxygen mask, and was breathing easily enough. He smiled weakly at Truchaud, who he had seen though his right eye.

'Not going to be able to play distraction with Natalie in the immediate future. Sorry, boss.' It had been a take-down technique that Truchaud and his squad had used more than once. The two attractive young members of his squad would create a distraction — and very good and entertaining they were at it too — while he, Leclerc and the inspector snapped the trap shut.

'Never mind about that. What happened?'

'Well, funny that, boss. I've never had a tyre go flat on the motorway on me ever, and to have two go at the same time … Well, I don't know.'

'How do you mean?'

'Well, I was doing nearly 130 clicks an hour, the maximum you're allowed to do without flashing blues and twos, and was aware of this big old black Merc slowly gaining on me. As he pulled past, my left rear blew, and the car started to fishtail, then almost immediately the left front went too, and I lost it. The car started to roll, and I don't remember much after that. I must have got out of the car before I lost consciousness, or maybe I was thrown out, which they tell me was fortunate, because the car was burning when they got to me.'

At this point a severe looking senior nurse appeared, and suggested that that was it for the day unless the policemen wanted to sit and hold the patient's hand quietly without talking, as he needed to rest. Neither policeman felt like arguing with her, even if they were minded to try. 'You can have another five minutes tomorrow if you like,' she added as she followed them out.

The next stop on their itinerary was the local gendarmerie, which made them feel welcome and filled them with coffee, much to Captain Duquesne's pleasure. A Lieutenant-Colonel greeted them formally. Auxerre, being the prefecture of the

Yonne Département was entitled to one of those. In fact, it had the right to a number of senior police officers, in much the same way as Dijon, despite it only being a tenth the size. Truchaud was also sure that the reason that he had appeared was that he outranked both his visitors, and therefore there would be no possible debate on his authority. He had the thin greying air of a rather elderly senior maths teacher, approaching the status of being a lean and slipper'd pantaloon, without having quite got there yet. He didn't have a lot more information to give them than Delacroix had given them himself.

What was left of the car was in a forensics lab, but stank of burnt rubber. Of the black Mercedes there was no sign, and it hadn't apparently stopped. The alarm had been raised by a passer-by, who had noted the tyre marks on the carriageway, the damaged crash barrier, and the smoke and flames down the declivity on the other side of the barrier. Having put two and two together, they had called the emergency service. The *SAMU* team had found Delacroix unconscious some distance from the wreckage of his car. It appeared that the detective had been very lucky.

'Do you have a telephone number I can call directly, to get further information?' asked Truchaud. 'As you understand, this is all part of an ongoing investigation in Nuits-Saint-Georges, in which Paris is also involved.'

The Lieutenant Colonel passed them both a card from his desk, and Duquesne returned the compliment with one of his own. They finished their coffees, and taking their leave of the officer, walked out of the gendarmerie. 'I would like to cast an eye on the wine merchants that Maréchale was dealing with. Now that we're here it would be a shame not to at least find out where it is.'

So they programmed the address into the satnav and it directed them round to an industrial estate round the back of the town. 'What did you think of all that?' asked Truchaud as they set off.

'Do you think an occupant of the big old Mercedes shot out Delacroix's tyres?'

'That occurred to me too, but we may never be able to prove even the shooting bit, as the Colonel did comment that there was a bad smell of burning rubber, suggesting that the tyres had been burnt. If only we'd got those wheels in our Paris lab, we might be able to find something.'

'Surely that's not a problem? Couldn't Paris request that the wheels be shipped up to your lab in Paris? After all, this was an incident involving a Paris detective.'

'Smart thinking, that man! When we stop, I'll phone the Divisional Commander and politely suggest he gets to work on that. Not least of which, he outranks a Lieutenant Colonel.'

Maison Dubois was a large square white block of nothing very much, with its name painted over a door to the side of it. There was a small car park in front of it with three small non-descript middle-aged cars parked in it. The BX didn't look out of place. Before they got out of the car, Truchaud phoned his commanding officer, and explained he had seen Delacroix, and that he wasn't in any danger. However, he did make the suggestion about, at the very least, requisitioning the offside wheels from the wreck to examine closely for evidence of bullet damage to the rims. The DC took it on board and Truchaud hung up.

They got out and walked up to the door. They saw a button beside it, which said, 'press' so they did. There was a clicking noise from behind the door. They looked at each other, shrugged, and Duquesne pushed the door. They walked through into a wide-open space. The area to which they were restricted was bordered by a waist-high counter. There was part of it that looked as if it would lift, but it didn't respond to Duquesne's attempt to do so. A rather care-worn, middle-aged man, greying round the rather unkempt edges, appeared from round a stack.

'I'm coming. Keep your buttons done up,' he said, sounding as if it was the last thing on earth that he really wanted to do.

Both detectives flashed warrant cards at him, not that Duquesne really needed to, dressed as he was as a Captain in the Gendarmerie. 'I don't suppose you gentlemen are here to buy a case of Chablis for the policeman's ball?'

'Sadly not,' replied Truchaud. 'However, if you had a nice bottle of Irancy red for me to try, I would be most obliged.'

The man disappeared back into the warehouse and almost immediately came back cradling a bottle which he wrapped in tissue paper. 'That'll be fifteen euros,' he said. 'Anything else I can do for you gentlemen?'

While Truchaud was fishing in his pocket for his wallet, Duquesne took over. 'We wondered if you knew the whereabouts of a certain Simon Maréchale, with whom you do business from time to time.'

'Simon?' he mumbled, 'Simon? We haven't got a Simon Maréchale working here, no.' He paused. 'The only Simon Maréchale I know works down at Laforge's in Nuits-Saint-Georges.'

'Yes, that's the one we're looking for. Have you seen him over the last day or so?'

'The last day or so you say?' He paused again. 'Could I say I've seen him in the last day or so? No, I couldn't say that.' His pauses seemed as if he was thinking very deeply about a very complex intellectual problem. 'About a week ago more likely; not the last day or so.'

'What sort of business do you do?' asked Truchaud.

'We're a wine merchants, sir. Says so over the door.' The reply came quickly this time, as if the clockwork was now fully wound.

'I mean, do you swap bottles from other areas, or does money change hands?' Truchaud was beginning to become quite irritated by the apparent simplicity of the man. If he were employing people, he certainly wouldn't trust this man to handle his money.

'Money changing hands?' said the man. 'When that happens it involves the taxman, doesn't it?' he said. 'Mind you, I know of taxmen who take their cut in wine, if you know what I mean.'

Duquesne and Truchaud exchanged glances. 'It was a fairly

simple question,' Truchaud replied testily. 'Is there any way you could give me an equally simple answer? Does money change hands or is it a simple barter transaction?'

The man looked back. 'Sometimes one; sometimes the other,' he said non-committedly.

Duquesne leaned over the counter and breathed coffee fumes and garlic at the man. He took hold of the man's shirt just below the top button to emphasize the point. 'And the other day between you and Maréchale?'

'That one was a barter transaction,' said the man and Duquesne let go of the shirt.

'Now that wasn't so difficult, was it?' said Duquesne. 'All you have to do is answer the questions we ask, and nobody gets hurt.'

They were both off-patch, but any further conversation of this sort would be likely to trigger unwelcome action from the local police. They probably had all the information that he could give them, being that Maréchale wasn't in the building. Any further activity would just make things difficult.

'Home?' said Truchaud. He put fifteen euros on the counter and picked up his bottle. With a 'thank you', they turned on their heels and left.

They drove back quietly to Nuits-Saint-Georges. 'I wonder whether the old boy at Dubois was as thick as he was having us believe,' remarked Duquesne.

'Either way, I don't want to get any deeper at the moment,' replied Truchaud. 'If we need to come back to Auxerre, we've got a stick we can brandish if we need to, and I can get authority from Paris myself if we really need it.'

The conversation dried up on the way back to Nuits-Saint-Georges. Their thoughts both drifted back to the injured Delacroix. The attempted killing of a Parisian detective, if that was what it had been, was either an indiscriminate potshot at law and order in general, or it suggested Paris was involved as well. Delacroix was not directly involved in the case. The one thing they did talk about was the Richebourg label, which had presumably been destroyed in the accident. The master was still in a filing cabinet in Duquesne's office so he agreed that he would e-mail a copy to the lab in Paris as a replacement.

Truchaud dropped Duquesne back at the gendarmerie and drove back home. It was now middle to late afternoon, and he had no particular urge to go back to Laforge's, or to face Montbard with the news. Either she would be very upset, or she wouldn't be. If she wasn't, then his judgement of female feelings had once again been found wanting, and he could do without having his face rubbed in that at that moment.

He went home, took off his trench coat, and put on his Domaine Truchaud hat. The tractor had been serviced, he was glad to know, and his father was busy putting the 'Bordeaux Mixture' into the tank and the spraying machine hanging off the back of the blue tractor. Winemaking tractors were tall devices, driven with a mix of gears and chains, and designed to straddle a row of vines, without actually coming in contact with them. Truchaud thought that they looked monumentally unstable. He had heard that there were parcels further up the *Côte* that were so steep that they were still ploughed and sprayed by hand, or with carthorses. This wasn't just because the by-products of the carthorse were a reasonable fertilizer, but also because a carthorse had not, in living memory, been seen to overbalance. The Truchaud parcels were relatively flat, apart from the *clos*, and compared to some of the higher plots on the *Côte*, even that wasn't steep.

Truchaud looked at his dad. 'Where is this destined for?' he asked.

'I've sprayed the Vosne already,' he replied. 'That went okay, so next we do the Clos, the Nuits and finally the far side of the Seventy-Four. The weather looks set fair for the next couple of days, so we'll get the whole lot done.'

'Do you want me to take over from here?'

The old man looked rather sadly at his son. 'Look, you've confiscated my secateurs, and you're very involved in your own activities. Let me do what I am still capable of and permitted to do. If I spray the wrong patch of grapes, no one gets upset. In fact, most people are grateful. Grapes from neighbouring parcels invariably get sprayed at least twice, once by their owner, and once by their neighbour who's spraying the next row along.'

'I had often wondered about that,' Truchaud thought out loud. 'If one vintner is biodynamic, and the other is chemical, what happens?'

'Well, there are only a few chemists left. Most of us are, at the very least, organic now, and we don't use synthetic fertilizers or pesticides. Whether you want to go the whole hog and do it by the phases of the moon using leaf-days and root-days is a matter of personal belief and individual taste.'

Dad was making far more sense today, much to Truchaud's relief. He had had similar thoughts himself. When he had bought biodynamic wine in the past, it was less because of its inherent belief system, and more because of the individual personal effort the individual winemaker had put in. There was no room for mass production in biodynamic or organic winemaking. 'The philosophy of the individual winemaker is paramount, and if a bit of chemical spray drifts on the wind over a biodynamic site, it washes off. That's what I think anyway,' continued the old man.

With an agility that belied his years, Truchaud Senior swung himself upwards into the saddle of the tractor, and started the engine. The tractor coughed and spluttered a bit like a twenty-a-day smoker on waking in the morning, belched out a few clouds of black smoke, and then caught. Once it was turning over properly the black smoke disappeared and the tractor started to smile. Father and tractor turned out of the courtyard and disappeared off into the street.

Truchaud sat and thought for a moment, and then followed him out in the car. He got to Vougeot first, having overtaken his father before he got to Vosne. 'What are you doing here? Are you spying on me?' his father shouted down at him as he drove past him on the road up to the Chateau. Truchaud was leaning lazily against the wall, having parked his car further along in front of the house.

'No, I'm just watching in the hope of learning something,' he replied. The old man *harrumphed*, but let it pass. Truchaud had worked out which were the family's vines, and which weren't. He had worked this out from looking at the nearest obvious border, and counting back. Dad had driven straight to the same row without stopping or apparently counting. He stopped and turned round to his son. 'I shouldn't stand there,' he shouted, 'it'll make your eyes water. I would sit in the car for a few minutes while I spray this lot.'

Once the cloud of spray had cleared his immediate vicinity, the detective walked back down to the wall again. Further down the row, the tractor was driving away from him, followed by the haze of spray covering at least three rows either side of the row it was straddling. At the bottom of the row, the tractor turned and then came back towards him, again straddling the next row. He reckoned each row would get at least three doses of Bordeaux mixture and maybe that was just right.

'Quite a spectacle, isn't it?' came a voice beside him. It was Molleau, who had crept up on him unawares.

'That's my father spraying his vines,' Truchaud replied, pretending he had known Molleau was there all along. 'But you're probably not here to admire my father's performance.'

'No, not really. I wondered whether you had any information to share.'

'You mean apart from Sergeant Delacroix's accident?'

'Oh yes, that was bad, wasn't it? Do you know how he is?'

'Very shaken, with a few minor cuts and bruises, but fortunately that's all. Very lucky indeed. Fingers crossed.'

Truchaud wasn't really thinking about anything else. In fact he was trying to concentrate on his dad's oncoming tractor, to shut out the events of the day. Molleau wouldn't go away though.

'Any thoughts about Laforge's cellar?'

'We've explored most of it. There are a couple of locked doors whose keys aren't on any key ring we found. Old Mr Laforge thinks that they maintain a border with someone else's cellar, but he can't remember whose. I'm not convinced, but old Mr Laforge's granddaughter would rather we didn't go in and

183

wreck the doors if we can help it, and for the moment, I can't think of any reason to override her wishes.'

Molleau said nothing for a moment. He then looked at Truchaud again. 'Any news of the missing Maréchale yet?' he asked.

'Not that I've heard,' Truchaud replied, still wondering exactly what Molleau was hunting for.

'Well, when you do,' he replied, 'be sure to let me know.' He turned on his heel and ambled off.

Truchaud couldn't decide whether to feel amused or cross about Molleau's patronizing attitude. *You had to hand it to the man*, he thought, *he wasn't short of a pair.*

There wasn't a lot of point in his waiting around any longer at the *clos*, watching his father on a tractor.

There was, however, one other person who might have known Maréchale, and no one had thought of asking him about Maréchale yet.

Chapter 24

Nuits-Saint-Georges, then Dijon, Tuesday afternoon

Truchaud returned home to the domaine and called Natalie in Paris. Somehow he wanted to be somewhere Molleau had no likelihood of cropping up out of the blue. He had no reason to distrust the man, but he just did; simple. He sat down in the chair by the dining table and dialled. She answered quickly, 'Oh it's you, *chef*. We've just heard about George. Awful, isn't it?'

Truchaud was aware from her voice that she might not be alone, so he said just to be sure, 'Say "no" if you're not alone and you can't talk.'

Her next sentence contained the word 'no' at least twice, so he continued, 'You'll be glad to know that I've seen George today in Auxerre, and he's a bit battered and bruised, but isn't seriously injured. He's a very lucky boy.'

'I'm very pleased to hear that, sir. Hey, guys, the *chef* has seen George today, and he's not seriously injured.' There was a moment's pause and then she said, 'Commander Lucas wants to know how the car is.'

She is so good at painting pictures with words, Truchaud thought, 'From what I gather it's a complete write-off. It caught fire after George got out.' He decided not to tell her George might have been thrown out. He then told her to call him back when she was next able to do so, which she naturally promised to do, and thanked him profusely for reassuring the squad about Delacroix's condition. They disconnected.

Truchaud climbed back into his BX, and drove into the eastern part of the little town. There weren't any obvious parking restrictions and, anyway the Girand house had a little courtyard in front of it for him to pull off the road. He got out of the car and rang the bell.

'Charlie!' Geneviève appeared delighted to see him again. 'What brings you back so soon? A cup of tea, an aperitif?'

'Oh, no thanks, I've got the car outside. I'm actually pretending to be a policeman today,' he apologized. 'Is Suzette here? I need to ask her a couple of questions. She's not in any trouble or anything, but she did find Mr Laforge's body, and there were a couple of things she might or might not have noticed. I thought it might come better from me than Captain Duquesne, who she didn't seem to like very much.'

'No, she didn't, did she?' she said, her green eyes glittering at Truchaud, probably unintentionally, he thought sadly. 'She isn't home. She's got a room near the university in Dijon, where she stays during the week. She only comes home at the weekends.'

'You wouldn't have her address to hand, would you?' he asked wondering about the hands of Fate. He had adored this woman from afar for the past twenty-five years without ever seeing her, and now, here she was in front of him, and he was interrogating her like a suspect. There were times, he felt, that he was missing a number of important psychological components.

She wrote the address down on a piece of paper for him. He looked at it, and recognized the street by name. Whether he would still do so when he was actually standing in it might be a different matter. The city had been quite extensively rebuilt near the university over the last few years.

'I'll see you again soon,' he said, 'hopefully for social rather than police matters next time.' He let himself out of the house, and went back to the car. He drove back down the street, until he almost reached the little road joining the motorway junction to the town centre. He phoned the gendarmerie on his mobile. A voice he didn't recognize answered it. 'Truchaud here. Just letting you know where I'm off to.' He gave them the address.

Over the years, when he was down staying with his family, he had watched the slow but inexorable construction of the Rocade, Dijon's eastern bypass. It now connected with the motorway, which was quicker than driving down the

Seventy-Four, so he drove through the tollbooth and took the exit that pointed him to Metz. He was amused that the direction to Paris was signed as south towards Beaune. The distances should have been marginal, he thought, at the very most. Driving north on the motorway, he was just that bit further from the *Côte* than if he had been on the Seventy-Four, and it looked proud and magnificent on his left. He could imagine Napoléon's army marching along it, with their eyes looking directly at Le Chambertin. There was a story, probably apocryphal, that the little general had woken up too soon, and had called the 'eyes right' at Fixin, some five kilometres to the north. He wondered idly whether the marching troops had tripped over each other as they covered that distance without ever looking where they were going.

Once he had pulled off the motorway and driven through the tollbooth, this time registering on the automatic Dart, he headed up onto the Rocade. The road was already too busy for its own good, with the traffic density on its two lanes considerably greater than the three lanes of the motorway. This would have been because travelling on the Rocade didn't impose a toll, whereas on the motorway it did.

He pulled off at the rather unnecessarily complicated junction, which depending on your throw of the dice, pointed a driver at the hypermarket at Quétigny, or the university campus. The complexity of the junction seemed to have been designed to cause maximal confusion and bloodshed. They must have resuscitated the street designer from Paris for that junction, he chuckled to himself.

Once he'd escaped the junction and passed the edge of the campus, he crossed the old inner ring road and found himself in the street where Suzette lived. He was pleased to notice that the block of flats was a building at least a century old, and not a modern synthetic box.

The block had a narrow gateway, which, he supposed, was designed for a *chevalier* and his squire to ride through side by side, or perhaps through which a farmer could drive his ox-cart. The BX just about fitted without making contact with either side, but not by much. That was a very effective traffic-calming method, he thought. He'd have never got the Divisional Commander's Jag through. There was a courtyard in the middle, where he parked the car and got out. The concierge had already been woken by the arrival of an unknown car though her sacred gates, with an equally unknown driver in a shabby trench coat.

'Yes, sir?' she asked, without appearing to want an answer, just an immediate departure.

Truchaud extracted his warrant card and asked for directions to Suzette Girand's flat. 'Fourth floor on your left,' the concierge replied. 'The lift's through there.'

The lift was a cage surrounded by the circular staircase. Truchaud thought it looked as old as the rest of the building. 'When you get to the floor,' said the concierge, 'remember to close both sets of gates properly. The lift doesn't work for anyone else unless you do that. In the old days, we had a man who ran the lift for us, but when he died, the students we now have as tenants, all voted not to replace him, to save money. Every resident agrees to pay the agreed fine if they don't shut the gates properly. We don't want to be fined, do we?' she added patronizingly.

Truchaud looked at the old woman politely, 'No of course not. I promise to close the doors properly.' He wondered how many francs the fine was exactly. The whole thing seemed so last-century. He opened both sets of scissor gates and walked into the cage. He then closed the outer gate so that it clicked into place, before he closed the inner gate. He pressed the number four. The lift was slow, much slower than the one in his flat in Paris, but then his own block of flats had been fully renovated after the war; this one probably hadn't needed it.

The big double oak door at the entrance to the flat looked magnificent. Even the bell pull had an antique look to it, and when he pulled it, it sounded like an old-fashioned clapper on a real bell. A rather hairy unkempt head looked round one half of the door. 'Yes?'

'Is Suzette Girand here?' he asked.

The head looked back into the flat and bellowed. 'Suze,

188

you'd better get your pants on. There's an old geezer out here looking for you.'

A female voice he recognized shouted back. 'Out in a moment. I'm on the phone.'

The head nodded him in. 'Third door on the left,' he said. Truchaud wondered whether it was to the hairy young man, or Suzette herself to whom he ought to be delivering a safety lecture on security. Probably both, he thought. He could have been anyone.

He walked down the polished wooden floor and tapped on the door. There was a shout from within which could have been 'Come in!', but when he actually did so, he wondered whether it might have been 'Hang on!'

He was not sure who was more surprised, Truchaud himself, Suzette, sitting half-dressed at a dressing table, with a cell phone held to her left ear; or the young man, in an ill-fitting t-shirt which read simply 'Merde!' He wasn't wearing any shoes, and was lounging on the bed. He took one look at Truchaud, shouted, 'Oh fuck!' and leaped off the bed, trying to get to the door before Truchaud shut it. He didn't succeed. By the time he had hit the door, collapsed on the floor, and regained his senses again, Truchaud had immobilized him. The detective manhandled him back to the bed, and pinned him there face down. It was then that Suzette started to move. 'Let him go!' she screamed.

'Everybody just calm down,' said Truchaud.

'What are you doing here?' she asked still fairly loudly.

'Looking for you, to see if you might know where he is,' he replied, jerking his free thumb at the prone figure on the bed, which he recognized as Simon Maréchale.

The door opened, and the hairy young man put his head through the frame. 'Is there a problem in here?' he asked. Truchaud also thought that a squeal of ecstasy might be a problem here in this flat, but maybe that didn't happen too often.

Truchaud nudged the prone figure underneath him. 'The man asked a question. Is there a problem in here?'

'N … no,' he replied.

'Do I have to hold you down any more?'

'No.'

Truchaud let go, and looked up at the hairy young man. 'No problem,' he said, pulling out his warrant card. 'I'm the police.' The hairy young man gave him a look of abject terror, and he could have sworn that he also muttered, 'Oh fuck!' as he disappeared out of the door, slamming it fairly hard.

Maréchale glared at Truchaud. 'What?' he said crossly.

'I'm not even going to ask about the episode in the cellar,' he replied. 'I'm sure we'll get to that further down the line, but there are more important issues we need to discuss.'

'Like what?'

'The execution of Jérome Laforge, of which you're obviously not guilty as you're hiding in here with Suzette Girand. There is no way that she could have put on that show of distress at finding the body, being, at the same time, aware of who had done it. I'm sure, at the same time, that if you had been guilty of that, then the cellar episode would never have played out as it did. You know I ended up locked in there overnight?'

'Oh, I'm sorry about that.'

'I am sure the Richebourg is the clue to Laforge's murder, so I would like to take it one step further. You took me to that cellar so that I'd find the Richebourg, didn't you?'

Maréchale looked up at him interestedly. 'Yes, that's right. May I ask a question? If you got locked in behind that door, how did you get out?'

'It involved a great deal of noise and some destruction,' he replied. 'Some of the contents of those poor barrels will take a little time to recover from the shock. However, if there's any breeding in them at all, they will get better over time.'

Maréchale looked at him. 'I'm relieved to hear that,' he said.

'Who was it that called out for you that had you running so fast? I didn't recognize the voice.'

'For a most unpleasant moment, I thought it was my previous employer. I thought he had come looking for me again. Actually, it was some dealer that young Mr Laforge knew, who had just heard about his death, and was worried about the state of one of his orders, and whether it would still go through.'

'So, satisfy my curiosity, how long have you been hiding here?' asked the policeman.

'Ever since you got locked in,' he replied. 'Suze is a good girl, and looks out for me.'

Truchaud looked at the girl by the dressing table, and then looked away again. He found it far more disconcerting looking past her perfectly shaped bare legs, than she appeared to find his looking at them. They were certainly not on display for his benefit, maybe not for Maréchale's either, but she may well have been in the process of changing her state of dress or undress when the phone went. The shirt she was wearing was far too big to be hers, so was it his shirt? That would explain why he was wearing a slightly ill-fitting and inappropriate t-shirt. But if it was his shirt, then was she completely naked underneath it? Had they both grabbed the first item of clothing available when her flatmate shouted out his warning? Were they post-coital or were they just about to start? Natalie Dutoit would have known; she could smell the progress of sex a mile away, in a way he never could.

'And Suzette, how did you get involved in all this?' Truchaud asked, perhaps to move away from the pictures in his head. Suzette waved a hand at Maréchale. 'He was very kind when I was taken on by young M. Laforge, and he showed me the ropes. I was sort of expected to know everything, coming as I do from my family's domaine, without being taught anything. Customers ask you all sorts of strange questions,' she continued.

'So it was the presence of Simon here that was the real reason that you went to work at Laforge's rather than working with your uncle Jean?' asked the detective.

'No,' she said. 'I met Simon after I started there.' She looked at the young winemaker with an expression of tenderness. His expression was more difficult to read, but he hoped he felt similarly for the girl.

'It was handy that she has a working knowledge of English and Catalan,' said Maréchale. 'I always feel very sorry for the wine the Americans buy in the middle of a summer holiday to drive away with. It must boil in their hand luggage, and be a poor memory of the wine they tasted when they were still in the cellar.'

'So what do you know about that Richebourg?' asked Truchaud.

'Absolutely nothing, but I knew it couldn't be genuine. If you add the number of cases made by all the different domaines that have parcels in the plot called Richebourg, you'd get less than 3,000. There was no way that you could get the sort of quantity that is in our cellars. It just couldn't be genuine. Then Laforge went and got himself killed. I have to say I got really scared. I didn't know who to trust apart from Suze here, and I didn't want to put her in any danger. Then you appeared out of the blue. It seemed like a gift from the gods. All I had to do was to make sure that no one else knew that I was on your side. Really pissing you off and then disappearing seemed like a good move on the spur of the moment.'

'Do you know who killed Laforge?'

'Haven't got the faintest idea. First thing I knew about it was Friday evening, when Suze gave me a bell after she got home. She didn't take to your gendarme mate, you know.'

'Yes, I got that.'

'Well, she said you were all right, if a little creepy — sorry — but probably on the side of the angels. That night I had to try to work out how to find a way of getting myself between you and the bad guys, to use you as a shield, so to speak. So Suze phoned her uncle.'

'Jean?'

'Yes that's right, and you walked right into it.'

'You see, there are just too many coincidences in there. The only reason why I went to see Jean was because my father had been pruning his vines, and I went round to apologize. Now you can't tell me that my father was involved in all this, or my nephew who caught him with the smoking secateurs?'

'I agree that that was quick, but I assure you, I would have made contact with you within the following twelve hours. You were already linked with Laforge's yourself, and you'd already met Suze.'

'You mean that Jean was already involved in all this?'

'As far as I know he doesn't know anything at all, apart from the fact that I was educating his niece in the ways of the vintner.'

Truchaud raised his eyes at the partly clad girl. 'And this?' he asked.

'Err, that might have come as a bit of a surprise, yes. Actually, came as a bit of a surprise to me too. Not complaining though.'

Truchaud wasn't sure quite how to take that either, so he didn't react at all, apart from suggesting to Suzette that she might get dressed, just to reduce the level of tension in the room. She pulled on a pair of jeans, to cover her lissom limbs, and a couple of trainers. Whether they too were a pair, Truchaud couldn't tell, he didn't know much about shoes. It didn't seem to make it any easier to think either way. He still couldn't work out how the pieces fitted together. He tried a different tack.

'Tell me about Maison Dubois in Auxerre,' he said.

'Nice little firm: buys, bottles and deals in Chablis. Why?'

'I was up there yesterday.'

'Must have been a pleasant drive. I hesitate to ask why, again.'

Truchaud thought for a moment. He didn't really want to bring up Delacroix at the moment. Then it came to him. 'We were looking for you, as you might imagine, and the only piece of paper with anything to do with you at Laforge's was a receipt from last week, from Maison Dubois with your counter-signature on it.'

'Yes, we did a bit of business last Friday afternoon. I bought some Chablis for our shop. Did a swap for some red.'

'Did you ever sell them any Richebourg?'

'No. I never sold anyone anything labelled Richebourg.' He looked Truchaud directly in the eyes as he said that. Truchaud glanced at the winemaker's hands to see whether he was giving away any hints with them as to the veracity of his statement that he wasn't giving with his eyes. Not that he noticed.

'Did you ever *give* anyone any Richebourg?' Truchaud asked equally severely.

'Again, no. I had only been aware of its existence for a few weeks, and I have to say I was very interested to find out what it was, and as you can imagine, in particular, I wanted to know what it was like. I was working up to a way of asking young Mr Laforge for a tasting. You know, I would have liked to have known in advance so to speak, if it was something I had made myself, but then last Friday happened. He wasn't going to tell me anything after that.'

'Do you think Marie-Claire, his niece, might have known anything about the Richebourg?'

'I have no idea what she knows or doesn't know. She really doesn't appear very much at the premises, despite the fact that she lives in the flat at the back.'

'She and Celestine seem to know each other quite well.'

'Celestine would. She hangs round every leading family member in the building. I think she wants to get her hands on a share of the family wealth. I'm sure she would be willing to sleep her way into it. Ironic really: she's lost all the men in the family apart from old Mr Laforge, and he is really old.' He thought for a moment. 'That is, unless she's going to hang on for Jacquot.'

'Are you saying she was sleeping with Jérome?'

'I doubt it. She's been somewhat too old to suit his tastes for several years, or so I understand.' *So*, thought Truchaud, *he knows about young Mr Laforge's taste for young girls too.*

He looked at Suzette. 'Did he make a pass at you then?'

'No. He probably understood that I know exactly how to deal with unwanted attention. I've had some experience in that. I also already knew from one or two of my girlfriends that that might be a game he wanted to play.'

Truchaud looked at her for a moment. *Yes*, he thought, *I imagine you did. I can see you're very aware of the fact that how you look affects the space around you.* He returned his questioning to Maréchale, 'Are you saying that Celestine sleeps with Marie-Claire then?'

'I have no idea on which side of the fence Marie-Claire currently sits. The fact that she's got a kid suggests that there has been a man present in her life at some time in the past, but there's never been any evidence of one while I've been around.'

'Celestine's orientation?'

'Strictly fiscal. I don't think she is particularly concerned about gender,' he replied. 'I did toss my hat at her soon after I arrived. Sorry, love,' he glanced sideways at Suzette, 'before you got there. She wasn't interested. I haven't got any money, you see.'

'So how did you get into Laforge's?' Truchaud asked.

'Talent, pure talent, mate. They advertised for a winemaker, I applied, and got the job.'

'Where were you before?'

'Down in the Languedoc, but working in Nuits-Saint-Georges looks really good on a winemaker's CV. I'm now just one job away from working in a five-star establishment, or at least I was until last week. I can't help thinking that Domaine de la Romanée-Conti in Vosne or Chateau Margaux in Bordeaux probably aren't so likely now to pass a positive eye over my credentials when their rare job opportunity comes up in the *Winemaker.*'

'Can you explain why no information about you is to hand in the winery office today? It's like you don't exist.'

'Oh god!' The young man sagged. 'I'm already off all the papers?' He looked sadly at Suzette. 'I think it would be safer for you, Suze, if I moved on straight away. If they've already deleted me, then I shall need to disappear once again, and start again at the bottom of another ladder.'

'No, Simon. Don't even think that way. I'm sure Uncle Jean will be able to find something for you. I'm also sure the Commander will protect you, won't you, Commander?' She opened her eyes unscrupulously wide. Even though she wasn't wearing the green contact lenses that day, she knew exactly how to work her physical advantages. Truchaud was damned if he was going to let on.

'You've already been in a situation like this?' he asked.

'Not exactly the same, but similar I suppose. There weren't any murders involved if that's what you mean. But selling

195

wines as something they're not? Yes, I've been there before in the Languedoc. I'm beginning to think that that's why I was recruited to work here. My CV obviously didn't advertise that I had any scruples, so that's why I'm here.'

'As in, in my room?' asked Suzette sharply, looking up at Maréchale.

Maréchale looked sadly at her. 'Indirectly I suppose. I wouldn't have met you if I hadn't got this damn job. Once I got the job, I was on the way to us all sitting in this room just where we are now.'

'The question I have to ask at this point,' Truchaud interjected, 'is whether you are both happy keeping this going for a little while. Suzette, are there rules that you are going to get in trouble with, about keeping a man in your room?'

She looked at him amused, 'Mr Truchaud, this is France, not an American frat-house film.'

'Simon, would you feel safe here for the moment? I could take you into protective custody if you prefer, but I would rather not do that locally. I'm not sure how safe you would be with the local police round here.'

'See?' said Suzette, 'I told you that gendarme was trouble.'

Truchaud grinned at her, 'My dear young lady, Captain Duquesne is the one other policeman in this area whom I'm sure I could trust with my life. He may be a little bumptious and very competitive, but I think he is completely trustworthy. Can you let Mr Maréchale stay here for the time being? I promise I will tell no one he is here, not even your mother.'

She smiled at the young winemaker. 'Do you want to stay?' she asked wide-eyed.

Truchaud had no idea how he could have said 'no' if he had been asked that question in that way, and Maréchale gave him no hints as to how to do it either.

'In that case, I would like you to consider yourself under house arrest here. Don't go out, Simon, under any circumstances. If you need me, here's my number. Call me. I will tell no one you are here, and if I come back, I will be either alone or with Captain Duquesne only, and I will have warned you

196

in advance. If I'm with anyone else, hide. I need both of your phones programmed into mine.'

'Am I in that much danger?'

'To be honest, I really don't know yet, but I need you to be safe. I don't want what happened to Laforge to happen to either of you two. One thing I would like to know. Apart from Esau out there, is there anyone else living in the flat?'

'Esau?'

'The hairy hippie who reeks of cannabis. You know, "My brother Esau is an hairy man, but I am a smooth man?" It's somewhere in Genesis, but I can't give you the exact chapter and verse.'

'There are three more usually, but they're not around at the moment.'

'Can you call him in?' She did and he came sheepishly as summoned, as if he had been sitting just outside the door, listening in.

'I'm not looking for cannabis,' he told them. 'What I am doing is trying to protect this chap,' he said jerking a thumb at Maréchale. 'Your security here sucks. Now if anyone turns up who isn't me, claiming to be from the police, they may well actually be so, but that doesn't necessarily mean they are on the side of the angels. So make lots of noise, so that at least young Maréchale can get out of the fire escape or something. Suzette, make your room smell really girly with lots of Eau de Cologne or something. And you, Esau, two things: wash both yourself and your clothes; and secondly if you must smoke that stuff, don't do it in the flat. The drug dogs would go half-crazy from the second floor upwards. If I can smell it that easily, they need no excuse whatever to tear this place apart room by room, and that would be a shame.'

He turned on his heel. 'I will call before I return, but rest assured I will be back within twenty-four hours, and if I'm not, something has gone wrong, and you really need to get out of town, like you originally planned.'

Chapter 25

Nuits-Saint-Georges, Tuesday night; Dijon, Wednesday morning

Truchaud left the flat, well aware that there was a whole slew of questions that still needed answering, but he was also aware that he was expected for supper shortly and that the questions he would be asked when he got home were the ones he would rather not be answering right now.

'Your Captain Duquesne phoned and asked if you were all right,' remarked Michelle as soon as he walked through the door, and tossed his coat onto the hook in the hall. *Hmm,* he thought, *I'm getting quite good at that!*

He called Duquesne right back on his mobile, who asked, 'Did you find her?'

'Of course,' he replied. 'Not a lot to go on, but wonderful old flat,' he replied. 'Any news from your end?'

'Well, I'm happy to be able to report that your Sergeant Delacroix is still on the mend. The car is a total write-off, and the tyres are long past any definitive forensic examination, but they're hanging on to the metal parts of the wheel rims to study them.'

'And the Maison Dubois?' asked the detective.

'I've been digging around a little, but there's no obvious dirt on them. They seem a genuine enough erstwhile little family firm that has been keeping its nose clean down the ages, making and selling some nice, if not spectacular Chablis. They set up their warehouse business fairly recently, selling wines from other parts of eastern France, including, as part of their portfolio, some Laforge Bourgogne.'

'Did the kids find anything at Laforge's after we'd left?'

'No, still nothing about Maréchale, and I think we're going to have to approach the judge to get a warrant if we want to break down those doors. At the moment I don't think I can justify it. One of the more interesting things might be to crack open the gates at the wharf and go up or downstream in the underwater canal in a canoe, and see where that leads us. Ever been to Disneyland?'

'Err, no,' replied a puzzled Truchaud.

'Well, we took the kids there at the end of last summer.'

'What, you took Lenoir and Montbard to Eurodisney?' exclaimed Truchaud stunned.

'No, my wife and I took *our* children to Disneyland Paris,' Duquesne explained in a rather tired voice. 'They had this ride there called "The Pirates of the Caribbean", which was very up and down, with cannon shells going off all round the boat you're riding on. The kids had a great time.'

'I knew there was another good reason for not procreating!' replied the detective drily. 'Thank you for reminding me what it is.'

'Then there was the Great Schplouf at Parc Astérix,' continued Duquesne, totally ignoring him, 'where you potter quietly round on your flat-bottomed boat with soft music and pretty flowers all around and everybody goes 'aah!' Suddenly the water drops away and you're going down a waterfall … *schplouf!* It's onomatopoeic, you see. The kids really loved that one!'

'And you want to go *schplouf* under the streets of Nuits-Saint-Georges?' enquired Truchaud in disbelief. He was beginning to think the gendarme was trying to waste the National Police's telephone account on purpose.

'No, no, but it's something that needs to be done, and we won't need to create a case to the judge to do it. Are you intending to go out again tonight?'

'I wasn't planning to.'

'Good, then I'll see you in the morning.' The phone clicked and went silent.

He went back to the family, to find supper on the table.

'Did that nice Sergeant Delacroix get off all right,' Michelle asked once they had all sat down.

'He had a car accident on the way back, and he's in hospital in Auxerre,' he replied drily. He went on to explain that Delacroix wasn't seriously hurt, but it was the last meaningful conversation he had that evening and he went to bed.

He dreamed of many things that night, very few of which had anything to do with any other. For the second time that week he woke in a knot with a mouth that tasted like the bottom of a parrot's cage.

Breakfast the following morning was the usual quiet affair. For Truchaud himself it was croissants, jam, coffee and the morning paper. Once again it appeared that the paper really ought to be interviewing the local grapevine. There was far more local news in the air outside the house than he had read in that paper. However, if he wanted to buy anything, anything at all, he would probably find an advertisement for it within its pages.

He had been allocated a parking space round the back of the gendarmerie, and a key to let himself in. He didn't need to wake the gendarme on the desk any more, and let himself directly into Captain Duquesne's office. 'Ah! Coffee time,' came from the figure behind the desk. He pressed the buzzer, 'Truchaud's usual, and mine,' he said.

'What news?' Truchaud asked.

'Well, they couldn't be sure that the metal-on-metal scarring they saw on the inner rim of the left front wheel was from a bullet. It could just have been from a bolt from the crash barrier as the car ran over the top of it. They don't think they're going to be sure either way.'

'But it doesn't exclude anything either. Anything else?'

'They've put out an all-points bulletin for the big old black Merc, but so far they've drawn a blank.'

'It will probably be well over the border into Germany by now. It's the home country of big old black Mercs. It will be quietly undercover out of sight, or exactly the opposite; in plain sight in a museum. But as far as Maréchale is concerned …?'

'Still no sign of Maréchale anywhere,' Duquesne interrupted as the coffee made its appearance, carried by the ever-present constable Montbard. She didn't show any outward signs of either lethargy or distress. When she left the room, Truchaud asked if she knew about Delacroix.

Duquesne said that he expected so, but why should it worry Montbard? Truchaud explained his thoughts about the glimmer of mutual interest between them that he thought he had spotted in the office the previous morning.

'Well, she's a girl; he's a man. As long as it's on their own time, what's the worry? I don't think she has any particular interests in anyone she can't see in a mirror. Far too absorbed in herself, that one, to worry too much about anyone else.'

Truchaud thought about that for a moment, and then shrugged Gallicly, and continued quietly to Duquesne. 'I've seen Maréchale, and talked to him,' he said. 'At the moment, he's undercover, perhaps like the big old black Merc, though not on display, and I'd like to keep him that way. He is one scared young man.' Truchaud explained what had gone on late the previous afternoon.

'You want to keep him in hiding there?' asked Duquesne.

'If you don't mind. I think I trust the pair of them. I'll soon find out, won't I? Do you have any questions you want me to put to him?'

'Not at the moment, but I would be grateful if you would tell me before you move him out of wherever it is you've got him hidden.'

'I'm sure the only place I will be moving him to will be formally into protective custody with you.'

'And that's where you're going next?'

Truchaud took a large mouthful of coffee and agreed that that was where he was going next. He left again out of the back door of the gendarmerie, and drove to Dijon that morning via the Seventy-Four. Once he had passed through the bottom end of Brochon, he pulled into a layby and called the flat in Dijon. 'I'm about ten minutes away, plus the ride in the lift. Are you both dressed and decent?'

202

'What do you think we get up to up here?' giggled Suzette who had answered the phone.

'I have a very shrewd idea, and have no wish to see a live performance. Satisfy my curiosity. Oughtn't you to have been at university at least an hour ago?'

'My first lecture is at eleven o'clock this morning, so I was having a lazy start.'

'Get the kettle on, young lady. I'll be with you shortly.'

Hairy Eddie looked and smelled like he had scrubbed himself with a wire brush. This morning he positively reeked of carbolic soap, and his hair was combed, and he must have been up all night polishing himself and his fangs. Truchaud was pointed to the communal kitchen where a fully dressed for study Suzette and a tidy Maréchale were sitting nursing fresh hot cups of coffee. 'Yours is still in the pot,' she said.

'How are you all this morning? Sleep well?'

'Not very,' replied Maréchale. 'I don't know whether being caught by you was easier or worse than being caught by the cops in general.'

'I'm a pretty class act,' Truchaud replied. 'You can take it as a compliment to your hiding skills that it took a policeman of my calibre to run you to ground.'

'What's Nuits-Saint-Georges like today?'

'Grey, moist, without it actually raining. Much the same as it is here actually.' Suzette swallowed the rest of her coffee, and put the mug in the sink.

'Can I leave you to do the washing up?' she asked. 'I've got to help the new lightweight Eddie across to the chemistry laboratory. I think he's a little bewildered about how you persuaded him to scrub up. He's still getting used to the change the effect of gravity on his new physique.' She walked out of the kitchen 'Come along, Eddie,' she called, as if summoning a lapdog.

'Whoa, yeah, right, whatever,' and various other incoherent mumblings emanated from Eddie as they left. 'I think we ought to walk down the stairs rather than take the lift. It'll help you sober up,' they heard her say as the front door closed.

'Quite a girl!' exclaimed Truchaud as he settled back down in the kitchen. Maréchale agreed, and waited for the Truchaud inquisition to begin again. 'Now,' the inquisition recommenced, 'what I want to talk about today is the role of my family in all this.'

Maréchale looked at him expecting him to continue. They looked at each other for a moment. 'I was mostly an observer, you understand … at least to start with,' he said after a moment's uncomfortable silence. 'Young Mr Laforge was the negotiator in all this from our side.'

'You know it amuses me how you can describe someone at least thirty years your senior as *young Mr Laforge*.'

'Well it's to distinguish him from *old Mr Laforge*, his father, who while he'll never see eighty again, can still be found from time to time roaming about the shop a bit.'

Truchaud let that pass. 'And the negotiator from our side?'

'Your father.'

An answer he had expected and dreaded at the same time. 'So what happened, and how?'

'Well, the two domaines already had a business arrangement set up between themselves long before I arrived on the scene. Your family produced the lion's share of the grapes, being from the east side, which we harvested, vinified and bottled.'

'Yes, I've always wondered. What did you actually do with that?'

'I'm coming to that in a minute.'

'Go on.'

'You also made two village wines and a Grand Cru Vougeot from start to finish. On our side of the fence, we grow and vinify a Grand Cru Echézeaux. As you know, in these large multi-owner Grand Crus like Echézeaux and Clos de Vougeot, the quality is distinctly variable. It depends on where in the Cru your vines are, and, to be honest, how good the individual winemakers are at working the plot. Now, your *clos* is in a pretty good location, and your dad has always been a very good winemaker. We have plots throughout the whole of the fifty hectares that are Echézeaux, the sum total of which, lumped together, could never have been described as better than 'average Echézeaux'. We weren't sure whether it was the *terroir*, or the hand of the man who made it. That was where I came in.' He paused for a moment. 'I need to be sure from this point onwards that I don't need a lawyer present.'

'This discussion is with me as a Truchaud, not as a policeman. Does that help?'

'A bit. What will you do with it?'

'Until I know what *it* is, I can't really answer that. What I can say is that I could have you banged to rights for aiding and abetting an assault on a police officer already, but I'm not pressing those charges. I think you're already in serious trouble with person or persons unknown, and at this moment in time, I'm trying to work out a way of keeping you alive. I suggest you keep working with me on that.'

Maréchale looked at the man he was still having difficulty in thinking of as 'the winemaker's son', and continued.

'I had a reasonable record as a winemaker on the Languedoc, and when this job came up, I applied for it. They wanted to know if I thought I could improve the Echézeaux that was their flagship wine. I thought when I joined that they wanted me to upgrade the *terroir*, like Jacky Rigaux.'

'Jacky Rigaux?' Truchaud asked. 'I don't know that name.'

'All winemakers who have been through Beaune do. He's a lecturer there and has written a number of definitive works on the subject. He also co-authored the *Ode to the great wines of Burgundy*, with Henri Jayer; a wonderful book. Anyway, it rapidly became obvious that it was a job in which it wouldn't do me any favours to ask too many difficult questions. One of the things they had spotted in my CV was that I had some experience of blending. Now, that's no big deal in the winemaking world. All the good Languedoc wines are blends of different grape varieties, mainly Merlot, Cinsault and Grenache. All the red Burgundies of higher ranking than *Passe-Tout-Grains*, however, are all vinified from a single variety, the Pinot Noir. However, as you well know, there is a vast difference in how the same breed of grape expresses its own micro-climate. That's what is meant by the word *"terroir"*. It can be no more than 500 metres from the grapes in your *clos* up top, to downhill and the ordinary wines on the east side of the Seventy-Four. They're the same kind of vines, but the wine you make from them is totally different.' He took a breath for a moment.

'Go on,' Truchaud encouraged.

'Well, as I said, we own a few separate holdings in the large Grand Cru that is Echézeaux. They wanted me to work out which of them would be best blended together, to make the best possible bottles of wine. That is all perfectly above board provided all the grapes are Pinot Noir and come from within the vineyard called Echézeaux. Then they wanted me to make use of the wine I had discarded. Now that stuff, I have to say, wasn't bad or anything, it just didn't fit in with the other stuff. Anyway, I was asked to see which grapes we harvested on the east side of the Seventy-Four were worthy of *upgrading* with this declassified Echézeaux. I assumed at the time, that the boss was looking at doing an *old vines* type of branding with a flashy label, to sell to the tourists, like we did in the Languedoc, and that we would be badging it something like "Laforge's Old Special Reserve". We knew your dad's patch on the east side in Vosne would have fitted in there, so I was just looking for a few more to blend in with them. A couple of years ago, your dad offered to market his bigger wines through us too, as long as he kept his labels on the bottle.' They exchanged knowing looks.

He continued. 'Well, there's a saying that "there are no ordinary wines from Vosne". There are, however, vineyards on the east side of the Seventy-Four in Vosne that do not qualify, by reason of location, to be called anything more than "Bourgogne". As you know, some of those vines are yours.'

'I know. Bertin was very fond of those vines. Laforge's may have harvested them and vinified them, but to him they were his babies, and I wonder whether he might have taken them back off you when he took over Truchaud's, had he lived.'

'They were certainly good vines, and it was a good *terroir*; very good considering they were from the wrong side of the Seventy-Four. He also treated them well and we made good wine with them, which certainly did not deserve to be tipped into the vat with all the other rubbish with which we make ordinary table wine.

'Young Mr Laforge and your dad were in total agreement there. Then I was tasked with looking into working out how to *upgrade* all the wines we made. There were a number of other small family domaines like yours that we dealt with, but, to be honest, yours is head and shoulders above the rest. You had good *terroir* on your side, and you also had a couple of really good farmers to express it. What young Mr Laforge wanted was more "Fine Wine" for the export market. What he needed, however, was the right quantity of quality wine to go through the French wine censors first. Once wine has crossed the French border, the *Institut National des Appellations d'Origine* and French customs quickly lose interest.

'So you can see, my job was primarily to make our Echézeaux better by cutting and pasting within the holding. I was well aware by now that I was getting in over my head but I found it an interesting challenge, so I thought, "what the hell?"

'So we swapped a bit of it with a bit of your village Vosne, which came our way last winter still in its barrels, and which I have to say, I thought was the flagship of the fleet. Your Clos de Vougeot, for the time being we left alone, and let your dad get on with the bottling of it all. We hadn't yet worked out how we were going to get your dad to pass the responsibility for that patch over to us. Pressure and seduction was on our agenda for the next couple of years. It was my job to get to know Bertin and make friends with him. We got on all right, I guess, but we certainly weren't bosom buddies.

In order to replace the Vosne, we upgraded some of your Vosne from east of the Seventy-Four, and popped that into the Village Vosne vat. Sorry about that. I did what I was told! Your Village Nuits was also pretty good and I was keeping an eye on that too.'

'How much was my father aware of what was going on?'

Maréchale looked sadly at Truchaud. 'I think he was more aware of the implications of what was happening at that time than I was,' he replied. 'He and young Mr Laforge were part-ners in all but name. At that time, remember, the project was to upgrade the quality, and thus the value of Laforge's Echézeaux. Remember Grand Cru Echézeaux is generally worth more on the marketplace than Village-ranked Vosne. Mr Laforge explained the improved quality of his Grand Cru away by praising this bright young winemaker they'd been lucky enough to find.'

'You?'

'Me! Exactly.'

'But that wasn't where it ended, was it?'

'No. At that point there was someone else taking an interest in the activities at Laforge's. As you probably know, Laforge's was involved in the international market too, as they also liked our Echézeaux; it's nice wine, especially since I took over. But there were a couple problems: one, there wasn't enough of it, especially as I had reduced the yield, and they wanted more; and secondly, the dealer didn't like the name. It's actually a bit of a tongue-twister in English. There was a heated discus-sion which I heard bits of. The bottom line was that if Laforge wanted to continue the relationship, there had to be more wine, and it had to be badged differently. I doubt if Laforge could have pulled out of the relationship anyway; he was already in too deep, so he went to talk to your dad.

'That was late last summer … when your father started get-ting ill for the first time. Young Mr Laforge came back from your dad's swearing like a man possessed, having totally failed to make your dad understand the problem in which he found himself. He wanted to use your dad's Clos de Vougeot as the flagship badge, and your dad simply wasn't having any of it.'

'I'm pleased to hear it. That parcel has been our family's pride ever since the *clos* was broken up in the nineteenth cen-tury, when my great-great-grandfather acquired our parcel at that time. It's the start of our family's involvement in Burgundy. The old boy wanted to make wine, and acquired that parcel and the Vosne parcel at the same time. We have been slowly increas-ing the size of the domaine ever since. There's just not enough yet for two kids and the dad to be kept with it.'

'Maybe that's what your dad was working towards.'

'How do you mean?'

'Well, if he made more money from his business, then he could buy some more vineyards. They do come on the market from time to time. Somebody dies, or gets into financial difficulties and has to sell a parcel.'

'Do you think that's what he was doing?'

'I have no idea for sure, but that's the aim of all winemakers: to increase the size of their holding. If you don't continually try to do that, the holding shrinks. It splits into pieces at the death of every senior family member anyway, so there must be enough growth to keep the next generation involved.'

'Another coffee?'

'Why not?' And so the conversation came to a hiatus.

Chapter 26

Dijon, Wednesday morning

With refilled mugs, Truchaud and Maréchale sat down at the kitchen table again. They adjusted their seating and locked eyes, like wrestlers at the onset of the next round.

'I think it was young Mr Laforge who was the first person who realized your dad was getting ill. Perhaps your brother had already spotted the signs, but he wasn't letting on; certainly not to the likes of me.'

'Didn't you get on with Bertin?'

'We didn't *not* get on as such. I was trying to become his pal, partly because that was what I was being paid to do, but partly also because I did actually like the guy, and was concerned about what I was beginning to understand young Mr Laforge was trying to do to your family.'

'Was there a bit of self-preservation in there too?'

'You may be right, although that wasn't consciously on top of my mind. Trouble was, I am considerably younger than he was, and he treated me rather like you would treat your little brother's chum; someone to be tolerated rather than interacted with. But if Bertin had worked out what was going on and had shouted "foul!" I guess it would have been handy for me to be able to count him as a friend. Truchaud's was going to be his one day, and until you showed up, I thought it was all going to be his. I don't know what you had agreed between you.'

'We hadn't agreed anything,' said Truchaud sadly. 'I suspect that would have come up first at Dad's funeral.'

'Well, hired help certainly wasn't a role he would have relished. He was a good winemaker in his own right. His version of your family Vosne told us all about that this winter.'

'You tasted it yourself then?'

211

'Of course. How else would I have known where it fitted in with my blending plans? Very good it was too.'

'I'm so relieved to hear that, and his widow will be too.'

'Didn't any of you get to taste it?'

'No. Dad told Bertin and Michelle it was disgusting muck and was an insult to the name Vosne-Romanée, and gave the whole batch, lock, stock and barrel to young Mr Laforge. He logged it as failed declassified stock.'

'Oh dear, he really was losing the plot, wasn't he? That actually sounds more like a rant of jealousy rather than anything else. Maybe he was trying to justify to Bertin why he was putting all your Vosne into young Mr Laforge's Project Richebourg.'

'That occurred to me too. Tell me … was the wine that good?'

'We tasted the wine as soon as it got into our cellars and it was truly excellent stuff, and just the ingredient I needed to exercise my skills as a blender to add to the spare Echézeaux, to make Laforge's Special Cru in reasonable quantities. Young Mr Laforge told me he didn't mind too much if I didn't have such a good year with the Echézeaux, as long as the new stuff was top-notch, and that it needed to be wine to lay down in the cellar and forget about till a later date. So the Echézeaux was a blend of itself and some okay stuff east of the Seventy-Four. The new super-wine was a blend of the best of the east of the Seventy-Four — your Vosne — and the rest of the Echézeaux.'

'The one thing it didn't have in it was any Richebourg.'

He agreed. 'The one thing it didn't have in it was any Richebourg.'

'What did you tell the INAO had happened to the Village Vosne?'

'I didn't tell them anything, but I gather young Mr Laforge told them that it had failed as Vosne, just like your dad had said, and had been downgraded and tipped into the vat marked "Ordinaire".'

'The thing that amazes me is how good that Richebourg tasted, considering its provenance and its extreme youth.'

Maréchale smiled. 'That is the skill of the blender, sir.' He flicked his forelock. 'Any Burgundy worth the name tastes good and fruity when it's really young. The wine to keep then goes into its shell for a while to reorganize the tannins. It's when the wines wake up again that people then talk about the greatness of red Burgundy. However, it's at that first tasting after about a year in the bottle, that the critics get their initial ideas about a vintage. The winemakers themselves, of course, know already.'

'You're that good?'

Maréchale grinned self-deprecatingly, 'I'm that good. Mind you, have you ever tasted a real Richebourg to compare?'

'No,' said Truchaud. 'I must admit I haven't. Have you?'

Maréchale tapped the side of his nose and continued. 'It was not my idea to call the wine "Richebourg". I had planned on calling it something like "The Great Red Wonder", putting *"Appellation controlée Bourgogne"* on the label, and getting in a good graphic designer. Then it would all have been pukka and above board. Young Mr Laforge had to get greedy.'

'There is a chap that young Mr Laforge introduced me to once. He called him the *regional dealer,* a sort of agent, called Massener, who comes by from time to time. From what I gather, he's got well-trained taste buds. He was most impressed by this new wine, which is why young Mr Laforge lost it for a moment and introduced me to him. I gather this Mr Massener puts international buyers in touch with local merchants like Laforge. I think they knew each other quite well.'

'Massener? Sounds like an Alsatian name, perhaps even German.'

'Possibly. I only met him once, but I'm kind of surprised he hasn't been round snooping about since young Mr Laforge's death.'

Truchaud took out his notebook and noted the name. 'Do you have a forename?'

'Presumably he's got one, but I don't know what it is, and there appears to be nothing on paper in the domaine office. That struck me as odd too. Presumably the firm he works for isn't called "Massener". I hadn't got round to working out what the name actually is.'

'So, Laforge's deals with all sorts of firms then?'

'A fair number, yes.'

'And then?'

'Well, once I found the bottles in the cellar — about a fortnight ago — I must admit my sense of humour took a battering when I saw the Richebourg labels for the first time. I still have no idea where he got them made, as they couldn't have been local. The people from the *Big Domaine* would have been round, loaded for bear as soon as they heard about it … and they would have.'

'The Big Domaine?'

'The Domaine de la Romanée-Conti, also known in the trade as 'the DRC'. They make the most prestigious wines in the area, and if you get one of their bottles for less than a thousand euros apiece, it's a good bet that it's either a fake or an Echézeaux. Even winemakers who aren't DRC sell their Richebourgs at several hundred euros a bottle. Anyway, I went and had it out with young Mr Laforge. We drove around a bit in his car so no one would overhear. I tried to explain that there was no way that every single one of those bottles would be drunk by someone who didn't understand the Burgundy wine laws.

'He tried to say that by the time they were opened, and where they were opened, the trail would have gone cold, and people would be more interested in what this strange bottle actually tasted like than where it had come from, considering how much they had actually paid for it. People are very sensitive about being made to look like fools. He reassured me that, thanks to me, however dubious the wine looked on paper, the drinker wouldn't be disappointed. However, he did go on to say, that if I really didn't like it he would give me a reference and I could go somewhere else, outside Burgundy. I was still thinking about that suggestion when he was killed. At that point I knew I was right, and got very scared.'

'So who did you think was responsible for killing him?'

'I have no idea. I doubt it would be any of the local people who make Richebourg, and I'm sure the DRC people wouldn't have actually committed murder, although they might have stood over him while he systematically broke every single bottle in front of them, and then told him to get out of town, fast. But it's not as if young Mr Laforge would have been stupid enough to try to sell any of it round here.

'Giving it that name ruled out the local market, and by local, I mean European. So it needed to be a distant foreign market. It would probably have travelled about incognito for a while in various dealers' portfolios, and would have resurfaced again a couple of years later, for sale in markets outside Europe. In the States, India, China ... Tokyo maybe.'

'So let me see if I've got it straight? He makes, with our help, a pretty good bottle of wine, and a good deal of it. It was probably better than the wine whose most prestigious label it has a right to; "le Bourgogne".'

'It was certainly that. There are other wines that the makers have declassified to basic Bourgogne because, for one reason or another, they deem it not right for top labelling. I know of a top-rank winemaker who does that very thing. He downgrades his wine until he thinks it is as good as it can be. His white Grand Cru Musigny is currently just a Bourgogne Blanc, but all the wine marked as his Bourgogne Blanc is, in fact, declassified white Musigny, and its price tag will tell you that. It boosts the value of your top wines if people know that you do that sort of thing. The problem is that your name does need to be well-known.'

'Okay so carrying on. He has this very large quantity of very nice tasting but unfortunately not very prestigious wine in his cellars, and he's now trying to increase the value of the wine so he can get more money for it.'

'Got it in one.'

'But if he's going to commit the fraud anyway, why didn't he go the whole hog and stick a prestigious label on it?'

'I don't know. Obviously he wouldn't use somebody who doesn't make any Richebourg, but if you're going to sell a fake to the Yanks or the Asians, then bung a DRC label on it and to hell with it, I agree with you. If you want to look it up on the Internet you can, it'll be all there: DRC and Richebourg in the same entry. Now, you can put Chateau la Nuitoise into Google, and you'll find nothing. I don't get it either.'

'However, I can't see any of these people physically killing Mr Laforge for his role in all this, although I could see them all ganging up and killing his business perhaps. But not murder, no! I think, however, you getting involved right now may be seen by some observers as a reaction in the nick of time, to save your own family business.'

'So where do I go from here then?'

'Well, the first thing *you* have to do is to find the wine itself and bring it back.'

'And if the money has already changed hands, to try to send that back in the right direction.' Truchaud sounded doubtful. 'Actually I think the first thing I have to do is to do a formal audit on my own family's bank balance, to try to work out how long we've been involved in this fraud. Michelle told me that she had no access to the grape business accounts, only the wine business. That was the Clos, Vosne and Nuits we harvested, vinified and bottled ourselves. The grape business is the stuff from the east side of the Seventy-Four, which wasn't supposed to have even started fermenting by the time it left our ownership. I understood that the point of all this was supposed to have been Dad selling grapes to you to bring up the quality of your Bourgogne and your Ordinaire. It's times like this that I wish I wasn't a policeman.'

'Huh?'

'It is strongly frowned upon to swear unless you are using it to increase the tension in an interrogation.'

'Is this a formal police interrogation?'

'We've already agreed that it's not. What I am is full of information that I'm not sure what I'm going to do with. One thing I really need to know is how much my brother was involved in all this.'

'As far as I know your brother didn't know very much. As I said, he didn't talk to me much, apart from farmer stuff, like the weather, spray supplies and mildew. We never talked about the wine business. During the summer months we winemakers are all great mates: we talk about vines and how to get the best out of them; we drop each other hints on how to keep the pests at bay; we work in teams to keep the wild boars out of the vineyards; and take a share in the armed nightshifts to keep the rampant porkers away from the grapes that are just about to be picked. It's in all our best interests to maximize the general quality of the crop. Come the harvest, we all retreat into our shells again, and only speak to those we have business links with. Usually, the first time we talk to unlinked winemakers about a particular vintage is during an international dealer's tasting somewhere like London, a year later. If you were to ask for my personal opinion, I don't think your brother was very much involved.'

'I'm glad to hear that. It does explain why Michelle didn't seem to know anything about what you've been telling me. The next thing I have to do, however, is investigate my family's finances in depth.'

'What would you do as a policeman if you found the depth of your family's involvement was intentional in a case like this?'

'I would have to declare a conflict of interest and recuse myself from the case. I have to say that I would rather do that as late as possible. I am sure I would be better placed to protect Bruno's interests while I'm still in the game than when I'm outside on the substitutes' bench, looking in.'

'So what are you going to do about me?'

'At this moment, absolutely nothing. This conversation hasn't taken place until I say it has, and that won't be a while yet. I would recommend you stay here. When I come back, I'll call you before I arrive, on your mobile phone. When Suzette or Hairy Eddie come in, they've got keys. If anyone else comes, I would hide. If Captain Duquesne wants to see you, I'll bring him with me. Nobody else knows you're here as far as I know. I know you're innocent of murder, and that's my bottom line. The local fraud squad doesn't even know it's in business yet, and if I have to involve them at all, I would like to be able to present them with a completed case, done and dusted.'

'What do you see happening to me in the end?'

'Well, you're not guilty of murder, are you?'

Maréchale looked at the detective and shook him by the hand. 'Thank you,' he said.

'I will see you again within twenty-four hours from now,' he said, looking at his watch. 'If I'm not back by then, disappear. But I would be grateful if you took Suzette and Hairy Eddie with you, when you go.'

'Rest assured … they'll be okay.'

Truchaud grinned, and with a 'See you,' he left the flat.

Chapter 27

Nuits-Saint-Georges, Wednesday morning, later

Michelle looked a little pensive as he came in.

'What's the matter?' Truchaud asked.

'I've been summoned to the doctor's this afternoon,' she said. 'I'm running out of insulin, and his receptionist doesn't sound best pleased. She doesn't think I should be running low for at least another week or so.'

'Do you want me to come with you? If the doctor's going to get difficult, I can lean on him. He can't say no to more insulin, surely? That would be tantamount to attempted murder.'

'Would you? I'd appreciate that.'

They broke bread and put fresh pâté on it, while he tried to broach the subject of money with her. He knew she and his brother had a shared bank account, which slightly askance, she showed him. There was nothing to cause concern on the statements. Certainly there were no big swings in incomings and outgoings. 'What's this all about?' she asked.

'Laforge's seems to have been quite deeply involved in a fraud of international proportions. I am trying to reassure myself that it didn't rub off on us too,' he said.

'You mean that's why poor Mr Laforge was murdered?'

'Could well be part of the story, yes.'

'Are we in any danger?'

'That's what I'm trying to find out, and if so, whether you and Bruno would be better off staying with your parents for the next few days.'

'I couldn't leave Dad, not in his condition.' He noted that she called his father 'Dad', a dutiful daughter-in-law.

'He wouldn't go with you?'

'He gets very confused if you take him out of his local space. For example, if you were to leave him at the top end of Beaune or the bottom end of Dijon, even on the correct side of the Seventy-Four, he'd never get back, and it's a straight road. He'd be hopeless at my parents and probably wouldn't even recognize them. It really wouldn't be kind.'

Truchaud thought about that for a moment. What might end up happening to his father might not be kind either, he thought drily.

Michelle produced the domaine books, which all looked above board as far as he could see. There were notes on the number of barrels of each wine, and the Vosne crossed out, with 'failed' and 'declassified' in Dad's handwriting. 'No values on the barrels?' he asked.

'Not yet. That depends on how the vintage sells overall, I suppose,' she replied.

'Does that depend on those all-important auctions in Beaune next November?' Truchaud asked.

'Not really. The auctions for last year happened last November, and that was really only about the wine donated to the almshouses by the great and the good of Burgundy. It doesn't really have a lot to do with our wine, nor does the Nuits-Saint-Georges' charity auction, which happened the other day. I suppose the auctions are the first time that a particular vintage shows its face in public, and the rich and generous want the wine they donated to the auctions to be top-quality stuff. I would imagine that, in a normal year, young Mr Laforge might have donated a barrel of our wine from the east side of the Seventy-Four, but I don't think he went this year. I suppose if the price rocketed ludicrously, we might have a rethink. But the price we charge for our bottles is our decision; one we haven't yet made for last year's wine for one reason or another.'

So it appeared that these accounts were up to date as they usually were at this time of year, and there was no evidence that Dad's failing intellect was the reason for their falling behind. He asked Michelle how the accounts were presented each year.

'Dad takes both sets of accounts to the accountant — that's the wine accounts and the grape accounts — and the accountant signs them off each year.'

'So, where are the grape accounts?'

'Dad will have them.'

'Will he let you have them?'

'Well, he showed them to Bertin about three weeks ago ... Oh!' she stopped.

'What?'

'That was the first time Bertin didn't come to bed that night. He spent the whole night roaming around very upset, mumbling to himself.'

'Did he tell you what had upset him so much the following morning?'

'No. He seemed okay the next day so I didn't push it. When Bertin gets upset, he either gets over it, or he tells me about it when he's good and ready. It never does to push it, so I didn't.'

'Do we know where Dad is at the moment?'

'You obviously don't, but I think he's in his room sulking. There's nothing for him to do, the weather's pretty grey, and so nothing's growing today. He was cleaning out fermentation tanks a bit this morning, but they don't need doing now, and will all need doing again in full before the harvest.'

'Poor soul. He's bored. I've got something that will interest him, I think.'

He went out into the yard and up to his father's flat. It was untidy, and could use a good clean in its own right. Dad was sitting in his chair staring into space. 'Dad?' Truchaud asked.

The old man looked around, registered who it was, said, 'Oh, it's you,' then turned back again and resumed staring into space.

'Dad, I've got something I need to talk to you about.'

'Oh? What?'

'I need to look at the books for the grape sales side of the business.'

'Why do you want to do that?'

'Because I think there are errors in there, which if we don't correct them now could get us all into a great deal of trouble.'

Truchaud thought that was the most tactful way of broaching the subject.

'Like what exactly?'

'Would you like me to be straight and to the point?'

'Please do.' The old man was still looking in front of him, making no attempt to look his son in the eye.

'I think you have been contributing our wines to a fraud of international proportions. Furthermore, this fraud appears to have played a part in the murder of young Mr Laforge. What I need to know is whether you have put the lives of Michelle and young Bruno at risk as well.'

'You don't mince your words do you, boy?'

'Now is not the time to be playing nice. I have to discuss this with the law by the end of today, and I'm trying to work out how to do so with the least possible collateral damage to our family. Now look at me and talk to me.'

The old man turned around slowly and with intense sadness asked Truchaud what he actually wanted to know. 'Where are the accounts for the grape business? I've already seen the wine accounts, which seem genuine enough, even if the wine you sold wasn't.'

The old man's face screwed up in anger. 'What exactly do you mean by that?' he asked.

'You know only too well that our wines have been used in blends that Laforge's was putting out there fraudulently. Laforge's made up the quantities we sold so that our figures looked correct. When did this all start? I would really like to know whether the wine I've been so proud of for so long was really anything to do with us at all.'

'You can say some hurtful things, you know.' Truchaud wasn't in the mood to listen to his father attempting to pull on his sympathies. It wasn't going to work.

'When did you tell Bertin what you had been getting up to?'

His father looked at him, and had obviously realized where the conversation was going before Truchaud did. 'It was about three weeks ago, wasn't it? You were probably boasting to him about how clever you thought you had been, weren't you. It hadn't occurred to you that you were losing the plot. You've got Alzheimer's, Dad. You shouldn't have been making decisions about the family business, especially such bad ones.'

'But I've made a lot of money, son. I've got enough to buy another plot of land.'

Truchaud let his head fall into his hands. 'Oh dear god!' he sighed. 'From whom?'

'Mr Laforge. I haven't decided yet, but when the time comes it'll be a good one you'll see. Bertin will be really pleased. He'll really enjoy working that land. It'll be really easy for him to work you see. It'll be a Grand Cru plot, and grapes grow naturally on that. You'll see.'

'Dad!' he said despairingly, 'they're both dead. It's not going to happen. Where is the money?'

'Well, Mr Laforge's got it, of course. That way, when the right plot of land comes on the market, he can just buy it before anyone else can get a look in.'

Truchaud didn't know whether to laugh or cry. Laforge had been defrauding his family too. If somebody hadn't already done the job for him, he would have blown a hole in Laforge's head himself. He had no idea whether his father would have been interested in this scam himself when he was fully *compos mentis.* He didn't think he would have been so stupid, but he was certainly involved in it now.

'I shall have to think about this, Dad. I will also have to discuss it with Captain Duquesne. I have to tell you, you're in a deep hole, right up to the eyeballs.' Truchaud got up from his chair, turned on his heel and left the flat. As he was crossing the courtyard, just passing the sleeping tractor and his equally drowsy car, the phone woke up in his pocket.

'Yes?' he asked.

'Natalie Dutoit here. Is it convenient your end?' she asked.

'Absolutely fine,' he said, 'but please forgive me if I sound a little abrupt. It appears that there are temporary residents in Purgatory who have been trying to wind me up, and I have to say that they're doing quite a good job of it. How are you?'

'Fine, fine.'

'Tell me, what was Commander Lucas doing in our crew room?'

'Ah, well it wasn't quite like that. You see, when you called me on my mobile, I was in his crew room.'

'Oh yes?'

'Because I'm having to go to court on one of his cases.'

'Go on.'

'Do you remember the chap I questioned about the "Fox" just before we arrested him? Well, it appears that I also cracked Commander Lucas's case wide open at the same time. He has been trying very hard to recruit me to his squad ever since.'

'Tell him "no", not even if he can arrange your promotion to Chief Superintendent. You're still working for me.'

'Well, that's what I told him too, *chef*, but that did require me to tell him that I was actively working for you at this moment, and he did get fairly aggressive. You know, he can get really unpleasantly close to you when he's trying to make a point. You not only hear the words he's saying, but you can also feel them and smell them, especially when he's been eating something spicy. I am much less threatened, and my personal space is less invaded when I'm working with you, *chef*.'

'Don't worry. Your job in our squad is quite safe. Anyway, did you find out why your Karl-Heinz is looking through Laforge's affairs so diligently?'

'Oh yes, *chef*, that's very simple. It appears that his dissertation is not a dissertation he *was* doing, but is very much in the present tense. He reckoned that using the angle of investigating the activities of an individual unknown Frenchman within the Red Army Faction framework put an interesting twist on what he was writing. Does that help?'

'It does indeed, though in some ways it's rather disappointing,' replied Truchaud. 'What else have you both found?'

'We've found some odd banking anomalies in Domaine Laforge; not least that it seems to be sending an inordinate amount of money to a numbered bank account in Zürich. It takes a slightly convoluted route there, as we discussed yesterday. There doesn't appear to be a name on this account, just a serial number. The money didn't spend any time at all in Laforge's account in Beaune before bouncing on, so it might be quite interesting to find out where this came from and where it went.'

'What sort of figures are we talking about?'

'Several million euros already this year alone,' she said. 'I haven't managed to find any sums before then to the same scale, but it may just be that I haven't looked in the right place yet.'

Truchaud whistled. Several million? He wondered how much of that had come from advance sales of the wine Laforge had labelled as 'Richebourg', and how much therefore belonged to Domaine Truchaud Père et Fils. Was that the money Dad had been talking about a few minutes before? 'Concentrate on those sums, Constable, for the moment. I would be fascinated to know more about them, and I may need to go to Zürich in the not too distant future.'

'Yes, *chef*. You know something, sir. If you're looking for a volunteer to go to Switzerland, bear me in mind. A change of air would be most agreeable, if you know what I mean?'

'I'll bear your offer in mind,' Truchaud chuckled, 'I'll talk to you again soon.'

The phone went dead.

Chapter 28

Nuits-Saint-Georges, Wednesday, after lunch

Michelle and Truchaud headed out to the surgery. The receptionist didn't look particularly upset with Michelle when they walked in. Perhaps she was being professional; perhaps it was a different receptionist.

'Madame Truchaud for Dr Girand,' Michelle announced. They were pointed to the waiting room chairs. It wasn't long before the doctor himself put his head out and motioned her through into his consulting room. Truchaud followed his sister-in-law in. Dr Girand looked up at her questioningly.

'I seem to have been getting through my insulin too fast,' she said.

'You've certainly got through this lot a week quicker than you usually do,' he said. 'Have you needed to increase the dose at all?'

'Not that I'm aware of.'

'I mean, I can totally understand if the stress of the last week has been pushing you to comfort eat or something. Chocolate?'

'Er, no, thank you. I've just had lunch.'

'No, I wasn't offering you one. I was wondering whether you had been comfort-eating chocolate or something. A lot of people do.'

'No, no, not at all. I haven't noticed my blood sugar going up recently either. I have been measuring it, just like you showed me, and it seems to have been stable.'

Not understanding a lot of this, Truchaud asked, 'Measuring it?'

'Yes, I've got this little device, and I prick my finger with it. I put a stick in the machine and a drop of blood on the other end of the stick, and the machine tells me what my blood sugar is. I then work out how much insulin I have to give myself. It's really quite clever.'

'The intelligent diabetic has a better survival rate, which, in this respect at least, makes your sister-in-law a fortunate woman.' Dr Girand was being professionally polite. 'Well, we're going to have to keep a close eye on your insulin intake over the next few weeks, and I'm going to arrange a blood test just to see what your HbA1C is doing.'

Again Truchaud was defeated by the medical jargon. 'HbA1C?' he asked.

'A rolling average blood sugar, over a fortnight. It's the amount of sugar that's stuck onto the haemoglobin.' The doctor returned to Michelle. 'Meanwhile, you need some more insulin now,' he said tapping at his computer, which in the fullness of time generated a prescription from the printer. He signed it, and gave it to Michelle. He also gave her a form to take to the receptionist to book the blood test. 'If anything untoward comes from that, we'll be in touch.'

'Thank you, Doctor,' she said and they left his room. They had said nothing about his father at all, which was probably a good thing. She turned to her brother-in-law. 'I'm going to have to go to the chemist to pick this up. It may take a little while,' she said.

'And I'm going to see Duquesne,' he replied. 'That may take some time too.' With that they went their separate ways.

He walked across the Seventy-Four as it meandered through the little town of Nuits-Saint-Georges. He found the bell push at the front door. He walked through the door. 'You don't have to push the button, you're one of us now,' said Lenoir, now back on front desk duty.

'Ah yes,' he replied, 'but if I had wanted just to walk in, I would have had to go all the way round the block and come in through the back of the building, and as it's drizzling, I would have been fairly soaked by the time I got under cover.'

Truchaud had got in ahead of Duquesne, and as the Captain walked through into his own office, Truchaud said from behind Duquesne's desk, 'Coffee?'

'Why not?' he said. 'Creamy, like you like it.' They changed places. Having settled, Duquesne looked up at him. 'News?' he asked the detective.

'Lots,' he replied. 'You?'

'No change. Delacroix's comfortable enough … and getting bored. They're thinking of transferring him back to Paris in the next couple of days.'

'Well, I've got a lot to tell you, so we can wait until the coffee arrives.' It duly did, and then Truchaud started his narrative. 'Basically, I now know about what's been going on at Laforge's.'

'Yes, they've been making fake Richebourg,' replied Duquesne.

'A large component of which has been Truchaud-sourced Village Vosne.'

'I imagine you find that rather embarrassing.'

'So sooner or later I shall have to excuse myself from this case, and probably go back to Paris.'

'Not yet, you don't. I really do need you to stick around for the time being.'

'In which case we'd better get a move on. Have the kids been down the tunnel yet?'

'Not yet, but we've called in our tunnellers. They'll be going down tomorrow. Do you want to come?'

'Not tomorrow; it's my brother's funeral. Somehow I think Bruno's granddaughter would be most annoyed with me if I was somewhere else, like down a hole for instance.'

'Bruno's granddaughter? I thought he was only twelve.' Duquesne thought for a moment and then the proverbial light went on. 'Oh, I see; the future family history and stuff. Fair enough. Well, we'll see where we get to.'

Truchaud started by saying, 'You remember that constable in Paris that my Divisional Commander offered us a few days ago?'

'The one you said was way too pretty to go undercover in Nuits-Saint-Georges?'

'Well, she's been hitting the computers on our behalf in a fairly major way in Paris, and has been following the activities of Laforge from his young days as a student in the late sixties, until he finally got back to Nuits-Saint-Georges, twenty years later.'

'Even the most sluggish of people would have taken less than twenty years to travel the distance from Paris to Nuits-Saint-Georges, even if they were using random Brownian motion,' observed the gendarme drily.

'Yes, and in his case, he wasn't being particularly random,' remarked Truchaud, and went on to tell the story as Natalie Dutoit had told it to him, right down to the considerable sums of money that had been passing through young Mr Laforge's hands recently. He then went into fairly fine details about the discussions he had had with Maréchale and his father. He concluded with, 'The one thing we're no closer to is who killed Laforge.'

'But I think we now know the sort of organization he or she works for.'

'Do we?'

'Yes, one that needs, or at least wants lots of money. This case is about money, hence the very complicated banking arrangements.'

Truchaud thought for a moment. 'No, that's what Laforge was about. It's not necessarily the killer's angle. Laforge was trying to make money out of nothing. All I think we know about the actual killer is that he stopped him.'

'I see what you mean. You have to say that it did look like a contract execution; low-velocity round to the back of the head.'

Truchaud had been invaded momentarily by a thought that refused to go away while he was doing his spiel to Captain Duquesne. He tossed it out there just to see if it would fly. 'My brother's still in the path lab fridge till tomorrow morning. You don't think he died of low blood sugar, do you?'

'Go on?'

He told Duquesne the story of his sister-in-law's missing insulin, and wondered if it had, in fact ended up in his brother.

Duquesne picked up the phone and dialled a number. He spoke social inconsequentialities into the phone for a moment. Then he said, 'I've got Commander Truchaud sitting in here with me at the moment, and he's just had an interesting idea. Is there any way it can be checked out before the funeral tomorrow, that is, if you haven't done it already? It's about his blood sugar.' Duquesne pulled the phone away from his ear with a shocked expression on his face.

'Really? I didn't know forensic pathologists knew such language! I thought that was why you hide in the laboratory, rather than face the criminal population at large.'

Truchaud cocked an eye at the Captain. 'He asked why you waited till now to ask him this,' said Duquesne.

'I didn't know till lunchtime today that there was any insulin missing.'

Duquesne relayed that message back to the pathologist, and again withdrew the receiver from his ear, before putting it back and listening more intently. 'White cells, right. The eye. Okay, okay, I'll tell him. I think he'll be relieved to know that. Yes, thank you. Bye'

Truchaud looked at him. 'What was all that about?'

'Well, it's like this. When the body dies, not everything dies at the same rate. We all work to the policy that the official moment of death is brain death. That, however, is difficult to measure exactly, so it is measured at the moment the heart stops beating. From that moment, the brain dies very quickly owing to the lack of oxygen. Other bits, however, go on for days, weeks, even months after the official death of the body.'

'Yes, I've heard all about people exhuming corpses and a couple of months later their hair had grown and they had a full beard and stuff.'

'Yes, exactly that. Well, the body's white cells and the invading bacteria still carry on their battles after the death of the body. That's why the body decays. The most important nutrient the body has to feed this battlefield is the sugar in the blood, so it continues to reduce after death. They didn't find your brother for several hours after he had died, and so they assumed his blood sugar would have dropped significantly from the moment of death, so they didn't bother to test it. It's been a week since the body was delivered to them, so you can understand the technicolor language. There is one particular source of body fluid where they could take a sample that might still be instructive, though it will take a while to get the results back.'

'Oh yes? Where from?'

'The vitreous chamber at the back of the eye. That place will still be sterile and there won't be any bacteria or white cells in there. He suggests that they put a needle in and draw off some of the vitreous humour and send that off to the reference lab in London for them to do some tests on.'

'You mean we haven't got a lab here in France?'

'There is one in Paris, but he thought that you might find that one a little too close to home, bearing in mind it will have the name Truchaud all over it. The other one is in Geneva, but he thinks the one in London would be cheaper.'

'Tell him to get on with it, and let's get the funeral over and done with before people start slinging words such as "suicide" or "homicide" about the place, and go all Catholic on us.'

Duquesne picked up the receiver again. 'Truchaud says, let's get on with it,' he said. 'Personally, I think we need to know one way or the other, even if we don't actually do anything with it. Cheers. See you soon.'

'Well, that's settled,' said Duquesne grimly. 'Where do we go from here?'

'Well, I'm going round to the funeral directors just to make sure all is set for tomorrow, and then you'll probably find me at home.'

'What would you do if they haven't got it all set up for tomorrow?'

'You know, I haven't the faintest idea. Swear and scream would probably be the first things that come into my head, and then in all probability, I would start throwing all my teddies out of my pram, before I start conjuring up some nasty little spells.'

'We will collide tomorrow. If not before, I'll see you at your place at the wake.'

Truchaud nodded and wandered out. The trench coat was useful at least for keeping the drizzle off him, and as he walked home via the funeral parlour, he felt fairly miserable, even despite the reassurances that Saint Symphorien's church was ready for them tomorrow, and the crypt had been opened. On a sunny day he might have walked up to the graveyard just to see what they had done, but today was not a sunny day, and right now he simply wasn't in the mood.

When he got home, he phoned Maréchale to confirm he was safe. Maréchale confirmed that he was, as were Suze and Hairy Eddie. Truchaud then said he would be a bit out of contact tomorrow, as it was his brother's funeral, which he intended to attend. He gave him Duquesne's contact number in case he needed to contact a policeman in a hurry, but promised he would see them both by the following evening.

Maréchale wished him all the best for the funeral on the following day, and they both hung up.

Chapter 29

Nuits-Saint-Georges, Thursday morning

The inside of the little church was sombre. *It would always be sombre,* he thought, *even when there wasn't a funeral taking place within its walls.* It was a church after all. There was a small choir, which Truchaud was pleased to see the family had qualified for. They had obviously put enough into the coffers over the years. Maybe he was just being cynical.

The boy treble had a beautiful innocent voice and his solo rendering of the 'Pie Jesu' from Fauré's *Requiem* was almost heart-breaking. Apart from the boy, and the soft *obbligato* on the organ there was complete silence. Not a breath could be heard. Everybody's sore throat had been instantly cured by the sound. He looked down the pew at Bruno. A little tear trickled down his cheek. His mother was sitting next to him, dressed in black, looking softly sad. Beyond her sat Dad, betraying no emotion whatever.

Truchaud was impressed by how many people from Nuits-Saint-Georges had turned out to say 'goodbye' to his brother. There were people from the wine community, some of whom had a considerable reputation. There was Jean Parnault and his wife. There were also people he had just met, such as the baker down the road who had made the wonderful croissants, and Mrs Albrand, the lady that lived next door, who had piled in to help his family in its hour of need. A receptionist from the medical practice was on funeral duty, but the doctor himself wasn't there, he was probably doing a surgery. The survivors of the Laforge family were present further back in the nave, including Marie-Claire and old Mr Laforge. He assumed that the rather angular teenage boy was Marie-Claire's son who he had heard about, but as yet never seen.

He was pleased to see that there was no police presence, not even a Molleau in mufti. He turned back round to the front and listened to the boy singing.

He didn't really listen to the curate's address, and was still in his own space when the congregation filed out behind the pall-bearers and the coffin. He was uncertain who the pall-bearers were, but he knew he wasn't one of them. With military precision, they marched in slow time from the church to the graveyard.

There was a narrow manufactured chicane in the Rue Caumont Bréon from the town up into the Hautes-Côtes, where the path crossed out from the churchyard itself, across to the graveyard on the other side of the road. This chicane had been blocked while the sad little procession crossed to the graveyard beyond. The gravestone had been removed, and was lying beside the entrance to the crypt.

The curate said some more Latin by the graveside, and with 'In nomine Patris et Spiritus Sancti' his brother was lowered into the ground. Everyone walked slowly away. 'Was that what you wanted?' asked the lady with the sad kindly eyes from the funeral parlour.

'Exactly,' he replied. 'It was gentle, and hopefully he is now at peace.' This he actually somewhat doubted. Assuming the existence of an afterlife, he thought it was unlikely that his brother would be at any form of peace until this Laforge stuff had been sorted out once and for all. Not that he would say anything like that out loud, however. He wasn't sure who might be listening.

They walked back past the church and down into the west end of the town to the domaine. There was food on the dining table, and some of the '99 Vosne had been opened. It wasn't wine that Bertin had made himself, but it had been made by the family, and was certainly a wine he had enjoyed drinking when he was alive. Toasts were drunk to Bertin's memory, and the polite little canapés were eaten, or at least their edges were nibbled at.

Duquesne chose that moment to make his arrival. 'We've got

a result down in the tunnel,' he said. He pulled Truchaud out into the courtyard and produced another bottle of 'Richebourg'.

'Not now!' hissed Truchaud; 'We've got most of the great and the good of the local wine business in there. If anybody sees that they'll go thermonuclear!'

'Which is why I didn't put it on the kitchen table.' He whistled softly towards the gate, and Lenoir poked his head round the gatepost. 'Lenoir, take this bottle back and put it somewhere out of sight.'

The young gendarme, snapped to attention, clicked his heels and saluted. 'Sir!' he said.

'Okay, okay,' said Duquesne. 'Joke over.' The bottle was passed across and Lenoir hid it in his uniform and scuttled off. A moment or so later the familiar squeal of tyres that invariably accompanied Lenoir's driving could be heard, disappearing off into the distance.

'How many of those did you find?'

'Several thousand, I imagine,' replied Duquesne. 'We haven't actually counted them yet. We went down the tunnel just a little way, and just round the first bend there was another wharf. We went ashore there, where we found the cases, all stacked up just inside the archway. The bottles hadn't actually been moved more than fifty metres.'

'What was that cellar like?'

'Much the same as Laforge's. I have no idea whose it is, but it might be an extension of Laforge's. It only contained the fake Richebourg. If you go down the other end of it there's another locked door, and once again, none of our keys actually fitted the lock.'

'I tell you what we'll do. You slip a note under that locked door, and I'll go back to Laforge's cellar, and we'll see which door it comes out under.'

'And if it doesn't come out under either, we'll know that isn't the whole story.'

The two men looked at each other like a pair of schoolboy conspirators plotting together on a wizard jape. The solemnity of the day was already a thing of the past. Truchaud was more interested in what had taken his brother's life than in bidding him farewell from it. Being a detective, he supposed, had had this effect on him over the years, and perhaps, he felt, that was part of the reason for his inability to feel much in the way of any genuine emotion. Yes, being a detective could do that to a man, that and a Geneviève. Or a man like Molleau came rapidly to mind, as the same crept up from outside the domaine gate. Truchaud didn't think he had been invited, but there he was all the same. 'My old friend, it's so good to see you.' That had to be ironic thought Truchaud.

'Inspector Molleau, how kind of you to come,' Truchaud replied with a touch of acidity. 'Just inside the door you'll find the canapés. I'm told they're most diverting.'

'That sounded almost corked,' Molleau replied. 'Has today gone according to plan?'

Truchaud deflated, he really couldn't be bothered to argue with the man. Today was about so much more than that. 'Yes, I think so; so far anyway,' he replied. 'Pretty much everyone who's anyone has been by to pay their respects to my brother. I'm touched that so many people will miss him so much. I don't think everyone's here to see what the family was up to last year, and even if they are, they'll be disappointed, as the wine that's out there is well-aged.' Truchaud led both policemen back into the house, and cut the capsule off another couple of bottles. He drew both corks, and remarking that it was a shame that the wine really hadn't had enough time to breathe, poured a tasting into three clean dry glasses. He handed one to Molleau and another to Duquesne, who, glancing at Molleau, started to mutter about being in uniform and therefore he really shouldn't.

Truchaud hissed, 'Take it. Everyone's watching!' and laughed, 'Well I never!' he said loudly. Duquesne picked up on the hint and laughed too, and Molleau laughed with them too. Truchaud hoped that the message that they were trying to give out — that the policemen here present were just friends of the family in its time of distress, and Duquesne just happened to be wearing a uniform — had gone down as it had been intended. Molleau sniffed his glass and then looked at it, and having nodded at it, he then took a mouthful, sloshed it around his mouth and swallowed.

'Nice,' he said, and having picked up a sandwich, he wandered off munching happily. Duquesne and Truchaud exchanged glances as if to say, 'What was that all about?'

David Clark, a young winemaker from Morey-Saint-Denis, came over and joined them for a moment. 'It's good to see so many people turning out for Bertin,' he said in his soft Scottish burr. 'If anyone had any doubts, the turnout has certainly proved he was one of us.'

'Thank you, David, I appreciate that.'

'We understand he had made a great wine last year.' David had obviously heard something interesting.

Truchaud didn't miss a beat. 'Yes, he was trying out an experimental blended wine as a brand for the foreign market place. It's too early as yet to see how it has worked out, but the concept was quite promising. You know, the same sort of thing as Alain in Gevrey's *My Favourite Old Vines,* which doesn't tell you anything much about the contents of the bottle, but everybody knows it's a nice blended Village Gevrey.'

'But you don't make a Gevrey,' replied the young winemaker.

'No, we don't, but that was the concept. It won't be released or anything this year, but one day we hope you'll be enjoying a bottle called 'Bertin's Next Big Idea from the Côte de Nuits' or something like that, perhaps in a year or so.'

'I hope it all works out for you. See you soon,' he said, and walked off back into the party.

'Elegant,' muttered Duquesne.

'What? David, or my argument?' replied Truchaud.

'Both. Was that all complete BS, or was there a vein of truth in all that?'

'I think everybody does a few experiments at harvest time to see if there are any special ideas that may have a place in the future market. Maybe there's a place there for a re-relabelled Wine-that's-not-a-Richebourg.'

'Uncle Shammang, thank you. I think that was nice for Dad.' Bruno had caught up with them and was trying to smile,

239

hoping that his uncle felt like doing so a bit too. 'You're not going straight back to Paris straight away, are you?'

Duquesne smiled at the lad. 'No, Bruno, your uncle has agreed to stay on and do a little work with me. You have to understand that your uncle is still on holiday, and his boss in Paris asked me very politely to keep him on holiday for as long as I can. How better can I keep your uncle on holiday than to give him some work to do?'

'Oh, thank you, Captain Duquesne. Uncle Shammang, can we walk the vineyards this evening then?'

'There are one or two people I have to see this evening, but tomorrow, you, your granddad and I will all go and walk the domaine. How does that sound?'

'Cool. And after that we'll find Suzette Girand and play some Tarot. The guys will be so-o-o jealous.' And with that he wandered off to find one of the boys of a similar age.

'I think my nephew is developing his first adolescent crush,' Truchaud remarked drily.

'I can think of a number of less agreeable girls for him to cut his teeth on,' replied Duquesne. 'But maybe it would be safer for him to find someone a little younger, and a little further from the danger zone.'

'Quite,' replied Truchaud. 'But he did remind me that I had to go and see them. Two questions: firstly, do you want to come too; and secondly, can I soak a label off one of our special bottles, and take it to them? I really would like Maréchale to confirm that this really is the bottle he thinks it is.'

'Why take the label off it then?'

'In case I get into an accident on the way over there. I would hate a traffic policeman to think that an officer from the Paris serious crimes division could actually afford a bottle of Richebourg, or that I might be involved in trafficking fake wine across a parish border. The other thing I would like to do is make sure Maréchale doesn't get any hints of what it is from the label.'

They climbed into his BX and went back to the gendarmerie. In the end they soaked three labels off three bottles, and then stuck a plain label on to each bottle, on which they wrote the numbers 'one', 'two' and 'three'. Truchaud phoned Maréchale, and told him he was coming over. He told him to warn Suzette that he was bringing Capitaine Duquesne with him, and that they'd have a little surprise with them as well.

Chapter 30

Dijon, Thursday evening, then Nuits-Saint-Georges

The detectives rang the doorbell, and as usual, Hairy Eddie answered it. He obviously hadn't been warned that Duquesne was coming over too, or perhaps nobody had communicated that he would be in uniform. He wore a look of abject terror for a few moments.

'I'll tell them you're here,' he said. This time he scuttled off into the kitchen, and there was no shouting about getting dressed this time. Suzette put her brown bob round the kitchen door, and said, 'We're in here.'

They followed her in. 'This is Captain Duquesne,' said Truchaud. 'Please believe me, he's one of the good guys,' he reassured both Suzette and Hairy Eddie.

'And this is my mother,' she said, pointing her mother out. Truchaud couldn't quite believe he'd not noticed her, or perhaps his consciousness had refused to accept she was there. He nodded at her.

'Good evening,' he said. 'We've just been talking to Jean. He was at my brother's funeral.'

Duquesne rather assertively reclaimed the conversation, by putting the bag of bottles loudly on the kitchen table. 'Now,' he said, 'we're all going to do a little wine-tasting. Anybody got a corkscrew and some glasses?' the gendarme added, sensing that there was enough subtext going on around the table in which he wanted no involvement, and which anyway was none of his business.

Maréchale took over the bottle-opening duty. He looked at the bottles, and their totally uninformative labels. 'I assume number one is the first bottle you want opened,' he said.

'That's a good start,' replied Duquesne. There were no

243

capsules on the top of any of the bottles, so the corkscrew was just inserted and pulled. Maréchale poured a little wine into each of the six glasses he had found and put on the table. They weren't matching glasses, but what would you expect from a house full of students?

'Do you recognize the wine?' Truchaud asked him, looking Maréchale directly in the eye.

Suzette and Maréchale looked at the detectives. 'It certainly could be,' he said. 'Nice round nose, almost flowery, lots of wild cherries in there, blackcurrants too. Can I detect just a touch of liquorice in there in the background? It's absurdly young, of course. This stuff shouldn't have been let out of the wine-maker's cellar yet.'

'Summery,' said Suzette. 'It reminds me of a hot summer's day with birds singing in the background. Perhaps there's a slight breeze in there too.' She giggled, gently mocking the pretentiousness of the men, but then continued. 'I really like this. What do you think, Mum?' *She is really trying hard to work her mother into the conversation,* thought Truchaud, *and I'm trying to keep her out.*

'Madame Girand, may I ask you if you have known the whereabouts of this Monsieur Maréchale all along?' That was Duquesne asking the awkward hanging question.

She answered it honestly in reply. 'Yes, if I'm correct in thinking that by "all along" you mean since Suzette and this Monsieur Truchaud found the body of Mr Laforge.'

'Exactly that,' he replied.

'Yes,' she replied without going any further.

Truchaud chipped in, 'If it had transpired that Mr Maréchale was the one who had killed Mr Laforge, would you have turned him in?'

'I know he isn't the killer, so that question doesn't arise,' she replied evenly. 'And I thought that it was important for us all that you worked that out for yourselves.'

'May I know exactly how you are so sure of his innocence?'

'My daughter said so, and I believe her.'

'May I ask you to justify that?' Duquesne asked.

244

'Simple,' she replied. 'Simon was with us all that day, and then she went and opened up the shop. She was in the shop, or watching it until Charlie here joined her there, and they found Mr Laforge's body together. I have known my daughter all her life and I know exactly when she is lying, on the rare occasions she does so.'

Neither policeman wanted to take that line of questioning any further, but probably for different reasons. Truchaud took them back to the wine. He opened the bottle marked with a '2'. 'What do you think of this?'

Maréchale took a sniff at it. 'Corked,' he replied. Truchaud took a sniff at his glass. He was certainly right there. An unpleasant corky aroma came up from his glass, dominating everything else. Truchaud pulled the cork on number '3'. He took all the glasses with the corked wine to the sink and tipped the unfortunate wine down the drain, and rinsed them all out under the tap. The tea cloth was dry and moderately clean, so he wiped them down with that. He then poured a mouthful of number '3' into each glass. Maréchale sniffed it, put it down, and then found another glass, and put a little from the first bottle into it and sniffed at that one. Truchaud didn't need his answer; he knew what it was going to be anyway. 'They're the same wine, aren't they?' he asked.

'So you recognized the two bottles as being of the same provenance. Now do you recognize them as being from the blend that you put together?' continued Truchaud.

'If you asked me if it is likely, I would say yes. If you were to ask me if I was a 100 per cent certain, I wouldn't stake my life on it. I'm not as sure about that, as I am, for example, to state that these two bottles came from the same barrel as each other. That I can say, as I tasted the two bottles together. I think they're the same wine that I tasted three weeks ago, but I'm relying on memory here, and a great deal of unpleasant stuff has happened during these last three weeks, so I wouldn't like to trust my memory as much as I might. Incidentally, the cork taint in the second bottle came after bottling, so it too may be from the same piece.'

'Well,' said Duquesne, 'I can certainly reassure you that all three bottles came from the same case anyway.'

'That answers that then,' said Maréchale. 'I would not be ashamed if you were to tell me that I made these bottles. It's a nice agreeable glass of Burgundy, fresh on the tongue and fills the mouth very well. I would certainly rate it as a Village Cru, probably from Vosne, and I've tasted Premier Crus and even Grand Crus from the area around Nuits, which I wouldn't have enjoyed as much as this. What are you going to do with it?'

'I think we're going to make them wards of court for a while,' remarked Duquesne drily.

'Can we finish these off?' asked Suzette with a smile, tossing a glance at Truchaud. 'It would be a shame to let them go to waste now they've been exposed to the air.'

'I see no reason why not,' replied Truchaud. 'I agree, it would be a complete waste if we didn't give them a good send-off. What do you think, boss? You're in charge?' he asked Duquesne, who shrugged.

'As long as I don't have to drink the corked bottle,' he replied, and grinned back at the present company. 'That is the point of a glass of wine as good as this; to make such convivial company smile.'

'Cool,' said Hairy Eddie, and poured himself some more. 'I might even drink the corked one too if no one else wants it. Free booze is still free booze.'

Maréchale thought about the bottles, and continued. 'If these were a real Grand Cru Richebourg from Vosne, I might be somewhat less impressed,' he said after a while. 'This is good, but it isn't that good.'

'You can tell that and I can tell that, and Mr Truchaud can tell that,' said Geneviève. 'But do you think that an average wine drinker in Shanghai or Hollywood could tell you that? As you say, this is a rather nice, distinctive tasting bottle of Burgundy wine, and most people would like it and respect it.'

'What would you pay for it?' Truchaud came back at her.

'Difficult to say. Remember, I come from a family that makes a Grand Cru wine or two, like you do. We have far more experience of what a particular wine *should* taste like and its value than the average man in the street. If you look carefully at the wine listings, the cost of a bottle of wine seems to be far more linked to the fame of the label, than what the tasting critics think when they have tasted a bottle in a blind tasting.'

'And it is the man in the street, with money in his pocket, who is the designated victim of this con,' remarked Maréchale.

'So,' said Truchaud, 'what's the next step?'

'Well,' replied Duquesne, 'all we have removed from the hidden cellar was the case we've got at the gendarmerie: half the contents of which we've got here. We've left most of the wine in the cellar, so I think the next step is to follow the wine and see where it leads us.'

'I agree,' said Truchaud. He turned to look at Maréchale. 'Will you be safe here?'

'Sure, provided the wrong somebody doesn't know where we are.'

'And will you look after the ladies and Hairy Eddie?'

'I don't need looking after,' said Geneviève. 'I'm coming with you.'

'Oh no, you're not!' spluttered Truchaud. 'This is police business and dangerous. You are a civilian, and it doesn't even involve your family. You can stay here or go home, I don't mind which, but accompanying us is not an option.' *What was she thinking?* the detective wondered to himself. Come to think of it, why was she there?

He could understand the other three, but why Geneviève? He wasn't going to ask anyone, he would rather not know. If she were on the other side, then surely she would have sold out Maréchale before Truchaud had found him. So she wasn't and presumably Jean Parnault wasn't, so why did she want to get more involved than she is already.

'Simon, please be in charge of the ladies, and Eddie, just as far as safety is concerned, count yourself as a lady. If you have to get out of here in a hurry, give me a call or a text, and go. We'll find each other again. Geneviève, do you have a car here?'

'Yes.'

247

'I think it would be wise to have a car available to make a quick escape, and it may as well be yours, as it's newer. So if you wouldn't mind moving it to near the bottom of the fire escape outside the courtyard for easy egress, that would be the best for all. If you don't mind returning home in a police car, Captain Duquesne will drop you off at home now.'

'And how will I get back here without a car?' she asked.

'Hopefully, either Captain Duquesne here or I will be back in touch tomorrow, and whichever one of us is coming will bring you back.' He turned to Maréchale. 'If we don't contact you by this time tomorrow, at the very least by telephone, get out.'

Chapter 31

Nuits-Saint-Georges, later Thursday evening

Duquesne and Truchaud discussed the pros and cons of leaving Truchaud's BX parked in the street near Laforge's shop, and generally felt the tatty old car was the lesser of the two evils. Duquesne still had a key to the place, and they went in.

For the first time that Truchaud had been in there, there was no one else in the building except the two of them. They did not light anything upstairs, even though it was already early evening when they went in, and it was likely to be night when they came out again.

They went downstairs into the cellars, and switched on the lights down there, then went down into the smuggle cellars, and made their way to the wharf. The punt that Lenoir had used to explore that morning was still there, so they climbed aboard, and pushed off. When they reached the police chains, Duquesne unlocked them, and put the padlock in his pocket and they pushed on through. The bend in the tunnel was much sharper than it had appeared from the wharf, and they followed it round. No more than 100 metres further on they came to another wharf, still on their right. Duquesne got out his torch, and pointing it at the wharf, improved its details for the policeman to see. There was a very similar archway and behind it, and up a few steps, they could make out the unmistakable outline of wine cases. Truchaud got out of the punt and Duquesne lit his way to the boxes. He picked up a box to reassure himself that they were still full of bottles. They were. The temptation to hold up a box up to his ear, and give it a shake like a Christmas present was almost too much to resist, but resist it Truchaud did.

The boxes were sealed but they had the Richebourg label they had got to know so well, stuck on one end. Truchaud put the case back exactly how he had found it. He went back to the wharf and sat down on his haunches facing Duquesne, who was still in the punt. 'The question is how long are we going to have to sit here waiting for someone to come along? It could be months.'

'Bearing in mind that it claims to be Richebourg, we could be talking years,' replied Duquesne glumly.

Duquesne had spotted a rather different looking metal case at the back of the cellar. It was very heavy and had a completely different aroma, that of old oil, they thought. The two police-men looked at each other. 'Guns?' they said at the same time. Duquesne added, '*Maquis*? Or do you think it's more recent?' It appeared to be sealed and locked with a padlock. Neither of them was particularly happy about shooting the lock off, both feeling that if it was Second World War ordnance from the French Resistance time frame, that it might be distinctly unstable sixty years down the line. They looked at each other, shook their heads and said simultaneously: 'Expert explosives disposal unit required, I think.'

'I'm not sure we are going to let the sappers loose in here until we have sorted out what we are going to do with all this wine. A controlled explosion could well destroy the whole place, even if it doesn't destroy the ceiling and the street above it.' Truchaud was very concerned indeed about what they were sitting on.

'So, if we ignore it and it does spontaneously blow up and take out half of Nuits-Saint-Georges, won't we be responsible for the wholesale slaughter of innocent people?'

'Therefore we've got to make something happen,' replied Truchaud. 'I wonder where this little tunnel comes out. That's a question that really needs answering,' he said and climbed back into the punt. He settled back down to the paddles and Duquesne pointed his torch forwards into the darkness. The waterway was indeed quite meandering. Downstream they found another wharf and went ashore. It didn't contain any fake Richebourg, they were pleased to note, though they were concerned for the security of the winemakers whose wine they did find. They walked around the cellar, and Truchaud sniffed the delicious air. The scent of old oak and the distinctive aroma of the vine underneath was the sort of experience of which Truchaud had dreamed throughout his life in Paris. They resolved to have a quiet word in the owner's ears at the next opportunity. If Laforge's were willing to sell fake Richebourg from their cellars, he couldn't think of any reason why Laforge's or their co-conspirators should baulk at stealing perfectly legitimately made wine and selling that off in the same markets, if the bottles were just sitting there with a sign saying 'steal me'.

They headed back to the punt having decided to see where the tunnel went. The answer was, not very far. Just after the next bend they ran into a wall. This was a bricked-up wall that was not new. The water that lapped up and down revealed a green algae waterline.

'But the water is still flowing gently,' observed Duquesne, 'and it's definitely going that way,' he added pointing to the wall. He shone his police-issue halogen torch down through the water at the base of the wall. Down below the waterline there appeared to be a hole in the wall, or perhaps a pipe beneath it. The gendarme let out a strangled oath.

'I totally agree,' replied Truchaud. 'A quantity of counterfeit wine, a cache of weapons and now a waterway, which you need a submarine to navigate; the whole thing does appear a little out of a wartime thriller.'

'I'm not going to succumb to the temptation of even thinking that at this moment,' replied Duquesne. 'I think Mrs Duquesne will be waiting for me.' He pulled out his mobile phone, and presumably called the gendarmerie. 'Ah, Lenoir,' he said, 'I'm glad it's you. You wouldn't mind coming down and taking over from me, would you? My wife will have my supper on now, and I would prefer to eat it than wear it. Do you know if we have a scuba suit at the gendarmerie?' There was a pause, and then, 'Oh well, you'd better call Dijon then. We do have use for it, and if they want to know why, it is not a matter of life and death, so there is no immediate hurry. What we may need, however, is hands to move the cases back into the cellar they came from. Can you round up the cadets and equip them with waders? I've got a job for them to do.' Pause. 'Thanks, we'll see you upstairs shortly.'

The two men paddled back to Laforge's smuggle cellar and wandered back upstairs to the office. 'What I could really use is a cup of coffee,' muttered Duquesne as he sat down at the desk with the laptop on it.

'Did the occupying forces leave a jar of instant behind when they were camped here?' enquired Truchaud mischievously.

'Don't know. I'll ask Lenoir when he gets here, but actually when he gets here, I'll be wandering off and getting my supper. Would you like me to ask him for you anyway?'

'I shouldn't worry too much. I don't usually drink instant unless I'm absolutely desperate, and I'll be off shortly to take an evening meal myself.'

They sat and looked at each other. The plot was getting more complicated by the minute. The possibility of a weapons cache was a whole new twist and maybe a sign that the international gang was getting clumsy. The wine had been moved after Laforge's death, into a cellar already in use. The gang was very aware that Truchaud and Duquesne were on its tail.

'Evening, sirs,' came Lenoir's cheery voice from the shop, and he walked through the door. They had been warned of his arrival with a slightly different timbre of protesting tyres. 'That'll be the Espace,' Duquesne remarked. The big van was full of the terrified gendarme cadets that Lenoir had rounded up to shift the wine back into the old cellar.

'Evening, Captain,' they replied.

'Good evening, boys,' came Molleau's voice, as he climbed out of the passenger side. 'I hitched a ride to come and see what you were getting up to these days. Haven't seen you for ages.' Truchaud looked at Duquesne and the latter thought for a horrible moment that the policeman from Paris was going to roll his eyes.

'Where did he come from?' mumbled Duquesne softly.

'Good evening, Inspector,' replied Truchaud unenthusiastically. A conversation almost entirely between two pairs of eyebrows then took place, finally ending up with a frown on Molleau's face that very explicitly said, "Tell me!" with as many expletives as either policeman could imagine unspoken.

'We think we might have found what may be a locked cache of weapons in a cellar just round the corner from Laforge's,' Truchaud explained. 'We haven't any idea how old they are, or how stable they might be, but some clown has just moved a large quantity of wine, which we consider to be evidence in this case, into the same location from where we found it originally. It is our intention to move the wine back to the original site so that if this box of weapons does detonate, it won't blow the evidence up too, which would be a shame.'

'The last thing we would want to do would be to blow the wine up,' agreed Molleau smoothly. 'May I cast an eye over this weapons cache?'

'Of course. Constable Lenoir, can you take the Inspector round to the cellar round the corner? But before you go, there are one or two other things we need to discuss with you.'

'Sirs?' he replied.

'The waterway appears to have been walled up downstream some time ago. Your thoughts on what would be the best way through and where it might come out would be appreciated.'

'Right, sir, I'll nip round and have a look.' Lenoir looked Molleau up and down. 'You will have noticed that the Inspector's not dressed in waders or anything practical,' he remarked drily.

'Nor were we, but we've left the punt at the wharf in Laforge's,' he replied, watching with considerable interest the movement of Molleau's eyebrows. It would have been fascinating to be a spare brain cell in his skull, to try to work out what was going on in there. Molleau followed Lenoir down the stairs into the cellar. 'I wonder what he makes of it all,' he remarked to Duquesne as the gendarme was putting on his cap on the way out.

253

'I wonder too. I shall see you tomorrow,' remarked Duquesne, and, grinning, he left the building. Truchaud sat at the desk for a moment. Molleau was far too young to have been alive when the *Maquis* was active round here, he thought, but he wasn't wholly convinced by the expression of complete bewilderment. He was beginning to think that Molleau knew more than he was letting on.

Chapter 32

Nuits-Saint-Georges, Friday morning

Truchaud was back in the gendarmerie the following morning, full of ideas. Apparently it was rather too early for Duquesne to be actively thinking yet. 'What would you think of passing old Mr Laforge and his granddaughter over to Mr Lemaître? We've got enough evidence surely?'

'Well, rather than blundering around like a bull in a china shop, how about I go and have another chat with the grand-daughter first. I'm sure she has more to tell us.'

'Fair enough, would you like to take a chaperone with you?'

'Only if you can spare her,' he replied; the red-haired gendarme would have got used to his ways by now. Captain Duquesne readily agreed, and summoned the ever-present Montbard. The two of them set off in Truchaud's old BX again from the gendarmerie to the Laforge shop. One question that had remained in Truchaud's head since the beginning of the affair was had it been Montbard who had sat with Michelle on the night that Bertin had died?

'I'm not the only girl in the gendarmerie here, you know,' she replied, after telling him that it hadn't been her.

'You're the only one I've seen,' he replied.

'I shall quietly contemplate the implications of that, sir,' she replied carefully. There was, however, a ghost of a smile in her voice.

They drew up at the front door of Laforge's, which had a half-open air to it. There was a plain, rather sad-faced girl that Truchaud hadn't seen before behind the counter.

'Good afternoon, sir. What can I do for you?' she asked becoming aware rather slowly that the female companion of the man in the trench coat with rather bulky pockets was dressed in a blue uniform. 'Oh!' she said. Truchaud flicked open his wallet at her and flashed his warrant card.

'Commander Truchaud. Gendarme Montbard. Is Madame Laforge in the house?' he asked.

'Would you like me to go and see?'

'Whichever way you find the most agreeable to get us out of your shop at the greatest speed, with the least possible inconvenience to anyone. I imagine it's your job to sell all the wine that your firm wasn't able to sell all last week, owing to the … ah … unpleasantness and my colleague's colleagues' presence in here.'

The girl gave him a terrified expression as if he was dangerously insane, and deciding that she wasn't going to understand any other words he was going to say anyway, she said, 'Wait here,' and went through the back door of the shop into the office. She wasn't away for more than a minute, and then returned. 'Would you like to go on through?' she said, and held open the office door for them.

'Good luck,' Truchaud wished her over his shoulder as he went into the back of the building. Her eyes gave him a sad reply without words.

At the back of the office was a door which led into the house proper. In that door stood Marie-Claire Laforge. 'Come on through,' she said, and 'Tea?' when they did.

Truchaud introduced the Constable to Madame Laforge, and accepted the offer of tea. Whether Montbard would have liked a cup of something else instead wasn't explored. 'I hope you don't mind, but there are a couple of questions I would like to ask,' Truchaud started without further ado. 'It's about your father's accident.'

'Oh dear,' she said, 'How did you hear about that? That must be over twenty years ago,' she said.

'You would be impressed at our sources of information,' agreed Truchaud. 'I often am. Now, what I would like to know is what you remember about your father's accident. What sort of driver was he? Was he a good driver?'

'I always thought so,' she said. 'It was something he used to say regularly that he would always look through the car in front at the idiot in front of him. There was always someone out there who hadn't the faintest idea what they were doing, and one day he was going to pick a winner.'

'And he did.'

'I suppose so, yes.'

'What sort of person was he?'

'Like Granddad really; an old-school winemaker and dealer. Some of the grapes we grew, and made wine from our own vines; some of the grapes we bought and made wine from them; and some of the wine we bought ready-made from elsewhere as an investment, already bottled and then stored in our cellars, and sold from our shop when we thought they were ready. We also had links with other wine merchants further away from the *Côte,* both nationally and internationally. This was how it had been certainly since the Revolution, and each generation had increased the business. I think we were fortunate in the inheritance situation, as either our descendants were really good at wine, or chose to be somewhere else, and to do something else. The various wars that France got involved in in the twentieth century helped the inheritance problem too, and the Laforge family lost a number of potential heirs during those. The battlefields of the Somme were strewn with the bodies of Laforges who died trying to be heroic, before their time came to reproduce.'

'Was it heroic, Madame?' asked Montbard softly.

'Well, you know,' she replied shrugging a shoulder. 'You, being a woman, realize immediately the pointless waste the whole thing was anyway. Anyway, Granddad survived. He was a teenager during the Second World War. In fact, he was a teenager for rather longer than most people are supposed to be. As far as the Germans were concerned, he was still at school, and too young to be drafted into the STO.'

'The STO?' enquired Truchaud.

'The *Service du Travail Obligatoire.* It was a law enacted in 1943, where French males aged between sixteen and sixty could be rounded up and sent off to work in factories in Germany. Granddad has always been a small chap, and they acquired a forged birth certificate to say he had been born two years later, so he stayed at school, learning the trade of being a vintner, so that when peace finally came, he could serve the Third Reich with the wine that it felt it deserved. He was at least two years older than he claimed to be, but they never caught on. Our cellars were used by the Resistance and the 'not quite a boy' Granddad could often be found down there, if you knew where to look. As we all now know, the Third Reich actually lost, and the French are still their own masters.

Granddad grew up very rapidly, and got married as soon as the war was over, and had two sons. He had a daughter too, but she went off to become a nun. She's dead now, and I don't think I ever met her. My father, the elder son, went into the wine trade like his dad, and the younger son, Jérome, went to Paris.' She stopped for a moment with her narrative and took a mouthful of tea.

'Over the next thirty years, Dad grew up, became a winemaker like his father before him and got married, and I came along. Mother was never very well. I remember her as a rather diaphanous little thing. Whether she had any physical illness, they never told me, but she often cried a lot. Then Dad got killed on the motorway linking Dijon and the A6; the motorway to the sun. It was a strange bit of road being neither one thing nor the other even then. There was never a lot of traffic on it, and Dad was always such a good driver. I never could understand why his car had left the road in broad daylight on a nice bright sunny day in June, on the way to Auxerre. It wasn't as if he had a particularly fast or racy car either; he wasn't into speed.'

'I take it, Madame, that you are wondering if he was murdered?' suggested Truchaud, thinking that it wasn't so far from that spot that Delacroix had recently had his accident. Whether he had taken that route to the A6 he would make sure to find out when he next saw him.

'Well, it has often crossed my mind, but at the same time, I also wondered if I was just blaming my uncle for his death as, with Dad's death, everything changed for me. I came to blame my uncle for practically everything that I didn't like happening to me.'

Truchaud was becoming aware that she was finally getting to a part in the narrative that she was going to find difficult. 'Go on,' he said gently.

'With Dad being dead, and Granddad getting on in years, Uncle Jérome was summoned back from his perennial studies to do a job of work. Granddad told him, I gather, that he was no longer going to fund his life of doing nothing very much, and that he had to come back and help run the business that had subsidized his lifestyle. I had really only seen my uncle from a distance the whole of my life, and really didn't know him at all. At the same time my mother, poor sad little Mum, went off to stay with her parents near Vézelay, and for one reason or another never came back. She died at least ten years ago, and we only heard about it after the funeral was done and dusted. We weren't invited. I went to the churchyard there once. She's buried in their family crypt under her maiden name. I often wonder what the Laforges did to her to make them that bitter towards us. Granddad never mentioned her again, and wouldn't talk about her if I ever brought her up. So I became the family's Orphan Annie, and learned the trade from the inside. Does that help?'

'How did your uncle take to being summoned back to work at the domaine?'

'Well, as I didn't really know him before he came back, it's a little difficult to say. He wasn't very like my father, shall we put it like that? And he and Granddad didn't appear to get on especially well, but as the money kept on coming in, things were relatively calm between them.'

'What sort of things were you expected to do at the domaine?'

'Well, to start with, I worked in the vineyards when it was really needed, but as you can see, we generally employ girls in the shop, so as soon as I was legally old enough to work in the shop, that's where you would have found me.'

'So how old were you when your father died?'

'I was fourteen,' she replied, 'so I was still at school during the day.'

Truchaud did a bit of maths in his head, and realized that she was somewhat younger than she actually looked. 'And then you went on to Beaune University?'

'No. I learned all about wine from Granddad, and the various managers we employed over the years.' Truchaud said nothing but he wondered whether it was one of the managers who was responsible for her son. He filed that thought for later if necessary. 'My other job, of course, was running the household, which I had had to do long before Dad died and Mum left. I was already doing the cooking, and laundry and stuff. Fortunately, Granddad was supportive enough to actually spend some money on things like washing machines and tumble dryers. My school homework wasn't going to be very high on anybody's priority list, so a baccalaureate was out of the question anyway.'

'The women in your family had a fairly rough time one way or the other, didn't they?' Truchaud remarked drily, and Montbard gave a little cough in agreement.

'How do you mean?' she said looking up slightly surprised.

'Well, your mum disappeared as soon as your dad died, never to be seen again. Your aunt went off to become a nun, again never to be seen again. And you, well, you don't appear to have had much of a childhood, and were expected to skivvy for the men in your family.'

'It was expected.' Truchaud's thoughts again drifted towards the rather angular teenage boy he had seen in the church at his brother's funeral. His presence would have certainly kept her in the household.

'I never thought about it like that,' she said, 'but I suppose you could be right.' She looked rather sadly off into the middle distance for a moment, perhaps thinking of all the fun things she could have done during the youth that had been denied her, and was now behind her. Truchaud began to feel a little guilty having sowed the seeds of doubt about her father and grandfather, but then he stopped thinking that way. Certainly his own father had first fallen under the influence of old Mr Laforge, and look where that had got them all. He knew that young Mr Laforge had helped himself quite liberally to the coffers of Domaine Truchaud recently, and it was quite possible that old Mr Laforge was still the driving force, using the son as a front.

'Did you do any negotiating with wine merchants?'

'No, that was the men. Later on, I did do some of the work in the back office, especially as my uncle started employing younger girls to work in the shop. Payroll and stuff, you know, especially during the harvest and vintage. There's a lot of extra casual labour that we take on board at that time, many of them students, who need to be fed and lodged, and that doesn't happen overnight.' Truchaud certainly acknowledged that. His own family's little domaine doubled its workforce from two to four plus Michelle at harvest time, so bigger organizations would need far more people. He'd never really thought of the logistics of all that.

'Yes, that was my main role later on. We needed pickers for our own, and your vineyards. We needed sorters and then people to run the fermenting tanks, and while our *Maréchales* actually oversaw the winemaking process, alongside the men, I needed to make sure that the workforce was fed, watered, bedded and generally content to be when and where we needed them to be at any point in time.'

Truchaud tried to steer her back to Richebourg, bearing in mind she had had no idea of the extent of the family cellars when he asked her last. 'Did you have any idea about the merchandising side of the business?'

'Rather less so over the past decade, when I stopped working in the shop. Of course we talked about wine and the business over supper. That was probably more for Jacquot's benefit than mine.'

'Jacquot?' enquired Truchaud.

'My son.'

'Oh yes, I remember him. He was with you all at my brother's funeral.'

'Yes, that's him.'

'Thank you, incidentally, for coming, it was much appreciated. Do you have any idea when you are going to have Jérome's funeral?'

'The police haven't given us any idea yet when they're going to release the body. Will you have a word with them?'

'I don't know how much influence I can bring to bear, but I'll certainly have a word to make sure they haven't forgotten.' He thought that there wouldn't be any even slight risk that the presence of a body in the lab would be forgotten by any of the technicians in the forensics laboratory.

There was a knock at the door from the outside. 'Come in,' called Marie-Claire. It was the girl from the shop.

'If it's all right, Madame, I thought I would go off for lunch now. I've locked up, and I'll be back at three to open up for the afternoon.'

'Any sales?'

'A couple of interested gawpers came in and then got embarrassed and bought a couple of bottles they never wanted in the first place, but otherwise, no, not really.'

'That's fine, Mélodie, we'll see you this afternoon.' The girl left, shutting the door behind her. 'At least we could find her at short notice,' she remarked to Truchaud. 'The other girl has just vanished off the face of the planet, and I haven't seen hide nor hair of that damned Maréchale man either over the last few days.'

'Don't panic about either of them,' replied Truchaud. 'I know where they are and they're safe, but sort of in protective custody. We weren't quite sure who to tell at your end, until today.'

'Are they together?' After a moment's silence from Truchaud, she continued. 'I only asked, because they seemed to be an item when they were working here, and it seemed quite a constructive relationship.'

Truchaud still didn't comment, but changed the subject. 'Is there anywhere I can look to see if you've got any records of wine stocks you hold for other people still in bond? It would be instructive to see if you have any listed buyers for stock you still have in the cellar. They may, after all, need to be told that there may be a delay in their receiving their wines.'

'I think they should all be on the laptop in the office. Do you want to have a look?'

Chapter 33

Nuits-Saint-Georges, Friday morning

Truchaud looked over Marie-Claire's shoulder as she tapped at the keyboard. He wasn't quite sure what she was doing, but she appeared to be completely in control. Montbard at that moment was out the back washing the teacups. 'There,' she said suddenly. 'Is that what you're looking for?'

Truchaud looked carefully at the entries in front of him. He couldn't see any use of the word 'Richebourg', but there was certainly an 'Echézeaux' and the recent vintage beside it with a list of names, quantities and bottle sizes. 'That looks like it,' he said. 'May I?' he asked and made as if to change places. Marie-Claire stood up and he slid into the place she had vacated.

'Call me if you need me again. I'll just make sure your gendarme is all right,' she said and slipped out of the door from the office into her house. He smiled quietly to himself. *Poor woman,* he thought, *she's got two prowling policemen in different parts of her house, and she's only got herself to watch what they're doing.*

Truchaud tapped at the computer thoughtfully. *Echézeaux,* he thought. He tried to find the last year's reports to see if they had made a lot more Echézeaux the previous year. They had, but the previous year had been a very productive year, and anyway, Maréchale had already admitted that he had added some lesser wine into his blend, so that extra was probably within the variables of the two years.

Truchaud suddenly had the feeling that someone was walking over his grave. He remembered his lecturer in the Police College telling the cadets to be aware of their sixth senses, and to acknowledge them. It wasn't necessary to be sensitive about having 'spidey senses', they didn't have to talk about having them, or be worried that their partners would tease them about being jumpy. He advised them that when their minds or bodies warned them to be afraid, then they were worth listening to. The mind acquired a lot of information, some of which it didn't waste time processing into the laborious form of words.

He became aware of movement behind him, he didn't exactly hear anything as such, but was aware of movement, and this particular movement was trying not to be heard. He tapped at the keyboard with his left hand, while feeling with his right hand in the pocket of his trench coat. The butt of the pistol slipped gently into the palm of his right hand, and his thumb, more automatically than it had ever done before, flicked off the safety catch. He hoped that the movement behind him didn't notice he wasn't actually looking at the screen all that time. What he wasn't expecting was the cold hard feeling of metal at the nape of his neck. He did, however, know exactly what it was. He dived to his left, feeling the butt of his own pistol, and pulled his right hand out of his pocket. In the most fluid movement he had ever achieved in his life, twisting in his fall, he fired a shot back over his left shoulder from whence he had come. The chances were not good: he probably would only have hit the target if he had been aiming on a shooting range one time in a hundred. Sometimes you just got lucky.

Montbard came tearing into the room. 'Sir! Are you all right?'

'Get down!' Truchaud heard himself shout. *Oh! That's good,* he thought, *I can still make some noise.* 'There's someone in here with a gun.'

'I know,' she said from the floor over by the door, 'Where?'

From his position on the floor, lying on his back, looking up with his own pistol out in front of him, Truchaud could see nothing. To his left, however he heard an unpleasant sizzling noise. There was a wisp of smoke coming out of the middle of the computer screen. There was no one in front of him. 'I don't know,' he replied, 'He was right behind me.' He gingerly got to his knees, his left shoulder hurt like hell, why his left shoulder? He wondered.

As his eye line rose he saw the person who had shot at him, bent backwards over the fallen chair. Truchaud stood up. There was no way that Molleau would ever do that again. Truchaud was stunned. He had, by sheer luck, put his bullet straight through Molleau's forehead. He looked over his left shoulder, and saw that Molleau had put his bullet straight through the monitor which, moments before, Truchaud had been looking into. 'You can stand up, constable, it's all over,' he said.

Montbard stood up wide-eyed. 'Are you all right, sir?' she asked.

'Well, apart from trying to work out how he put one bullet into my right shoulder and another into the computer monitor, yes I'm fine.'

'Your right shoulder?'

'Hurts like a mother,' he muttered. 'Is it a through and through? No, it can't have been. I dived to my left, and that side went away from the screen.'

'It's not bleeding, sir.'

Truchaud pulled his hand away from it, still holding his pistol, albeit loosely. He checked the safety catch, and put the pistol down on the desk. He then looked at his hand. No blood. 'Nor there is,' he muttered. He wiped the hand over his very painful shoulder. Painful it still was but moist it wasn't. Satisfied that he wasn't bleeding, they both looked at the dead policeman in front of them. Truchaud checked for a pulse in the neck. It was still, as was the radial pulse at the wrist.

'Inspector Molleau?' she enquired. 'How did that happen?'

'I haven't the faintest idea, but what I do know is that he executed his victims with a bullet through the back of the head. It looks like I was to be his second intended in a week.'

'You mean he also killed Mr Laforge?'

'It looks like it. It's exactly the same modus operandi, and I do know he was very handy with a firearm.'

'Oh thank god!' came a voice from the door. 'Does that mean it's finally all over?'

Truchaud and Montbard both looked up over their shoulders. Framed in the doorway to the house stood Marie-Claire Laforge. She was wearing an expression of complete relief on her face, which suddenly looked younger and less drawn.

'Madame,' said Truchaud standing up, 'is there something more you want to tell us?'

'Yes, I think so,' she replied.

'If I may ask the constable here to put down in her notebook the timings of the incidents of the last few minutes, then we'll come through, and I think we've all earned another cup of tea.'

Montbard was already scribbling notes, when Truchaud added, 'He's not going anywhere. Just check that the girl did lock up the shop when she left, and then come on through to the house. I think we will have one very big story to tell your *Capitaine* in the next half an hour. Are you going to call him, or shall I?'

'Whichever you want, sir, she replied,' and having agreed that it would be she who called Duquesne, she slipped through the side door into the shop.

Truchaud walked through the office into the back of the house and into the sitting room again, whose door Madame Laforge had left open. He was still rubbing his shoulder, which was still really sore. Had he cracked something when he landed on it in his dive to the left? Montbard arrived.

'Yes, sir, all properly locked up.'

Madame Laforge came through with three rather old-fashioned looking bone-china teacups, all steaming with tea. There was a jug with milk in it, and a couple of slices of cut lemon on a saucer. There was also a small plate with some plain biscuits.

'There are things that I am going to tell you that I would rather were kept confidential, but it will explain to you why what happened actually happened. Does that make any sense?'

'I'm sure it will, Madame, when you have finished.' His reply sounded reassuring, but wasn't promising anything he might be unable to deliver.

'We were talking about your father a little while ago,' she said. 'He has been part of the business for quite some time, as you know. He may actually own quite a lot of Laforge's you know.'

'Huh?' asked Truchaud incredulously. 'What do you mean?'

'Well, Uncle Jérome remarked at table the other day to Granddad that he should keep his eye open for any interesting parcel of Grand Cru vineyard that might come onto the market, because he thought they might have enough cash in hand to be able to grab it before anyone else could put in a bid. Granddad asked him where he had got that sort of money from, and he mentioned your father's name, and explained that they had been doing some investing together.'

'And that was ready cash in hand?'

'That's what he said.'

'Do you know where it is?' Truchaud asked, wondering if that was the contents of the Zürich account, and why the complicated pathway, was that what was needed just to evade the taxman?

'Presumably in a bank somewhere. I can't see Uncle Jérome sticking it in a sock in his bedroom drawer.'

'Well, it will be frozen if it's in a bank until the probate lawyers have got their hands on it all, but if it's cash, in a sock drawer, then that shouldn't include the value of the cellar stock you've got, or we've got. Was there some sort of deed of partnership that you know of?'

'If there was, I don't know where it is now. It's always possible that it was one of the many documents the gendarmes took away when Uncle was killed. Does your father have a copy?'

'Well, now I know such a document might exist, I'll know what to ask for, but he never mentioned anything about it when I was talking to him about stuff yesterday. His memory isn't quite what it was, you see. Anyway, you say this business arrangement was set up between my father and your uncle, and it didn't involve your grandfather at all?'

'As far as I understand, no, although I can't believe that Granddad didn't know all about it. Granddad may be physically quite tottery, but he's all there upstairs. There isn't very much that goes on here that Granddad doesn't know about, and doesn't have an opinion on.' The way she said the last bit suggested that she was about to add something, but had second thoughts on the matter.

269

'Go on,' said Truchaud, picking up on that. 'You were going to say something else.'

She looked around uncertainly, almost as if she was making sure that everyone was where they were supposed to be. She caught Gendarme Montbard's eye, 'I would rather you don't take notes for the moment,' she said. Truchaud nodded at Montbard in agreement. 'You may have heard that my uncle made life a little difficult for the girls in the shop?'

'I have heard it said that his hands were somewhat overactive yes. It was also quite well-known among the girls themselves. I gather that was why there was quite a rapid turnover of them.'

'He didn't like the girls getting older,' she remarked drily. 'He also didn't like them getting pregnant.' Her replies were getting drier by the moment.

'Did he get a lot of them pregnant?' Truchaud asked, cocking an eyebrow.

And she dropped her next bombshell. 'Well, me for a kick off.'

'Jacquot?' asked Montbard, before Truchaud could get the question in himself.

'Jacquot,' she replied dully. 'May I request that you both keep that seriously under your hats? I cannot see how that piece of evidence will help anyone's case in court.'

'May I ask, Madame, how old you were at the time?'

'I was fourteen when I became pregnant, and the same age Jacquot is now when he was born.'

Montbard sucked air between her teeth. 'And you say your uncle was definitely the father?' she asked. 'Why didn't you tell your grandfather?'

'I did,' she replied. 'He would rather not have believed me, but my condition became obvious fairly quickly. Up until that point, there hadn't been a lot of me. That sort of shame and scandal didn't go down well in Nuits-Saint-Georges. I left school and became instantly two years older. That was something that needed Grandfather to arrange. One of the farm workers disappeared under a cloud. Offhand I can't remember who, poor lad, and everybody looked the other way, shrugged and said, "C'est la vie". I hope my grandfather made sure he was well looked after, but I don't know for sure.

'Grandfather is very good at making things he doesn't want to talk about simply not exist, or at the very least go away. The one plus point of getting pregnant was that my uncle never interfered with me again. That probably was my grandfather having a quiet word in one ear, while holding the other one very hard indeed.'

Truchaud said, 'Madame I think we can safely say that we will keep that information under our hats. Does Jacquot know?'

'He thinks his father was an itinerant worker in transit, and he was the result of a moment when I was not best in command of my faculties.'

'What does he think of that?'

'He's happy enough to be alive and part of this family. It could have been a lot worse as far as he's concerned. He also thinks I am somewhat older than I actually am, and that is the way I would like it to stay, please.'

'We will do our best,' Truchaud replied. 'Montbard?'

'Yes sir,' she assented.

'Now coming back to Molleau,' he continued. 'You said, "thank god it's all over". What exactly did you mean by that, Madame?'

'Molleau appeared to be a very close friend of my uncle's, and they did a lot of things together.'

'Including sex?' asked Montbard from her place by the sofa.

'Er, no,' she replied slightly drily. 'My uncle did not have sex with Molleau; my uncle was into teenage girls. Moreover, I didn't have sex with Molleau either. I meant their political views were of the left-wing variety, or rather they supported the politicians that the press labelled "Gauchistes". I have that feeling that they supported the Gauchistes rather like middle-aged men support the football team from the town where they grew up: out of loyalty and ignorance of the facts rather than from any enthusiasm or commitment.

'However they did get together and mutter amongst themselves, at the same time threatening that if ever I said anything

271

about what I *hadn't* just heard, I would be in very serious trouble. It is, however, not very difficult to say nothing about something you haven't actually heard, because you don't actually know what it is you have to be discreet about. After a while, I did become fairly anxious about it all.'

'I can imagine, Madame. Have you even any idea what they might have been talking about?'

'Wine, I imagine: wine and money.'

'Do you think Molleau was buying untaxed wine from your uncle?'

'No, I don't think we're talking about small quantities for their own consumption. I think it involved shifting fairly considerable amounts from one country to another, for much larger sums of money.'

'If it's the wine that we're interested in, then it's very considerable quantities indeed. I am asking for your assistance here. Do you think that this was an illegal export without the involvement of the customs?'

'Well, if it wasn't illicit, why threaten to injure me if I spoke up about it?'

'Why indeed?' replied Truchaud slowly. 'Tell me, Madame, did Molleau actually injure you.'

'No, surprisingly,' she replied. 'But for years the threat was there, and I always thought it was just around the corner. It wasn't just that I believed he would if I didn't do as I was told. I was sort of expecting it anyway; I was just lucky that he was too busy to knock my head off today. Does that make sense to you?'

At this point there was a rapid knock at the door. 'Open up! Police!' Truchaud got up and walked to the front door. Duquesne looked him up and down. 'I am informed you've got another body here,' he said. 'I suppose it's as good a place as any. That way we don't have to go around learning new places.'

'Follow me,' replied Truchaud, and led him through into the office.

'Nobody's touched the body?' asked the gendarme.

'Only me to ensure that life was extinct, and I was under the direct observation of Constable Montbard here.'

'And the body hasn't been moved?'

'No, sir,' she replied from behind Marie-Claire.

'Can you tell me exactly what happened, in your own words? Please, Commander, consider yourself under caution, just in case we need to come back to this in court.'

Truchaud narrated the incident in the office to the best of his memory, and by the act of narrating it he began to realize how close to his Maker he had come. He didn't mention the conversation with Marie-Claire about Jacquot's conception, and Montbard didn't bring it up either; neither was asked. Duquesne handed over the scene to the scene-of-crime officer and his camera.

They walked through into the sitting room and asked Marie-Claire if she wouldn't mind creating a cup of coffee.

Chapter 34

Nuits-Saint-Georges, Friday morning

There were still things Truchaud didn't understand completely. He could understand Duquesne's discomfort too. 'If Molleau and Laforge were such good friends, why did Molleau execute him?' he asked.

'That was one thing that was worrying me too,' assented Duquesne. 'There is someone we haven't seen yet who might have an answer for us on that.'

'Old Mr Laforge?' enquired Truchaud.

'The same. Is he around?'

'We could ask his granddaughter when she comes back.'

Marie-Claire reappeared on cue with three cups of coffee for the police.

'Is your grandfather on the premises?' asked Duquesne.

'I'll see if I can find him,' she replied. 'He doesn't usually go very far. His joints no longer let him get about much.'

Old Mr Laforge lived up to his name. Wizened he was and lined. He had a coarse tremor in his hands, but if he was trying to give an image of elderly frailty he had to do something about the eyes, which, looking at least fifty years younger, were razor-sharp and very watchful. His voice was slightly tremulous maybe, but not the content of what he said. 'Gentlemen, I understand you have a few questions for me.'

'Firstly, we have found a cache of weapons in one of your cellars. We would like to know about those, and their age.' Duquesne opened the questioning.

'Which cellar, may I ask?' the old man replied.

'The second cellar to which you can only gain access via the waterway,' came the reply from Duquesne, who then added. 'Are there many caches of weapons in your cellars?'

Old Mr Laforge ignored the second question but asked, 'You mean you can still only get to that one via the waterway?' he replied. 'I would have thought that the boys would have knocked down all the plasterworks by now.'

'I don't understand. When were you last down there?'

'Well over ten years ago I imagine. I have a very wobbly hip, and even going down the main steps into the upper cellar isn't something I have attempted for years.' He tapped his left hip. 'Hurts too.'

'Have you thought of getting it fixed?'

'What? Let some idiot at me with a knife? What kind of fool do you think I am? Anyway,' he continued changing the subject back, 'if the plasterworks are still standing, then those weapons will be from the Second World War, maybe even before that, which is presumably what your original question was about.'

'I understand you had experience of the Second World War,' Duquesne pushed gently.

The old man dug into his pocket, produced a small medal box and opened it. Suspended from a rather faded red and black ribbon was a bronze disc with a cross of Lorraine embossed on it. 'There, what do you think of that?' he asked.

'It's a Medal of the Resistance,' said Truchaud. 'You were awarded one of those?'

'Why do you sound so surprised, young man?' old Mr Laforge replied tetchily.

'I was not in any way trying to impugn your valour,' Truchaud wriggled uneasily. 'It's just that I didn't think that General de Gaulle awarded those to the Communist Resistance.'

'What makes you think I was a communist?'

'Your son ...'

'Ah yes, my son. Jérome joined the Communist Party in the 1970s, yes. Exactly how does that make me a communist?' The old man grinned, and continued. 'My boy being a champagne socialist doesn't say anything at all about me. I really wasn't political; I was a *Maquis* boy, pure and simple. I fought the Boche because that was who they were: the Boche.' He managed to infuse a great deal of venom into the word. He looked around at the others who were aware he was going to tell them a story, and it might be worth a listen.

'I was still at school when the Boche came. This part of France was occupied, as Goering wanted the wine to fill his own fat belly. He was only interested in wine with a name that idiots recognized for quality, which was why the Boche occupied the Champagne and the Côte d'Or. For some reason,' he added with a chuckle, 'he also persuaded Hitler that the Bordelais was worth hanging on to.' Truchaud thought that his colleague, Inspector Leclerc in Paris, would have liked that comment.

'The first thing they wanted was wine. And to start with we had a lot of wine that we would have objected to them having, even if they were willing to pay for it. They had no sense of taste, the Boche; Goering, perhaps, I don't know, I never met him. If we had met, that would have been a meeting only one of us would have survived, that's for certain! Anyway, the '39 vintage, which was in the barrels when the Boche walked in, was the worst year that my father could ever remember. Tradition says that a vintage at the beginning of a war is invariably bad. I never tasted the 1914, but he told me that that was not a good year either. The Boche did pay us for the wine to start with, and we had a fair amount of 1939, because it was a wet year, and to add to that there hadn't been much sun to ripen the grapes. We were technically at war during the harvest, but it was a funny sort of war in 1939. There was also snow during the harvest that year. Our poor vines didn't stand a chance.

'It was thin dull wine, but it was a perfect thin dull wine to sell to an invader who couldn't tell bilge water from diesel fuel. We'd never have been able to sell the stuff in peacetime. It wasn't even strong enough to be worth distilling for industrial alcohol. We had no idea what was going to happen, but certainly my father had less faith in the Maginot Line than most French politicians, so we got to building in our cellars.'

The old man took a breath and looked around. He had his audience hooked. 'Sitting in our cellars was a number of bottles of older finer wine: some of it grown by us; and some of it bought from other winemakers when they were very new, for us to mature, and sell on when they were ready. Call them the first *en primeur* investments if you like. My father took the whole family down into the cellar. He and my older brother laid the bricks, while my mother, sister and I looked for spiders and things to make the wall look older so that when the Boche came, they wouldn't think this was a new construction. There were one or two other tricks he came up with. We sprayed milk at the new walls, so that mortar and stone became rapidly covered in mould, which helped to age them, and those of us who had, shall we say, fully amiable hoses, were encouraged to pee at the wall too, to help age the aroma.

'He insisted that we didn't tell anyone — anyone at all — what we were doing; he didn't want anyone to know. Everyone knew that the Boche were ruthless from their experience of them in the Great War. So if people didn't know what we had done in our cellars, then that information couldn't be tortured out of them. The '38 wasn't a bad year, and that all went behind the wall. My father also hid all the glorious '28 that he'd still got behind the wall. We got quite good at building walls to hide things behind, and by the time the Boche did actually arrive, we had walled off a whole cellar, which you could only get to via the waterway.'

'What did the Germans make of the waterway?' Truchaud asked.

'They never knew anything about it,' he replied. 'They appeared to be rather afraid of our cellars. If they wanted something from the cellar, they would send someone down there to get it, usually me, and threaten to shoot my sister if I didn't get back up there with it, *chop chop*. Good little boy that I was, I did as I was told. Mind you, by the time the Boche arrived, we'd even walled up the doorway that you blew up the other day, so our cellars were nowhere near as big as they are on paper now. The way that we got into the deeper cellars was down the wellhead you can still see at the bottom of the stairs. If you look down that well you see water. That water you can see at the bottom of the well is, in fact, the waterway itself. So when the Resistance arrived they went down into the well in buckets, and hid weapons and people down there too.'

'So it was during the war you learned how to mislabel wine?' remarked Truchaud drily.

'I know what you are trying to say,' the old man replied, 'and up to a point that was true, in that any of the wine they took from our upper cellar was likely to have been 1939 Ordinaire, no matter what it said on the label, if that's what you mean. The Boche couldn't tell the difference. Later vintages weren't so good either, but for different reasons. We couldn't get any copper salts to kill the downy mildew in 1940. You know … yellow oil spots on the topside of the leaves, followed by white furry spots on their undersides. Anyway the Boche often wouldn't even let us into the vineyards to do the basics. For a nation that claimed to be wine-savvy, as Germans were supposed to be, they were pretty useless. Mind you, they probably kept the Rhine wine men on the Rhine making their wine, rather than dressing them up as Boche and sending them off into Bourgogne to police us.

'The bottom line was that our cellars, and a lot of others I got to know after the war, were places where all sorts of things were hidden from the Boche. Ours was certainly a weapons cache for the *Maquis*. I was only a little fellow, and not very well fed. You weren't very well fed in Bourgogne during the occupation if you were French. I managed to remain young and still at school, and was a well-rat until we were liberated in 1944.'

'You mentioned you had a brother. What happened to him?'

'Ah, yes, Armand,' he sighed. 'He was *recruited* by the *Service du Travail Obligatoire* and sent off to Germany to work in a factory. That was the last that we heard of him. My son, Jérome, did try to find some records of him when he went to study in Germany in the seventies, but he said he never found anything. The trouble was that they never told any of us where they had sent them. A lot of the forced labour camps, like Buchenwald, were in the Russian Sector after the war, so that wasn't easy to investigate either. Even though my son told them he was a communist, it didn't seem to make the East Germans any more helpful towards him or his search for his uncle.'

'And your sister?'

'She managed to avoid getting pregnant during the war. She was younger than me, so it wasn't so difficult for her to remain childish and of no interest to the Boche during the occupation, apart from as a hostage to ensure I came back from the cellars nice and quickly. After the war she trained as a nurse, and went out as a fully trained matron to Indo-China during the unpleasantness out there. She died at the battle of Dien Bien Phu in 1954. What a waste! She was due to come back and get married, and had a post already set up for her in the hospice in Beaune on her return.'

'Was the chap she was going to marry in the wine business?'

'Of course. She wouldn't have thought of anyone else. Nor, I suspect, would our father.'

'What happened to the fiancé?'

'He married someone else, and thus married into their vineyard instead.'

'Your family had its fair share of bad luck, didn't it?' remarked Duquesne drily. 'Are there other *Maquis* weapons walled up in your cellar somewhere that we haven't found yet?' he asked changing the subject.

'For all I know, there may even be *Maquis* themselves still down there,' he replied with a twinkle, then added, 'Well, I never moved them when I was younger, and I never told the boys about them, especially when Jérome joined the Communists. The last thing I would have wanted was that lot getting hold of proper guns. You never knew which idiot's hands they might end up in. When I last went down there, as I say about fifteen years ago, they were still as bricked up as they ever were.'

'So those doors at the bottom of your main cellar …?' Truchaud enquired.

'Ah yes, I heard you were interested in them. They're a different story altogether. My father and I did open them up after the war, like the route down to the wharf, and we replaced them with the old oak doors we had removed in early '39. I'm afraid we sold, or occasionally drank the contents of them after the war. They reactivated the business. I've got the keys somewhere,

I think, but I don't think there's much in them apart from empty bottles that we might need to use one day, and empty barrels. You know,' he added drifting off at a tangent again, 'those were things we couldn't get during the war: empty bottles! Towards the end of the occupation people had to bring their own bottles in to get them refilled, even the Boche.

'Just think, those wooden doors survived both world wars in some location or another, and then young Truchaud's boy comes in here, and I gather they were blown to pieces.'

'One of them is. I'm afraid, yes.'

'Oh well, these things happen. Will you arrange for its replacement?'

'Of course. I will discuss it with Mr Maréchale when I next see him.'

'Oh you know where he is then?'

'Of course. I forgot to tell you I knew.'

'He's with that Parnault girl, I suppose?'

'Girand her name is.'

'Yes, that's the name her father gave her, but she's from the Parnault wine family. Funny that, you know. Back in the day we always thought that Parnault's daughter was going to marry one of you two lads, and then she went and married a doctor, and you went off to play at cops and robbers. Strange place the world has turned into.'

'So you followed the story of my life then?'

'Most of my working life was spent sitting over a barrel with your father, and his father before him, tasting glasses in our hands. What else was there for us to talk about but the next generations?'

'Did you know your son was trying to sell off some straight Bourgogne as Grand Cru Richebourg?' asked Truchaud getting down to his own version of the nitty-gritty.

'I had heard something about that, yes. Our Mr Maréchale did try to fill me in, but I think I pretended to have lost rather more of my memory than I had at the time. I wasn't sure whether I wanted to know about it to be honest. I did try to discuss it with my son, but he didn't want to talk to me about it.

It made me think he was trying to create some money for that damn party of his.'

'You mean,' Truchaud exploded, 'that your son was going to use our wine to fund the Communist Party?'

'Yes, I thought so for a while perhaps, but I don't actually think he was. It took him some time, but I actually think he had finally grown out of all that communist clap-trap, and he was trying to rustle up some capital to buy a new parcel of land.'

'So where did Inspector Molleau fit in with all this?' enquired Duquesne, reminding the other two that he was still there.

'*Inspector* Molleau?' enquired the old man, full of contempt. 'I would never believe a single word that he had to say. He probably wasn't even a qualified inspector.'

Truchaud and Duquesne exchanged expressions, 'He wasn't?' they chorused simultaneously.

'No, he was a party activist through and through. The party probably bought the rank for him to set him up here to spy on the community.'

'So he was fooling us all this time? You know none of us checked. We just assumed he was who he said he was. I suppose we ought to check and see if Mr Lemaître is who he claims to be too.'

'Oh, you can count on that,' replied Duquesne, 'we go way back. Anyway, Mr Laforge, you were saying, about Molleau?'

'His grandfather was certainly a member of the Francs-Tireurs,' he explained.

'Les Francs-Tireurs?'

'The free-shooters. They were a group of partisans in the Second World War, and the Communist Party of the Soviet Union funded them. I think they were supposed to maintain a posture of neutrality against the Nazis, while the non-aggression pact between the Boche and the Russians was still in place. That all went down the pan when Hitler invaded Russia. Molleau's grandfather was caught by the Nazis and executed. His son survived, but with a fierce anti-Nazi chip on his shoulder. He will have grown up in Nuits-Saint-Georges, but I wasn't particularly aware of him; there were a lot of fatherless children around in the fifties. He would have gone off to university I suppose, to Paris at the end of the fifties, and become active in the sixties. I'm sure he was one of those who made friends with my son when he was there in '68, and presumably recruited him. I suppose he had a son while he was in Paris, and the child's mother will have acknowledged the father enough to give him Molleau's name at least. No, that's not fair. I have no reason to believe that they weren't all happily married in Notre-Dame itself. However, when a youngish chap turned up out of the blue soon after Louis had his accident and Jérome had come back to take his place, calling himself Molleau, I remembered the name. The chap you just disposed of must have been that grandson. Which side of the political fence he actually sat on, I don't know, but he was fairly often in our front room discussing things with Jérome, and the conversations went quiet when I arrived.'

'Now supposing he was trying to re-recruit Jérome into the Party, do you think that would fit what you knew?' asked Duquesne.

'And then when he knew he had failed, he shot him?' added Truchaud. 'But if that is so, then how did he know he had failed? The only thing that had gone wrong before then was Bertin's death. How did that fit in? If anything, that would have improved the situation. And one other question I have to ask is why did he wait until the weekend before he got involved? He must have known what was going on right from the beginning.'

'Perhaps he was trying to find out how much you knew about the fraud when you came down.' Duquesne was thinking out loud. 'Supposing Bertin was in collusion with Jérome, and was involved in the fraud.'

'But Bertin wasn't politically minded,' objected Truchaud.

'He didn't have to be,' explained Duquesne. 'He need not have known about Jérome Laforge's communist past to have become involved in this. He might actually have been the reason that Jérome *grew out of the Party,* as his grandfather here so delicately put it. He could simply have seen that Jérome was a potential source of wealth for himself and his family.

283

Meanwhile, maybe Molleau's thoughts were that Jérome was planning to con Bertin out of his share to repay his debts to the Party, and of course access to Bertin's share was no longer possible once Bertin was dead. Molleau may or may not have known in advance that Bertin's brother is a Commander of the National Police. That might have been a bit of a facer for him if he didn't.

'What he then needed to find out was if you had any twists in your nature or not. It would have been easier to dig around there if you didn't know he was actually doing it. What do you reckon?'

The police and the old man exchanged expressions. Old Mr Laforge looked at Montbard for a moment and said, 'You've been very quiet, my dear, what do you think?'

Chapter 35

Nuits-Saint-Georges, Friday morning, later

'Am I under arrest?' enquired Truchaud. 'I think I ought to be,' he added to Duquesne as they looked at each other across the steaming cups of coffee on the gendarme's desk.

'I think your pistol certainly ought to be in police custody,' replied Lemaître, waving his hand at Duquesne, 'pending official investigations.'

Truchaud removed the pistol from his pocket, checked the safety catch as always and handed the pistol, holding the barrel, butt first, to Duquesne over the desk, who took the magazine out of the pistol, and seeing that there was one shell in the chamber, and only one missing, he said, 'Note that down, Constable Montbard: one shot fired.'

'Yes, sir,' replied the gendarme. Duquesne meanwhile locked the pistol in his drawer.

'Would you like me to tell the old man in Paris that I'm suspended from active duty?' Truchaud asked.

'Would you?' replied the Captain of Gendarmes. 'That would be much appreciated. I'm sure you would explain it so much better.'

It was at about this point that Montbard finally broke down into a fit of the giggles.

'Something amusing you, constable?'

'If only you could hear yourselves, and how ridiculous you both sound. Commander, you shot someone in self-defence. If you hadn't done so, you wouldn't be here now.'

Truchaud looked at the constable thoughtfully for a moment, and, deciding not to say anything, he let her chuckle to herself if that was the sort of thing that amused her. 'Tell me,' he asked her finally, changing the subject, 'I could have sworn you were about to ask old Mr Laforge a fairly significant question when he commented on your silence, and then you stopped.'

She looked at him for a moment. 'And then I stopped.' She paused. 'Is that an order?' she asked.

'Would it need to be an order?' asked Captain Duquesne, as he glanced at Truchaud, 'even if he were in a position to give you one?'

'This is all getting a little tense, and probably unnecessarily so,' said Lemaître trying to clear the air. 'There are a number of questions that have gone unanswered in this case, the solutions to which may be of interest, but may create even more problems in the long run, for very little, if any, gain. For that reason, would it be better if they weren't asked in the first place? Is that one of those sorts of questions, constable?'

'Yes, sir.' The red-haired policewoman looked relieved at the Judge's sensitivity in finding a solution to her discomfort.

'Meanwhile, Commander Truchaud, would you phone your Divisional Commander in Paris. We will all remain present, in case he asks you a question which you can't answer.' Without further ado Truchaud dialled on his mobile phone. The amiable bluff tones of his superior replied, and Truchaud explained that he had been relieved of his weapon by the local gendarmerie and why.

'Well, Commander,' replied the Divisional Commander. 'I have to say I never saw that one coming: you being suspended for shooting a policeman; shooting anybody really, apart from by accident. I always thought you achieved your promotions *despite* your ability with a firearm.'

'Well, fortunately he wasn't actually a policeman, but it was sheer good luck on my part that I am here to talk to you at all.'

'I'm pleased you are, but we may need to look at your current status on the force for the time being. It occurs to me that I need to be discussing your future with the local departmental commander in Dijon. It would be useful if you were to find your way back here, then we could continue this conversation face to face. However, I suspect you consider yourself to be under open arrest by your Captain Duquesne. I will send down an officer to escort you home. Anyone you had in mind?'

'Constable Dutoit was very helpful during the investigation, so if the good Captain were to hand me over into her custody over dinner in the next couple of days, I think all would find that an acceptable arrangement. That is, of course, unless you want to come down to dinner yourself? The local cuisine here is particularly excellent.' Truchaud was relieved when the DC declined the offer. Dinner for twenty at *La Cabotte* would not have come cheap, and he doubted that the DC would have expected anything less.

Duquesne cocked an eyebrow at Truchaud who explained his Paris squad's tradition of a semi-formal dinner at the conclusion of a case. He added that he would like to invite everyone to a similar dinner in Nuits-Saint-Georges, and during the meal, for Duquesne to hand him over to his Parisian custodian as part of the entrée. Lemaître then suggested that they continued their current conversation, off duty in a café somewhere. He also suggested that Constable Montbard should accompany them too.

The idea that two gendarmes in uniform were off duty in a café with a judge and another man in a trench coat was fairly difficult to swallow for the owner of the café they chose, especially as it was the one opposite Laforge's shop, which had been fairly seriously disrupted by the police over the past few days. These three then had the temerity to want a booth where they could sit and talk privately without being overheard, and all for the price of four cups of coffee! The owner wasn't amused. The police didn't appear to be particularly bothered what his feelings were; he was lucky that none of them wanted to smoke.

Truchaud, stirring his *café au lait,* started the ball rolling.

'I think my brother killed himself,' he said. 'I wonder whether he couldn't see any way out of what he had got himself involved in with Laforge. And Laforge hadn't told my father or my brother that he was secretly negotiating with both of them as individuals. It was all getting out of control. He was a gentle fellow and was soon to take over the domaine, which

287

had always been his one ambition in life. At that point in time, he was told that the first batch that he had made all by himself of the wine that had always been his favourite, was rubbish, and that his father had thrown it away. I think that would have upset most people, but he wasn't the sort of fellow to voice his feelings in public, and certainly not those sort of negative ones. I suppose he never talked to his wife about things when they got desperate either.'

'How sad,' remarked Duquesne. 'If I were ever that unhappy, my wife would be the first person I would turn to.'

'I am pleased to hear it,' replied Truchaud. 'She sounds a remarkable woman, your wife.' He paused for a moment as if to honour *'Madame la Capitaine'*, and then continued, 'Going back to Bertin, though. We know he was suffering inside, because he wasn't sleeping, and had gone to see Doctor Girand about that. The good doctor's solution was a small box of sleeping pills. How intensive his consultation had actually been isn't clear, but he did seem genuinely surprised that Bertin had died, and the thought of suicide never appeared to have crossed his mind. It occurs to me that his solution was a, "well let's just tap the symptom on the head a little, and when he comes back for some more sleepers, then we'll discuss it again" sort of thought process. He certainly hadn't considered the situation to be terribly serious and thought a softly, softly programme was appropriate. Sadly, it wasn't.'

'So, what do you think actually happened?' asked Duquesne.

'Well, as you know, he didn't take very many of those pills at all. Supposing he took most of them that last night …'

'But sir,' interjected Montbard, 'those sleepers are really pretty safe, and even if you took the whole prescription at once, which he didn't, the worst you could expect is that you would wake up the following morning with a bit of a hangover, and a very dry mouth, if you slept with it open.'

'Quite, but during that period of unconsciousness, you would be well and truly unconscious, and not just asleep.'

'Go on,' added Duquesne sounding more and more interested.

'So what else was missing in the household?' Truchaud asked. When she continued to look lost, 'The insulin.'

'The insulin?' queried Montbard wide-eyed. 'You mean someone murdered him with the insulin while he was asleep?'

'Not necessarily murdered. I think that's the way he killed himself though, and killed himself in a way that his suicide wouldn't be discovered as such. That was probably why he picked insulin as his method of suicide in the first place. He obviously thought long and hard how his killing himself would affect everyone around him, and he didn't want to be telling Bruno, and perhaps Michelle as well, that they weren't an adequate reason for him to stick around, or that he didn't care for them enough to go on living. This wasn't a suicide to punish anyone else, only himself, for failure.

'He also knew that his death wouldn't affect Dad greatly, as his Alzheimer's has already progressed too far for him to fully understand what had happened. Here's a question … tell me what the usual finding is that points we police towards think-ing about suicide in a sudden unexplained death case?'

'The suicide note?'

'Exactly, and they're usually a revenge sort of thing, "Look what you made me do, you bleeps! I couldn't cope any longer, nobody loves me yadda, yadda …" You know the sort of thing. He may well have believed what Dad told him, and really took it to heart that he hadn't got the winemaking gift. That would have really upset him, to realize in his mid-forties that he had absolutely no talent in the life he had chosen for himself.'

'So?'

'He decided that night to kill himself. He took a few sleeping tablets that he knew would knock himself out over the next half hour, then drew up a syringe full of insulin from Michelle's vial, and injected it into the loose tissue between his toes. He then disposed of the insulin vial and syringe in Michelle's insulin disposal bin with all the others she had used already herself, and went to bed. The low blood sugar caused by the insulin would normally have woken him, making him shake and feel desperately hungry. However, he wasn't asleep, he was unconscious and his vital organs couldn't work with such a low blood sugar. Thus he died. At the autopsy, the only foreign drug they found on board was the sleeping pill, in a fairly low and certainly non-fatal concentration.

'They didn't look for insulin, and why should they? We've all got insulin on board? And the blood sugar levels continue to drop off after death, as the systems continue to shut down, so the blood sugar level at autopsy is always considerably lower than it is at the moment of death. That is what I think happened, and if Laforge were still alive, I think he would be the person I would be going after, for justice. I just don't see what the point would be for raking all that up, now that Laforge himself is dead. We've got a natural causes certificate, and for Bruno and Michelle's benefit, I would like to let sleeping dogs lie. Thoughts?'

'I can see why you wanted us to discuss this while we are off duty,' remarked Lemaître drily, 'but actually I agree. It would cost a fair amount to prove your suggestion one way or the other, and if we actually did so, I can't see what would be gained, so I accept your suggestion that we leave that well alone. I think there was something else you wanted to discuss too?'

'Not me actually. I think Constable Montbard had a suggestion she wanted to put … off the record too.' Both senior policemen looked at the girl who looked uncomfortable for a moment.

'Well, it was just an idea that crossed my mind, as an explanation for a number of rather odd things that happened in the Laforge family, and in the lead up to the particular one that led Jérôme Laforge returning to Nuits-Saint-Georges in the first place.'

'Go on,' encouraged Duquesne.

'Well, when Commander Truchaud and I were with Madame Laforge before the incident with Molleau, she was talking about her mother going off to Vézelay and abandoning her daughter and the rest of the Laforges for ever, and never coming back. Eventually she died in Vézelay and was buried in the local churchyard under her maiden name. I felt that was as complete a rejection of part of a person's life as I have ever heard. I have to say I wondered why someone would reject her own child so completely. What could Marie-Claire have done that was so terrible, especially as she was still a child when her mother departed? There was a solution that occurred to me: she simply *was*. I have no proof of what I mean, and again, if proof was uncovered, it is information that would hurt innocent people for no obvious gain.'

'You're not making a lot of sense at the moment, but you've got us both very intrigued. Please explain.'

'Well, supposing her father was not Louis Laforge, but old Mr Laforge himself, that would have made Jérome, the father of her son, not her uncle but …'

'Oh lord, her brother.'

'Well to be precise, her half-brother. But can you see how that sort of information being proved would, in any shape or form, be of any help to the investigation?'

'I think the investigation is complete without any of this extra information being added to it,' declared Lemaître, 'apart possibly from a further cup of coffee all round.' He waved at the girl at the bar. 'Any chance of a refill all round?'

The girl looked at him without smiling, shrugged and wandered back to the bar. At least the hissing noise from the coffee machine told them that coffee was being made. 'I think we have to decide exactly the limits of the case. To me it is simple,' said Lemaître. 'It started with the death of Jérome Laforge, and I think its conclusion was the death of his killer, at your hands Monsieur Truchaud, in self-defence.

'We could enlarge the story to include Andreas Baader and Hermann Goering, if you like, and we could expand it to include Louis XVI, Adam and Eve if we really wanted to get carried away, as they say that there are a maximum of six degrees of separation between everyone who has ever lived. I have never asked anyone to prove that to me, but I'll take their word for it. I will put my case to the prosecutor and see whether he's happy that that's that. I don't think there's anyone left alive to try any more. The maximum, Commander, I see that you're guilty of is self-defence. I think we will probably leave the decision as to the status of the wine up to the prosecutor, but if he were to ask me, I would recommend that the fluid itself still belongs to the two families, but that it should never appear in a public place labelled as "Richebourg", though I wouldn't object to being able to give a bottle labelled as such to my wife as a souvenir.

'May I also suggest that you and Michelle, representing your family, meet with Marie-Claire, representing hers, get round a table and come to an amicable agreement? I would probably agree to the presence of a corporate lawyer, but would not recommend a criminal one to be present too.' He looked at the others around the table.

Truchaud looked at him and the young gendarme. 'To me that sounds fine, but I am aware that it is very much in my interest.'

'It is also in the national interest. It would be an inexpensive judgment, and the only people who might feel hard done by such a judgment are all dead, apart from old Mr Laforge, and if he were to think about it carefully, he would probably think he has come out of it okay too. I suspect he would not want questions about the paternity of Marie-Claire and Jacquot to appear in the newspapers, which they inevitably would, if it ever went anywhere near a court.'

'In which case may I invite you all to dinner?' said Truchaud. 'I would like to take over the back of the Café du Centre. *Capitaine*, at the very least that you could allow Constable Montbard here and also Lenoir to be off duty to be able to attend, should they so wish. Moreover, I would like to invite your wife, as I shall be inviting my sister-in-law, nephew and people involved in the case like, Marie-Claire, Maréchale and Suzette. They are the future of the domaines that are responsible for those bottles unfortunately labelled as "Richebourg".'

Chapter 36

Nuits-Saint-Georges, Saturday and a few days after

Truchaud leaned back in his chair. The second cup of *café au lait* had slipped down a treat, and the croissants had been up to their usual standard. Marie-Claire Laforge had already arrived and had introduced herself and Jacquot to Michelle. The boys were currently shadow-boxing, as boys who know of each other, but who had, as yet never really spoken to each other, often do.

To the Commander, it appeared that the two women were getting on fine, and it looked like the future of both domaines was becoming secure. He wasn't really sure how skilled viticulturally either woman actually was, or for that matter how good *he* was at making such a judgement himself. He was counting on Simon Maréchale to make that difference. That was of course, always assuming that young Maréchale actually turned up.

'Anybody at home?' came a familiar voice from the door.

'On time too,' observed Truchaud getting to his feet. 'That is, I assume you are turning up for work.'

'Do you think I would be stupid enough to be showing my face here, if I wasn't planning on doing any work?' The two of them walked through into the dining room where the two women had covered the dining table with papers and maps. In particular, the local map of the vineyards of the Côte de Nuits was unrolled and pinned to the table with a solid-bottomed whisky tumbler at each corner.

'Michelle, may I introduce you to Simon Maréchale?' said Truchaud.

293

'Monsieur Maréchale, welcome. I have heard lots about you from my brother-in-law, and now from Marie-Claire, most of it very favourable.'

'Please, Madame, call me Simon,' the young man replied. Truchaud did note that she didn't yet respond in kind. No doubt that would come.

'I think the first thing he needs from both of you ladies is a contract of employment,' continued the policeman. 'One of the problems we had over the past fortnight was the absence of a contract, and I don't think anyone was helped by that.' *Was it only a fortnight,* he thought? Somehow he had never been as personally involved in a case as this one, and he really hoped he never would be again. 'Come to think of it too, I think you ladies need to come up with a contract of agreement between yourselves.'

'And you, Shammang, will sign whatever we come up with?' Michelle asked.

'Provided you allow me to read it to confirm that it doesn't require me to boil myself in sesame oil or some such nonsense. Of course, I will.'

'See?' Michelle said to her new best friend and business partner, 'I told you we could count on my brother-in-law. On Monday we will call round a solicitor and we'll get everything signed.'

'Madame Laforge, I have delivered Suzette round to the shop and she's opened up. There are still a few police in there, but they don't seem to object to the shop being open.'

'They won't unless they find something in particular to excite them that they didn't expect to find,' said Truchaud.

'So,' said Maréchale, 'where do we go from here?'

'I think the boys should show you round our domaine,' said Michelle, and called for Bruno. When the boy arrived, she said, 'Go and dig your grandfather, and then take Simon here and show him our vineyards, and tell him all about how they're currently doing.'

'Take Jacquot with you. He should find that interesting too,' added Marie-Claire. All three young males and a very elderly male, all piled into Simon's little car and headed off, presumably to the Clos de Vougeot to start the tour.

Michelle grinned at Truchaud. 'How do you think Bruno will react when he realizes that we've just taken on Suzette's boyfriend as the new winemaker, and he's just finished showing him around?'

'To start with, I imagine he will think we have both betrayed him badly, but he'll calm down a bit once he realizes he'll probably see more of her this way.'

'Bruno has a thing about Suzette?' asked Marie-Claire with concern in her voice.

'In the way that twelve-year-old boys do,' replied Michelle. 'He's getting his first experience of hormones.'

'Oh dear,' said Marie-Claire, a note of concern in her voice 'Jacquot's got a crush on her too. Let's hope they form an alliance in their collective misery, rather than get all competitive about it.'

Truchaud looked up just as a tall young man dressed as a gendarme walked between the uprights of the gates to the yard. He got up to go and meet him; it was Lenoir. 'I have come to accept responsibility for you, and to tell you I have a flat-bottomed boat with an outboard attached in my new van outside.' Truchaud — being technically under house arrest for the moment — needed to be accompanied by a named policeman if he were to leave the property of the domaine itself. Lenoir was accepting that responsibility. Both of them knew he wouldn't betray that trust.

'Remember that small loading dock just upstream of the town centre? Well, we've blocked it off so we can load some of the wine formerly known as "Richebourg", and bring it round here to do some surgery on the labelling, and store it in your cellars.'

'Sounds very promising,' said Truchaud, and led him to the entrance to the cellars of the domaine. Michelle and Marie-Claire followed. 'What do you think?' he asked.

Lenoir looked at the space quizzically. There was a space on the left side of the wall, presumably where the Vosne was intended to have gone, had all have gone according to plan. 'I reckon we could probably get half of it along that wall if we stacked it from floor to ceiling. We'll leave the other half in the Laforge cellars if that is okay with Madame?' he added.

'You mean there's that much of it?' asked Michelle, her eyes forming big round Os in her face.

'Oh yes, there's that much of it,' said Truchaud. 'It's a blend of all Bertin's Vosne, some of the best wine from the wrong side of the Seventy-Four, a splash of the Nuits and our Clos de Vougeot.'

'And a bit of our Echézeaux as well,' added Marie-Claire.

'Quite,' continued Truchaud. 'It's all Burgundy, and it's all ours. You tasted it. Do you think Bertin would have been proud?'

'Yes, I think he would have liked it lots,' Michelle replied with a wistful smile. 'What a waste.'

Lenoir and Truchaud looked at each other, slightly uncomfortably, 'Shall we start moving wine?' They unloaded collapsed crates from the back of the outhouse into the back of the new Renault Trafic parked just outside the gates. It would have caused significant problems with circulation, had it not been painted with 'Gendarmes' all over it. *Stick the right labels on things and you can get away with anything*, Truchaud thought. But if you overdid it like the 'Richebourg', then it all went belly up.

Lenoir drove the van down to the slipway, which was blocked off with marker cones, and backed down to the stream. They launched the punt, and loaded it with just enough packing cases to leave space for the pair of them in the boat, and puttered off downstream. Truchaud wondered what people might think of a gendarmerie van parked on the slipway, but he needn't have worried. Further downstream there were smiling faces leaning over the car park wall at them. It seemed that all the staff at the domaines that overlooked the stream had come out to wave. They then disappeared under the bridge, and turned left into the underground culvert. Under the power of the little engine, it only took them fifteen minutes to get to Laforge's cellar. The two walls in the culvert, the nearer of which Truchaud had already seen, now had large holes in them to let the boat through.

'I showed them a lump hammer,' said Lenoir drily, 'and they decided that resistance wasn't such a good idea. They thought about it for a moment maybe, and then just fell over.'

On their way past them Truchaud noted that the other cellars that opened up onto the culvert had all grown steel gates to protect their stock. 'That was quick,' he observed laconically.

'I think they were all in individual cellars somewhere, just not in the right place,' replied Lenoir. 'When the Captain remarked to some individuals what they had in their cellars, how old they were and how much they'd got, and how easy it was to get at them, I think they were very easily persuaded to tighten up on security. It probably explains why one or two of them were waving at us outside.'

As soon as they reached Laforge's first wharf, Lenoir tied the boat up to the stone bollard and switched off the engine. 'We must be careful about pollution,' he remarked, and they started unloading the cartons off the boat. There were one or two other familiar faces in the cellar already, including a couple of off-duty gendarmes in mufti, and Jean Parnault himself.

'I've come down to get a free look at what one of our rival operations is getting up to,' he grinned, waving a corkscrew and a little box of tasting glasses, which he parked on the top of an upturned barrel.

'But fortunately, not what they're actually going to call it when it gets out into the market place,' replied Truchaud with a laugh.

There was a stack of bottles which had Richebourg labels on them, and next to them Lenoir placed the cartons he had just unloaded from the boat. The crew, which included one or two of Jean Parnault's employees, as well as the gendarmes, were busy packing them into the cases.

'It's all right if we reuse the packing filler from the old boxes, isn't it?' asked one of the men. 'It'll be safer for the bottles.'

'They don't have the word Richebourg on them anywhere, do they?' asked Lenoir.

'No, they're just plain cardboard filler.'

'Then use them,' replied Lenoir, carrying the first filled boxes to the boat. 'Are you coming back with me in the boat, or can we put a few more cases in here?' he asked.

'It's up to you, you're running this show. Whatever you need to do to make sure it's all above board.'

'Savioli?' Lenoir called. A young fair-haired off-duty gendarme looked up.

'Lenoir?' he replied.

'Can I pass on the responsibility for keeping an eye on Commander Truchaud here? He is technically under house arrest, and is only allowed out under my supervision.

'Can I trust you?' Savioli asked Truchaud.

'Of course,' Truchaud replied.

'Only I would hate to have to shoot the owner of all this lovely wine.'

'I would hate for you to have to do that too,' Truchaud replied with a grin.

'The last chap who tried to shoot him didn't come out of it very well,' added Lenoir.

'Mind you,' Truchaud added, 'I was armed at the time.' He hoped Savioli knew the whole story, and that he and Lenoir were just joking. And with that little exchange Lenoir clambered into the boat and puttered back off downstream.

Parnault leaned on the upturned barrel, holding a bottle still wearing its 'Richebourg' label. He cut the capsule, noting that it didn't have a tax stamp on its top. He inserted his corkscrew into its cork and gently pulled it. 'You can tell me the house arrest story in a moment,' he said. 'First, you tasted my new wine the other day, so it's only fair that I should try yours, especially as there seems to be so much of a hoo-ha about it.' He poured a splash into a glass, and looked at it.

'Nice bright purple colour,' he said and then he took a sniff. He stopped and looked at it quizzically, and then took another sniff. 'Oh yes,' he said and looked at Truchaud. 'I see what you mean,' and took a mouthful. He swirled it round his mouth, then stopped for a moment looking upwards and to the right.

He then appeared to swirl backwards, and nodded. He then looked around for a spittoon, and failing to find one, finally swallowed. 'May I say that I'm impressed?' he asked Truchaud.

'That was my brother's wine, which Suzette's boyfriend finished, and now we just have to wait for time to weave its magic.' Truchaud replied.

'It's a wine of great quality,' remarked Parnault. 'You can't call it this though,' he said pointing at the label.

'I wasn't going to, though quite what we are going to call it, I don't know yet.' He explained its provenance and that all it qualified to be was a basic Bourgogne.

'Yes, that's the problem with the regulations,' agreed Parnault. 'You can't even call it a Nuits-Villages, despite the fact that it's a blend of wines from the greatest Villages in the Nuits area. Ironically, it contains absolutely nothing from the Villages that constitute the Côtes de Nuits-Villages, being Brochon and Fixin to the north and Corgoloin and Comblanchien in the south. You know, I think the wines from the bottom end of Prémeaux have to call themselves Côtes de Nuits-Villages too.'

'I think it's partly to avoid confusing the foreign buyers too much.'

'You reckon?' replied Parnault. 'Since when did we ever care whether we confused the English or not? They have their LBW law; we have our Burgundy wine laws.'

'LBW?' asked Truchaud confused.

'I don't know whether you've ever seen cricket played, but if you do, expect to be bewildered. One of the most complex regulations, in a singularly bureaucratic game, is the LBW law. I have a friend who's a wine merchant in London, and is quite into the game, explained to me that it was invented in the early nineteenth century to weed out French spies during the Napoleonic War. You get the picture? Explain the LBW law, and if they couldn't, they were in trouble.' Parnault took a breath, and then continued. 'Well, we retaliated with the Burgundy wine laws.'

'Do you understand this LBW law?' asked Truchaud.

'Haven't the faintest idea, old boy. I don't even know what

it's short for,' he replied, 'but I believe he really does. Anyway, what are you going to do with this?' He poured a little into the other glasses and beckoned Savioli over. 'You can at least see what this whole affair is all about,' he remarked to the young gendarme, who took a large swig and swallowed. Parnault grinned and enquired as to whether he was from the north.

'It is our intention to market it. As it's a blend of four different appellations, all we can do is call it what all four qualify as being: straight Bourgogne. But provided the marketing is right, we can price it how we like. Remember the white Musigny? Until the vines were old enough to rank as a Grand Cru, the Count de Vogüé could only call it a white Bourgogne, as Chambolle wasn't allocated a certificate for a white wine with a lesser status than Grand Cru. It was still the richest, smoothest and most expensive ordinary white Burgundy on the market. Everyone knew it was made from Chardonnay grapes that grew in one corner of his mystically brilliant red wine vineyard, whose produce was described by one lunatic, desperately in need of therapy, as "Little Jesus, slipping down the throat in velvet trousers".

'Sorry about that, I was drifting off into my own little dreamland for a moment. There is something about Burgundy wine that grabs me there, and for a while, won't let go.' The two men grinned at each other and chuckled.

'Your brother and your new sidekick combined to make a magical bottle of wine. If you think you need someone to sell it at the level it deserves, may I offer you my services?' While Parnault was producing his pitch, each of them had filled more cases with unlabelled bottles, and had carried them over to the wharf to await the return of Lenoir. Truchaud's thoughts to that offer were for the most part positive, but before he did so, he thought he ought to discuss it with his family and his new partners who, after all, had a shop of their own.

A couple of days later, an unmarked police car drew up into the yard of the domaine, and a gorgeous young blonde woman got out of it. Truchaud walked out of the back door to greet her, followed by a stocky young woman with reddish hair, far from unattractive herself, despite being dressed in the uniform of a gendarme. He introduced them to each other. 'Detective Constable Dutoit. Gendarme Montbard,' he said.

'Detective Constable Dutoit,' asked Montbard. 'Are you willing to accept into your custody Commander Charlemagne Truchaud?'

'Charlemagne?' she mused, 'You know, *chef*, I don't think I ever knew that.' Her voice then switched tones, 'Yes, Constable Montbard, I am.'

'Do you want to bring your bags in?' he asked. 'We have a spare room for you tonight, and then we'll go back to Paris tomorrow. Tonight, I owe these good people a dinner, and I'm sure they'll be very interested to get to put a face to the person who was doing all the work in Paris for the case.'

'That's fine, provided you aren't a naughty *chef* and try to run away from me in a place I don't know my way around.'

'Don't worry about that,' said Montbard. 'We'll help you catch him if he does try to do a runner. We'll find him. We've got all the keys to the cellar now.'

And so another few days passed in the quiet little wine town of Nuits-Saint-Georges. The little café in the Place de la République hosted a dinner the like of which was only seen hosted by a squad of detectives in Paris. However, the diners this time weren't just detectives and gendarmes on this occasion, though if you looked carefully, you might have recognized one or two of those out of uniform. There were one or two civilians as well, including a couple of boys just on the cusp of manhood, who were finding it quite difficult to decide which of the young women present to gape at in rapt adoration. If the local criminal fraternity had had advance notice of this particular shindig, there might have been a crime wave in Nuits-Saint-Georges. After all, most of the police were there. But there weren't any

301

criminal masterminds based in Nuits; it simply wasn't that sort of place.

The man who picked up the tab for this dinner was a policeman from Paris, who was beginning to acquire some credibility in the local winemaking community, and also as a private eye. He had sold some of his family's wine to the restaurant, and then bought most of it back to accompany the dinner, even though, to be honest, the wine was really too young to be used like that. Soon it would go to sleep, and really wouldn't be worth drinking for a good five years, but at least the labels had been stuck on more or less straight.

Oh, what was that? Oh the name of the wine, you ask? Printed on the label in large capital letters was the word 'Bourgogne', and underneath it in smaller letters were the words 'Bertin's Pride'.

Notes on the ranks in the French Police

The Gendarmerie is a branch of the armed services, and as a result, is answerable primarily to the Ministry of Defence, though the Ministry of the Interior has some input too. It can, as in this book, be seen to be synonymous with the police in uniform. The local force is run by a *Capitaine*, with a couple of lieutenants, a sergeant or two and some 'guardians of the peace'; standard coppers in uniform. The problem I ran into, as a writer in English, is that the name of the rank of Sergeant is in fact, *'Brigadier'* in French. The word 'Brigadier' in English is a very senior field rank, so, to avoid confusion, on the odd occasion that an NCO appears I call him 'Sergeant'. Having anglicized that, I then anglicized Duquesne's rank to 'Captain' to be consistent. *'Gardien de la paix'* translated to 'Constable' so easily, that I took that liberty too.

The Civilian Police Force *(la Police Nationale)* is a national civilian force answerable to the Department of the Interior (The Home Office). It also has a ranking system. Truchaud would be a *Commandant*, roughly the British equivalent of a Detective Chief Inspector. I kept him as a *Commandant* in the first draft of the book, but the first two or three people I recruited to test-read it asked me why I was giving him the same rank as a German WWII prison-camp commandant, and declared they were happier with 'Commander'. From there the other ranks followed this logic. The Chief Superintendent is called *'Commissaire Divisionnaire'* in France, and again my friends wondered if he had a desk by the front door, and arranged things. I translated his rank into English as 'Divisional Commander' to preserve the old man's dignity. Truchaud's underlings in Paris, who appear occasionally on the phone are 'Inspectors', 'sergeants' and 'constables'.

The Municipal Police is a local service answering to the local Mayor. It is responsible for local traffic enforcement, building regulations, pest control, and general crime prevention

The Investigating Magistrate (termed in France as an Investigating Judge) is a civilian role that we do not have in the UK, and is somewhat like an American District Attorney. They are independent of the police, and manage all parts of a police investigation. If they feel that there is adequate evidence to proceed, they then refer the case to the Public Prosecutor *(Procureur)* who takes the case to trial. The investigating judge takes no further part in the proceedings, and the prosecutor can't call them as a witness, but can and usually does call the police. To watch these characters in action, I strongly recommend watching the TV series *Spiral (Engrenages,* or links (in a chain) in French). The *Procureur* doesn't have a role in *The Richebourg Affair,* but Monsieur le Juge crops up from time to time.

Dramatis Personæ

Commander Charlemagne Truchaud, *A detective; our hero*

His team in Paris

Inspector Leclerc, *His sidekick, a real Parisian*

Constable Natalie Dutoit, *A beautiful blonde detective; sharp as a tack*

Constable Georges Delacroix, *A detective who has an accident*

His family in Nuits-Saint-Georges

Dad, [Philibert] *His father, not as well as he used to be*

Bertin, *His brother, tragically dead*

Michelle, *His brother's widow; an insulin-dependent diabetic*

Bruno, *His brother's son, a twelve-year-old boy, who thinks his uncle is wonderful*

Other police officers in Paris

The Divisional Commander; *Truchaud's ageing boss*

Commander Lucas, *Another team leader going places*

At the Gendarmerie in Nuits-Saint-Georges

Captain Duquesne, *The chief*

Constable Lenoir, *A policeman who is a frightening driver*

Constable Montbard, *A policewoman with strawberry blonde hair*

Constable Savioli, *Another policeman, new to Burgundy*

Civilian law enforcement in Nuits-Saint-Georges

Monsieur le Juge Lemaître, *An investigating judge*

Inspector Molleau, *The Chief of the Municipal Police; dismantles pistols*

At Maison Laforge, where the Truchauds did business

Old Mr [Émile] Laforge, *Who is indeed very old*

Young Mr [Jérome] Laforge, *Who would be middle-aged if he were not already a corpse*

Marie-Claire Laforge, *Old Mr Laforge's granddaughter, and Louis's daughter*

Louis Laforge, *Marie-Claire's father; victim of a road accident twenty-five years earlier*

Jacquot Laforge, *Her son, a lad of fourteen years; a slave to his hormones*

Armand Laforge, *Emile's brother, abducted by the Boche during the war*

Simon Maréchale, *The winemaker and blender*

Celestine, *Who works in the office; on the lookout for a ladder to climb*

Suzette Girand, *A university student, who works in the shop sometimes*

Other people in and around Nuits-Saint-Georges

Doctor Girand, *Suzette's father and the local GP*

Geneviève Girand, *Suzette's mother; a very old friend of Commander Truchaud*

Jean Parnault, *A winemaker, Geneviève's brother and an old friend of Bertin*

Hairy Eddie, *A student who flat-shares with Suzette in Dijon*

A sad-faced woman who works at the Funeral Directors

People who exist outside the author's imagination! (but their parts in this book are as fictitious as all the rest)

David Clark, *Who really does make wine in Morey-Saint-Denis*

Christine Tournier, *Who owns and runs the Café du Centre in Nuits-Saint-Georges*

Pierre Vincent, *Who really does make wine in Prémeaux-Prissey*

About the author

R.M. Cartmel has been a writer one way and another since being a medical student at Oxford. After a long career as a successful and much sought-after GP, R.M. Cartmel decided to retire from practice and dedicate himself full-time to the creation of crime fiction. This is his first novel.